ZERO HAPPILY EVER AFTERS

MN BENNET

Copyright © 2025 MN Bennet
This edition is published by M.N. Bennet LLC

Hardback ISBN: 978-1-967397-07-5
Paperback ISBN: 979-8-9901493-6-6
Ebook ISBN: 979-8-9901493-5-9

Edited by Charlie Knight (https://cknightwrites.carrd.co/)
Paperback cover art by Miblart (miblart.com)
Hardback cover art by GraphicSoul (https://www.graphicsoulart.com)
Formatting by Mayonaka Designs (mayonakadesigns.com)

www.mnbennet.com/

To everyone who has followed Dorian, Milo, and the entire homeroom coven the last three books. It's truly been an honor sharing this world with you. I can't wait until you see the adventures I have in store for this installment.

READERS BE ADVISED

You've returned for the fourth installment in the Branches of Past and Future series. That makes me so truly delighted. I've included a list of content warnings on the following page for those interested, and I will say they are mostly the same as previous installments. However, there are some darker elements added to this book.

You may know by now from reading this series—or even my others—that I very much believe in HEA and HFN in all my works. It's something I strive to bring no matter how long winding the journey is, and with a title like Zero Happily Ever Afters, you can probably guess the path will be painful at times. That said, I think there are some absolutely lovely scenes, adorable moments, and way too many laugh out loud lines. I can't wait for you to see what's in store for Dorian, Milo, the students, and all the other wonderful characters popping onto the page.

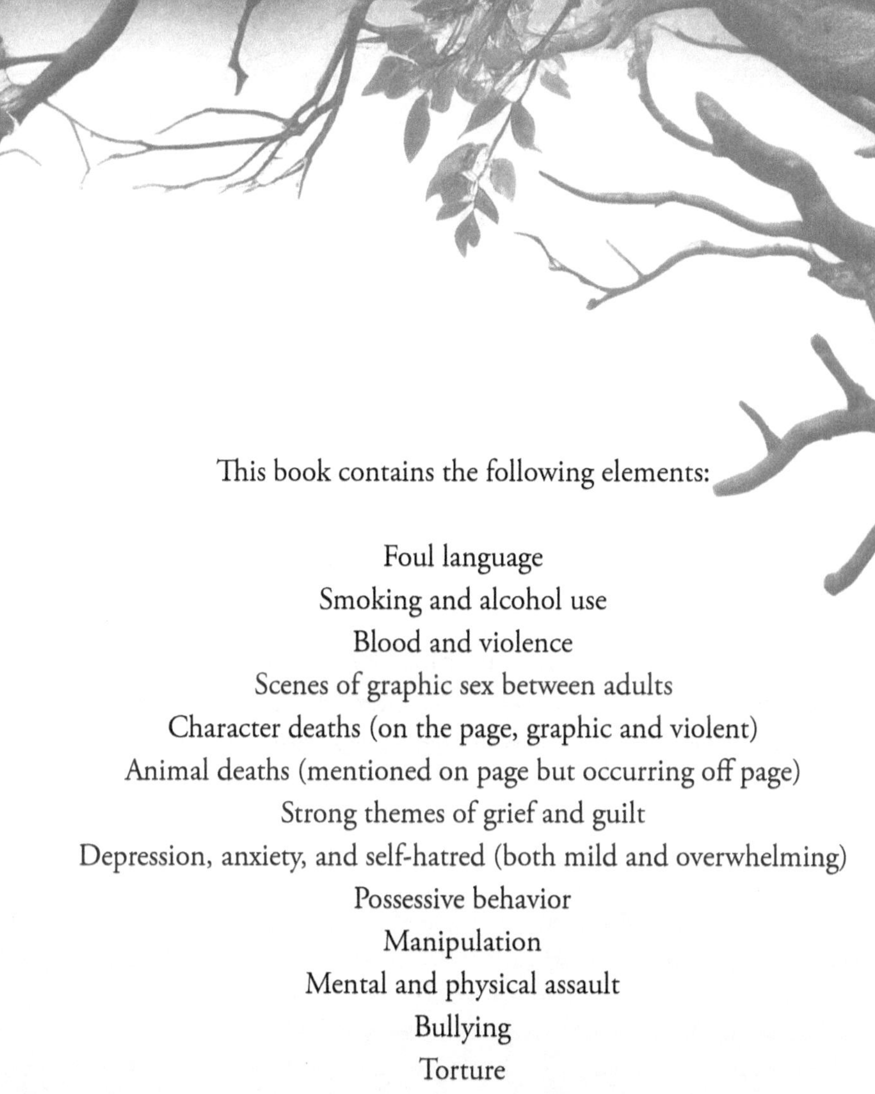

This book contains the following elements:

Foul language
Smoking and alcohol use
Blood and violence
Scenes of graphic sex between adults
Character deaths (on the page, graphic and violent)
Animal deaths (mentioned on page but occurring off page)
Strong themes of grief and guilt
Depression, anxiety, and self-hatred (both mild and overwhelming)
Possessive behavior
Manipulation
Mental and physical assault
Bullying
Torture

I hope you'll enjoy this installment as much as I did.

There is a codex in the back of the book
explaining the magic and world in a bit more
detail for anyone who is interested.

WARD
REJUVENATION
PRIMAL
PSYCHIC
HEX
ENCHANTMENT
AUGMENTATION
BESTIAL
COSMIK
ENTROPY
ALTERATION
ARCANE
TELEKINESIS
SENSORY
BANISHMENT
LEVITATION

CHAPTER ONE

FINN'S boyish grin always lit up his entire face, even when his thoughts held sour notes of irritation. I stood in this dream, reminiscing about the countless possibilities that might unfold. There were many memories of my life at Gemini Academy as a student. I gathered my bearings, assessing the clean-cut uniform of my younger self and how he hadn't added goth embellishments yet. How *I* hadn't. That meant this memory came from my first year at the academy.

The way Finn's eyes glimmered, studying the sky, I knew his magic had locked onto some type of historical fact floating in the air. Here he'd stormed over, ready to bite my head off for something I couldn't recall, and now, he'd been left to fight back a giggle fit over something no one but him would understand, thanks to a thousand inside jokes he shared with the secret histories of the world.

Realizing Finn was lost in a daze, I watched my younger self turn on his heel, ready to walk away and avoid any scolding. No. Not scolding. Work. It came back to me as I spun away from Finn; the sunlight cut through the courtyard at the perfect angle, shining against Finn's glorious face and highlighting his hazel eyes that'd stopped shimmering from the effect of his magic.

"You can't keep dodging me." Finn looped his arm through mine and dragged me across the academy courtyard.

My heart raced and surged with excitement because Finn's grip held me tight, and each breath carried a deep inhale of his cologne. I never wanted this moment to end. The me of then, at sixteen, still sorting through my feelings, and the me of now, at damn near thirty-five, dreaming of what life used to be.

"If I'd known you were gonna be this difficult, I'd have partnered with someone else." Finn released me once we reached one of the outdoor lunch tables and squared my shoulders before shoving me down into a seat.

"Fine. Trade partners." I shrugged, pretending not to care because despite busting my ass my first year at Gemini Academy, I remained aloof about anything this place had to offer. "Work with Milo."

I nodded to the curly, blond-haired mop top sitting across from us and stuffing his face with food.

"Yeah, right." Finn scoffed. "He's even worse than you on this peer project."

"Not uh." Milo glowered, still eating. Geez, I'd forgotten how much he stuffed his face. Guess he still had quite an appetite but got better about shoveling food in his mouth at all hours of the day.

"Look, I don't care if you're above the whole sharing details about your life." Finn crossed his arms, giving me a very surly expression, which from Finn always brought a smile to my face.

Even when I worked my hardest to scowl and glare and pretend I hated everything, seeing a pouty Finn made it impossible, and the tiniest of smiles nearly crept out. That said, I knew how this memory played out and that I fought Finn tooth and nail when it came to sharing my life story—hell, it took him until we graduated, and I shared what a sad sack kid I was with no friends except some imaginary one who eventually ran off too. How that was even remotely vital to instruction for some history project on ourselves still eluded me. Personally, I thought our instructor ran out of lesson plans and tossed together the most exhausting self-assessed project possible.

"Mrs. Valson will take off a whole letter grade if it's turned in late." Finn pointed an accusatory finger at me, practically ready to jab me in the chest. And I invited it because back then, my telepathy worked best when making physical contact with another person, and I wanted to know Finn's every thought. Even the supposedly grumpy ones.

"A ooole lebber graade?" Milo asked, mouth full of food. When I turned and glared, he simply hummed a tune in his head and stuffed his face with another ridiculously big bite of his sandwich.

"Yes, and I'm not failing a history class," Finn said, practically embarrassed at the idea someone with his branch could ever struggle in a course framed around historical facts.

I sank into this dream, indulging in Finn's rant to my younger self as he pretended not to care what Finn said, but in truth, he did. I did. I loved him so much by this point in my life, and even now, all these years later, I found myself enamored by this memory, relishing each passing second relived.

For so many years, memories such as this haunted my sleeping hours, filling my mind with recollections of all the days wasted, not truly valuing the time I had with Finn. Then, I found closure. Closure given to me by a piece of Finn's magic tucked away in my subconscious. Closure granted by Milo's unyielding presence. Closure found after spending years dodging it at all costs.

But memories and moments with Finn had eluded my slumber since the revelation of my manifestation's actions. He'd stolen Finn away, a piece of Finn that had been bound to the most dangerous devil I'd ever had the misfortune of encountering. My manifestation wrought havoc onto the city, onto the lives of so many, and he did it all without an ounce of remorse until it was too late, and the blood of Jamie Novak had been spilled.

I believed that was why dreams of Finn had stopped so abruptly. He didn't haunt my memories because he haunted my choices. The lengths I went to save him, to bring him back. And yes, I fully grasp the manifestation acted of his own accord, but I remain culpable. Part of me knew he was out there. I could feel his presence like pin prickles against the nape of my neck. I sensed our connection in the faintest ways. Hell, I'd recognized the effect his absence had on my branch yet ignored it. I told myself I wanted to focus on the evolution of my branch, the way my telepathy had advanced. In truth, I think I wanted an excuse to ignore the horrors my manifestation intended to unleash because of my selfishness, my arrogance, my—

"You're too hard on yourself," Finn said, eyes glowing subtly as he studied my mind for the peer project.

"Don't use your goddamn magic on me," I snapped because it terrified me that Finn's retrocognition would glimpse every sordid and confused feeling I had for him.

At sixteen, I'd come to realize I was very gay. I had a hundred thousand different fantasies about what I wanted to do with Finn, with Milo, with Finn and Milo, but despite having telepathy, I had no clue if either of my close friends were, in fact, queer.

Turned out that at that age, Milo often focused on his sexual urges for women when around his nosy telepath because he didn't know what to make of his own desires. Sorting out erections for women was one thing, but he didn't grasp why he got just as aroused when with Finn and myself or when staring at his male enchanter idols on the TV screen.

Being bisexual must be utterly exhausting to decipher as a teenager. Hell, I'd heard my share of thirty-somethings still trying to gain an understanding of their bi-thought processes.

"Well, if you spent less time beating yourself up and more time answering my questions, then I wouldn't have to pry," Finn said with a smile, hazel eyes still glowing as he rooted through my history or someone else's. He had this nonchalance when casting, when talking, when revealing the deepest truths he'd unraveled.

I didn't recall what I beat myself up over instead of focusing on our peer project, but my self-loathing hatred for all my choices or lack thereof wasn't something I'd developed overnight. Oh no, I spent years cultivating and finetuning the art of blaming myself for all the world's problems. It was a true skill.

I chuckled—internally, of course, since in reality, my younger self simply scowled at Finn, and my slumbering body merely gurgled a bit while my eyes fluttered open before the darkness of the dream memory took hold again.

Memories of Finn were always so timely, so perfectly planned. Here, I'd been beating myself up for the actions of my manifestation, and so my subconscious sent a message through Finn to remind me not to blame myself for everything. From what I recalled about this memory, it involved Finn scolding me throughout our peer interview for withholding answers and for berating myself, while Milo scarfed a sandwich and dodged his peer partner for a project he didn't want to do—since he knew it held no value to our grades, but he didn't share that with us at the time, damn clairvoyants—and a lot of placating us instead of taking a side when Finn and I inevitably broke out into bickering arguments.

Every fiber of my being wanted to settle into the memory, into this simpler time, and indulge in the monotony that came with youth.

A pitter-patter of frantic footsteps scampering in the distance pulled my attention. Of course they did. The universe loved to steal shining moments from me at any chance it had to take them.

I huffed hard enough that it almost roused me from my sleep, but the weight of this goddamn vision held me down and ensured I had the displeasure of watching it unfold.

Caleb ran toward me, carrying a black void of nothingness that ate away at all the scenery of my dreamscape. The sunlight faded. The academy crumbled to pieces. Finn and Milo vanished in a breath.

Each step carried the weight of death. Caleb's sweaty face engrained itself in my mind, his frantic expression, the muddy snow-white hair from a bad dye job he'd gotten as a first-year student. When he winced in pain, silently shouting in the darkness, I rolled my eyes. Figuratively. Maybe literally. All I knew was by the time he'd hit the shadowed ground and Kenzo stood beside him, retrieving the bloody dagger embedded in his back to show to Tara, who'd also appeared in the void vision, I'd lost all interest.

This damn premonition of the future haunted me for months on end, but I'd somehow helped in averting it. Unfortunately, whether Milo's visions were prevented or ended up cementing into reality, the vision itself never faded away. I mean, this was clearly my students during their first year at fifteen. It wasn't possible for this specific vision to happen anymore.

It was a terrible fucking magic, and since I had the misfortune of absorbing tens of thousands of Milo's clairvoyant musings of potential outcomes when we shared a kiss last year, that meant I had to deal with these visions regularly. Everything Milo did to store them in a less inconvenient place within my mind was only temporary. The tethers holding the visions at bay often snapped, and I was always greeted with the void vision, one I'd now had the misfortune of seeing close to a hundred times over.

Even as I sighed with annoyance, the damn thing replayed on a loop five more times. It just kept reminding me of what could've been.

I understood that with so many visions stored in my mind, they were bound to wriggle loose and flood my thoughts, but I didn't understand why the void vision always had to pop out first. It came to me like a harbinger of ill tidings, bringing with it a cluster fuck of countless other visions.

One by one, they clouded the darkness surrounding the void vision. My mind became a collection of puzzles where each piece stemmed from a different work of art. Sightings of burning buildings. Images of bloody battles. Singing in the rain for surprising days off. Dancing at the club with a nauseous stomach—*damn sandwich*. Clammy hands as I approached a podium, clearing my throat. A trophy so close to my grasp, I'd finally achieved accolades for my inventions. Dogs barking and chasing a familiar up a tree. Fiends everywhere, feasting on traces of magic before exploding into wisps of fluttering white light. Magic cast with precision during exams. Magic cast carelessly during a case. City streets erupting as destruction swept through Chicago. People honked, cursing the construction they knew was bound to start soon, yet blamed the lazy bastards fixing the roads for why they'd be late to work.

Every vision burst through my mind so quickly, I barely grasped the fleeting sights. Some of them felt like they belonged to me, like these outcomes could be mine, but none of these visions held my story. No, it was merely an awful way of perceiving the future for Milo. Some of his visions were over the shoulder of those he observed, like catching a short film. But others…others pulled him into the driver's seat, peering through the eyes of the would-be could-be person in question.

I had no idea how Milo made sense of any of those visions, sorted them from urgent to mundane, figured out which potentials were outdated and which could still come to pass.

"Such an exhausting fucking headache," I grumbled, groggy and finally waking from the dreadful lack of sleep. Sleep had almost found me, allowing me to feel well-rested while locked in a dream, yet those damn visions stole away any semblance of rest I'd found.

"Bad dream?" Milo asked with a yawn, rolling over from his corner of the bed where Charlie had forced him after wedging himself between us at two in the morning. His hind feet were stretched far, jabbed into Milo's back to maintain a proper distance that Charlie approved of.

Charlie chirped when I rubbed the orange fluff on his face. Carlie chirped too, my fat little tabby cat sitting at the edge of the bed with doe eyes of desperation. She wanted food and pretended to be sweet. Another minute and she'd be rubbing against my feet. Another two minutes and she'd be biting them. Three minutes and the claws would come out.

Still, I struggled to gain my composure. Between the blobs of orange representing my cats, the bright inferno of sunlight piercing through my bedroom window, and the countless visions still swimming through my head, it was any wonder I hadn't passed out. Okay, passing out would be a reward, something that allowed me to sleep, even if restless.

"Well?" Milo asked again, scratching his facial scruff. He'd been stretched so thin making a thousand different arrangements on short notice that he'd barely had time to rest, let alone focus on grooming habits.

I liked the five o'clock shadow, though. I also liked his curly, blond hair, which I could only ever truly run my fingers through first thing in the morning before he tossed in a ton of product to establish the Enchanter Evergreen look.

"Maybe he needs a new look," I whispered.

"Dodging my question." Milo smiled with tightly closed eyes, the goofy type of grin like a dog enjoying pets as I massaged his scalp.

"The visions came loose again," I answered Milo's question.

He responded by brushing the sleep from his eyes, an action that proved a most difficult battle. The war on a good night's rest plagued us both. And guilt pinched at me, stealing the bit of sleep Milo had left before starting his next big case. A case that'd be unlike any other. A case that'd change everything. A case that'd steal him from me. Even if only for a few weeks. I didn't like it.

"Lemme see what I can do." Milo wrapped his arms around me. They were so much bigger than mine, firm and powerful, carrying the weight of the world and all his love for me.

"I gotta learn how to do this on my own." I pulled away, almost as reluctantly as Carlie would whenever I picked her up and held her captive with affection.

Milo smirked, scooting closer and sending Charlie trotting to the edge of the bed to join his sister. He meowed in protest, furious to have his sleep and cuddle pillow taken from him.

"You don't have to learn today."

"I have to learn soon. I mean, you're leaving today, so now is basically—"

"Is basically," Milo interrupted. "Is basically the perfect time for a last-minute tune-up on the creaky floorboards of your brain."

I huffed, which only invited Milo to scoot closer. Telekinetically, he pulled out an enchantment he'd bought specifically for diving into my mind with ease. Gently, he placed the symbol on my shoulder. I shuddered at the warm vibrance radiating off the magic, magic that merged Milo and me into a unified consciousness. He pressed his forehead against mine and then tumbled into my mind.

Here we stood, surrounded by messy, shattered visions floating around my inner core, shimmering and blaring and doing everything they could to steal my attention to the urgency of their potential future.

"This shouldn't take too long."

"Good." I crossed my arms. "Wouldn't want you to miss your flight."

"You're so sassy this morning." Milo's smile filled his face, making my cheeks heat and burn with flustered frustration. "I like sassy Dorian. You gonna get like this every time the Global Guild calls on me for an out-of-town trip?"

"Don't know," I practically growled, attempting to show his absence wouldn't bother me, which obviously had the opposite effect since Milo giggled. "How many trips are you planning?"

"However many the Global Guild requires my assistance on." Milo channeled his magic, sending it into the enchantment he'd placed on my shoulder and cascading through my body. "Or however many I deem appropriate for the best possible future. Only happily ever afters if I have anything to do with it."

Milo waved a hand, herding the loose visions like wrangling cattle. He had such a knack for it.

"Like a Border Collie," Milo said, playfully panting with his tongue out. "Except I think they herd sheep."

I tsked, reminded how unified our minds were when he dived into my inner core with that enchantment. He'd gotten better at reading the exposed frequencies of thoughts floating inside my head; it was as if he'd read my mind.

While he worked on restoring order in my head, I sat and watched. Whenever I gestured, commanded, or demanded for the visions to move, they ignored my actions. It was enough to make me feel impotent in a psychic sense. As a telepath, controlling things within a mind was supposed to be easy. Controlling things in my own head—I should've held complete and total mastery, but I sat and studied Milo like a novice.

The way he pulled the visions, some in big sweeping groups, others he'd pluck one at a time, but everything he did held some specific arrangement. I couldn't see the system behind his method. There was a purpose, though. He stacked visions on top of each other meticulously. He sorted which piles sat beside each other and which were placed furthest apart. He hummed as he worked. Not to keep me out of his thoughts, which he willingly shared. No, he enjoyed the melody in his head. It helped ignore that what he did was work, instead thinking of it like a treat.

A day inside the head of your grumpy boyfriend. What a field trip.

"Someone's extra sassy this morning."

I sighed. My thoughts rang a little louder than intended.

"Loving it." Milo winked, then continued working. "*Wish I had time to show you what happens to sassy boys who mouth off.*"

I took an immediate deep exhale, forcing a breath to settle the sudden shudder of exhilaration that traveled across my skin. A tingling sensation of lust and love and kink all roused tightly in my chest before blood flow found another outlet, making it difficult to hide how much I enjoyed Milo's thoughts when my morning boner rubbed against his inner thigh as he worked.

We lay together while Milo finished locking away the visions, slamming them together with such force they appeared welded. It wouldn't last, it never did, but I'd slowly learned to adapt to the presence of Milo's visions in my head.

"They'll hold long enough," Milo said, turning to me and smirking from the shadows of my inner core. "And when I return from my case, I'll make my next mission helping you master the art of clairvoyant Tetris."

"Seriously?"

"Seriously. Each potential future needs to fit together just right so they don't stack too high and crumble in your mind."

"Then why do they keep crumbling? Or exploding. Or whatever."

"Because visions are also like cats," Milo said, grimacing as Carlie bit his toes outside my mind. She'd grown impatient and planned to drag us out of the depths of my inner core if it was the last thing she did. Anything for breakfast.

"Tetris cats?" I quirked a brow, telekinetically removing the fat cat from the bed so she didn't claw up Milo's leg.

He moved closer, cuddling against me. The scruff on his face rubbed against mine while inside my head, he swaggered closer, bringing us together in an embrace inside and outside my mind.

"You have to get ready," I whispered.

Milo's mind buzzed with a checklist of a thousand different things he needed to get finished before going to the airport, yet the highest priority sang in his mind. He wanted to enjoy every second in bed we had together. He wanted to hold me so tightly that I'd feel this hug for the next several weeks in his absence.

"We still have a few minutes left." Milo kissed my neck.

With Milo heading off for this Global Guild mission, I'd have to learn how to be independent again. I wouldn't have him around for weeks. Longer maybe. After pushing him away for over a decade, the idea of spending more than a few days without his light, his joy, his love—it felt impossible. I didn't know how I'd cope without having him here, so I lay in bed soaking up a few more minutes of cuddling and doing my best to savor these precious moments.

Chapter Two

EVERYTHING about this second and final semester of working with my homeroom coven moved too quickly. Between lessons, meetings, grading, check-ins, alternating trainings, and research into potential enchanters for internships, my mind fell into a fog. It was already February, and I hadn't accomplished half of what I set out to cross off my to-do list.

It didn't help matters that my telepathy coiled at the back of my head, squeezing against my skull and ready to burst. Milo's trip had only just begun, yet his absence left me craving his presence. I'd become completely reliant on his joy, his love, his everything. Milo completed the missing pieces in my heart and mind, and as such, my branch ached for the comfort he offered. Even so, I wouldn't find him. I couldn't reach across the country to follow his thoughts while he worked on a case with the Global Guild in California. Or wherever the hell in the airport he currently waited around before his flight took off.

It didn't deter my magic to make the attempt. Hence, the fog of auto-pilot on my drive to work. While I remained firmly planted in my car, absent-mindedly driving through traffic and barely focused, my telepathy soared across the city of Chicago.

Fluttering above the morning crowds in the thick of downtown, weaving between the busy district of guilds, stalking enchanters in hopes they'd taken on a case accompanying Milo in some unknown venture. Even searching the halls of Cerberus Guild presented no new intel. I very much knew Milo wasn't in the city. I had complete and total awareness of that fact. I knew exactly where he was located—or would be when his plane landed—but my magic hunted for him all the same, like a sad, lonely dog desperate for affection and companionship.

"Fuck." I slammed my foot on the brakes, bracing against my steering wheel as I whipped forward from the sudden halt. It rattled my telepathy back into place but sent an ache coursing through my bones.

I blinked a few times until the last specks of the city faded from my vision, and the full depth of the academy parking lot settled in.

Chanelle stood in front of her parked SUV, wide-eyed and her long braids outstretched, appearing almost like sentient serpents. But in reality, the braids were merely caught in the sudden, heavy entanglement of channeled telekinesis. The subtle flow of her waist-length passion twists around her body cast a calming allure to the tense situation. She pressed her telekinesis against the hood of my car so precisely that it left a large handlike indent, almost as if Chanelle's slender fingers had suddenly extended the length of my car and wrapped around it like a mere toy in her path.

I lifted my hands and tilted my head apologetically. "*My bad.*"

"*Damn, Dorian. I know you like this parking space, but Jesus Christ, you can't just...*"

Letting out an exuberant sigh, I nodded profusely during Chanelle's incredibly long-winded rant. I was at fault, lost in a daze of nonsense. Her thoughts helped keep my mind attentive and focused on the here and now. I supposed today's lesson would do the same, keeping me locked on whether my students were ready for their first big upcoming test before the ticking clock of saying farewell to them this summer and hoping for the best.

"*Today is not the day.*" And with that, Chanelle lifted my car into the air, hurled it across the parking lot to the furthest space she could find, and then delicately dropped it.

Okay, not such a delicate drop, considering the way my head whipped side-to-side, braced only by the collision with the cushion of my seat head-rest.

"Oh, come on," I grumbled half aloud and half still linked to Chanelle, who really didn't have the patience to continue or ask where my head was this morning since her thoughts were already lost on a long list of tasks she needed to complete, double check, redo since the person assigned likely fucked it up, and a thousand other things she needed done before eight o'clock.

Yeesh. I sucked my teeth, breaking the connection that tethered our minds because that much work fried my brain this early in the day.

> Milo: Hope you have a good day.

He'd attached a close-up photo of him grinning.

> Milo: Well, a productive day.

He sent a second photo, and this one had him holding a notebook while telekinetically floating pens above it. I almost chuckled. Was that his idea of being productive? Writing in a random notebook that he impulsively paid way too much for at the airport.

> Milo: A stress free day.

And he'd attached a third photo, this one of his legs propped up like he was lounging at the airport, which he likely was while waiting for his flight.

> Milo: Just try not to overthink your day.

No photo. Just a follow-up of three heart emojis.

Overthink today? Like how my magic decided to become erratic in your slight absence, searching for you across the city and swiftly making its way toward O'Hare? I didn't send that. Instead, I sulked, redistributing my channeling efforts into my roots to drain my overactive telepathy.

Me: Have a safe flight.

After sending Milo the message, I headed inside the building. I shuffled between students in the hallway and had the misfortune of enduring Kenzo's scowl as I reached my classroom and opened the door. He huffed, keeping his stare trained on me and sending his most judgmental surface thoughts for my lack of punctuality.

I glared back at him, eyeing the short tyrant. Gray static coursed across his slender body, zipping from his fists to his pale face all the way through his jet-black hair, adding a sheen, then underneath his academy uniform down to his shoes and back around again, ensuring his training never ceased.

```
Name: Kenzo Ito
Branch: Hex (Disruption)
Ranking: 1
```

He wasn't actually as short and slender as he used to be. It'd been almost two years since he'd first stepped into my classroom. Kenzo had grown since then. Seventeen years old, like most of my homeroom students, his shoulders were broader, his biceps more muscular, and he'd even shot up a bit in height too, now standing at my height of 5'11. He merely looked deceptively small when standing beside Gael. But didn't we all?

"Morning, Mr. Frost." Gael smiled with his shark-like teeth, towering over Kenzo and me as he stood outside the classroom.

Thankfully, Kenzo's chatty boyfriend always seemed to wrangle him in before the angry prick became too tiresome. Gael also served as a literal bright beacon of positivity around Kenzo; his sunshiny orange aura bled into the black and whites of Kenzo's inner core. It didn't change Kenzo, didn't stay very long, but it stirred a calmness in his thoughts, allowing him to release the bitterness in his throat for the many rude things he sought to say.

Gael kept his brown eyes locked on me, smile intact, and thoughts screaming for a compliment. Even in Spanish, I caught enough to understand. Okay—that was an utter lie. I recognized at most three of the words zipping around Gael's head, but the yearning on his face, the fluctuation in his aura, and those damn pleading eyes.

"Nice hair." I nodded to the spiky pink hair he sported for the upcoming holiday.

"Yeah, and?" Gael stepped closer, blocking the doorway and eagerly turning side to side, showing off his large spikes.

```
Name: Gael Martinez
Branch: Augmentation (Spikes)
Ranking: 35
```

The biggest pair sat on either of his shoulders, weighing heavy on him, but given his broad chest and very muscular physique, Gael handled the extra twenty pounds with ease. The way he flexed his forearms was intentional, and suddenly, I caught what he wanted to flaunt.

"You've finally figured out how to redistribute your spikes." I nearly smiled. We'd worked on that after winter break and to see how Gael masterfully handled altering the set-in pathways of his augmentation in a few weeks for a training I anticipated would take the entire semester—if not a few years to follow. "Quite impressive."

Gael couldn't simply remove the flow of magic or the protrusions of spikes across his body, but from the training we'd done with Milo's acolytes last semester, I finally gained a better understanding of Gael's branch.

Instead of hundreds of tiny spikes lining his forearms, Gael had about a half dozen bigger spikes around his wrists. They curved slightly backward so as to not interfere with his hands, and they resembled the angry rocker bracelets I used to buy when I was Gael's age in some desperate attempt to seem edgy.

"Come on, porcupine." Kenzo grabbed Gael's hand and dragged him into the classroom.

Sweet and almost endearing, except it became clear that Kenzo simply wanted to beat everyone else to class since he treated everything like a competition—including attendance. I swear, Kenzo gave me the biggest headache.

I clenched my teeth from the barrage of questions circulating around a familiar mind. Namely, Caleb who carried a stack of books in his arms and kept four weighted blocks hovering above his head.

Okay, Caleb's curiosity occasionally made him a bigger headache. A lot of occasions.

His thoughts stirred in a hundred different directions, replaying training scenarios, buzzing with questions on today's possible lesson, and paraphrasing the texts he carried to class. He barely resembled the boy from the vision last year, having shot up more than a foot in height and doubling in muscle mass. Seriously, the scrawny, nerdy teen who walked into my class with a frazzled face and curly hair then now had a jock build with a sharp jawline and a stylish new hairstyle where he'd shaved the sides while allowing the top to grow out, keeping the curls tamed with product.

One of the books in the mountain Caleb carried had tipped and tilted and nearly fallen from the stack until I waved a hand, steadying what he carried since his attention drifted every which way.

"Oh, thanks so much, Mr. Frost." Caleb smiled, sincere yet nervous, adjusting his books and putting the thin, flimsy copy of Fundamentals to Root Casting under a much thicker hardback copy of some intricate research about the History of Banishment in the French Parliament.

I scrunched my face. Caleb really decided to dive into every possible account on root magic in hopes of accessing his perfected banishment casting again. His copy of the fundamentals circulated through his thoughts, every word, even the acknowledgments, memorized. He'd read each book in his stack a dozen times over, the worn spines an obvious indication, but also the massive amounts of information floating along his surface thoughts, interlocking with a web of knowledge he tied together, hoping to learn more mastery over his four root magics and prove his worth.

```
Name: Caleb Huxley
Branch: N/A
Ranking: 100
```

I wanted to ensure Caleb demonstrated his perfected banishment technique again. Preferably with enchanters in attendance. Something told me Caleb wouldn't master his perfected root casting by the end of his second year, but I believed he'd access it a second time. I believed his use of the perfected banishment was more than a fluke. If I could help him use that level of magic again, it'd draw in a lot of enchanter interest, and among them, I'd certainly find one worthy of helping Caleb succeed during his third year. As a branchless student, I could already see the pile of polite rejection letters to the inquiries we'd make about him working as an intern. Too many enchanters would see him as a burden, a waste of resources, a charity case they didn't quite see the benefit of offering their time toward.

They were wrong, though. Caleb would make for a fantastic addition to any guild in Chicago, and I wanted to ensure the best enchanters and the strongest guilds wanted to work with him. They'd help him cultivate his talents, offer him the best opportunities, and finally demonstrate how goddamn overrated branches were in this world.

Even as the thought of irksome branch magic crossed my mind, my telepathy pulsed, tugging and seeking Milo despite the impossibility.

Caleb gulped. *"The forehead wrinkles are setting in, which can only mean he's extra angry. I can only imagine what that means for today's lesson."*

I scowled. Did Caleb just analyze my expression like he knew what it meant?

"Check us out, Mr. Frosty!" Gael shouted, accompanied by the ear-piercing crow of his rooster familiar.

Caleb took my weary face and the turn of my attention to scurry into the classroom and avoid my telepathy. Whatever.

Gael floated through the hallway on his side, almost as if he were sprawled out on a couch, keeping one arm resting under his head to prop it upward and another hand planted on his hip. Since him and his familiar had stopped actively avoiding his levitation root, Gael now took every opportunity to show off his immediate proficiency with the magic.

```
Name: Gael Rios-Vega
Branch: Bestial (Familiar)
Ranking: 92
```

He didn't wear his academy blazer, making the flex of his biceps very obvious. That, and the strained expression on his face, but to be fair, he did well to hide the exertion with a mischievous grin. Gael's blazer sat neatly folded on his hip bone, offering King Clucks a comfy seat as he steered Gael through the sea of children in the hallways. Seriously, the damn bird looked like a ship captain cawing at anyone and everyone in their path.

"Is there a reason you're flying through the hallways?" I sighed, gesturing for him to stop and stand appropriately.

"Cl-cl-cluck."

"*Exactly,*" Gael thought, sticking his tongue out, showing off his piercing while also making a disgusted expression. "*He spends forever whining about us not levitating, and now he's gonna bitch when we are levitating.*"

"Ba-ba-ba."

The pair continued blocking the hallway for nearly everyone since Gael remained stretched out horizontally with King Clucks on his partner's hip, ready to squint with fury at anyone who dared complain about the inconvenience.

"*Yep. Some folks are only ever happy when they have something to complain about.*" Gael waggled his brows, and my gaze fell to his eyebrow ring, then the industrial piercing on the opposite side of his face, through his upper left ear. He'd gotten both over winter break. Since returning to school, he'd also changed out his subtle earrings for flashier diamond studs.

"*Don't know how my boy Evergreen handles all that whining...and the talking. Nonstop. Lecture this, rules that, life lesson moral thingy...*"

His rooster puffed his chest, imitating a laughing gesture.

"Right. Mr. Frosty must lay it down, backing it up hard, because you know that's the only way—"

I glared, waving a hand to tilt Gael's trajectory while King Clucks squawked and furiously flapped his wings as he scampered up Gael's body, scaling his human partner until he planted himself atop Gael's head.

"Chill out, Clucks!" Gael's shoulders tensed, and he grinded his teeth as his familiar dug his claws into Gael's fauxhawk.

"Ba-ba-bawk!"

"Yeah, I know he's a dick. Doesn't mean you gotta be a total mother hen."

Gael cringed, bracing for the inevitable pecks that left bright red marks along his forehead and stood out from his deep bronze complexion.

"Look what you did, Mr. Frosty."

"What can I say? I don't like it when students block the hallway all lounged out." I brushed a hand through my hair, knocking the long, brown locks behind my ear. Dramatic flair, but something about Gael's angst brought it out of me.

"Who knew you had those bad bitch moves." Gael nodded approvingly as he swaggered into the classroom with his familiar on his shoulder.

I rolled my eyes. Only Gael.

As they shuffled inside, I counted down the seconds until the bell rang. All the minds in the air today made it difficult to focus, though that might have more to do with the tug from my branch, searching far and wide in a barren city. A city without Milo.

"Morning, Mr. Frost." Tara stopped in front of the door, rifling through her bag. "Here you go."

Still the beautiful, leggy blonde with the features and build of a model. She wore perfectly styled accessories and makeup like the first time she walked into my class almost two years ago, but she didn't wear a fake smile now. No mask to hide her pain. This smile was genuine. The ocean in Tara's mind still existed, but the storms didn't seem overwhelming like they once had. It was almost like Tara had finally found herself, found a way to live with her depression, and hang onto those happy moments in between.

"Well, well." I held up the updated fledgling permit Tara had gotten.

She couldn't take the test over winter break, but I didn't expect her to find an open slot on such short notice—usually, even the academy had to reserve review times months in advance. Guess the Whitlocks really could do anything they wanted.

```
Name: Tara Whitlock
Branch: Ward (Sealing)
Branch: Cosmic (Shadows)
Branch: Arcane (Intangibility)
Branch: Primal (Icicles)
Branch: Psychic (Banshee's Wail)
Ranking: 9
```

"I'll make a copy of your newly approved branch and then return this by the end of the day."

Tara nodded, more annoyed she'd have approval for her fifth branch than stressed by the idea of mastering five branches. As her magic continued to blossom, so did her confidence.

"Tara!" Katherine darted down the hallway. Her athletic build helped her weave between others in the hall as she waved goodbye to a group of friends.

Pining permeated the air off the classmates she stepped away from when racing toward Tara. Most students at the academy seemed captivated by Katherine's presence. Whether because of her sweet smile, her genuine interest in other's conversations, or her highly competitive skills that didn't come with the same cocky personality as most students in the top ten. Even though Tara was kind, she was so reserved that most confused it for an air of arrogance, whereas Katherine's giddy, extroverted personality shined through, and that attracted friendship.

Sunlight shimmered through the windows, dancing along Katherine's light brown complexion and resonating with the bright yellow of her aura. "So glad I caught you."

"You realize we have class together?" Tara quirked an eyebrow.

"Right." Katherine bopped her head. "I'm super scattered today, but I managed to make the updated sigils. Sorry it took so long."

Katherine retrieved a small cube, similar to the weighted blocks Caleb trained with, though the enchantment sigils differed. Unlike his that helped hone root casting, Katherine had created this block to absorb casting from Tara's magics. Each side represented a different branch, allowing her to continuously train without the casting disrupting or destroying anything nearby. That'd helped a lot with Tara's confidence. I'd seen it. The way she discreetly trained, always happiest when the pressure of everyone's eyes didn't fall on her.

"You know I don't actually need an updated enchantment box." Tara retrieved the one she currently used for casting practice. "I really only need this for the three that are overlapped. Otherwise, it's just harder to train all three at once."

Tara's overlap caused her shadows, her sealing, and her intangibility to become tangled together, which made it impossible for her to use one without using the other two in tandem. It didn't help they weren't the most compatible. Still, I'd watched her flourish since arriving at Gemini; even when the new branches she awakened worried or intimidated her, she kept strong and determined.

I believed that overlap caused so much stress in Tara's youth that she inadvertently suppressed her other branches. How many she currently had suppressed, I had no idea. But it reminded me of how I had the tendency to suppress the magnitudes of my telepathy branch, going most of my life without realizing the full extent of my casting ability. I wouldn't allow that to happen to Tara, not if I could help her learn from the mistakes I never had.

Katherine grimaced, then adjusted her glasses in some effort to stop staring at the worn scuffs lining the corners of the enchanted box she'd created while she judged herself for sloppy work on the sigils that she considered so basic a five-year-old with her branch could compose better spell work.

```
Name: Katherine Harris
Branch: Enchantment (Spell Craft)
Ranking: 7
```

"This one is sturdier than the last one and takes into account your fifth branch." Katherine laughed, handing Tara the cube. "Try not to get too many more branches—only one unused side left to the cube. But it's not unused. I added a rejuvenation protocol, hence the better reinforcement. Also, totally add as many branches as you want. I can just make a second block. Caleb's got four. Well, four for school. Then there's his home set, work set, and… And, yeah, I know he can just use the same set everywhere, but you wouldn't believe how much he burns through the weighted blocks. Practically destroyed the first set in like a month. So, I find it easier to make a couple sets for different places, which helps keep the wear and tear minimal. Thankfully, you're not as rough in your training, but if you need another set or want another set or just—"

"Thank you so much, Katherine." Tara forced a smile; the desire to smile was genuine, but the action took great effort on her part. The action made Tara anxious, flushing her fair skin with reddened cheeks.

"Anytime." Katherine adjusted the grimoire strapped to her side and looped her arm around Tara's. "Seriously, anytime, because you have no idea how much this is for my own benefit. Like, yay, helping people and training? Oh my god, don't even get me started…"

And with that, Katherine walked into class arm and arm with Tara.

Serene confidence cut through the hallway, drawing my attention as a bright neon blue aura of skylight happiness shined. Carter's smile had this infectious effect, as I fought to maintain a frown despite his many peers smiling when locking eyes with their classmate who strode down the halls without a care in the world. That wasn't true, though. I could hear his thoughts, the deep whispers tucked in the back of Carter's head. They ached to be heard, they craved the rattle of paranoia sparked by their presence, but they held no power in Carter's mind.

It'd taken more than a year, but I finally saw Carter return to the jovial young man he was before the fateful day when trauma nearly consumed him. The day he'd altered the purpose of his branch to heal my fatal injuries.

```
Name: Carter Howe
Branch: Rejuvenation (Vitality)
Ranking: 75
```

I rubbed the scar along my neck, remembering the splotchy, red face Carter had that day. The way every breath I took frightened him, fearful it'd be my last. All that seemed like a bad dream. Dream, not a nightmare. Nightmares were powerful things that haunted and consumed. Dreams faded faster.

Carter had cut his hair shorter, almost shaved like Caleb's, but blonder and with a silly duckbill of gelled bangs in the front. This accounted for a lot of the attention he received walking the hallways. That and he'd landed some awe-inspired winning shot on the boy's tennis team. Ugh. I'd forgotten the few athletes we had scrambling to enjoy the fun extracurriculars while they still had time. I'd have to start bursting bubbles and reminding them they came here for guild success, not athletic careers.

So, despite his branch being perfect for draft picks or whatever, I'd be steering Carter to spend this final semester more wisely.

Carter smiled and high-fived nearly every person whose path he crossed, much to the discontent of Jennifer, who trailed behind him, ready to hiss or pounce on anyone foolish enough to strike up a morning greeting in her direction. Okay, maybe not that exactly, but Jennifer's angry eyes gave off complete and total cat energy. I knew there was something aside from her gothic wardrobe that I admired.

```
Name: Jennifer Jung
Branch: Psychic (Empathic)
Ranking: 18
```

"He's gonna be impossible today." Jennifer rolled her eyes and abandoned Carter to his adoring crowd before wincing at the doorway.

"You all right?" I asked, recognizing the agony of linking onto psychic energy unintended. It was sort of like when drinking water down the wrong pipe or breathing in a scratchy cough or banging your head against a fucking brick wall full force. Basically, it sucked.

"I'm fine, Nurse Frost." Jennifer glared, giving off the most menacing expression she could muster, before cutting her gaze down to the opposite side of the hallway. *"And that goofy fuck better reel in his lust. I do not have the energy to combat pining today."*

Jennifer buried her thoughts quickly after that, realizing she stood too close to me, and nearly revealed where her pining emotions fell. I already knew about her crush on Carter, Carter's crush on her, how the pair couldn't say it out loud because they both loved their friendship—even if they spent most of their time together teasing the other one for being a preppy prince or an emo queen.

I turned my head to where the irritating flutter of a crush had come. The feelings had latched onto Jennifer, who now sat in the classroom doing all she could to turn off her empathy.

At the end of the hall, Jamius turned out to be the culprit. I stared at him and three of his copies as they clustered around Layla, who was none too happy for his doting.

I scrunched my brow, genuinely perplexed Jamius had feelings for Layla. One, they'd never be reciprocated since she only liked girls. Two, Jamius was so nice and calm, whereas Layla was generally mean. Not like a distance herself from others kind of mean, but more of a mean girl who enjoyed picking and teasing and tearing down someone for sport.

```
Name: Jamius Watson
Branch: Alteration (Duplication)
Ranking: 52
```

Jamius brushed his hand across the twists that hung over his face like bangs and grinned. "I'm just curious what kind of guys she likes. I think we have a lot in common and..."

His thoughts trailed off almost as much as his rambling mouth when thinking of Layla's best friend, Amani Williams, one of Chanelle's home-room students. I didn't know what Jamius thought he had in common with Amani, but her image rippled in his surface thoughts, surrounding the well of his inner core, along with flashes of the pair somewhere snowy over winter break. I was surprised I hadn't seen it sooner, in the days since he returned to school, but for some reason, Jamius' desire practically overflowed, and with the help of a few duplicates, he decided to act on his crush.

"So, does she like funny guys?" A copy pointed to himself, grinning at Layla.

"Or how about charming?" A second copy adjusted his sleeves, rolling them down so as not to appear as uncouth as his fellows. Ugh—those were the copies' actual thoughts. Jamius had imprinted personality traits onto them specifically to gauge which would be the most helpful when trying to win over Amani.

"I bet she likes tough guys." The third and final copy blocked Layla's path, flexing his arms and scrunching his face in this bizarre, almost consti-pated expression.

"Oh, Jamius." Layla walked her fingers up the tough guy copy, a smile on her face and complete and utter contempt in her thoughts.

```
Name: Layla Smythe
Branch: Bestial (Therianthropy)
Ranking: 20
```

This wouldn't end well for Jamius.

"Your piqued interest is cute," Layla said. "Almost in an adorably pathetic kind of way. But now I'm bored."

Layla snarled, transforming into her full-size humanoid cougar form, which had immediately intimidated Jamius. So much so that even my legs quivered for a moment. When she roared, nearly everyone in the hall scampered in the opposite direction. Jamius' heart raced, and his magic waned; soon, his three copies exploded into puddles of muck on the floor.

"She likes confidence," Layla said with a deep, beast-like voice before shifting back into her petite human form and running her fingers through her low-hanging ponytails. "You shouldn't waste your time, Hun."

Layla strutted to the classroom and then adjusted her oversized blazer before stepping inside.

It didn't take long for everyone else to make it into the classroom afterward. Once the bell rang, I went directly to the front of the room and started my morning lesson. With a wave of my hand, I withdrew my laptop from my satchel and set it on my desk, rearranging the cords and getting the projector ready while I pulled up my PowerPoint.

"As most of you know by now, the Spring Showcase is just around the corner."

"Wait a second." Yaritza did a timeout gesture with her hands and quirked a brow. "It's barely February."

"Yeah, that's right." Jamius pointed to Yaritza as if to note she'd observed the most hidden secret of the world. "Didn't it start in like May last year?"

"April, actually." Caleb cleared his throat, prepared to elaborate on the exact date. The exact date of all three events.

"Yes, the first-year Spring Showcase lasts about a week, generally speaking," I explained. "But the second-year Student Showcase is meant to be a festive event that draws in enchanters."

"When you say festive, do you mean like a celebration?" Yaritza asked with wide eyes, curiosity piqued, and attention locked onto me. "Or is it just a bunch of combat rounds that'll be dragged out for months?"

I started to answer, "Well…"

"Because I'm fine with either," Yaritza said, summoning her magic from sheer excitement.

```
Name: Yaritza Vargas
Branch: Cosmic (Star Shower)
Ranking: 69
```

The glow of flaming rocks around her thick curls made me hesitate. I didn't know which was worse, the idea of Yaritza absentmindedly setting herself on fire or my classroom.

"Focus." I snapped my fingers and pointed to the fiery pebbles hovering around Yaritza.

"Oh, total attention span on it, Mr. Frost." Yaritza stood up and twirled, letting the flaming rocks circle her uniformed skirt as she spun. "It's a new gravitational effect I've been working on."

She whirled faster and faster, moving the rocks and herself with an added edge of telekinesis, and part of me thought she might very well drill her way through the floor like in the cartoons. But she didn't. Yaritza's mind called out, eyes locked on a central spot of the wall that kept her steady until she finished her demonstration and took a dramatic bow that got polite applause from half the class.

"I see how others are using their magics all the time." Yaritza's eyes fell to Kenzo's gray static bouncing around the corners of the room and the weighted blocks hovering around Caleb. "And I've been finding my own ways to keep my branch active and on full display. So, if we're doing something festive, I can definitely get behind that. Or in front of it. Or beside it. Really, whatever works best for the performance."

"You're not far off," I said. "After all, being an industry professional is about so much more than battle skills. Those are important, but how you interact with the public, how you engage with peers, and the way you carry yourself during interviews are all extremely important factors."

"I knew it!" Yaritza squealed, jumping in place as her star shower sprayed across the classroom, lighting everything ablaze. "I'm going to be amazing! Just you wait, Mr. Frost! I'm so ready to impress the enchanters this semester! I'm gonna rock every single interview and land all the internships!"

I stared at my flaming classroom, unable to hide the horror in my expression, the contempt, and the irritation that we were about five seconds away from a fire drill because this would definitely set off the sprinkler system in my classroom.

"Maybe you should work on your little rock show." Melanie snapped her fingers, smothering every single pebble scattered across the room. "It'd be a shame if you set someone on fire."

I crinkled my nose at the stench of soot or smoke or ash. It was strong, very strong if I smelled it, considering smoke rarely caught my attention.

```
Name: Melanie Dawson
Branch: Primal (Fire)
Ranking: 50
```

Yaritza had a tight, uncomfortable grin to match Melanie's, hoping she didn't appear fazed.

"Then again, that's one way to be remembered in an interview." Melanie smiled wider.

Layla snickered, which only further fueled Melanie.

"Thank you so much for the assistance, Melanie," I interjected because I didn't need a back-and-forth of snide comments from those two. Not this early.

"Sure thing, Mr. Frosty." Melanie winked, then ran her fingers through her red hair, missing the long locks but internally agreeing that Layla had a point. She always had a point. Melanie's face was definitely made for a pixie cut. She'd learn to like it. She'd learn to love it like all the things Layla showed her.

Those two really needed their schedules switched around. It wouldn't help. They'd still have homeroom together. And no one ever had their homeroom switched unless it was the most dire of circumstances. Still, the way Melanie sat at the altar of Layla, losing pieces of herself each and every day. I couldn't even blame Layla for it. She had an alpha mentality and fed on beta energy like Melanie's.

I sighed, appearing unenthused and angry according to the eyes watching me. "Back to the showcase. It's coming up. Phase one. There'll be lots of phases. Lots of events. They're all important. No, you can't goof off." I turned and glared at Gael, who grabbed his chest in shock—even though he hadn't been paying attention since texting at the start of class—and his familiar clucked to support Gael's obnoxiousness. "There'll be no do-overs this semester. Every day, each week, each event will be a moving piece to a larger score that will determine who picks you for an internship. Land the right internship, you might get a job offer after graduation next year. Land a shitty internship and enjoy paying for that casting license out of pocket for the rest of your life because you won't get another chance at a guild."

A few gulped, bit back a gasp, or merely fidgeted from my declaration. Everyone quietly straightened up, paying full attention to the words I spoke.

"Every student at Gemini Academy and every other academy in the city will be competing to catch the attention of enchanters. No. Every student across the state. Everyone wants to land a guild career, and if you want to stand out, then you need to treat every lesson this semester like your entire future depends on it because it very much does."

Even my most reluctant students paid attention. Kenzo cracked his neck and pulled out a notebook. Gael handed his phone to King Clucks and held onto the edge of his desk so his hands wouldn't wander. Layla put her hands on her lap and locked her eyes on me, enhancing her senses with branch magic to further her focus. Jamius dug deep into the well of his inner core, pulling from it every motivating thought he had, every speck of confidence, and all the memories of duplicates who excelled in classwork.

It was absolutely mesmerizing to see my students fully engaged—fearful, sure, but ready to take this next and final step with me leading the helm. I was so proud of them. Every single one of them. But I sure as fuck had zero intention of letting them know that. I rather enjoyed the fear as I went over this lesson. I hadn't seen this group so docile since the first day when I dragged them to the auxiliary gym and watched them scramble over how to handle banishing wisps.

I couldn't believe that in just a few short months, I'd have to say goodbye, send them off to internships, and hope for the best.

"Let's discuss how each of you plans on standing out during the second-year showcase."

CHAPTER THREE

WHEN work ended, I drove home, keeping my sensory root locked onto all the nearby wisps while also channeling my banishment root. No, I didn't plan on casting either magic. There weren't nearly enough wisps to form a fiend-leveled threat. Hell, the cluster of their white light barely created more than an irritating glint like the high beams of an asshole driver. But focusing on my roots did help temper the full force of my active telepathy, which still hunted for Milo in the sea of the city.

My students helped keep my mind and body too busy for my overactive branch to stir too much trouble, but my root casting would have to do the trick once I got home. That and my very needy cats, who immediately barreled toward the front door once I stepped inside.

Charlie meowed his hellos, lifting his front legs and digging his paws and claws into my slacks. I lifted him and pressed his head into the crook of my neck, where he cuddled and purred. It did little to drown out the loud cries of Carlie, famished and demanding her meal this instant. She rubbed against my legs, circling me like a shark and ready to bite me as hard as one, too, if her gentle nudges didn't drive me toward the kitchen soon.

After contending with the two of them, I was able to finally unwind. Carlie was easy enough. Once she had her food, her fill, and a follow-up treat—because of Milo and his need to buy her love—she mellowed out and slept. Charlie, on the other hand, required a full hour of attention. Pets, brushing, encouragement to go eat and drink water, and lots of affectionate words. After he'd been basked in love, he abandoned me to go sleep on the bed.

"All right," I said, cracking my neck and grabbing my book. "Time to master this telepathy bullshit once and for all."

I couldn't very well spend each day of this semester demanding my homeroom coven to properly control their branches, their magics, when I couldn't. It was hypocritical, which didn't bother me nearly as much as the fact it was also incredibly dangerous. I already had the misfortune of experiencing how dangerous it was. What my manifestation wrought onto the world would never happen again. Since the day his memories synced to mine, restoring a full understanding of the capabilities of my magic, I'd made it a priority to research telepathy.

Just as all twelve branches of magic are unique, every magic within a branch held a different skill. My telepathy differed from Milo's clairvoyance, from Jennifer's empathy, from Tara's Banshee's Wail, but it wasn't simply how different psychic branches varied from each other, but how the same psychic magic reacted differently for each individual. My telepathy was similar to many of the case studies I read in the archives of research I dug through, but there were components of my branch that didn't compare. Aspects I'd have to learn to control without guidance.

I read until my eyes blurred. Pages melted together in my head, knocking so much information around I thought it might very well make my head explode. Sinking back into the cushions of the couch, I got as comfortable as I could despite the fact the only part of me that ached came from within my skull.

Finn's smile washed over my mind as I flipped through the pages of this worn text on The Mythos Behind the Psychic Wall. I didn't care much about the research on the history of my magic, but I did enjoy the old lore. And it was the oldest of old lore.

Finn gave me this book, told the story to Milo and me, painted imagery

I never could when recounting the legends behind the first three psychic witches in recorded history. They weren't, most likely, but they survived the test of time.

"The Sisters of Fate," Finn had explained, hazel eyes fluttering as he recounted mysteries even the text of this special edition didn't hold. "Three goddesses in their own right."

"Wait, they're goddesses?" Milo had asked, picking food out of his braces. "I thought they were witches."

"Well, of course." Finn smirked. "Lore often answered the mysteries we've solved today with the more wonderous. They were witches—some of the most powerful, they say."

I'd dozed off into a beautiful memory with a beautiful young man.

"Although, some historians believe the actual deities existed, and the witches merely adopted the persona to pose as figures of divine authority."

"Christ, are you going to give an extra lesson after every single history class?" I scoffed, hiding behind a textbook and pretending not to listen, even if, in truth, I found Finn's recaps far more entertaining than our history teacher's droning.

"Aaaaaanyway, the Sisters of Fate," Finn said, boastful in his lesson. "Or the Moirai actually have ties to more than simply Greek and Roman lore."

"The Moriarty?" Milo asked, befuddled and unable to hide it on his face or in his thoughts.

"The Moirai," I said.

"How they're commonly referred."

My younger self rolled his eyes at that. They weren't more commonly known by that name. They weren't even commonly known other than the occasional pop culture reference because someone somewhere revamped Greek Mythology for the thousandth time into a movie or book or game.

"Sooooo," Finn said, stealing my attention. "They've found themselves in lots of different cultures, which begs the question of what these three knew, why they traveled the world, and how much of society were they pushing toward embracing our witch destiny."

Our witch destiny. Ugh. Finn, along with every history buff, studied the gap where magic faded away. Gone from the world for centuries. No one knew why it happened. Not even branches like Finn's could read the history on the centuries where magic died. His retrocognition required the touch of magic woven into the past to read its story.

All anyone really knew was that many beings for thousands of years were referred to as deities, as monsters, as mythical beasts, and we didn't have clear-cut answers for all those mysteries. Hell, we didn't even know why magic fizzled out for a damn near millennium. When magic had finally returned, when it graced society barely more than two centuries ago, everything changed again. We didn't remain a world that painted pretty lore. Nations embraced the new reality, the new way of life, and many considered that our witch destiny had finally begun.

Our world was divided into two entities. The witches who possessed magic, born of this world, and the demons who tore through the planes of reality, desperate to feed upon our strength and devour everything. All the other mysteries could remain forgotten by time, except by curious souls such as Finn, who sought to unravel the truth of the forgotten past.

Echoed whispers called out, pulling me out of my dozed-off state. I didn't want to surrender my dream, though. Not yet. I wanted to finish this memory; I wanted to follow it to another, let it lead me down a path of cherished days at the academy with Finn and Milo.

The words stirred more loudly. I snapped my eyes open, feeling the dry air sting as even dim lights lashed out. I squinted, taking in a fuzzy image of my living room as suddenly, violently, my sight whirled through the evening sky of the city. Everything whipped by in a hazy blur, and the thoughts of a thousand nearby strangers clouded my head.

"Fuck," I groaned.

My telepathy traveled the length of the city in search of Milo once again. Unwilling or unable to accept his absence, my magic searched for him like it had a will of its own. That made my heart skip a beat, a rhythmic terror, a fright that made my chest and throat burn.

"This is just the lack of a manifestation to deal with the bullshit I was too lazy to handle." That was what this was. But a part of me feared a new manifestation had blossomed in the back of my mind, plotting and preparing. How could I be expected to master the intricacies of my branch when I couldn't even trust my casting?

My vision barreled through the city until it reached the main building of Cerberus Guild. They'd begun construction on additional buildings neighboring their main headquarters, almost as if they sought to take the entire city block, which seemed absurd. Even their tenacious guild master couldn't poach that many enchanters. But Campbell did have a way of wrangling every witch she wanted.

It didn't take long for my magic to fly through the front entrance, up the stairwell, and onto the floor of Milo's office. Of course, my magic went to Cerberus Guild, searching and hunting for any leads like a bloodhound in pursuit of the one man in the world who calmed my unstable mind.

With no leads on Milo, my telepathy faltered, and I began to slowly reel it back.

"Let me be as clear as possible," Guild Master Campbell's voice rang loud but not as loud as her thoughts on Milo.

Campbell stood at a podium in a sleek white suit, addressing her acolytes in a meeting. Her mention of Milo pulled my telepathy toward her, searching her mind for any faint trace.

Her surface thoughts were focused on the rearrangement of her acolytes, moving around hundreds of pieces simultaneously to where I couldn't keep up or comprehend much of anything beating around her head. Well, one thing stood out. Campbell had pulled all the acolytes off the recent volunteering they'd done at Gemini Academy, where they worked with students, so they could prioritize their casework. I was already aware I wouldn't have access to Milo's acolytes this semester, which was fine. Their additional lessons did add some insight into helping my homeroom coven improve their skills, but I didn't have as much energy to wedge in extra learning opportunities with industry pros. Especially since I had to balance getting my homeroom ready for internships while finally controlling my own branch.

"With Enchanter Evergreen's absence, everyone will be stepping up." Her thoughts on Milo became clearer as she spoke about him, helping my telepathy delve deeper into the busy buzz of her mind. "No guild is defined by one witch. No city relies on one witch. Make sure the city of Chicago sees that. Each of you is just as capable as Enchanter Evergreen. If you weren't, I wouldn't keep you here."

She hadn't seen him in days, not since being debriefed on potential difficulties while he was away. Nothing Milo considered threatening but enough for Campbell to assemble her acolytes, schedule meetings all week with her enchanters, and ensure that Chicago ran as smoothly as it did with Enchanter Evergreen on the scene. No. Even better in his absence.

That sparked a sour note in my thoughts. I buried the feeling and reminded myself—and hopefully my magic by extension—that Milo wasn't here.

Campbell's phone pinged. She checked it, catching sight of the name, and then stuffed her phone back into her pocket to continue her speech. Milo had messaged her well over an hour past when she instructed him to check in with her. Enchanter Evergreen's official itinerary danced along Guild Master Campbell's surface thoughts, and suddenly, everything disappeared.

Campbell's sullen scowl faded. Cerberus Guild vanished. Chicago's buildings and busy streets fizzled away. Somehow, someway, my branch took the specific knowledge of Milo's supposed location and propelled my mind far past the bounds of the city. My heart hitched, terrified as the world whipped by and my thoughts propelled further and further across the country. City lines crossed; state lines crossed. How the hell was this even possible?

Any second, I'd collapse. Break. Crumble to pieces. Still, with Milo in my mind, it came with the slightest tug of his thoughts. Too faint to hear. But he must've been close. That meant we had to be in California at this point or near it. As frightening as the idea that my magic carried my mind halfway across the country was, I didn't feel like a balloon floating through the sky, aimless and toward doom. There was direction and purpose, and maybe, just maybe, if I latched to Milo's mind, then everything would be fine.

This wasn't nearly as bad as I anticipated. I mean, sure, my telepathy completely superseded the laws of physics, even by magical standards. But maybe the full extent of my branch didn't wane by distance. This could be tied to the strength that my deranged manifestation alluded to keeping from me. I'd searched memories for his recollections on what else my telepathy could do. Unfortunately, most of his memories were sordid, hateful thoughts for me, cruel conspiring, calculated manipulations, and callous beliefs.

I supposed, at the very least, this proved an unexpected learning opportunity for the limitations surrounding my branch or lack thereof.

I'd finally caught up to Milo, reached his mind, hovered over his shoulder, and heard his thoughts. It didn't matter that I sat in my living room thousands of miles away. It didn't matter that he walked through a crowded airport, bustling with people and noise. Everything except for Milo faded away.

The happiness along the surface hid the tiny glint of frustration that came with a long flight and a long evening ahead. The way he refused to feed the anger had this breathtaking effect on me, stilling my mind and soothing my magic that circled him as he trailed through the airport in search of the representatives meant to meet him for the upcoming mission.

And in this lull of calm illusions, the band that stretched thin, linking Milo and me, snapped. It hit so hard, every bone in my body rattled. My living room burst with a pulse of psychic magic. The walls cracked and crumbled. Or…maybe that was me. My skull. It throbbed and ached, but did it explode? It felt like that until I sank into the shadows of my mind. Deeper than the inner core, away from every single memory and down the tunnel of the subconscious, I traveled.

The endless darkness cooled my aching body. More like the lack of awareness that came with the subconscious disconnected me from my body, a body that lay broken and bruised after the ricochet of magic bouncing back at me from over a thousand miles like a rocket.

"This isn't so bad." I took a deep, shaky breath. "All I have to do is find my way back into my conscious core."

From there, I'd be able to reel my telepathy back. I'd have to. I'd go to the hospital. Maybe get put on some damper meds until I figured out how to properly control my branch. If I lingered in the subconscious, I might never find my way out.

"Everything will be okay. This isn't so bad," I repeated to myself.

"Oh, honey," a hauntingly familiar voice said. "It's so much worse than you think."

I knew that voice. It was mine. A lighter lilt, but that gruff undertone came from me. Only not me.

The person who spoke stepped from the shadows. Another version of me. My manifestation.

CHAPTER FOUR

HE didn't look like himself…well, not entirely. I'd seen all the images of how he portrayed himself when deceiving the last fragment of Finn's being. My manifestation took on the guise of me in my early twenties, back when I worked for Cerberus Guild as Enchanter Frost.

No, my manifestation no longer reflected my youthful appearance but instead looked more like the me of now. Only he had on this ridiculous My Chemical Romance T-shirt that was two sizes too small, exposing my…his… urh…our pale stomach and hairy happy trail. The magenta lettering popped against the black shirt, matching the edges of his heavier makeup. Mostly black with hints of pink. The rest of his getup was very high school me in the body of a man on the verge of a midlife crisis, from the mesh sleeves to the Tripp pants that were so tight at the hips and wide at the bottom, he looked like a mermaid.

"A gothy mermaid. I like it." He smiled, big and wide and filling his whole face.

I cringed in response, hating my smile more than anything and finding it an unnatural expression that didn't fit my face.

"You know I'm not that manifestation," he said, pressing his thoughts against mine to reveal how entangled we were, how similar. "I'm nothing like him."

"You're all the same." I bared my teeth, forcing my way to my feet.

"We're really not," another voice rasped from the shadows. Deeper. Meaner. A hint of all the rage I swallowed most days.

Every ounce of the anger buried oozed from the darkness where this new manifestation festered. It sent a tremble through my body, not my body—no. I lacked a connection to my muscles. That fear etched through my psychic energy, and in turn, I cast my magic into the darkness, snooping and seeking sight of the dangers hidden from me.

"How many of you are there?"

"A few hundred, I think," the gothic getup manifestation said. "We don't really keep a census here. Some fizzle out, some evolve, most just linger like myself."

"Linger?" I asked, wary of trusting the words from his mouth or thoughts revealed with ease.

"Not much else to do in the subconscious."

"And what about when you leave?"

"We don't."

I squinted, delving deeper into his thoughts, what could be considered thoughts. He possessed this hollow form, shallow in depth, and no real place to hide his lies. Yet I knew for a fact how powerful a manifestation could be. I'd had one that tiptoed around me, unraveled itself from me, and carried on around the city, conspiring unconscionable things.

"He did that by taking from you," the manifestation answered. "Your hubris…hmm, let's just call him what he was: the Ego. The arrogant."

"The Ego?" I shook my head. "The ego, the id—they're a part of a person. He was never part of me, not really. More of a cancer, a shadow. A doppler."

"Doppler?" My gothic manifestation quirked a pierced eyebrow, reminding me of the one I'd let close years ago. "Hmmm. Interesting, I suppose."

"Just sounds right." I couldn't explain it. The word, the meaning. It jumped out like a stranglehold.

"Whatever, Doppler, Ego, Asshole, the point is the bastard believed his worth more than what it was, thus why he abandoned the subconscious."

"And he's alone in that thought? Desire?" I asked, not looking for an answer but listening for one. Listening to the whispered thoughts hidden in shadows, determining the degree of threats surrounding me.

"You act like there's anything worth leaving the subconscious for." The manifestation twirled, transforming his clothes into something new. A tiny white shirt with bloody x'ed out eyes and a smiley face, and a pair of equally tight skinny jeans with neon green suspenders dangling around his legs. "We have all we need here."

"Illusions." I scoffed. "Unimpressive ones at that."

"And what does reality really have to offer anyone? If you're any indication, it's not that great." He pursed his lips in a twisted, snarky expression, then let his face fall flat before continuing. "Anyway, Doppler Dorian siphoned off a smidge of your magic, your power, and fled. The audacity. The sheer level of arrogance and spite that required. You don't have to worry about that from the rest of us."

"That so?"

"We're personas. Hollow, fragmented pieces of the whole," he explained. "Everyone has personas in their head, sides of themselves they never reveal, never explore. You know this."

Yes. I'd seen hidden shades of people, but rarely. I supposed that had to do with the fact those facets of others didn't often linger in the conscious mind but rather within the subconscious. And the distinct difference between my personas and others was how sometimes those expressions of identity stepped out of the mind and into the world. Causing havoc. Changing futures.

"I embody pieces of yourself you'd rather keep buried." The persona posed either for flair or to pull me from my thoughts. Possibly both. "The wardrobe, the makeup, the femineity."

"Excuse me?"

"It's not like you're suffering from toxic masculinity. Well, not too much. No one's perfect." He winked, playful and almost reminiscent of Milo, minus the charm because there was absolutely no way I could pull off charming.

Not ever. "Oh, there it is," he said, nodding to the thoughts I expressed floating in the dark between us. "You always doubt yourself, your ability, and as such, you box away every piece that doesn't fit in the world you're striving so desperately to appease."

"You don't know me."

"You don't know yourself, sweetheart." He ran his fingers through his ruffled hair; streaks of purple, red, and blue shimmered against the shadows. "I'm living the life you closed the door on far too long ago."

He meant how my attire in high school shifted. Sure, I kept the goth getup for far too long, but I tamed myself. I stopped painting my nails black because of the whispers on the surface of many minds. I toned down the eyeshadow and liner for a time. I picked my wardrobe very carefully—especially for someone who wanted the world to think I spent little to no time thinking about his outfit.

"It's not really living here, though, is it?" I asked, searching the darkness for thoughts from other manifestations, these personas lying dormant in my subconscious.

"We're not really alive, so what's it matter?" The gothic persona put his hands on his hips and raised his shoulders with a shrug. "I don't mean that in some introspective form of self-loathing depression. After all, I don't embody your depression. Pretty sure no one is running to fill out an application for that persona's role. You can keep your sad sack ways right there on the surface of your mind."

He gestured upward like he was pointing to my inner core, like either of us could see anything in the abyss of the subconscious.

"What do you mean then?"

"We have a very limited range in identity, mainly because we're cutouts of yours. Part of how you controlled your magic as a child and how you dealt with all the encroaching thoughts of others. Children are impressionable. I suppose it was your way of keeping other people's personalities from becoming yours. So down here in the depths of your psyche, I, along with all the other personas, remain in the subconscious, attached to different emotional and psychological aspects of you."

"Everyone here is some repressed piece of me?"

"Absolutely not, darling." He pointed to the shadows where the heavy, angry breaths continued from the aggressive persona. "Some avenues you actively pursue. I mean, you're a real dickhead."

"*Fuck off,*" I thought. "*I'm nowhere near that level of aggression.*"

The aggro persona, the manifestation made of anger, was like a wall of rage—a tower, really. Fury grew higher than most buildings, and I was grateful he kept to the darkness.

"Okay, maybe he's a slightly grumpier version of you." The gothic copy laughed, carefree like he didn't have a concern in the world. So completely contrasted to everything about me. It was strange to see a side of me dressed so dark, so angry, yet filled with a smile that would outshine Milo or Finn.

"As fascinating as all of this is, can you tell me how to get out?"

"Your mind is fracturing. You can feel that, correct?"

I nodded, doing my best not to let my thoughts twist into fear and paranoia.

"Your magic isn't abiding by the limitations of your body, and if this continues, you'll die."

"Unless?" I asked, waiting for the offer. It practically danced on his tongue in the whispers of the shadows from other personas. All this led to an offer he really believed me foolish enough to accept.

"You need to summon a manifestation."

"Not happening. Not on your life."

"I don't really have a life—haven't you been listening?" He rolled his eyes. "All the same, I enjoy the current arrangement surrounding my existence. You dying hinders that."

I channeled my magic, attempting to reel back my telepathy so I'd have enough psychic power to drag myself out of the subconscious.

"Kind of hard to do when you decided to hurl your magic across the country."

"I didn't decide anything."

He tsked. "Don't remind me of your utter incompetence. I was trying to give you some credit for your failures."

Ouch. That felt excessive and unnecessary.

"You need a manifestation to serve as a proxy, an extension to the distance you've stretched your magic. Let us help you."

"I'm not giving you a foothold outside my body," I said. "You can claim not to be like the other manifestation, but you could be lying like he lied. You could be deceiving me, manipulating me, attempting to—"

"I'm gonna stop you there, sweetheart," he said with raised hands, gesturing his offense. "No one is trying to take over your life. We've all seen it. It's pretty shitty, and you do your damnedest to keep it that way."

Goddamn.

"Here's how a manifestation is supposed to work," the persona said. "You summon us for an extension of magic, and we provide it. From there, the magic travels and performs whatever service you require. Usually stalking the mind of some random person for some inconsequential thing."

That was putting it lightly. The last time I harnessed a manifestation, it was to follow my students, which, to be fair, was probably creepier than delving into the mind of some random stranger, but it certainly wasn't for something inconsequential. I was attempting to stop a murder. That was far from trivial curiosity.

"Wait. Earlier, you said the Doppler took my magic."

"He took a piece, pieces to add to his own, which was how he untethered himself from you to begin with. We all have our own magic."

"What?" I couldn't hide the confusion in my voice or thoughts. "How?"

"You," he said bluntly. "You poured your branch magic into your subconscious, breaking off countless pieces."

"Why?" I didn't remember doing any of that. Ever. I wouldn't... I wouldn't even know how.

"Too much power. The mind of a child can sometimes be easily overwhelmed." His expression shifted to something soft, somber. "Hearing an entire city all at once when you're still too young to properly spell the word city can be excruciating. So, as a simple toddler, all you wanted was to make it go away. And you did."

"No. A toddler?" I shook my head. I remembered when my branch was triggered. I was much older when that happened.

"When you stopped talking to your imaginary friend? When you started looking outward to the world instead of inward?"

I stared at him, at his accusatory face, at his irritating surface thoughts that drifted between us and whispered more secrets about more things I'd never known about myself.

"Oh, yes. Dorian Frost definitely has a handle on his memories. It's not like he spends all his time evading them, dodging them, pushing them away at all costs."

Fucking hell. This guy. This persona. My manifestations were always shoving memories back at me in the form of my dreams. I supposed it gave them all a good laugh down here.

"You really just have no fucking clue how any of this works, do you?" He moved his hand, whirling his finger in a circular motion. "We can circle back to all this, but for now, let's return to how manifestations work." He pointed to himself. "We don't leave the subconscious. When you summon a manifestation, you're calling forth the magic you've loaned us."

I focused on his thoughts, completely transparent and synced with what he explained out loud. He twisted his hand, conjuring the illusion of light in the form of a purple flame. It flickered in the darkness but revealed nothing in the shadows. And I knew there were things in the shadows. I could hear their whispers, feel their presence. Other personas kept distant, studying me.

"This is the magic. The magic leaves, returns to you temporarily, and we wait here in the dark for our flicker of light to reawaken us." He handed me the purple flame, letting it hover close since I refused his offering. Then he pointed to himself again. "In other words, the persona stays."

It made sense, more or less. I'd summoned countless manifestations, but they were always me. It wasn't some new identity I'd conjured. They didn't dress differently or act differently. They were simply tools. Eyes for me to peer through when sending them into the deep recesses of another person's mind.

The only problem was…

"One of you already proved that manifestations don't stick to the subconscious."

"That's because of his persona, Doppler Dorian and all that. Narcissism, arrogance, cockiness. Obsession. Let's be honest, just a whole bag of dicks. Who would've thought all your bad habits wrapped into one big asshole would ever happen? I mean, the odds, right?"

"Most of us are only interested in your wellbeing," a young, light voice said.

It startled me. Shook me to the very core. That voice.

"Nico," I said, having a mountain of memories hit me all at once.

I hadn't thought about Nicholas Jenkins since I was a little kid. He'd left. He'd never really been there.

"Imaginary friend or helpful persona to a child in need?" the gothic manifestation asked teasingly. "Sorry to burst the bubble of cherished childhood memories."

"I created you." I stared at Nico, taking in his appearance.

He was small and lanky with shaggy brown hair and missing one of his front teeth, which didn't lessen the smile on his face. Unlike me, he never shied away from a smile; he never allowed the world to intimidate him into boxing away his feelings.

"Nico worked as a proxy, the first manifestation you created, but unlike the rest of us, you interacted with him."

I remembered that. We used to do everything together back when my parents were still married. God, I must've been four or five. It was so long ago.

"Nico helped shield you from the immense force of everyone else's thoughts."

"He always had a secret to share." I half-smiled, recalling all the things he used to whisper about people we'd never met. He had a thousand stories, and they were always filled with jokes.

"Until he shared the story about your father," the persona said. "The one where he'd found love. A new romance. A life fulfilled."

"A cliché mid-life crisis with his secretary of all people." I bit back a snarl because that man was not worth my anger, my energy. I'd already dedicated too many youthful years wondering if he'd return, if he missed me, if he ever cared. He didn't.

"I wish I could've helped more." Nico kicked his feet into the shadowed flooring the same way he used to in the dirt outside when we played.

He was really just a figment. A piece of my magic manifested. I couldn't believe it.

"So, everything Nico told me, every secret he whispered and shared, was just my way of comprehending the thoughts of everyone around me?" I asked, realizing how simple things were with Nico around. My head never hurt. But when he told me about my father. I ground my teeth, ignoring the flashes of our argument, the surfacing memories I wanted to keep buried. He'd tried to tell me what he had learned about my father, what he'd learned about my parents, why my mom was always crying. I didn't want to hear it then. I had yelled at Nico, blamed him for everything. "That's when Nico left."

"I didn't leave." He grimaced. "You sent me away, sent me here."

"I'm so sorry."

"It's okay." He smiled, so bright and cheerful it practically illuminated the shadows of the subconscious.

Even being cast into the depths of darkness because of my childish tantrum couldn't wash away the kind, joyful spirit he had. Did I make him this positive, this happy? Did he learn that outlook on his own?

"I made a lot of friends here," Nico said, reminding me more and more of Milo and Finn with every passing second.

Old memories continued to surface. Flashes of every conversation, from the silly topics we had in my bedroom to the reassurance he offered when my mom would drag me to the park all the way to every instance when the presence of another person frightened me, overwhelmed me, stressed me out. Long before I mastered the art of a scary scowl to force someone to distance themselves from me, I relied on hiding my face, my feelings, my fears.

Nico kept me calm during those days. In fact, it was his absence that taught me how to push others away through intimidation. Still, I missed my old friend, one I'd literally tucked away into the subconscious of my memories. Nico's thoughts radiated with bold confidence and friendly encouragement.

Had this imaginary friend sparked my interest in genuinely happy people, or was that something I'd always been drawn to, seeking the friendship and company of the cheerful? People like Milo, like Chanelle. And Finn, who held my heart but not my grief.

Nico continued, sharing anecdotes about the personas he'd met over the years deep in the darkness. Solemn souls who expressed my passion for poetry. Yuck. Athletes who were obsessed with the joy and health benefits of fitness. Exhausting. Every word built my trust in these personas, even if only in the smallest ways. I trusted Nico. He spoke fast, like a whirlwind trying to get every thought out of his head as if there were an expiration date on our conversation.

"There sort of is since I can't exactly stay here."

Nico's cheeks twitched, fighting to maintain his smile and pulling me from my thoughts. "And I learned that while I tried to help you handle all the world's words, you needed to help yourself and learn to control the telepathy on your own."

"Which you did." The gothic persona rocked his head from side to side, not even remotely hiding the judgment in his tone. "More or less."

"You can't stay here, Dorian. The subconscious is an easy place to get lost," Nico explained, like I didn't have a full understanding of how the mind worked.

The subconscious of every person led to the same dark realm of silence, an empty space that seemed infinite. I didn't know if they were actually endless, but I certainly had no desire to get lost in my own head.

"Even we're wary not to venture too far. Wandering in the depths can be fatal," the gothic persona added. "It's our connection to you, the magic that's drawn to your mind, that keeps us from drifting lost in the abyss."

"I can't," I said through gritted teeth. "I can't give you access to—"

"What the persona did," Nico interjected. "It hurt you. He abandoned you. He hid things from you. He tried to hurt you. He did hurt other people, even when he tried not to."

Christ. His words cut through me to the core of how anxious this made me. How frightened I was to lack an answer. Hell, I didn't know the questions I should be asking.

"It soured your experience, twisted your trust." Nico nodded with this solemn knowledge; it reflected off him in waves, giving me a chance to digest what came next.

Without a manifestation, I would die, lost in my own mind. I could feel it, feel it in my fading thoughts, in my outstretched magic, in my aching bones that became more distant with each passing moment.

"Your branch has always been too powerful," Nico said. "It created pressure, expectations, but maybe now is the time to sort through everything you're capable of? All you need is to trust your magic, your manifestations."

I didn't trust my magic or manifestations, though. I didn't trust these personas, not really. I didn't trust myself, either. But if I didn't make a decision soon, the choice would be made for me, and I'd find myself locked inside my own mind. If I managed to claw my way out without the aid of the personas, it wouldn't be enough for me to keep a solid footing.

My telepathy still moved independently of my will, erratically stretching across the country, and would certainly require a manifestation to alleviate the burden it brought down on my mind. There were dampener meds. If I found the right dose, nullified my magic… No. Even the best medications left psychics lost in a fog day in and day out. It was really the only way to dull the casting receptors.

Swallowing hard, I ran through every single option again and again, weighing the hellish outcomes over and over. There really weren't any other choices.

"Occasionally, a persona will step out with the manifestation you conjure," the gothic persona said, attempting to ease my anxiety. "But mostly, personas such as myself have no desire to fuse with the summoned magic necessary to step out into the real world. We have no interest in observing the world and performing trivial tasks for your bidding. That Doppler, though. Hmmm. He believed himself more than a persona, so he stepped into the role of manifestation, always flocking to fill the shoes when you drew upon magic in the subconscious. He spent so much time above I believe he deluded himself into thinking he was more than what he was. He went from being a persona to believing himself a special manifestation, a real man, and if he'd attained the impossible, I'm certain the fool would've grown bored with it and kept chasing new delusions of grandeur."

"You don't think you're real?" I asked.

"No, darling. And that's not a bad thing." The persona flipped his hair back, moving it from covering his eyes. "I understand my purpose in the world. I've seen behind the curtain and solved the mystery of my existence. It's more than I can say for you so-called living beings. We personas enjoy playing in the shadows. You've no worries about us stealing your life."

I believed him, too. Full-heartedly or foolheartedly? Either way, I decided to trust these personas, these pieces of my being, these echoes of unexplored experiences.

With certainty and wariness wrapped hand in hand, I stepped toward my persona who radiated with magic. My magic. My frequency. My signature. It would offer me the pulse and push I required to wake up, to regain my footing, to find a way forward.

The magic fused to the gothic persona glowed as it untwined from his being, forming and reshaping into a carbon copy of myself. It was strange, seeing a perfect reflection frozen and without any thought standing next to the persona who now appeared withered and faded, like a wilting flower.

"What happens to you while I use your magic?"

"Firstly, it is not *my* magic," he answered. The edge of attitude was lessened from his state of exhaustion. "Secondly, I sleep. I dream. Well, they're not dreams so much as flashes of what the magic connected to me witnesses. Memories, I suppose, that belong to you. Mostly, I wait until the magic is returned."

"Thank you," I said, sending the manifestation made of purple magic to the surface of my mind and following behind, dragging myself to the surface of my own mind.

"No rush," the persona said, sinking into the shadows. "It's been some time since I truly slumbered. I quite prefer it."

He faded beneath the darkness, and only whispers of his thoughts remained, much like the many personas of my magic around us. I floated away, leaving them behind, along with so many questions I had about my magic, my telepathy, my branch. Right now, I needed to breathe. I needed to free my mind from this dark prison. I needed to establish a proper connection to Milo's mind and figure out how a link that spanned more than a thousand miles of distance would work.

My eyes snapped open, and I sat on the living room couch, staring at a reflection of myself in the form of a conjured manifestation. Our vision synced, casting a mirror-like effect, looking back at each other infinitely.

"Go."

I sent the manifestation hurling from my home and following the tether that'd latched itself to Milo. It didn't matter that my branch spanned a thread halfway across the country; each second that passed, with the manifestation moving closer to Milo, eased my trembling body. I inhaled, deep and freeing, as my lungs had a slight reprieve from the stress of the overactive casting my branch had caused. The cramp in my muscles lessened. The fog in my mind faded. The manifestation's presence had alleviated the pain coursing through me.

Now I could follow Milo over a thousand miles away, working with the Global Guild while focusing on my final semester with my homeroom coven. The same group of kids that sparked the growth in my branch. The children I put my life on the line to protect and, in the process, found a reason to finally live my life again for myself. I was grateful to each and every one of those students. I was grateful for Milo. I wanted to give everyone my all, and with the help of these manifestations, maybe I finally could.

CHAPTER FIVE

I SOARED through the evening sky, zipping across the land in a blur of psychic energy. It didn't take long to pinpoint Milo's mind. He was a single star in the cluster of the cosmos, but he burned as bright as the sun. It didn't matter that a galaxy of minds buzzed around me. It didn't matter that I traveled faster than light and further than sound or that my branch should've stretched thin and shattered a hundred times over from the distance. I breezed ahead, fixating on what I'd learned.

Manifestations weren't a separate entity. In retrospect, I always knew that to a degree. I mean, they were me. They were my thoughts split into two forms at the same time. Forms that allowed me to use my telepathy without restraint or distraction in my day-to-day life by turning the volume down, so to speak. I left my other half to his devices, making observations and then informing me later when we merged back as one entity. But then there was the vile manifestation, the one who plotted and conspired and brought death where he walked. I'd met him before, an active, engaging manifestation who warped my perception of how my psychic energy worked.

But he was never a manifestation, merely a persona. A figment of personality traits, an arrogant piece of my imagination that sprouted real desires. And while I knew everyone had personas, fantastical sides to themselves that dwelled in their imagination, I didn't spend a lot of time in people's imaginations. Either they ran wild with chaos or were dim and depressing, dying a slow death as reality seeped into every waking thought, preventing a mental escape.

One day, someday, I'd need to delve into the deepest recesses of my subconscious and account for every possible persona lurking in those shadows. What happened with the Doppler would never happen again. While I knew attaching to Milo was a priority and teaching my students another, I'd ensure that both halves of my conscious mind worked to master my magic. I'd strive to make sense of it once and for all.

For now, I focused on Milo. Having finally reached him, I sighed a deep exhale of relief. Sure, I was nothing but magical energy, and breathing didn't actually fill my nonexistent lungs in this psychic phantom-like form, but it still offered me a reprieve, a chance to think and compose myself before attaching to Milo. My other half was probably already wondering when he'd need to message Milo about this development and creating a schedule on when to check the memories and observations I made.

Milo walked through the airport, a swagger in his steps, even though exhaustion weighed heavy on his shoulders. His flight had an unexpected layover thanks to some high-flying fiends. Waiting for the airport in Kansas to get a half-decent enchanter to banish the demonic energy took forever, and Milo hated the restrictions on licensing across state lines. Sure, in the case of an emergency, Enchanter Evergreen could've swooped in and cleared away this threat in minutes without fear of a fine or penalties. But since everything The Inevitable Future gleaned from his potential outcomes, it seemed the only way their state's general attorney would consider the incident an actual emergency was if those fiends formed into a demon and ripped one of the plane's wings off.

Not every state, every branch of government, worked well with guilds and enchanters. Turned out Kansas was quite adamant their local authorities could handle any threats, which explained why they had the highest warlock mortality rate in the country and often required National Guard intervention on their demon populace.

None of that mattered now. Milo had arrived. It didn't take long for the Global Guild representatives to find him and make swift introductions as they escorted him out of the airport.

A group of fifteen people circled Milo, taking pictures, measurements, jotting notes, feeling the skin of his hands, his cheeks—one even squeezed the tips of his hair then played with the gel between their fingers. It was as if they only had one job to do. An invasive one at that, but Milo didn't seem too shocked by their actions since he'd caught glimpses of the possibility and had years of experience with the Cerberus Guild PR team. Granted, they weren't as handsy.

"I'm Ronald MacDonald," a short, stout man said with a chuckle. "And no relation. But you best believe I trademarked my name, too. That's how good I am at my brand."

He was a round man. Quite literally very rounded, almost perfectly symmetrical like an ornament. It must've been his magic, an augmentation branch, perhaps. It didn't hinder him any. He had a sturdy build and a quick pace as he led the pack that continued evaluating Milo. I assumed because he assumed and, well, he understood the industry far better than I did.

"You'll wish to familiarize yourself with these." Ronald snapped his fingers, and the young woman to his left scuddled around and handed Milo a stack of papers.

Milo sighed, skimming through the confidential case files. The last thing he expected when getting tapped by the biggest and strongest guild in the world was paperwork. To be fair, they hadn't given him paperwork. It was research and intel, so it was more like homework.

I snickered, floating alongside him as he read through the documents. The team of representatives ushered him outside of the airport and toward a parking strip where cars pulled in and out for pickups and drop-offs.

"Geez, this is a lot," Milo said, eyeing the traffic. "Like, a lot a lot. It's just so much."

"The number of times I'm sure you've heard that, Enchanter Evergreen." Ronald winked—not in a suggestive, flirty manner, but playful and definitely with a hint of winning over his audience.

Which worked. Milo laughed, then went right to work diving into the reading material. I rolled my eyes because, at the end of the day, Milo was an easy audience to appease. If I weren't so closely attached to Milo at the moment, I'd consider delving into Ronald MacDonald's thoughts, where I was certain I'd find a list of ways to appeal to Enchanter Evergreen's ego. This guy was a "yes" man on the Global Guild level, so winning over top-ranked witches was a sport for him.

"I'm not sure what your team expects from me." Milo flipped through a few pages, heart elevating with each passing second. I wanted to reach out, console him, offer him some type of reprieve from the dread that consumed him with each word he read. "I can't see the potential futures of the dead."

Not them directly, anyway. He needed a living anchor to read their possible outcomes. The most tragic part of Milo's clairvoyance was he could still see the futures where dead loved ones could've played a role. There were hundreds of futures with Finn floating around Milo's mind. They were like knives stabbing me in the stomach every time I stumbled onto one of those possibilities that would never be.

"Oh, not to worry," Ronald said, grabbing a file from the stack while nonchalantly shrugging off the mountain of reported deaths in the papers Milo held.

Ronald had the appearance of a man who never dealt directly with death. Sure, he worked for the Global Guild, clearly handling dangerous cases like this one regularly, but he maintained a healthy distance from murder. Milo noted how it made Ronald oblivious to the weight and horror. Not in an insulting way, merely a uniformed, desensitized manner. After all, people died every day, and Ronald didn't even know them, so why should those deaths sting? Milo understood not everyone could carry the guilt.

I reached out as the psychic phantom I was and consoled Milo, wishing to send him waves of comfort and healing and hopeful one day he'd stop blaming himself for every atrocity that struck the world. He couldn't be everywhere, he couldn't predict everything, and he couldn't save everyone.

"See." Ronald pointed to a section of the file he'd snatched up. "There's a survivor."

Benjamin Oxland. He didn't look very old from the portrait they had on file. Maybe four or five. It was hard to say. I typically avoided little children as their thoughts were wonky, and their voices were loud. Plus, I didn't have much patience for anyone.

Milo came to a stop, rereading the state of the child. The magic that'd killed all those people in the novel of papers he clutched hadn't struck down Benjamin Oxland. This kid survived, if one could call it that. Apparently, the attack left him physically unscathed while in a vegetative state.

"What happened to him exactly?" Milo's mind whirled through every magic he knew from years in the industry, from years of listening to Finn's branch history lessons, but he'd never heard of a magic that could attack multiple minds at once and slaughter them, of a magic that could keep the victim trapped even after the witch who cast the magic had fled the scene of the crime. "What kind of magic traps someone inside their own head?"

"That'd be—"

"Oceanic Collapse," a feminine voice answered from above.

Milo spun around, catching full sight of the woman floating above him. She wore a golden cape with the Global Guild emblem on display for all those nearby. It matched her makeup and complimented her dark brown complexion. She'd appeared from literal thin air, moving so quickly and silently that neither mine nor Milo's magic detected her presence until she was right on top of us.

Milo's mind turned to mush, fanboying with a thousand different thoughts on Alicia Lawrence, best known to the public as Global Gladiatrix. Which made sense as a gladiatrix was the female version of a gladiator, and gladiators were renowned for their skill as warriors and champions of entertainment. Something every enchanter these days strived for. Of course Milo would be a fan for a fellow witch in love with the absurdity of stage names like The Inevitable Future.

"Gladiatrix," someone shouted, waving their hand and flashing the pink, light blue, and white bracelet they wore with two golden Gs.

The globally ranked enchanter posed, hands on her hips, chin held high, and chest proudly raised, displaying the heart-shaped trans flag on the front of her shirt. Her slow descent drew many eyes, many minds, and soon, people approached the internationally famous witch.

"She's one of the…"   "Whoa, I know her."

"What's she doing here?"

"Doesn't she work like halfway across the world?"

"She works all over the world."   "I can't believe she's here."

"Must be something big happening."

"You heard what happened in…"

"What? That was here?"   "Not here here, but yeah."

"Heard hundreds died."

"Try thousands."

The chatty group nearly swarmed Milo as they crowded around Gladiatrix, each eager to stand beside her for a picture, for an autograph, for a chance to talk with one of the strongest witches in the world.

```
Name: Alicia Lawrence
Branch: Alteration (Supreme Physicality)
```

Physicality came in varying degrees, so much so that the licensing committee created different titles based on the level of enhancement the witch possessed. Physicality, in the most basic sense, gave a person more physical ability than those around them. It differed from mere enhanced strength or speed. It was a combination of overall physical enhancements throughout the body: strength, speed, reflexes, senses, channeling, and healing.

That, in turn, gave them greater access to their root magics. I'd seen several differing levels of physicality over the years that included enhanced physicality, major physicality, and ultimate physicality—which came from a coach between jobs and trying to earn his way back into guild life—but I'd never encountered someone with supreme physicality. I couldn't even fathom how powerful Gladiatrix truly was. They say a single punch from her could hit harder than a semi-truck at full speed. And that was only if she held back some.

Milo had noticed how no one in this crowd paid attention to him, recognized him, or even acknowledged his presence. It was odd, comforting, and a tinge insulting. Enchanter Evergreen knew his audience was mainly back in Illinois, but he believed he had some national fame. After all, he'd recently become globally ranked, and he'd always had an engaging online presence. Still, he enjoyed watching Gladiatrix interact with her audience. Her strong stance, her poised expression, her gentle smile, and the lightest laughter when someone spoke to her. Every interaction held finesse and expertise.

Ronald stood beside Milo and huffed. "I told her we didn't have time for a photo op."

Milo knew that was a lie. He knew sooner than me, simply studying Ronald's stance, the slight grin on his face, the way his eyes darted around the crowd, and every other thing that years in the industry had taught Milo to be observant on.

A quick glance into Ronald's surface thoughts revealed how the recent attack had shaken the state, and he'd been tasked with ensuring the public calmed. He staged Gladiatrix's arrival, a small gesture he believed would spread quickly, much like the wildfires he noted California currently contended with. I grimaced. Seriously? Even as the man's poor taste in a comparison sat on the surface of his mind, he weaved together ideas of stealing some time from Gladiatrix's current mission so she could assist the local guilds on the current fires that ate through suburban neighborhoods. His mind reminded me of Caleb's if Caleb fixated solely on one woman's career and ways to play on the public to push her approval ratings higher and higher.

"Don't worry." Milo smirked, pulling me from my snooping. "I predict it'll all work out."

"And you'd know, huh?" Ronald replied with a small chuckle.

Facts about Gladiatrix poured out onto the surface of Milo's mind as he admired how she held herself for her audience.

Enchanter Alicia Lawrence was the highest-ranked woman in the Global Guild, sitting at number four with only three witches in the whole world deemed officially stronger than her. She was also the only trans person in the top ten rankings.

That wasn't a detail I knew because of Milo, though he did find her queer activism admirable. But no, I knew quite a bit about Gladiatrix, such as her work to gain the trans community more recognition and acknowledgment for their history in the guild industry and how only six witches out of the several hundred listed in the Global Rankings were trans.

This insight came from Carter and Jennifer as they took on leading roles in Gemini's LGBTQ+ Club. Each researched the roles queer witches played in the industry, in the world, and how that had evolved recently. They weren't the only students in the club, but they were definitely the pair that made the most time for it. Each eager to share something with their members or each other, each buzzing with facts, each teeming with a desire to finally share their feelings.

Admittedly, I learned a lot about the queer community in the industry I had taken for granted when eavesdropping on Carter and Jennifer, awaiting the day one of them would confess their crush.

"You ready?" Gladiatrix asked Milo, stepping away from the thinning crowd.

"I'll pull the car around." Ronald snapped his fingers to instruct one of his nearby assistants to pull the car around.

Gladiatrix kept her gaze fixed on Milo, awaiting his answer. He stared at the stack of papers in his hands, then at Gladiatrix, then solemnly back to the papers, and then back to the young enchanter whose smile lightened Milo's mood. She curled her fingers, balling a fist, and sent a sturdy wave of telekinesis through the air that stole away the files and tossed them into the hands of several representatives at Ronald's side.

"Well, ready?" Gladiatrix asked.

"Always." He grinned.

"Let's go," she said, hovering in the air. "Traffic in this city is a bitch and a half."

With that, Milo took off alongside Gladiatrix, and both snickered and smirked as Ronald shouted at them to come back.

I kept close to Milo, enjoying the warm buzz radiating throughout him. Emotions were high, filled with excitement and energy. He focused on his casting, hoping to impress Gladiatrix. I hadn't realized, but her flight movement was absolutely flawless. Milo studied her long, sleek hair with a perfectly tied high bun and side part that didn't move a bit through their flight. She kept focused telekinesis around her body, basically bubbling herself with magic as a barrier that left her unaffected by the wind of flying. It also likely shielded her from surprise attacks.

"So, why didn't your agent come?" Gladiatrix asked, pulling Milo from his observations.

"I don't think my guild master wanted to send our PR team on a mission that'd last this long."

"No, not your guild rep, your rep?"

Milo didn't know how to answer. He'd never had personal representation. Guilds did all of that for their witches, helping them navigate their public image and careers.

"As a Global Guild member, you're gonna want your own representation."

He thought about how Ronald Macdonald and all those serving at his behest awaited Milo's arrival, but in actuality, it dawned on him that they worked for Gladiatrix, preparing every place to serve as a stage for her arrival.

"Look, guilds are lovely, but they're out for their best interest. You're a potentially high commodity. Ranked one hundred in the whole world, which means everyone should know your name by now."

Milo sheepishly smiled, honored and embarrassed that Gladiatrix knew his global ranking offhand. It paled in comparison to hers. He hadn't felt this small and young since working as an intern while still attending Gemini Academy. It was a bizarre and humbling feeling to realize how much room he still had to grow.

"Yet not one person glanced in your direction during my photo op," Gladiatrix continued.

Milo hadn't taken offense to that. He actually enjoyed the break that came from not being in the spotlight, not being the biggest name in the room, not being the one whose every breath was studied.

"You should be a household name, and with the right agent, you will be."

"Your agent taking clients?" he joked.

"Sure, if you're looking to relocate to DC." She spun in the air, posing, the wind blowing on her back, ruffling her golden cape, but careful not to touch a single hair on her head. "He doesn't usually travel with his enchanters, but I am his…"

"Biggest client."

"First client." She smiled. "And the biggest, but a girl's gotta stay humble."

Milo didn't want to relocate, though. He didn't want to grow so big that he'd outgrow his home. Chicago was the grandest stage he'd ever stepped onto, and the idea of walking away from it… No. The only reason he even agreed to this mission, to leave the city, was to protect his home. There were unknown pieces moving in ways he'd never seen, which happened because of my magic. That damn rogue manifestation—persona, whatever—had shifted fates Milo delicately balanced, making potential futures he couldn't account for, and he believed that the only way to save everyone, to offer the happiest ever after that aftered for everyone, was with the assistance of the Global Guild. The best witches in the world could guarantee Milo's home remained safe and sound. But the best witches in the world didn't hand out favors.

He wouldn't whore out Chicago's independence, making them reliant on the Global Guild, on the government's whims. But a favor for a favor… That was something the greatest guild did for their members, and as a member, an official member helping them solve a difficult case, he could rely on the same if and when the time came.

"You mentioned the magic at use earlier," Milo said, drawing his attention back to the case at hand. "I've never known of a branch that could kill so many people at once."

"I'm unsure of the full extent of the magic myself," Gladiatrix explained. "I merely know the name and basics thanks to the case files."

"Oceanic Collapse." Milo nodded with a serious expression, recalling the name Gladiatrix mentioned upon her arrival. Then Milo's face fell into an awkward grin, and he rubbed the back of his head playfully to add some boyish charm. Feigned embarrassment which, *dammit*, looked really cute on him. "I didn't get that far in the case files."

"No worries. You're better off. It was mostly an accounting of the fatalities since this witch landed in the country."

Milo's chest tightened, heart pounding harder, and he wondered how heavy the burden of pinpointing a witch so lethal would be. He worried he couldn't handle the weight, the pressure of standing alongside some of the top-ranked witches. The burden and fear and stress ate away at me, too. Partly because I couldn't fathom a threat so imposing that the best enchanters were tasked with finding and ending it, and partly because I couldn't imagine life without Milo or a foe this strong.

I took a deep breath. Even as the air didn't fill my lungs, the false sensation helped center my focus. Milo would be fine. He'd taken down countless warlocks and demons that stalked the streets of Chicago. He'd taken down a devil, not once but twice. He'd survived the pain of losing Finn and never wavered from it. He was the strongest person I knew, and he walked alongside champions for this case.

"Milo will be fine," I whispered to myself.

"*I will be fine.*" His bright blue eyes widened. "*I need to stop worrying.*"

I loosened my attachment to Milo. Not by much. I didn't have the energy to untether my telepathy, but enough to where my worries wouldn't pass to him. I didn't want him to have my doubts in the back of his head. I loved him far too much to burden him in that way.

The pair continued their flight, passing over an abandoned town. An empty suburb—no lights, no life. Milo's psychic energy and mine noted as much. He didn't sense an inkling of possible futures in the air, and the only thoughts I heard came from Milo and Gladiatrix.

"This is where it happened," Milo said, catching sight of a few nearby threads, fates not snuffed out by the recent massacre.

They flew toward the building where Milo's clairvoyance glimpsed people. One fate a fading ember of reds and yellows, the other a gnarled purplish blue that almost faded to a deep gray. Not quite, though.

Hmmm. I'd never noticed how the threads of potential futures weaved around people, around the area they stood, and interacted with other threads. As Milo approached, his silver thread spun around the fading ember-colored future, accompanied by a bright pink thread that came from Gladiatrix. Already, the brief interaction had created potential shifts in the futures Milo had long since foretold. I couldn't see them. Well, perhaps if I delved deeper into his mind as our bond had grown and I'd seen many of the potentials he'd predicted, but I didn't want to see all these maybe fates. I barely had the energy to contend with the thousands of visions neatly stacked and stuck in my head.

"So, this is the clairvoyant?" a gruff, wheezing voice asked, and an old man stepped from the building.

Milo's eyes widened as he realized another top-ranked enchanter from the Global Guild stood before him.

"You think you can predict The True Witch's next target before she slaughters another town in one fell swoop?"

Milo's pulse thrummed against the back of his ear, and he swallowed the lump of insecurity in his throat. Here stood another legendary enchanter who expected The Inevitable Future's help in stopping a threat before she struck again. A witch who already skirted the Global Guild. A witch who killed an entire town without fear of repercussion. A witch who held a frightening moniker.

The True Witch.

CHAPTER SIX

IGNORING the stress of expectation, Milo sank into a feeling of pure awe. Boyish excitement blossomed from his heart in waves, blurring his vision and clouding his mind as he tried to absorb who stood before him. Every part of Milo wanted to break out into a giggle fit, smile bright and big with admiration, or ask a thousand questions he'd always pondered. He'd rarely met witches, enchanters, or industry professionals who left him speechless, but here he was, standing before two legends.

Gladiatrix was one of the top thirty under thirty enchanters and had struck industry success at roughly the same age as Milo, yet she'd soared so much further and faster in her career, in her journey to protect the lives of others, to save the world. And the old man was Enchanter Wadsworth, someone I knew nearly as much about as Milo. Especially since this witch had been an idol of Milo's all the way back to his childhood, before he knew how to cast his roots, before he'd unlocked his branch, and before he even dreamed about wanting to be an enchanter when he grew up.

```
Name: Samual Wadsworth
Branch: Rejuvenation (Healing)
```

Milo's mind buzzed with admiration at how Enchanter Wadsworth maintained his position as one of the highest-ranked witches in the world—well, in America. Global Guild in name and presence only since their members stemmed from American guild witches exclusively. I rolled my eyes at how Milo fawned over this old man who maintained his ranking as the eighth most powerful witch in the world in name only. Seriously, he held onto his ranking because he also happened to be a founding member of the Global Guild. He literally had almost three decades on the fifty-year-old organization.

There was no way this wheezing man in his seventies, who trembled from the chill of the outdoors, still had skills equal to other members in the top ten, let alone members of any ranking. The thought wasn't mine alone. Gladiatrix shared the same sentiment; in fact, we held nearly identical emotional wavelengths on the subject, and that helped meld our minds, even if only briefly. A few seconds tied to her thoughts, and it unraveled quite the insight. Milo was in good hands with her, at the very least.

A cigarette dangled from Wadsworth's dry lips—so dry, in fact, the filter hung to the peeling skin like he'd have to tear the cigarette away when he'd finally smoked it to the butt. If the pack of littered cigarette butts on the ground around him were any indication, he didn't need another smoke. Ugh. The nausea his chain smoking caused almost made me gag at the thought of my next cigarette.

If Enchanter Wadsworth's smoking habit wasn't bad enough, the man could barely stand in his constant state of exhaustion. He kept himself propped with the portable oxygen tank that he treated like the walker he desperately needed as the pain surging through his body came off him in waves. Every thought was occupied by muscle aches, bones crackling, insides twisted into knots, and a thousand other chronic pains I couldn't identify between the sharp, stabby, burning agony that came and went like a short, shallow breath. Inhale horror, exhale relief, but the inhale would return, it had to, and this pain continued in its brutality.

"You aware of the case details?" Enchanter Wadsworth asked, turning to walk back inside.

"Yes," Milo said, rushing to walk beside his idol. Details on the town's massacre, names and faces from the files he read through, stuck to Milo's surface thoughts as he rooted through what he understood about this attack. "I'm not sure I understand how this branch works or who The True Witch is. Usually, my clairvoyance is fixed when I know the person of the future I'm glimpsing."

I scoffed, recalling the lack of insight his void vision on Caleb came with and how fickle Milo's clairvoyance could be when it chose. Actually, his branch was sort of a bigger dickhead than my telepathy and just as unpredictable.

"The True Witch possesses a powerful arcane branch that allowed her to slaughter this entire town without breaking a sweat or triggering any of the defensive wards lining every home here." Enchanter Wadsworth pointed to the sigils designed into the paint of the living room they stepped through, and suddenly, I realized the building we walked through was a massive home. Well, home and office? It seemed very techie, like everything here came from new money.

Milo had already gathered that, though. His mind processed things so quickly, so compartmentalized, that unless I was looking for it, I often missed a lot of the surface thoughts he shuffled through. Hell, he wasn't even aware of my presence and had no reason to playfully tuck his surface thoughts away behind music lyrics. It turned out the town of Harmony Valley was one of those tech giant suburban paradises where everyone worked to control magic by streamlining it with the future of science.

That made targeting them a big risk, Milo surmised from the few corporations and government holdings listed in the case file he barely had time to read through. Already, Milo's mind tried to put together a motive, tying to it the intel Enchanter Wadsworth shared on this so-called True Witch.

"More than twelve hundred residents killed in a single day," Wadsworth said with a sternness in his voice. "And I do mean day. She's not some simple demon or pathetic warlock skulking in the dead of night to target her prey from the shadows with a blitz attack. Oh no, she's bold and deadly when she wakes."

Milo had theorized as much considering her target, her victims, but he didn't grasp that last comment. "Wakes?"

"I haven't seen her in nearly fifty years—tends to go underground then make a grand entrance all over again—but it appears she hits as hard as once before."

If she was as old as Enchanter Wadsworth, then she certainly maintained herself. Not that old age hindered casting capability, but much of our channeling drew on the strength of the body and willpower of the mind, and as I got older, I began to realize that each of those slowed down. What I didn't understand was how many grand entrances this witch had made. If her last attack was more than fifty years ago, how old was she exactly?

"That's all right." Enchanter Wadsworth sucked in a deep inhale of smoke and exhaled with a laugh. "I'm looking forward to showing her what I've learned since the last time our paths crossed."

"How does her branch work?" Milo asked, wondering why or how there'd been a survivor against someone whose magic sounded as if she'd dropped a huge body of water onto her victims.

"Oceanic Collapse is an arcane magic, and as you may be aware, the arcane branch twists and merges the magics from other branches into something new, and in her case, something quite perverse," Enchanter Wadsworth explained, twirling the smoke of his cigarette with a precise touch of telekinesis into the form of a feminine silhouette. "Her branch allows her to cast the illusion and reality of an ocean in the mind of her victims."

The shape of the silhouette exploded into a tidal wave that crashed onto the floor.

"It mixes primal magic in the form of water creation and control, cosmic magic with her ability to slip elements between various layers of reality, and psychic magic as she can delve into the deepest recesses of one's mind."

"Wait." Milo pieced together the explanation along with the crude show Enchanter Wadsworth had conjured as smokey men flailed on the floor before dissipating to nothingness. "She makes people think they're drowning, and they do?"

"Exactly. Her illusion can't be broken because it isn't an illusion. She is actually drawing in an ocean's worth of water hidden in the cosmic realm, dancing between stars or some bullshit." Wadsworth sucked a deep inhale of his cigarette, burning the last third down to the filter before he flicked the butt from his lips with his tongue. "The point is, there's no way around the threat she brings, which is why we need to find and neutralize her immediately."

"Agreed." Milo nodded.

"So, let's get you started on tracking her trail so I can kill the bitch." Enchanter Wadsworth patted Milo's back, ushering him to a room.

"Detain her," Gladiatrix said with crossed arms.

"Fucking witches of this generation." Wadsworth groaned and grumbled, muttering profanities under his breath. "So soft, all of 'em. You're not like that, are you, Enchanter Evergrand?"

"Evergreen," Milo corrected, utterly baffled to hear his name mispronounced.

"That's what I said." Wadsworth shook his head, legitimately offended at the correction when, in his old, ragged head, he knew he was right.

I huffed but released the annoyance because Milo had the cutest, most ridiculous, embarrassed expression, honestly believing he'd misheard Wadsworth. He hadn't. But I wasn't sure Milo, the great Enchanter Evergreen, had ever experienced being a nobody among celebrities.

Enchanter Wadsworth led them through the house to a bedroom where a home nurse stayed on standby with a group of medical staff all stationed, remaining vigilant if their services were necessary. I didn't require Wadsworth's quick explanation to piece together that they were Global Guild officials since the organization obviously wanted to remain in full control of the situation, including how it unfolded publicly. Plus, each medic had the fancy golden GG emblems embroidered on their uniform.

"How'd he survive?" Milo asked; the nagging question lingered in my head, too.

"His branch," Gladiatrix said. "He possesses some type of warding magic. When Oceanic Collapse activated, he triggered a seal or barrier to stop the water from reaching him. That's the most our psychics have been able to discern."

I saw it unfold in her mind, the explanation from the guild psychics who'd recently checked over the town. Everyone had water raging through their inner cores, minds shattered to nothingness, but somehow Benjamin's magic protected him from drowning, but it also kept him from waking. A team of telepaths had delved into Benjamin's mind, yet here he still lay locked in his own head, shielded and trapped by his own magic. How horrible.

"Why not bring him to a hospital?" Milo asked.

"We have the best of the best," Wadsworth said, visibly annoyed. "Hell, I'm one of them. Kid's got all he needs. Relocating him might impact the magic, and we wouldn't want to hinder our clairvoyant's chances of pinpointing our target."

Milo approached Benjamin Oxland, who lay in his bed attached to several monitors, all reading stable vital signs. There was nothing stable about him, though. Even with most of my psychic energy directed toward Milo, attached to his mind, I could feel those around me, and a war raged inside this boy's head. His fair complexion had gone ghostly in comparison to the file photo Milo had seen.

"All right." Milo cleared his throat, taking a seat on the bed next to Benjamin and searching through the child's potential futures while searching for threads of people he'd interacted with.

There'd be dozens, hundreds possibly, but Milo knew how to differentiate between familiar threads of fate and those wedged in momentarily. If The True Witch had any trace of her presence lingering in the magic of her victim that'd survived, Enchanter Evergreen would notice.

Unfortunately, before he saw anything tied to The True Witch, Milo grimaced at the futures lain ahead for the young boy. Pathways broke off, potentials fizzled away, and in every direction Milo stared, all he saw were the white walls of a barren hospital room. Milo searched through the decaying threads surrounding Benjamin's future. They weren't withered pathways like those that belonged to people with no future, but rather, the shimmer and light didn't radiate as brightly as once before. Well, as brightly as Milo had imagined those futures must've lit up before being attacked. Now, the potential possibilities were like wet concrete thrown carelessly, splattering and seeping into everything. Potential fates that soaked into every other possibility, futures that led nowhere except to a single, silent white room where the boy's thoughts no longer stirred.

Milo saw the dying embers of other futures, but the gravel bled over them, hardening until only one fate became prophesized for this kid.

"He's gonna stay trapped like this?" Milo stepped back, quelling his clairvoyance because the endless loop of life lost in a hospital bed after the horrors this kid survived seemed the cruelest twist of the blade from the universe.

"We've got some psychics on it." Enchanter Wadsworth waved a hand, blowing smoke at Milo from his newly lit cigarette. "Focus less on him and more on the witch that struck him down."

Milo bit back a comment because he was a psychic, the one they had on it. And he didn't need to be a telepath to grasp Enchanter Wadsworth only had one priority. The rogue witch he hunted.

"Are you gonna find her fate still looped around his?" he asked, already too impatient to pretend he cared about the kid locked inside his own head.

For a healer, Milo expected Enchanter Wadsworth to show more compassion. He expected someone with the rejuvenation branch to aim for saving a life, finding any means to heal, to help. But that wasn't Enchanter Wadsworth. Sure, Carter had stretched the limits of his vitality magic, even circumventing its ability to save my life, but if it had been a psychic injury versus a slashed throat… Well, there were many ailments even the best healers couldn't fix.

Milo's expression soured. Every nice thought he held for Enchanter Wadsworth crumbled to ashes, and suddenly, the idolizing transformed into a beast of unspoken words Milo wanted to hurl at the son of a bitch who hadn't even remotely lived up to his expectations.

"I know it's cruel," Gladiatrix said, a calm evenness to her tone. "It seems heartless. But the trail won't last. You can only glimpse potential futures connected by separated layers of interaction for so long, right?"

Yes. Milo nodded, unable to form the word to answer. Already, he tugged at the black thread weaved around the boy's mind. It shimmered and sparkled. And unlike every other thread surrounding the boy, it remained intact. All the other future threads had withered and turned a sour gray. They weren't lost entirely to Milo's sight, but he couldn't glean the potential futures from those gray strings since the lives they were once connected to had died. Every single person in Benjamin's life had died.

"We need your help, your expertise, to find The True Witch," Gladiatrix said with deep kindness and compassion. "She's never made an error such as this. There's never been a survivor to question, to observe. We need your branch to track her down."

"I understand." But Milo didn't see the boy as a survivor. He saw him as the victim who suffered the most, left trapped inside his own head with warding walls to keep him safe from drowning in his thoughts but unable to ever leave the deep recesses of his inner core.

"Good," Enchanter Wadsworth muttered. "We don't have time to cry over one victim when we're trying to prevent thousands more."

Milo began to dig through future threads, pulling at the black string that belonged to The True Witch. His eyes fluttered, searching, searching, searching, and when the light of possibility sprang forward, I caught glimpses. Fractured, shadowed, and veiled between countless layers of psychic energy between us, yet Milo's frequency had never beamed so vibrantly. I felt completely synchronized with him. We moved as one entity despite being thousands of miles apart.

I couldn't look at the futures Milo rooted through. They were grainy and dark, like staring at shadows in the night. But they were also impossibly bright, like the white dots that lined your vision while staring at the sun for too long. Milo made sense of it; he always made sense of the possibilities looped before him. Still, his mind stirred with pain, with sorrow, with a somber guilt that his mission had only just begun, and somehow, he'd already failed.

Clenching my teeth, I fought back the sensation. As a manifestation of myself, I had to steel my emotions, or they'd stretch and spread and reach out to my other half residing in Chicago, awaiting a proper report. We would link again, fuse as one entity, but I needed to do that on my other half's schedule, not because Milo's sadness cut deep into my heart and threatened to break me.

I worried what horrible futures he'd glimpsed to feel as if he'd already failed. There must be something awful wrapped in those bright shadows of infinitely dark sunlight. With so much pain in Milo's heart, I reached out to alleviate it, to take on the burden of such weight the grim futures must've painted. When my phantom touch reached Milo, I didn't see trembling thoughts on the visions he absorbed, the potentials he sorted, the threads he chased on leads of this supposed True Witch. No. The twisting knife came from guilt sparked on the child Milo couldn't help. On the young boy who sat trapped in his own mind. And Milo couldn't fathom walking away, ignoring this kid's fate as acceptable collateral to the greater good.

There was nothing Milo could do. Not one damn thing for this boy. He knew the Global Guild wouldn't have left this child in such a state with their resources at hand. They had the strongest psychics in the world in their coven. Three of the greatest telepaths sat in their ranks, other psychics with capabilities that far outmatched anything Milo had dreamed possible, but none that could chase the future like Enchanter Evergreen. That was why he was here. He could track an enemy, a threat, a looming danger with just the faintest glimmer of possibility. But he couldn't break the psychic damage that held this young boy captive.

He also knew the Global Guild didn't possess a psychic strong enough to shatter The True Witch's grip, her unyielding magic, her arcane branch that shattered minds, drowning them in their thoughts.

There was nothing Milo could do. It pained him that there was nothing anyone could do to free this child's mind. His sorrow ate away at me. I grasped my control was nothing compared to the psychics ranked among the Global Guild. My branch magic paled in comparison. My psychic energy couldn't compete, not with the help of manifestations or personas or a million years of training. I simply lacked the resolve for precision. Still, as Milo wept silently inside the confines of his inner core, I sought to free him and free this child.

I reached out to touch the mind of the imprisoned survivor. In order to delve into this boy's mind, I had to loosen the strings that kept me latched to Milo's being. I expected more pushback from my magic, considering how reluctantly it disobeyed me when searching for Milo in the city when my branch defied the laws of space and time to reach Milo. But my telepathy knew the suffering Milo endured, and as foolishly as me, my magic believed we could lessen that burden.

The second my psychic projection reached the boy's spirit, we collided, and I found myself heaved into an ocean storm so powerful that the currents nearly dragged me to the undertow of the subconscious. I gasped and choked and fought against the frigid tidal waves that rocked me from one end of this kid's mind to the other.

It was horrible, painful, but reminiscent of a mind I'd delved into once before. Tara's mind held an ocean of sorrow, which left her battling inner demons every single day of her life. When I had dived into her mind, her memories, I learned how to navigate the storms that brewed inside the minds of others. When I watched her fight against her depression each and every day, I learned how to handle the weight of the sea crashing down.

This ocean wasn't the same as Tara's, though. The ebb and flow were dreadfully similar, so I stopped resisting and allowed the current to drag me where it sought. But this horrible sea held a bitter taste of magic. Each drop of water burned with venomous hatred. I couldn't grasp how someone could despise a child they didn't even know. It wasn't that. No. It was disgust. Pity for those beneath her heel. Her shadow glowed in the dark corners of the ocean, too far to see but vibrant all the same. This came from Milo and me working in tandem to unravel her identity and location. Well, he worked toward that while I attempted to grasp how this godlike level of magic remained fully intact despite her being halfway across the world.

I gasped, taking a startling breath. Had I seen that because our magics collided with each other? Had it been from Milo using his clairvoyance to search and seek out the elusive witch? Or had she sensed my interference? Milo's attempt to see behind the curtain? There was an omnipotence to The

True Witch's magic. It burned or froze and offered a gentle hug all at once. The kindness was a lie, though, meant to deceive and take poor, unfortunate souls to the depths of their deaths.

I shook my head, raging against the ocean that spun me round and round, closer and closer to the seafloor where it'd pin me and drown me and destroy me as it'd done to countless others in this town.

A shiver of icy water traveled up my spine, sending a surge of every death this ocean had caused. The magic of The True Witch held a life of its own, much like my telepathy. Not sentient but primordial. When I dove into these waters, this fabricated illusion of drowning, the ocean magic sought to share some of its prized deaths, displaying atrocities soaked into each droplet.

This ocean wasn't like Tara's. It wasn't a construct of depression. It wasn't a coping mechanism for the horrors she'd endured in a family of monsters who painted themselves as idols.

"This is nothing more than a magical illusion," I called out, taking a deep breath of the bitter water meant to poison my lungs and harden my insides to stone. "You can't harm me. You can't harm anyone anymore."

I exhaled, releasing smoke and fire with each breath. As a projection, I didn't need the air, didn't need the cigarette either, yet I craved both. More than anything, I craved an end to this ocean of horrors. The fire I manifested burned away the water. Exhaling like a dragon, I cast enough fire to burn down every forest in the world.

"In the mind, a psychic reigns supreme." My flames manifested into a fiery giant of how I perceived myself as I strangled water between my hands. "Leave. Leave. Leave."

A gasp caught my attention. Above me, a glowing blue cube held the mind of Benjamin Oxland as he watched me wreak havoc on the ocean that threatened to drown him. He kept a fixed gaze on the fiery beast of a man I summoned to eradicate the water.

"Fire beats water?" He tilted his head, completely perplexed, and something about the shock made me smile.

I didn't understand why I picked fire. Perhaps it'd been the recent development of Melanie and Yaritza's branch magics. Maybe I missed the smell of smoke and craved the fire of nicotine in my lungs. Maybe I simply liked the irony of stomping out the water with flames.

"A true fuck you to the so-called True Witch," I whispered, but Benjamin heard.

His jaw had fallen slack, awed by the wonder unraveling in his mind.

"You're safe now," I said, resisting the smile and frowning at him.

The reverence he held collided against me, making me happy, making me proud of my actions, making me smile because he believed heroes should smile.

"I'm not a…" I turned away. I didn't have time to explain it to the kid. Chances were he wouldn't recall this anyway. The way his inner core had been slapped around by the ocean, my bet was he'd be struggling to recall his most concrete memories after such an ordeal, let alone the interaction he had with an annoyed telepath who really only did this to help ease the pain that ate away at his boyfriend.

Speaking of boyfriends… I disconnected from Benjamin's mind and went to return to Milo.

Electric blue ignited around the boy's body, sparking countless threads of potential futures that had returned now that the ocean meant to drown him had fizzled away. Milo's face lit up, smile wide and overjoyed, eyes darting about to study the possibilities, and thoughts absorbing what could've possibly happened to set this in motion.

"*Dorian?*" He tilted his head, truly believing this had been my doing, believing no one else could've possibly played a role or had the ability. "*How did you manage that?*"

I wanted to tell him, to reach out and tell him everything that I'd learned about my magic, about my manifestations, about my personas, and everything else. But my other half had a plan. I didn't know it. I couldn't fully comprehend what the sensation was or how to explain it. Even though we were split, with our consciousness divided and dwelling in separate parts of the country, I had this synchronized sensation for my other half. He—no, we—had a plan.

I'd share my truth with Milo soon, so for now, I would observe him silently and help where I could. Let him speculate. Let him wonder. Milo was always happiest when he could do both. He had a mission, a goal, and I wouldn't interfere.

"I love you," I whispered so silently I couldn't be sure my voice even formed sound.

"*I love you, too.*" Milo spun around to address Enchanter Wadsworth and Gladiatrix. "I've traced her threads, but her future's still pretty murky. It'll take time to unravel the potential outcomes, but hopefully, I'll have a location or potential location soon."

Enchanter Wadsworth tsked. "Useless. Told you there was no point in adding more damn psychics to our guild. Never understood why the Global Guild insisted on adding such magics to our ranks. In my day, we kept them on retainers." He ranted loudly, not talking to Gladiatrix or the medical staff nearby, but merely himself and every unsaid argument he'd never finished with fallen friends—hard to believe he ever had any. This was his way, bitching about the next generation of guild witches to the ghosts of former guild members. "Occasionally, they had useful leads. The psychics. Most of the time, it was 'maybe' and 'we'll see,' which is just a psychic way of saying they—"

Benjamin coughed and gasped, spurting out the water buried in his chest. He fell forward, gasping, choking, and unable to breathe out the last drops of the ocean embedded in his chest because the water was a lie. It was never there, and it wasn't there now.

"You…" Gladiatrix rushed to the kid's side, helping to steady his shaky body that quivered and shook as the reality of what had happened sank in. "Enchanter Evergreen, how'd you do that?"

"Just useless psychic nonsense." Milo smirked.

Enchanter Wadsworth crossed his arms, hiding his shame for not removing the damage done by Oceanic Collapse, unable to fathom how such a thing was possible. He'd studied the way the arcane magic had attached itself to the nervous system, the psyche, and threatened to implode if deactivated.

Well, goddamn. I stared with wide eyes. I wouldn't have dived in if I knew that.

This was why I needed to think before I acted. I sighed while Enchanter Wadsworth continued his rant on how useless psychic witches were, but not nearly as useless as some branches. Then he went on a tangent of listing and explaining how much each branch sucked while Milo read through the illuminated potential futures of The True Witch. He was determined to find her fates, track her locations, and prevent her from ever locking another soul in their mind to drown in a death of isolation.

I was also determined to stop this witch, maybe only as a phantom at Milo's side, but I'd use my understanding to help him and the Global Guild unravel her magic once and for all.

CHAPTER SEVEN

I SPENT an hour channeling my branch magic in the confines of my bedroom. Charlie chirped and cried and stuck his paws under the door for about ten minutes before finally giving up. I'd make time for him after I properly established a connection to my manifestation so our memories would sync up. Normally, drawing upon the observations of what my manifestation had seen didn't require so much effort. But normally, I didn't hurl a manifestation halfway across the country, so here I sat in my bedroom, on my floor, criss-crossed with my eyes shut in a meditative state.

Over the years, I'd learned lots of techniques from telepaths, from psychics. Things that helped when I first inherited my branch. And if I was being truthful, I'd become lax in these meditative trainings, traditions, since I was no longer a rookie witch. I shrugged off a lot of the suggestions as advice meant for a novice, an inexperienced fool with no understanding of their magic. It turned out I might've fit more in those categories than I cared to admit.

Slowly, patiently, I crawled along the thread of the tether that connected me to the manifestation I'd summoned. I wanted to see what he'd seen, to understand how Milo's mission went, and then reach out to him so we could discuss how truly invasive my branch had become. Seriously, poor baby couldn't even catch a break from my telepathy, no matter how far he went for work.

"This is taking so long." I ground my teeth, growing agitated instead of staying in a state of calm.

Calm took work. Calm was fucking annoying. But I needed my emotional state level if I wanted to follow the thread and reach my manifestation. It was too far to simply reel back and retrieve the intel, the memories. I mean, it wasn't. I kept a solid hook in my manifestation to ensure none would ever disappear to their own accord like the unruly one who'd tried to kill me for his own happy ending. And yes, I believed my personas weren't out for me…mostly. It was a weird sensation to hold trust and deceit in equal measure.

But if I reeled my manifestation into my mind, that'd leave my telepathy attached to Milo without an anchor for the magic, which would put me right back to step one, where my head felt like it was going to explode into a million pieces.

Carefully and calmly, I focused the tether until my connection with the manifestation had been established. Suddenly, memories collided together, filling in the gaps of what I'd missed from Milo's trip.

Images flashed like a collage of photo stills, filling the darkness of my mind with memories that became mine.

An exhausting flight. Arriving in California.

Meeting Global Gladiatrix.

Onlookers, adoring fans, and everyone captivated by her gracefulness.

Meeting Enchanter Wadsworth. Elation met with devastation.

Proof to never meet your idols.

A town of over twelve hundred dead.

Oceanic Collapse.

An arcane branch that merged together primal, cosmic, and psychic energy to drown a person inside their own mind.

The True Witch who eluded the Global Guild, arguably
the most powerful organization in the world.

A drowning boy hidden in a blue box meant to shield
him from a terrible ocean that sought to kill him.

Fire. Fire. Fire.

So many flames cast by my mind, my telepathy, my desire to ease the pain in Milo's heart.

Saved. I saved Benjamin Oxland and helped Enchanter Evergreen establish a connection to The True Witch, where he'd inform the others and find a way to stop her before she slaughtered anyone else.

I sat with the knowledge in a meditative state, hovering in the shadows of the tether that united myself and my manifestation. While I worked to sift through the memories, my other half floated behind Milo as he walked to the bedroom of an abandoned home that the Global Guild had commandeered during their investigation. Milo lay in the bed, stomach queasy with trepidation as he eyed the family photos. He considered asking to switch rooms but didn't want to burden the medical staff already making do with the living room as their sleeping quarters, and he didn't want to appear weak-willed in front of two of the highest-ranked enchanters.

Moving closer, I caressed his face, sending literal positive vibes as I wanted to assuage the looming dread that threatened to steal even a minute of sleep from him.

Milo began to undress, sliding off his slacks and folding them, then unbuttoning his dress shirt and tossing it. Before he removed his undershirt, he scrunched his face in thoughtful musings. With a smile, Milo pulled out his phone and texted me. The buzz didn't hit my pocket since I'd silenced it, but I fished out my phone and hit the dial-out button. All without opening my eyes. Milo would be proud of my little tech-savvy self who'd made him the only speed dial in my phone.

"Well damn, you must be desperate to explain yourself." Milo's smile twisted into a minxy grin.

I read his phone, seeing the question.

"I wasn't stalking you," I said into the phone, hearing the echo of my voice as I spoke to him in my bedroom while hovering in front of him in the room he slept inside.

"Consider me flattered." Milo let out a breathy chuckle, something that made his voice just scratchy enough to arouse me.

"It's not what you think."

"No?" he asked, quirking an eyebrow. "So you're not stretching your telepathy halfway across the world right now to see me?"

"You're not halfway across the world," I corrected.

"Might as well be. Admit it." He rubbed his hand up and down his torso, flashing his stomach a bit more each time his pinky caught onto the fabric of his shirt and yanked it up some. "You miss me."

"I'm not there, well I am, but it's not me."

Milo cocked his head.

"Well, it is me." I huffed, then proceeded to explain everything I'd learned recently about my telepathy.

How I couldn't control it, how my branch had always been too powerful for me, how pieces had been broken off years ago and dropped into the abyss of my subconscious. I explained what happened when I slipped into my subconscious, how I'd met some of my personas, and how it turned out my manifestation who went wild was nothing more than an unruly persona that dreamed of being more. More than a persona. More than a manifestation. More than me.

"Basically, I am trying to control my magic and really don't mean to interfere, but you know…" I cleared my throat. "How's that kid doing?"

"Better. Futures are looking bright, chaotic, full of all types of options, it'd seem." Milo nodded, pensive and lost in the visions of infinite possibilities, then smirked, minxy and full of snark. "And I'm okay with you interfering, as per usual. It's not my favorite thing, but I've grown used to the fact my boyfriend is quite possibly the most obsessive man on the planet."

I scoffed. "Untrue."

"And when someone says to him that something isn't possible, he's gotta prove them wrong."

"That's an exaggeration. This was a mitigating circumstance."

"And the void vision?"

I frowned. "Also, a random outlier."

"And when I went to face the devil of Chicago after telling you not to interfere?"

"Okay, three random occurrences do not make a pattern."

Milo squinted. "That's how patterns work. Literally. Once is a fluke. Twice is a coincidence. Three times is a pattern. Actually, two times is a pattern, but people just aren't ready to admit it, kind of like how you're not willing to admit you're toxically obsessive. But in a super-hot way. Especially when it comes to me."

I practically growled at his rambling explanation. "There are thousands of times I haven't interfered with something because I don't obsess over things."

"Name three."

I went to speak, went to formulate an answer, but my brain turned to mush. "You're an asshole."

"You are what you eat." Milo grinned, waiting for my breathing to ease. Even on the phone with only my voice, Milo quickly registered my feelings, my mood, and he wanted to ease my temperament before continuing. "Hmmm, so you didn't realize your personas and manifestations weren't the same thing?"

"No," I said very seriously, releasing my slight aggravation. "I don't exactly spend a lot of time with personas, mine or others. Mostly, they dwell in the subconscious, and no one wants to dive in there."

Occasionally, personas, images that folks painted for themselves, would appear on their surface thoughts, but they usually quickly faded away. We rarely spend enough time daydreaming about our ideal selves. The more time someone spent wondering who they could've been, the more depression seemed to cloud their thoughts.

"Do I have any personas?" Milo asked, truly engrossed by the topic, the idea his imagination and subconscious had made even more enchanting versions of himself.

"Yes. They're quite awesome and possibly the only reason I tolerate you." I smirked, just enough to savor the bubble I burst.

"Liar." Milo ran his hand down his stomach and slowly slid it under the elastic of his boxers. "I can think of at least one real reason you tolerate me."

The cockiness in his voice as he stroked his dick sent a shudder coursing through my body. I sucked my teeth, having a full view above him as he played with himself, hearing an echo of his breathy satisfaction from the room I floated in as a psychic manifestation and through the phone where his voice held this rhythmic allure that strengthened my concentration.

The pull I had for Milo was so strong, I'd forgotten my breathing in this meditative state. I'd forgotten to count, to focus, yet I still maintained a solid foothold in both spaces.

"I can't hold this for long," I said, explaining how I merely meant to check my memories connected to the manifestation.

"That psychic projection of yourself keeps you grounded, keeps you from breaking as your telepathy stretches out to reach me?"

"Yes." I bit back a panting breath as Milo stroked himself faster, enticing me with his voice, with the warmth that spread across his skin, with the desire dancing on the surface of his mind.

"And you can see me clearly?" The song danced on his surface thoughts, clouds parting as his sunshine vision filled my sight.

"Yes." I stared through my manifestation's eyes, keeping mine firmly closed so that the dual sensation of viewing my bedroom walls didn't splinter my hold.

"Well, I don't want you to hurt yourself." Milo teased me, tugging the elastic of his boxers to reveal his left hip fully but keeping the bulge of his cock tucked beneath the fabric. "I am curious, though…"

"About?" The seconds of silence felt infinitely long, like I'd never get an answer from those beautiful lips curled in the coyest smile a boy could make.

"Wanna test how long you'll last?"

"Excuse me?"

"Maintaining that tether." Milo playfully bit his lip, then brought his hand to his mouth, licking his palm and slathering it in spit in one quick motion before bringing his hand down to his crotch and playing with the head of his dick. "I mean, phone sex is hot. Facetime sex is hotter. But psychic sex has got to be the fucking hawtest."

I descended toward the bed, where Milo slid off his boxers. I barely gave him a chance to untangle them from his ankles before I landed on his hips, straddling him in the guise of a ghost. My psychic energy took form, filling him with the sensation of me. My body. My touch. My desire.

As he gained his bearings, I kissed him. Gently at first, light pecks across his chest, his arms, his stomach, his neck. Everywhere. I tasted him on my lips and wanted more. Craving his soft skin, his firm muscles. On the floor of my bedroom, I melted away and became engulfed by the scent of Milo, by his body heat, by my need to feel him entirely.

Milo quivered, enthralled by the kisses I left across his skin, but he couldn't find me, couldn't feel me more than the fleeting sensation here and then there, but he needed me everywhere. He wanted to grab my hair, yank it upward, and pull me into a kiss. I nearly leapt forward, granting that wish, offering him the kiss he desired, the pleasure, but there was something else he craved more.

I wrapped my lips around the tip of his cock, teasing and tasting every nerve with my tongue. Eagerly, I swallowed more, taking Milo's throbbing dick deep into my throat. Goddamn, I realized even as a projection, reality sank in quickly, and I gagged as I took in Milo all the way to the base far too fast. His moan, though. Fuck. He sounded delirious with pleasure as my throat constricted around his cock, and I struggled to breathe, gagging as I moved up and down his shaft.

"Fuck," Milo muttered, thrusting his hips.

He pumped slowly at first, relishing the sound of my choking breaths over the phone. When had that happened? I lost myself in his delight, in the faster motion of his hips as he thrust more quickly. His mind filled the empty air that he face fucked with my image. My teary eyes. My stretched jaw. My body pressed to his hips, grabbing hold as he pounded upward again and again.

But Milo wasn't fucking the air. It was me, my energy, my manifestation, my psychic extension. I twisted the magic that danced around us, linking to his frequency as I'd done so many times before. Soon, Milo caught sight of the invisible projection; he saw the illusion of my image.

This only further enticed him as he gripped a handful of hair and pumped into my mouth faster and harder, keeping a steady grip on my head with one hand wrapped under my jaw as he used my face and throat to bring himself closer and closer to cumming.

As I choked on the phone, Milo groaned with satisfied authority, and I knew it was my longing that sent these sensations. I loved to please him, I loved to feel his passion, and I loved the feeling of gagging on his beautiful cock.

I savored every second, sucking in air when I could but mainly sucking Milo off. He kept a steady pace of fucking my face, bringing himself closer to a climax, and while every part of me wanted to give him that satisfying release, feel his body quake and collapse deeper into the mattress, I wanted to tease him more.

His bright blue eyes shot open when my image vanished. No longer could he see me on his hips, cock in my mouth. He couldn't feel me either, the weight of my body pressed against his. I was there, though, a phantom of desire.

"Dorian?" He breathed heavily into the phone, gripping his hard cock. "Guess we lost the connection right when I was about to—"

I grabbed his hips, startling and arousing him, then flipped him onto his stomach. This surprised and confused Milo, who was fully prepared to slip his dick back in my mouth a moment ago.

"Not yet," I muttered into the phone, fueled by a surge of assertive long-ing.

Milo lay still, patient, and kept the phone close to his ear, listening to the spike of desire that'd shifted my mood. No longer had I linked us to serve his needs, but instead to command him to please my own. Moving down his body, my projection kissed his lower back before licking his crack.

I stared at his beautiful bubble butt, then slapped his left cheek.

"Oh." Milo chuckled. "Feisty."

"I'll show you feisty," I whispered, voice deep and gruff, so much so it carried a weight of authority that made Milo arch his back.

I slapped his ass a second time and then bit his other cheek so he wouldn't feel I favored either. I loved them both. Milo bent his left leg, moving it closer to his torso and spreading his cheeks. I kissed him, working my way to his hole, licking with long, lavish strokes that bathed Milo in a sensation of pure warmth. His teeth chattered as my tongue worked him over. His muscles tensed when I poked my tongue in his hole.

"Relax," I said into the phone.

The ease and ecstasy that released from Milo at the sound of my voice, my gentle order, only further fueled me. Using my tongue, I loosened and lubed Milo, listening intently to every hitched breath that came through the phone.

I supposed the sensation of my spit on his hole was purely psychic. It was as if we were inside his head, me weaving and controlling reality—an easy feat inside the mind of another—but we weren't inside his mind. It didn't matter; I had the power to shape everything he experienced. Each of his senses belonged to me.

"You're mine tonight."

Milo panted into the phone.

"Say it," I whispered into the phone, echoing my words inside his mind.

"I'm yours." He clenched his teeth. "Do what you want with me."

Milo sank into the mattress, completely lost in the pleasure. Each kiss, each tickle with my tongue, each soft breath was practiced and trained and meant to elicit more passion. Every second I spent rimming Milo only further enticed him.

I got hard listening to Milo moan, feeling him quiver and shake. I rose up, moving over Milo where I kept his ass spread as I slowly entered him. It wasn't skin-to-skin, not really, but the projection and imagery and fantasy of our bodies entwined helped strengthen my manifested hold over Milo.

Each thrust was deliberate and meant to push Milo closer to the edge. Milo hadn't lost a fraction of his erection from when he started with gentle kisses, turned into gagging deep-throating, and finished with a lathering rim job. Now, I held his hips in place as I pounded him, sensing the throbbing of his dick that rubbed against the sheets.

"Hold on," Milo groaned.

"Relax," I said into the phone despite being incapable of listening to my own words.

Milo whimpered and bit his lip when he finally came, unable to contain himself another second. I slowed my pace, moving one hand up his spine as he'd started to hunch, moving away from me as his body convulsed and twitched. I pulled him back into position.

"You're not going anywhere yet." The deep authority in my lowered voice sent an excited shiver through Milo's body. "What are you?"

"Yours."

Satisfied with his response, I took my hand to jerk his cock, savoring the pleased exhales Milo let out as I stroked the last sticky pearls.

Since Milo had cum a moment ago, his body quivered, turning into complete and total putty for me to play with. He wanted me to finish, to use him however I sought to achieve satisfaction. Part of me wanted to ram my dick in hard and fuck him fast and rough until I exploded. I started to, taking swift, brutal thrusts that made Milo bite his pillow as his eyes teared up. I grabbed his blond hair with both hands and yanked his head back, pounding into him as he lay there, completely obedient to my desires. The slap of skin became rhythmic, intoxicating.

I slowed, taking long, easy strokes. This allowed Milo's breathing to ease as he gained his bearings on the psychic cock that rammed him relentlessly. Kissing his nape, I caressed his shoulders, running my hands along his slick skin until I got to his lower back. I forced him into a deeper arch, adjusted his positioning, and reached around to jerk his flaccid dick.

"I'm not done with you, Enchanter Evergreen." I bit his earlobe, relishing the moan he released as I stroked him hard with each gentle thrust. I wanted him hard again; I wanted him throbbing like me. I wanted him to quake and beg and plead for me to cum, for him to reach the edge of his release and beg for more. His longing strengthened my psychic grip, allowing me complete and total control. "You're mine tonight."

"Yes." Milo moaned.

I gripped his jaw and turned him to face me, just enough so he could see me in the corner of his eye, the vision of my authority. "Yes, what?"

"Yes, sir."

I took long, slow thrusts because anything more and I'd have finished immediately. I didn't want that. I wanted to enjoy each second with Milo, wanted to get him off again, feel his pleasure, and watch the world fade away entirely for both of us.

Milo remained obedient to my direction as I fucked him, but it was me who served. I served Milo in every sexual fantasy, finding his bliss the most satisfying thing. Even controlling him now, shoving his face into the pillow while ordering him to stroke his dick as I moved faster, pounding him out and showing no mercy on his beautiful ass once again, I did it because I desired the hitch in his breath, the shudder in his body, the pleasure of his panting. Milo's mind whirled round and round, craving more from me, more authority, more control, more, more, more.

And I gave it to him. Rough.

I winced as my telepathy weakened, the bridge holding my mind together from two separate entities to one stretched across the nation. I didn't surrender yet. Not this close. I wanted to drag out Milo's second orgasm, wanted to watch him whimper when brought to the edge of his climax only to wait and serve my dick. But I didn't want to lose my hold mid fuck either.

Grabbing Milo by the back of his neck, I held him in place and took quick, sudden thrusts until I felt him about to cum, and then I buried myself deep in his ass and groaned. I sucked in a shaky breath as heat spread across my entire body. Our minds and magics collided and twisted together right as we came, and I felt his relief as he busted.

I clutched him tighter, holding onto him and the sensation, but as I exhaled, I came onto my chest, wishing it were inside Milo instead, I felt the tether connecting us snap and break.

All I had was Milo's haggard breaths into the phone, which kept us connected. "Damn, that was fucking amazing."

"Emphasis on the fucking," I said into the phone.

I heard him scrambling to retrieve his discarded device that'd slipped somewhere under the covers. "We have to do that again."

"Tonight?" I asked, barely able to hear my annoying neighbors after unleashing that much magic.

"No, I can wait a few days. A few weeks even." Milo rarely wanted to bottom, but when with me, he wanted to experience it all and explored it more frequently. "My ass could use the time to recover."

I chuckled. "I'll kiss it and make it all better."

Milo's grin hit so strong that even without my connection to see it, I felt it. I felt his happiness. We chatted until we dozed off, unsure who fell asleep first, but I knew even a world away that Milo had drifted into a happy dream dancing in his mind.

His peace made sleep easy for me.

CHAPTER EIGHT

I'D SPENT the week allowing my manifestation to follow Milo closely but hadn't reconnected with the thread that linked us. Enchanter Evergreen had an important case, and I didn't need to hover over his shoulder every second of it. Well, I supposed I was doing just that, but I'd resigned myself not to check the memories accumulated until the weekend hit. I wanted to prioritize my students, my job, and ensure they were all prepared for the first upcoming showcase event. A lead-in event that wasn't an actual part of the showcase but quite possibly the most important. It'd been pitched as a little game staff and admin had cooked up to ensure our students made a top-tier introduction to all the potential guilds out there.

"Good morning," Katherine and Caleb said in unison with bright-eyed smiles.

"Morning," I said with very little enthusiasm, sipping my coffee and hoping the caffeine would kick in soon.

Tara and Gael strolled toward the classroom, King Clucks plodding between them, crowing at any student foolish enough to stand in their path. The three of them came to a stop momentarily when Tiffany brushed past them, her long blonde hair tied back in a messy bun.

Name: Tiffany Sparks
Branch: Bestial (Familiar)

Her beaver partner chomped on a piece of wood, slapping its flat tail in the air to steady the flux of levitation that kept her floating beside her human companion.

"Tara." Tiffany nodded, then turned to address Gael's familiar. "King Clucks. Always a pleasure to see you two."

She turned on her heel and strutted away quickly before reaching another student, some third-year I'd never had in classes, and grabbed his hand. Tiffany made sure to shoot a dagger-eyed smile at Gael while conveying just how over him she was as she walked to class with her new boyfriend.

"She's still mad?" Tara asked.

"Not sure why. She's the one who ended things." Gael shrugged, glossing over any feelings he had for Tiffany and allowing them to fizzle out like a random thought. "Whatever. She's gonna be disappointed when she realizes Kevin's head game is weak."

I choked on my coffee, pounding my chest as it went down the wrong pipe.

"Wait." Tara paused, contemplating. "I thought he was straight."

"Tara? Really?" Gael cocked his head, a single judgmental eyebrow raised as if he'd taught her better by now, and she should have a full grasp on his god-level game—ugh, the ego running through Gael's surface thoughts. "You've seen me. I'm a whole damn snack. Of course he's gonna take a taste."

"And when Tiffany finds out you messed around with her new boyfriend?"

"Messed around?" Gael smirked. "Bestie, I had that curious boy on all fours, face down, and as—"

"Stop talking," I snapped, having finally composed myself enough to speak after the worst of the coffee had stopped scalding my throat. "I have no patience for it today."

"*When does he have the patience for it?*" Tara tilted her head, musing to herself and stifling a slight snicker.

"Sup, Mr. Frosty." Gael waggled his eyebrows. "You excited for the big day?"

"I'm prepared." I glowered. "Are you?"

"Always ready to fuck shit up." He balled a fist and punched his open palm.

"Go away." I waved my hand, a shooing gesture to usher him into the classroom, where I hoped he'd expel all his chatty energy before the bell rang. It wouldn't happen. It never happened. I sighed.

But goddamn, a guy can dream.

When the bell finally rang, I stepped into the classroom and immediately went to work discussing today's expectations. They'd be called down to the auxiliary gym soon, and I wanted to reiterate one final time how important today was for them.

"Today's event ties to the Spring Showcase as a baseline in a sense," I said, reminding those who'd lacked the attention span to focus during the other lectures I'd given about this activity. "There will be scouts from every guild in Chicago attending. Does anyone know what a scout does?"

"They're managerial recruiters that often work on the PR side of things," Katherine answered with a raised hand.

I nodded, gesturing for her to continue since she wanted to include a lot more in her response.

"They evaluate magic proficiency, collaboration, personality, extracurriculars, and anything else they deem noteworthy when deciding whether or not to list a potential candidate for an enchanter's observation." Katherine brushed a stray curl from the rim of her glasses, then tucked it behind her ear.

"Okay, that sounds like a lot," I said. "But why don't the enchanters just show up whenever?"

"Because they've got jobs."   *"Who has that kind of time?"*

"Is he really going over this again?"

"What the fuck, Frost? Kill me now."

"¿No repasamos esto ya? Incluso hubo una prueba."

"Wait. What's a scout? Like the sailors?"

"So is today actually part of the showcase or not?"

"Seriously? He's acting like we don't already know this."

"When did we learn this?"   *"Why is he just now going over it the day of?"*

"Well? Does anyone want to vocalize their answer?" I glared, letting them know their thoughts bounced around a little too loudly for my taste.

"Oh." Caleb raised his hand high, stretching his fingers as far up as possible like there was a cluster of eager people surrounding him, and he desperately wanted to be called on for the answer.

"Yes?" I looked at him.

"Enchanters simply don't have the time or resources to attend every event," Caleb said, tempering his hive of a mind that darted in a hundred different directions on an explanation, but he'd learned that sometimes less was more and focused on the key components of his response.

I practically smiled. Good job, Caleb.

"That's the reason scouts are so vital," he continued. "They're trained to understand several important needs. Guild interest, enchanter preferences, and market drive—basically, what magic and personality will appeal to the public. This allows the enchanter to prioritize the time they do have when they show up to the official competition later. Well, determining which events and dates they attend because they really only want to see their prospective candidates casting, so it's important…"

Caleb noticed the eyes of his classmates glaze over.

"For fuck's sake." Kenzo folded his arms and glared. "You're worse than Frost."

"And that's really the most important factor." Caleb grinned anxiously.

Katherine smiled. "I thought it was very interesting."

She would. I rolled my eyes.

At least the couple didn't drown the class in too many details. Today was stressful enough; I didn't want anyone going in too overwhelmed.

"Wait." Gael scrunched his face, lost deep in thoughts that merged with the silence of his familiar's mind. "Sooooo… If I don't impress any scouts during today's event, then they won't tell any enchanters to watch me during the actual showcase events, and they won't be at my round because there are multiple rounds at the same time?"

"Not the same time," I said. "More like enchanters don't have time to take off to sit and watch every single event play out. We've got hundreds of second-year students. Plus, try to remember we're not the only academy putting on a showcase for guilds."

"Right." Gael had a monotone voice, expression lost in a fog. It was a truly calming experience for me.

"Have you not listened to a single thing Mr. Frost has said for the past month?" Layla asked, rolling her eyes that'd shifted into her cat form as she practiced enhancing just her senses. "*What a **fucking** moron.*"

"He just never stops talking," Gael whined.

I scoffed. And the fog had lifted.

"Ba-ba-bawk."

"*Right?*" Gael's mind created an image of me droning on like one of those comic strip teachers who only said 'blah, blah, blah' the entire time. "*Always running his mouth like someone's got all day for those lectures.*"

I wanted to point out the irony of him suggesting that I talked too much considering who Gael was, but his mind darted and zipped and bounced about in a million different directions before he landed on his next concrete thought.

"*We gotta impress the scouts today, King Clucks. Make sure the Cerberus guys report back to Enchanter Evergreen about how awesome we were. If we fuck up, then he won't get to see our improved magics in action.*"

"Cl-cluck!"

"*You did not tell me that.*"

King Clucks crowed, clearly arguing with Gael about the parts of my lessons even the damn bird paid better attention to than Gael.

Thank goodness the intercom kicked in with a sharp buzzing sound that dulled Gael's obnoxious thoughts. Headmaster Dower came on, announcing that all the second-year students should make their way to the auxiliary gym. I led my students out of the classroom and through the crowded hallway as every second-year student made their way to the auxiliary gym in anticipation of this pre-emptive showcase event.

Aside from the semi-arena seating added to the outskirts of the auxiliary gym, the training facility remained completely intact, leaving each of the areas unchanged from the rock terrain with a cliffside to the fitness station and all the way to the forest terrain. It perplexed a lot of students who recalled everything had been renovated for the first-round obstacle course last year and the arena layout for the semi-finals and grand finale of the first-year Spring Showcase. This wasn't a first-year showcase, though, and the academy expected our students to demonstrate their abilities in any and all terrains.

Plus, today wasn't technically a showcase event. It was a pre-showcase event, hence the small, selective seating holding enough space for about three or four scouts from each of the prospective guilds in Chicago. I studied them, noting barely three hundred had shown up, which meant fewer enchanters were showing an interest in internships.

I sighed. Another year with another uphill battle.

"I know everyone's eager to get started with today's little event showcasing everything our second-year students are capable of," Chanelle said, opening with a speech she hoped would spark enthusiasm in the scouts attending. "Since Gemini Academy is the first in the city to kick off the Spring Showcase this year, we wanted to set the bar high and demonstrate the fantastic skills our students possess."

Unlike the first-year showcase, this event would be dragged out for the bulk of the semester, with lots of mini-rounds taking place whenever the academy could fit them in, which would also eat into instruction time. It came down to balancing things so enchanters could reasonably fit in attending rounds to see prospective student interns, not only at Gemini Academy but also every academy in the city, which meant we had to balance our tournament dates so they wouldn't interfere with any of the forty-three other academies also scheduling their showcases.

The real advantage to going first meant our students would catch the interest of scouts before they were bored and exhausted from attending endless competitions. Sure, some scouts already prioritized the to-do lists on their phones, multi-tasking all the things they needed to achieve during recruitment season, but once performance began, they'd take a lot of notes of students to keep an eye on for interested enchanters.

The biggest drawback to performing first was that the second semester had barely begun, which meant our students had less time to strategize and prepare for this event. An event that would determine if any enchanters came to observe them, cheer them on, recruit them as interns. I ran a hand through my shaggy brown hair, mentally preparing for all the polite emails I'd need to send to enchanters, all the wooing I'd have to suffer through to draw attention, and all the monotonous thoughts I'd have to read to gauge how I'd interest an enchanter into observing my second-year students. After all, I didn't simply rely on my homeroom's performance today. I played the game as well as any other teacher—better, in fact, because I had already made mental notes on the scouts in attendance so I could gauge which of my students wouldn't draw enough interest today.

Chanelle strutted across the makeshift stage crafted near the forest terrain, using the lush green trees as a backdrop to make her perfectly picked pink dress pop for the enchanters all the way in the stands. The outfit was meant to compliment her earth brown complexion and accentuate her curves without stealing focus from the students but definitely intended to make her a host those in attendance remembered. After all, the scouts would be visiting a dozen other academies this month alone. Not only that, but her vixen red lipstick matched her jeweled accessories and had a sheen almost as captivating as her voice. Chanelle was quite possibly the only person at Gemini better than me at strategizing which enchanters were worth her students' time and which weren't, so she kept close attention on the scouts she needed to wow. And she didn't even possess a psychic branch for deeper insight.

Oh, fuck me. Speaking of telepathy… Chanelle didn't even need to think the actual shades of her attire for the particular names to flicker in my mind.

Unfortunately, I'd become so attuned to her thoughts that my magic began to fill in the gaps that didn't flit about on her surface, offering me more insight.

"In today's thrilling preliminary ceremony of Gemini Academy's second-year student Showcase, we have 599 students eager to display their mastery over their magics."

That number hit hard. It practically silenced the crowd and the students, and it left a sour taste in my mouth. The aggravation from admin was palpable in the air, having already given Chanelle more delicate phrasing when referring to the number of students competing.

"*Nearly 600 students,*" popped in a lot of admin surface thoughts along with their frustrations. "*Just say 600. No one's gonna notice.*"

Chanelle didn't give a damn because she wanted that singular missing student to resonate, to be remembered. She didn't want to brush aside Jamie Novak's absence in a more palatable manner. The ache in her heart clouded her thoughts, giving a much longer pause than intended as she hoped this was enough…this gesture held as a meaningful reminder…a reminder of the student she believed more than anything she failed.

Once the moment passed, the somber silence for a few seconds, Chanelle reeled the students forward with a bright smile and enthusiastic tone. "In order to be a top-ranked enchanter someday, you have to prove proficiency over your root magics, your branch magic, your teammates' magics, and the world of magic around you!"

"*Christ, that's wordy as fuck,*" I thought, linking my mind instinctually, almost as if my telepathy sought the familiarity of someone, anyone since Milo had left the city.

"*Oh, shut up, Dorian. You're just pissy that I have you on proctoring detail.*" Chanelle strutted across the stage, gesturing to me and the other poor bastards she'd wrangled into proctoring today's ceremony. "Please make sure everyone's Cast-8-Watch is properly synced."

I made my way through my homeroom coven, double-checking their tech. Afterward, I made my way to the marble pillars Chanelle had the academy bring in for this showing. I wasn't sure why she demanded that proctors take their place atop the pillars during the competition, but I wagered it was for some outlandishly theatric reason. Everything Chanelle did was to ensure the audience remained mesmerized and lost in the performance.

"Today's game is a lot like Will-o'-the-Wisp tag," Chanelle said, which was met with a lot of groans of complaint.

Will-o'-the-Wisp tag was a simple game. Students chased wisps, and for each one they banished, they earned a single point. It was as elementary as it got. Hell, it was basically how I started day one with my homeroom coven, but I never treated it like a game.

Nothing about tag screamed proficiency. Nothing about wisps said these students were exceptionally talented. And absolutely nothing about Chanelle's game sounded like a fun thing. This was a childish waste of time; the thought soared collectively from hundreds of minds while Kenzo naturally led the pack declaring his utter contempt for Gemini Academy and their bullshit waste of time tactics.

I half-laughed to myself, quelling the minds of angry teens as Chanelle continued. I was careful not to silence their thoughts as I wanted to hear the revelation when she finished the directions and announced the biggest twist that'd leave them scrambling.

"But banishing a few wisps is only gonna demonstrate so much capability," Chanelle said. "We here at Gemini want to ensure that our students are prepared for threats from every direction, which is why every coven will stand on their own. Your survival in today's game depends on your coven mates, your success depends on your casting proficiency, and your likelihood will be determined by your rankings."

Chanelle shot a fist into the air, gesturing with all the obnoxious theatricality she could muster for the technicians to display the latest updates to the student rankings.

Most of my homeroom coven was fine, seeing their ranking hadn't changed like Kenzo and Katherine, who continued to place in the top ten. Some were pleasantly surprised to see their ranking had even improved slightly, such as the Gaels, who each showed growth in grades and casting, which paid off in the subtle bump. A few were disappointed, however, like poor Caleb, whose ranking had gone down.

I buried my guilt for withholding that information from him. Academy policy dictated that they should all be informed at the same time about their final set of rankings and when better to present that information than right before a competition that determined their future. Ugh. I hated it even if I agreed. Learning to digest difficult information and pivot was a necessary ability for any witch who wanted to work in the industry.

Caleb sank into his disappointment, wondering where he went wrong last semester and how he could prove he would do better this semester. He hadn't gone wrong anywhere, but unfortunately, I couldn't explain that to him. Not right now anyway.

"Now that you all see where you stand among the ranks," Chanelle said with a strut in her step. "It's time to explain the rules of this game."

A lot of students listened closely, attentively, even if they'd already formed theories on the obvious objective. After all, how complicated could Gemini Academy make a game of Will-o'-the-Wisp tag? The thin grin on my face grew because these poor bastards had absolutely no clue how sadistic and maniacal their kind, bubbly Mrs. Whitehurst could be. Even I didn't know the full extent of what she had in store, as she kept it guarded from all except for the admin team—mainly because they had to approve her ridiculous budget.

"Everyone will begin with a different number of points," Chanelle explained. "Your ranking will determine how many points you start off with."

I scoffed. Of course the academy would give an edge to those with higher rankings, allowing them an advantage over their peers. I mean, continuous hard work did deserve a reward, but this match gave them one opportunity to stand out to the scouts in attendance.

"Your beginning score will match your current ranking."

Well, fuck.

That meant the student ranked very last had already started the game with 599 points, and the student ranked number one had only one point to his name. I expected fury to boom from the crowd of teens, but a furious delight blossomed. Kenzo eyed his peers, calculating which weaklings would be worth eviscerating first. It wasn't merely about taking down the competition to improve his score in the game, but he wanted the weak witches who'd demonstrate his capability in combat. He knew in order to win, he'd have to raise his score quickly, his covens too, but he also had to keep an eye on those already hundreds of points ahead of him if he wanted to ensure they didn't win today's little game. Damn. Even now, Kenzo took into consideration who would help him shine the brightest in front of the scout audience.

"But a simple game of tag for points doesn't demonstrate how perfectly proficient this class of students truly is." Chanelle continued her strut, joining Headmaster Dower, who'd walked up to the stage. "I asked myself, how can I make this the most fun and engaging demonstration to date? Will-o'-the-Wisp tag is a blast, but then I think about the games I loved most as a kid: it was The Floor is Lava."

What?

I shook away the shock of everyone else as best I could. And suddenly, the pillars Chanelle demanded her proctors to stand atop made total sense.

Headmaster Dower took a deep, dragon-like breath. Her chest swelled three times the normal size, her veins glowed a golden red, and she spit literal lava from her mouth, spewing it across the entire auxiliary gym floor.

Everyone screamed and shouted and levitated as quickly as possible to avoid the deathly burn of the headmaster's primal magic.

"She could've killed us!" *"It's everywhere."*

"Hot damn. No, that wasn't a pun, King Clucks!"

"What would she have done if someone didn't levitate in time?"

"Ugh, falling into the lava is a whole ass mood right now."

"Worst. Teacher. Ever." *"Why is Mrs. Whitehurst like this?"*

"They're so dramatic. It's like no one here understands how Dower's primal branch works. Fucking morons."

"The lava swarmed the entire auxiliary gym in seconds."

"Makes sense. Headmaster Dower was a guild master candidate back in her day." Katherine's admiration grounded my mind, helping pull me from the collective surprise of surface thoughts stemming from every second-year student and the scouts in attendance. *"That is before they pushed her out of the industry and into education."*

I cocked my head in surprise. Few knew about that, myself among them purely by happenstance on the singular occasion Headmaster Dower's thoughts had twisted to past regrets during a staff training, wondering and wishing if she'd fought harder how things would have gone.

But as I dived deeper into Katherine's thoughts, steadying my own in the process, I grasped that she'd researched every guild master in Chicago, every potential guild master, and learned the number of women dictating the industry laws were few and far apart.

She quietly analyzed the lava casting, forming theories while also pulling from the stacks of research she'd done on empowered women throughout the industry. Katherine didn't want to simply be a talented enchanter like so many of her peers. She wanted to shape the industry, carve out the old, and introduce something new and better. To accomplish that, Katherine knew she'd need to become the best, which meant becoming a guild master in her own right.

Flashes of the youngest woman to run a guild rose in Katherine's mind. Guild Master Campbell, who steered the helm of Cerberus Guild. While every student here pondered how to impress the scouts, hoping they'd whisper wonderful things about them to the enchanter of their dreams, Katherine hoped to catch the eye of a guild master.

Huh. I'd never had a student who thought that far ahead in their career. They all dreamed of becoming enchanters, glossing over their internship, the years of service as an acolyte, and the difficult work of the industry. But Katherine ingrained it all in her mind, calculating every step to ensure she wouldn't falter on the way to the top.

"Don't worry." Chanelle hopped off the stage, and nearly everyone from the students to the scouts waited with bated breath as she landed in the molten pit and splashed her boots into the knee-high lava. "It's as soothing as a dip in a hot tub, which should be a lovely consolation to anyone who gets knocked out of the game before it ends."

Everyone paid complete and total attention to the rules Chanelle explained.

Scoring would be split into two forms. Individual scoring to show off the top ten students who excelled and coven scoring to show off the top ten teams that demonstrated the best collaboration.

Everyone started with a set number of points based on their ranking. The higher your ranking, the lower your starting score, and vice versa for low-ranked students.

Every wisp banished earned a point for a team member.

If a student fell into the lava pit, they lost all their points, and it wouldn't be added into the coven scoring.

If they were thrown into the lava pit, the student who knocked them out of the game would receive their points as a reward.

They had one hour to prove their skill.

An hour? That was a long time to maintain root magics in tandem. They'd have to keep their levitation and telekinesis active the entire time. They'd need their banishment root to remove wisps. As the competition thinned, they'd need their sensory root to locate more demonic energy for more points. Most of all, they needed to keep an eye on nearly every single classmate who was their enemy for the next hour.

"Hope you're all ready for a little fun." Chanelle kicked a leg, splattering lava ahead of her as she released a high-pitched gleeful, laughter. "Let the game begin!"

CHAPTER NINE

AFTER Chanelle's announcement, the big screen projectors above lit up and displayed every single student with their newly updated ranking for their second year second semester. The final ranking they'd carry to impress potential guilds for internships.

Cameras soared across the auxiliary gym, catching frazzled reactions to students surprised by their changed ranking. Some remained where they were last semester, a few moved up, but it was those who'd dropped that hesitated the longest. Microphones attached to the cameras caught the mutterings of students who quickly strategized.

With so many cameras moving around, they managed to keep every student in their sights, projecting an image of them on the borders of the massive screens above. The bulk of the screen would rotate on which students or scenes of combat to display, but when the game was over, every teacher would receive a copy of the full footage. We'd take that footage and have the students analyze it, pull out pieces of their own combat, and turn the event into a skills-based project presentation for homeroom.

When the timer ticked, everyone sprang into action, banishing wisps and collecting points. It turned into a frenzy almost immediately as students cast magic and collided with each other in a fight for points. Their Cast-8-

Watches synced to the tech that tracked everything. Their rankings were projected on the screens next to their image with a second matching number that sat beside their ranking indicating their current score. Once the competition began those numbers erupted as students banished wisps or knocked fellow competitors out of bounds and into the lava pit.

Several students among the top ten—including a few of my own—immediately targeted the lowest-ranked students who started with 500 or more points. They were the easiest targets, which seemed cruel, but the glint in Chanelle's eye drew my attention. She'd proposed this and silently observed the scouts who watched these low-ranked witches scramble to survive against the best of the best at Gemini Academy. Sure, they lost, but a few put up a good fight and drew the interest of a curious scout in the audience. Scouts who would've never looked twice at a student ranked so lowly. They were forced to, though, as they studied the best of the best tear apart competition to collect points.

My homeroom split apart into three four-person teams, sticking with their coven mates only similarly to most everyone else in the competition. They all wanted to impress the scouts in the audience, hit the top ten individually or as a team.

Following the cameras that displayed students on the big screen, rotating through multiple shots at once, I watched my students' performance. I needed to compile notes on how they handled themselves during this event, keep track of which scouts showed an interest in my students, and figure out what fine-tuning I needed to prioritize for my homeroom kids before the semester ended and they moved on to the industry as interns.

Jennifer leapt ahead of her coven mates, seeking out targets in the form of students versus wisps. While Caleb calculated the competition rules, weighing the pros and cons of striking down peers, Jennifer grasped the objective immediately.

Once Jennifer reached two classmates, she channeled telekinesis into her palms and slammed all the psychic energy she could into this interwoven strike. The expansion of my branch gave me insight into the colorful aura of emotions she struck.

```
Name: Jennifer Jung
Branch: Psychic (Empathic)
Ranking: 17
```

Not only did she knock the breath from their chests, but a white blob of energy circulating from Jennifer's aura devoured all the crimson confidence circulating from those she targeted, leaving them distraught and consumed by self-doubt. They stared at Jennifer, horrified due to their magnified emotional reactions, and in their surface thoughts, they truly believed her to be a monster. Jennifer's heavy black, scarlet, and purple makeup painted over her eyes and lips certainly fed into their fears as it gave her ghostly complexion a ghoulish appearance.

I chuckled, burying the pity I had for those students. It was a cruel, calculated tactic that proved just how impressive empathy could be when redirected into an offensive attack.

"Carter, if you don't get off the damn sidelines and—"

"Yeah, yeah, Emo Queen." Carter hadn't hesitated to strategize like Caleb. No, he'd looped his healing magics around each of his coven mates before entering the fray of chaos.

Flying from above, Carter swept past Jennifer and redistributed his roots into a precise strike of telekinesis to knock away the distraught pair that Jennifer had already immobilized.

As they crashed into the lava, their hopes were dashed, but their injuries remained mild since Carter had weaved a bit of his branch to lessen the pain of their impact.

```
Name: Carter Howe
Branch: Rejuvenation (Vitality)
Ranking: 75
```

He didn't care for Jennifer's approach of emotionally devastating anyone in their way, but he also refused to lose because of his own self-doubts. Anxiety quickly consumed by Jennifer and released back into the air for others to breathe in. *Christ.* She'd seriously mastered the emotional wavelengths of her peers well enough to literally weaponize their fucking feelings.

Wisps bounced against a blue barrier, blocking them from floating away. Carter and Jennifer eyed those around them, confused about whose branch this might be and how it benefited them.

"If you two want to actually earn some points, you got about ten seconds before that spell fades." Katherine held her open grimoire in one hand while extending her other arm toward her coven mates and casting a powerful banishment strike that took out a cluster of wisps, ensuring she maintained the highest score on her team.

```
Name: Katherine Harris
Branch: Enchantment (Spell Craft)
Ranking: 7
```

Since Katherine held such a high ranking, she had a lot of catching up to do to keep up with the point system in place. That didn't deter her or any of my students, each lashing out at competitors with masterful offensively combative techniques.

Tactically speaking, I'd screwed up with Katherine's coven. Each member had a support-style branch magic. Normally, I flipped student groupings around each semester so that by their final year at the academy, they'd grown used to working with others and had a well-balanced team of strategy, defense, offense, and support. However, after the warlock incursion their first semester, the way they bonded, the way they fought for their lives, for my life—I struggled breaking up their teams, rotating their partnerships.

That failure on my part didn't matter because my homeroom coven had done what they'd always done. They compensated for my faults and continued to impress me. Despite being a team best suited for support, Katherine, Jennifer, and Carter proved the versatility in their casting capabilities.

Caleb still hesitated. It wasn't his overactive mind making plans. Well, it was in part. He'd glanced at the big screen projecting all the names, branch magics, and rankings still in play. Some had already been crossed out with red Xs since they'd fallen into the lava pit below. What caused Caleb to freeze was the overwhelming shift of information displayed above; his ranking had dropped, and seeing it projected for everyone left him rattled.

```
Name: Caleb Huxley
Branch: N/A
Ranking: 106
```

Despite all his training, studying, and mastery over his roots, hitting the rank of 100 really was the peak of his potential according to Gemini's standards since he didn't have a branch to calculate. And since other students below him had shown blossoming improvements in their branch magics, rankings had shifted, and he dropped by six.

Get it together, Caleb.

I bit the inside of my cheek, resisting the impulse to reach out telepathically and knock some sense into his beehive of a mind.

Despite sinking into the shock of failing before he'd started, Caleb finally pulled it together and soared through the air. His heart fluttered, anxiously beating until he'd steadied his emotions by remembering what he'd always known.

Caleb was used to being overlooked, underestimated, and dismissed. He set his mind to showcasing why these scouts needed him, why they'd want him at their guild. Following along with his coven mates, Caleb countered a few competitors who'd moved in close to strike Jennifer, then pivoted to assist Carter in tackling an opponent before finally launching himself above Katherine and catching sight of the huge cluster of wisps just out of her casting range.

Caleb clapped his hands together, using the sound to precisely extend the huge wave of banishment cast. It cleared the area of wisps almost instantly.

Not that it impressed Caleb much since this was how he practiced with his fledging permit every day outside of school, yet nothing seemed to help him access that singular use of perfected banishment he'd demonstrated during the first-year showcase. It wasn't his fault. I should've focused more on studying perfected roots, searched for some information that'd help him access that skill set. Not that there was much to be found since very few witches ever perfected a root magic.

"You branchless bastard!" Kenzo shouted, flying directly toward Caleb. "Those were my damn points!"

Caleb eyed the area, noticing a bunch of students fighting against the disruption that'd knocked away their levitation roots. Most plummeted into the lava pits coated in gray static, while a few resisted, relying entirely on their telekinesis to stay afloat and desperately hoping the hex would fade before their channeling wavered.

```
Name: Kenzo Ito
Branch: Hex (Disruption)
Ranking: 1
```

Having cleared the area of opponents, Kenzo had planned on collecting a surplus of points that Caleb had unintentionally stolen with his widespread banishment.

Kenzo planted a foot on Caleb's face, kicked the stunned Caleb, and used the force as propulsion. It moved both boys in a backward flip through the air as Caleb descended until he gathered his bearings and Kenzo soared high using his former friend as a literal step while propelling himself further up into the highest trenches of students competing for points. Kenzo coated his entire body in gray static before lunging into the fray and tackling several students.

He didn't care what he hexed, so long as he disrupted magic around him and threw off his competition, which allowed him to claim another batch of points as he knocked more and more people into the lava pit.

Part of him longed to dart back down and face off against Caleb, but he'd already prepared a strategy with his coven mates to ensure they performed well today. As the other three members of his coven caught up to Kenzo, Layla and Melanie were convinced Kenzo only included them because he wanted to make sure his coven scored first place, whereas Gael believed Kenzo cared so much about each member of his team he was determined they'd all succeed.

I rolled my eyes and huffed. The reality of Kenzo's motives lay somewhere between those opposing theories in a mixed bag of angry emotions and utter arrogance.

Kenzo's erratic strikes of hex magic had cleared a path for his coven mates in every direction, tearing through the competition of unlucky foes. Soaring swiftly through the sky, Kenzo served as a vanguard and unleashed advanced combative techniques. He truly was the ultimate offensive tactician. So much so, the scouts studied his maneuvers, eyeing the trickling hex magic in the air meant to support his team that lagged behind. Many enchanters still had a chip on their shoulders for Kenzo's winning speech last year, where he declared them all incompetent fools. That didn't seem to matter, though. Some scouts weaved together ways to present Kenzo, put a spin on his cockiness, and convince their enchanters why he would make a valued intern.

Good. That'd make my job easier. Granted, every scout with an interest massively underestimated Kenzo's attitude.

Layla maintained minimal transformation, only shifting her eyes and her claws and enhancing all her senses so that she could sniff out magic usage and take down nearby classmates who encroached on her team.

```
Name: Layla Smythe
Branch: Bestial (Therianthropy)
Ranking: 14
```

As the second most aggressive member in their team—hell, in my homeroom class—she didn't hesitate to knock classmates out of the competition and into the lava pit if they got too close to Gael or Melanie, but it appeared sticking close to those two became her priority. Kenzo's plan flitted on Layla's surface thoughts along with a few choice words for how she felt about the annoying asshat she worked with.

"Layla," Gael shouted, telekinetically redirecting some of his spiked projectiles and luring the wisps he'd missed toward Layla.

```
Name: Gael Martinez
Branch: Augmentation (Spikes)
Ranking: 35
```

I understood.

While Layla focused on peers who posed a threat, she wasn't gaining many points for banishing wisps. That became Gael's main goal in the group, ensuring each member of the coven maintained similar scoring. His spikes were seeped in magic that drew the attention of wisps, and since he'd gotten better at channeling his root magics, Gael also soaked his spikes in banishment magic. Gael's precision aim allowed him to take out a vast number of wisps from a great distance and in nearly every direction.

Layla slashed the wisps Gael drew toward her, channeling banishment into her claws almost as proficiently as Gael had with his spikes.

This strategy also allowed Gael the opportunity to avoid attacking his peers, which remained his biggest weakness in the field. Gael was definitely too nice for someone with a combative branch and build. He stood taller than nearly everyone in our homeroom and had a broad, muscular jock build.

Flames engulfed Gael, consuming all the wisps drawn toward him.

"*¡Caliente! ¿Estás intentando matarme?*" Gael spun around, shaking the fire away with no effect since they only obeyed his teammate, who spent more time snickering at Gael's flailing than she did securing their position.

"Melanie, pay attention!" Layla snarled.

"Right." Melanie straightened her posture and returned the flames to their distant position as her tracker beeped, and the numbers shot up from the wisps she'd taken out.

```
Name: Melanie Dawson
Branch: Primal (Fire)
Ranking: 50
```

The versatility of her fire made her the best long-distance member of their team, controlling her flames in a spiral serpent shape that circled her coven mates and forced nearby students to hesitate over the threat of burning up or claiming points.

Their coven worked together like a machine, each focusing on one specific function to ensure their collective force overwhelmed the competition.

"Woohoo!" Yaritza tore through the flames, fanning them with the powerful swimmer's kick of her legs. The massive outpour of telekinesis spread the blaze and almost hid her fiery comets aimed for the cluster of nearby wisps. "Thanks for clearing the path, Mel."

"*She's so damn irritating.*" Melanie waved her arms, resecuring the flamed barrier meant to shield her team.

```
Name: Yaritza Vargas
Branch: Cosmic (Star Shower)
Ranking: 67
```

Wisps exploded into shimmery light when Yaritza's comets struck them, revealing the banishment she'd laced throughout her branch magic, similar to how Gael used his projectile spikes.

Yaritza's movements through the air were chaotic, but the technique held the same finesse that her coven mate Tara used when flying through levitation and telekinesis, which I took some pride in. After all, the best instruction often came from peers, and I enjoyed seeing how much my homeroom coven had grown in two years. They took the lessons I'd given them and fine-tuned their skills. They leaned on each other, offering techniques and support. They trusted each other implicitly.

Yaritza cackled, unleashing a flurry of comets in every direction. No method behind her surface thoughts aside from pure chaos meant to confuse and frighten those who'd moved in to take her out of the competition.

"Look out." Jamius spun in circles, holding a copy of himself by the arm before flinging the duplicate toward Yaritza.

The copy tackled the incoming student, nosediving into the lava pit as Jamius summoned a barrage of copies to sweep the area clear.

```
Name: Jamius Watson
Branch: Alteration (Duplication)
Ranking: 52
```

His copies shielded the original from magic and knocked a few students into the lava. Most of all, he selectively distributed his roots. Each clone held either telekinesis or levitation based on how the copies paired off to work together, which left Jamius enough control to keep from faltering while he used sensory to pinpoint wisps and banish them from the area. His Cast-8-Watch glowed, beeping again and again as his points shot up.

"You two are good." Gael hovered between Yaritza and Jamius, near a cluster of wisps the pair had lured with comets and clones. "But you can't outshine the glory of my cock."

"CLUCK!" The damned rooster extended his wings and flapped furiously, sending a breeze laced with banishment which gave Gael all the points.

"Ugh." Yaritza frowned. "*The duo of dumbassary is going off script.*"

I snorted.

```
Name: Gael Rios-Vega
Branch: Bestial (Familiar)
Ranking: 84
```

King Clucks remained perched between Gael's shoulder blades, looping telekinesis to hold himself in place while keeping his human partner secured in his grip. Gael fixated on levitation and sensory, while King Clucks prioritized telekinesis and banishment.

Gael and King Clucks dominated with their flying duet, something they learned from Jamie's lesson. Jamie still stirred in Gael's mind, grateful for the technique and holding a tiny piece of regret for the fact he'd never made things right with Jamie.

Tara unleashed a scream laced with telekinesis that knocked back a dozen students. It ate away at their sadness in a way only a Banshee's Wail could, which almost made the devastation of being eliminated from the competition bearable.

```
Name: Tara Whitlock
Branch: Ward (Sealing)
Branch: Cosmic (Shadows)
Branch: Arcane (Intangibility)
Branch: Primal (Icicles)
Branch: Psychic (Banshee's Wail)
Ranking: 4
```

With so much magic at her disposal, she put it all on display. She hurled icicles fused with banishment to strike wisps. It was nice seeing so many students take our lessons on fusing branch casting with particular root magics seriously. It wouldn't work for everyone, but this was perfect long-range precision practice for those with projectile branches.

Tara kept her other three branches held together in shadowy spheres. The overlap of her shadows, sealing, and intangibility didn't immobilize or deter her like it had in the past. Now, Tara kept a flow of magic coursing into each of her branches and roots, ensuring those protective spheres stayed close to her coven mates, shielding them from surprise strikes.

I took deep pride in my homeroom coven, chest swelling so much I had to double-check I hadn't triggered my levitation root. I floated on a high as scouts observed each of my students, showing an interest in reporting back to their enchanters. Their notes were furiously swift, keeping up with hundreds of competing students simultaneously, but I fixated on their comments for twelve.

*"Look at how succinctly she wields all those branches
simultaneously. Breathtaking."*

*"Almost certain the Martinez kid will end up at his
parents' guild, but he'd be perfect for Pegasus."*

*"Simply amazing. She's not even reading from
her grimoire as she recites countless spells."*

"For an empath, her ruthlessness is…delightful."

"His coordination with his copies is masterful."

"The precision with each flick of the flames—quite impressive."

"A cosmic magic like that is definitely something that'd intrigue audiences."

*"He's the one who manipulated
his vitality to save his teacher."*

*"That hex branch is flawless. No wonder
he held his own against warlocks."*

*"Not surprising from a Smythe. Her technique
is even more refined than her brothers."*

*"Not sure who has a more flawless
reaction time, the kid or his rooster."*

*"Where's that perfected banishment, though? I really
wanted to see what the kid who faced off against a
devil would unleash."*

I took notes of my own, accounting for every positive the scouts had for my homeroom students. I'd let them know, savor the happiness and pride they'd take on the compliments. But of course, I'd have to balance it out with some critiques on where they each floundered. They definitely had room to improve, and I would ensure they did.

A spike of fear drew my attention from my students.

Chanelle's focus waned, thoughts teetering away from her meticulous observations of the scouts in attendance. Admittedly, I might've been skimming her surface thoughts for easy notes on the audience. I mean, these scouts would be compiling lists for their enchanters, so I needed to know who among them was even worth pursuing and who I should politely thank for an interest in an internship before rejecting them. I only wanted the best opportunities for my homeroom coven, something that tugged at Chanelle with equal ferocity—so much so that it dragged my mind toward hers as panic swept through her.

Dammit, woman. I cracked my neck, attempting to sever the easy connection we'd built over the years, but my telepathy remained glued to her mind.

"Fuck," she muttered, nearly letting her mic catch it. Thankfully, Kenzo had sent a competitor plummeting so hard into the lava pit, all anyone caught was the rattling soundbite from nearby cameras.

Chanelle's gaze was locked onto three of her students.

Tia signed spells to create barriers for her coven mates.

```
Name: Tatiana Owens
Branch: Enchantment (Invocation)
Ranking: 158
```

Beside her, Vik bit their lip, unsure of themself or which magic they should mimic. Their shadow cats swirled playfully in the air, silhouettes of magic at the ready to copy any spell with mastery. Mastery Vik didn't believe they possessed at all.

```
Name: Vik Smythe
Branch: Arcane (Copycat)
Ranking: 156
```

They towered over Tia when standing upright, but the anxiety in their chest was so heavy that Vik hunched low, trying to hide themselves behind their coven mate. Tia was far too petite for Vik to disappear, but that was what they wanted to do. Disappear so everyone wouldn't witness them fail again.

The last member of their coven was probably the one I knew the least about. A lanky guy with a deep amber complexion and a frazzled expression.

```
Name: Emmanuel Delgado
Branch: Hex (Luck)
Ranking: 333
```

"Giving you all the luck in the world, try not to screw it up." He grabbed Tia and Vik by the arm, pulsating with luminescent black light. It radiated from his palms and into his coven mates' chests.

Tia read Emmanuel's lips, then nodded assuredly as she used the luck he passed along to reinforce her barriers. When the luck coursed through Vik's body, it sent a surge of confidence, allowing them to make a choice in the form of mimicking Tia's magic. Unfortunately, Emmanuel's legs wobbled, and he had to jump into Vik's arms to keep from falling into the lava pit.

"So sorry," he whined, realizing he'd sacrificed too much of his good luck and made his own fizzle out in the process.

It seemed the more luck Emmanuel provided others, the less he had himself, and vice versa. Since he could only hex others through physical contact, he couldn't exactly pass the bad luck onto the threat of competitors that closed in on their coven.

I swallowed hard, perhaps clinging to my own guilt for Jamie Novak's coven mates. They already struggled to properly collaborate with each other but after losing a member, they were at an extreme disadvantage in this competition.

Chanelle's fear for her students came from the fact that Peterson's homeroom coven swarmed around the three. All twelve stuck close together following a tactic Peterson had recommended for this game: unite as a class and dominate. It worked and they took out a few four person teams. Now, they'd found an easy target of three members who still struggled to collaborate like first-year students.

Unable to tune out the horror, I watched just like Chanelle, guilt ridden and unable to stop this tactical strategy to tear down competition.

Tia, Vik, and Emmanuel found themselves surrounded, with no defensive magic left, and bracing for the pain of being struck down into the lava pit by Peterson's homeroom.

A spike of calculating fury drew my attention.

It turned out Peterson's homeroom made a glaring error in assuming that Chanelle's homeroom wasn't collaborating. Sure, they stuck mainly to their four-person covens like everyone else, but they didn't remain idle once Tia, Vik, and Emmanuel ended up cornered.

"Let's fuck 'em up," Derrick shouted, swirling his arms to heighten the raging water he'd summoned.

```
Name: Derrick Lowe
Branch: Primal (Water)
Ranking: 78
```

"You think we'd just let you gang up on our class." Tiffany surfed along the tidal wave, swerving the direction of each drop of water alongside her beaver partner until the pair slammed into Peterson's entire homeroom coven.

```
Name: Tiffany Sparks
Branch: Bestial (Familiar)
Ranking: 60
```

"Eat it, bitches." Harrison had a cocky smile, arrogant in the most awkward way from a five-foot-nothing scrawny boy blaring the hardest profanities looped into song lyrics while rifling through the fanny pack strapped to his hip. Even hovering upside down as he swung past Tiffany from another angle, it didn't hinder his trajectory one bit as he hurled fragile glass bottles that exploded on contact with the water.

```
Name: Harrison Heywood
Branch: Enchantment (Potion Craft)
Ranking: 25
```

One of the scouts observed how Derrick altered the movement of the water to manipulate and strengthen its density, thus ensuring each potion shattered simultaneously.

"Blitz firework destruction. Hell yeeeeeeah!" Harrison cackled, delighting in the mayhem of carnage that swept across the tidal wave as Peterson's homeroom scrambled to escape the frenzy of explosion enchantment magic.

They couldn't find an exit, though. The water seemed to loop back around on itself, creating an infinite circle. Harrison's destructive onslaught appeared endless, too. Neither was true.

Amani stood at the edge of the water's depths, watching as students in Peterson's homeroom plummeted to their defeat. As they fell one by one, she released her illusion over them.

```
Name: Amani Williams
Branch: Psychic (Glamour)
Ranking: 5
```

Once the last student from Peterson's homeroom fell into the lava pit, Amani snapped her fingers. Her three coven mates flew to her side, ready to continue their strategy for winning the event now that Vik, Tia, and Emmanuel were no longer being unfairly targeted. *I wouldn't call it unfair. Hell, it was a smart strategy working as an entire class to eliminate competition.*

Amani turned her gaze toward the nearby cameras, ensuring the whole auditorium heard her next words. "Anyone fucks with our homeroom, and they're dead."

Tiffany popped a hip. "But, like, not in an actual dead kind of way."

"Fuck that." Harrison folded his arms and posed as tough as he could. "Six feet under, mofos."

"You can't say that, dumbass." Derrick smacked Harrison on the back of the head, then pointed to the cameras presenting to everyone.

Apparently, Derrick and Harrison often butted heads with each other quite literally since becoming coven mates, but before either could break out into a familiar tussle, gray static surged along their abdomens. With their levitation roots hexed, the shock of falling left each boy too immobilized to strategize with their telekinesis as a way to prevent their plummet.

Kenzo smirked, a wicked glint in his gaze as he descended from above and closed the distance between himself and Amani. "While you were running your mouth, per usual, I took out your beta boys."

Few held much competition for Kenzo, but Amani was among the top ten, and he believed she wasn't utterly incompetent. Too cautious for his liking, but skilled when she wasn't gossiping about people with his irritating teammate, Layla. He found both girls irksome, but he couldn't very well punch Layla without hindering his chances of winning the game. Amani would have to do.

"*I could take him,*" Amani thought before her mind twisted into countless variables, ones she'd likely encounter against someone of Kenzo's caliber, and she took the remaining time, along with her current score, into account. Most of all, the loss of Harrison and Derek left her vulnerable in comparison to other teams who still had a full coven.

With a snap of her fingers, Amani summoned more than thirty illusions of herself, Tiffany, and Duchess of Damnation.

Amani's glamour magic was fascinating in the sense that she didn't alter the perception of what an individual saw or experienced but more like she draped her magic in an area, manipulating the psychic plane and making it hers. Anyone who looked at her glamour was affected; even those well out of her range scattered throughout the auxiliary gym fell victim to the phony duplications Amani conjured. As an experienced psychic, I could see through her illusions, but it wasn't easy given her expertise.

The girls bolted to the other side of the auxiliary gym while a relentless Kenzo tore through the illusions one electrical strike of disruption at a time. Amani wanted to impress the scouts, which she couldn't do in a long, dragged-out battle against Kenzo. She accurately surmised that sometimes the most impressive strategy came in the form of knowing when to fall back.

By the time Kenzo had cleared a path forward, he'd already found a new quarry to hunt.

Sheesh. I grimaced. He really did treat this event like he was an apex predator slaughtering defenseless prey.

Seeing as they were both separated from their teammates, Kenzo raced toward his next opponent.

I flinched when his fist collided with an unsuspecting Caleb, who spun through the air in pain and shock and confusion. It took precious seconds to compose himself and determine where the attack came from. Kenzo allowed Caleb those seconds. With each tick of the clock, he strategized weaknesses of Caleb's he could exploit. The blitz attack wasn't meant to defeat Caleb or offer Kenzo an edge. It was, in the most sincerely absurd manner, Kenzo's way of saying hello, greeting someone he deemed worthy of eviscerating.

"Well, branchless." Kenzo coiled gray static over his arms, channeling it across his entire body. "Show me what you got. I wanna see those roots in action."

Kenzo could've struck Caleb with hex magic during his surprise strike. He could've projected it at a distance now. Two things Caleb surmised. He couldn't fathom why Kenzo held back, though, why he hadn't used the opportunity to knock Caleb out of bounds and into the lava pit below. The only thing that came to mind was that Kenzo still found him unworthy. Unworthy of attending Gemini, unworthy of joining the guild industry, and unworthy of being Kenzo's friend.

"You still think I don't deserve to be here?" Caleb ground his teeth, channeling a ferocious amount of telekinesis that knocked encroaching competitors away.

When the waves of energy reached Kenzo, his disruption shattered the pulse and fanned it in opposing directions.

"If I didn't think you belonged here, Branchless Blunder, I wouldn't be here to fuck you up personally." Kenzo smirked, gloating confidence radiated so brightly it hid the natural shades of fury that painted his aura. "I'm about to pound you into the ground, so consider this my way—"

"Hello, phrasing!" Gael shouted from nearby. "I might've gone with pummeled, but that's just me."

Caleb flew toward Kenzo, channeling concentrated telekinesis into his fists. "You won't be the one doing the pounding here."

"Am I the only one who hears it?" Gael hovered sideways, mind lost in perverse musings. "Get a room, you two. And make sure your partners are cool with it. Or better yet, in on it. Foursome fun, yum."

Kenzo hurled a bolt of hexed electricity at Gael, which he only evaded thanks to his clucking rooster, who kicked his human partner in the head and out of the path before dragging Gael away and back to their coven.

As much as Gael irritated the ever-living fuck out of Kenzo, he silently thanked the irksome boy for his awful timing. Kenzo tasted a bitter compliment lodged in his throat, mixed with memories and sentiment and a craving to bury their past. He didn't want to release his anger for Caleb, though. Not yet. He wanted to hold onto it, hold onto something between the two, as he believed they had nothing but Kenzo's rage connecting them anymore.

So Kenzo, being the dramatic, angry brat that he was, decided he'd use what remained of the competition time to beat Caleb to a bloody pulp as his way of acknowledging the branchless kid who he tried to cut out of his heart did, in fact, belong at Gemini Academy. Kenzo didn't know any other way to express how he saw Caleb as a worthy rival in the industry.

I did my best to pull my attention and telepathy from them, but unfortunately, the cameras and my magic remained locked on the conflict.

The instant their fists collided, they landed a solid hit on each other's jaw—enough to draw blood, enough to bruise, and almost enough to create a crack of bones. But the crackle came from the collision of their telekinesis.

It rippled in waves from the sheer force of their strikes, yet neither fell back. Instead, they redistributed the flow of telekinesis they kept synced with their levitation root, allowing them to maintain a steady stance in the air as they kicked and punched at one another.

I rubbed my temples, drowning out the prying surface thoughts of other students questioning why two people from the same homeroom coven would be attacking each other. The stories about each boy painted legends and rumors in the minds of their peers, believing more than anything they must've been friends.

After all, they'd faced off against warlocks together, they'd survived demons, devils, criminals, life-threatening ordeals, and stood victorious in last year's Spring Showcase side-by-side. Not to mention, they did all the same extracurriculars, spending nearly all their free time together. Surely, they were bonded, friends—much like their significant others Gael and Katherine, who connected many of these dots that others had concluded about their introverted boyfriends.

Few people knew Kenzo or the animosity he held toward Caleb. Even fewer knew Caleb or the regret he clung to because he believed he'd surrendered their friendship too easily all those years ago. Sure, everyone knew of the boys. Even the staff and scouts watched in awe of their continued combat.

Uff, speaking of… I winced at the hard kick to the chest Kenzo delivered before knocking Caleb into random bystanders.

The thing was, no one really knew either of the boys well. Kenzo's aggressive nature kept most at bay, while few had a chance to get to know Caleb since he kept his face buried in a book at all times. All they knew was their reputation.

Caleb headbutted Kenzo with a solid, concentrated blow of telekinesis that allowed him to move in closer and lock one of his arms around Kenzo's, so he'd have a harder time countering.

The two of them spun round and round, plummeting toward the lava pit, hearts racing, bodies locked in battle, senses distracted by observations of the other's next move. It didn't matter. Each boy fought with a fearlessness of consequences, believing failure couldn't touch them. Not in this moment.

Both of them pivoted, kicking at the other and casting a wide divide between themselves and the lava that splattered chaotically against their channeled telekinesis.

Kenzo cracked his knuckles, pressing his thumbs against his fingers and popping them one at a time, releasing static with each crack.

Caleb weaved around bolts of gray lightning, dodging trace amounts of static that darted across the auxiliary gym. Disruption Kenzo had laced throughout since the competition kicked off.

Once cornered by hex magic in all directions, Caleb closed his eyes and focused on his banishment root. Doing everything possible to draw on the same emotional release Caleb had the day he accessed his perfected casting, he released magic in waves.

Caleb's banishment cleared the wisps around them and sent the encroaching gray static curling backward on itself. Not enough to silence the magic, but Caleb stalled its pursuit of him. The technique hadn't gone unnoticed by anyone. Not me. Not the scouts in attendance. And certainly not by Kenzo.

While he didn't demonstrate a perfected banishment, Caleb came quite close and proved he still had access to such immense, skillful power.

It didn't take long for the effects on Kenzo's hex to fade, and he channeled his magic as he prepared to send forth endless bolts of disruption.

They'd each studied the other since day one of arriving at Gemini Academy, yet they'd only fought once, very briefly—because of my own stupidity of pairing them against each other—but now they'd both grown so much. This sparring between them was merely a warmup, an opportunity to gauge the strength and strategy of the other one.

Now, the true fight between them would begin.

BUZZZZZZZZ!

The timer screeched, and everyone froze.

Headmaster Dower took a deep breath, inhaling the tempered lava she'd lain about the floor of the auxiliary gym.

Chanelle cheered for everyone who'd remained afloat for the full hour.

The massive screen above whirled and whipped through names and faces as it calculated who finished among the top ten in each category.

I half-smiled, proud to see each of my homeroom students' covens land among the top ten, especially since only about a quarter of the students had full teams at this point. Then that glimmer of joy twisted into a snarled frown when Gael's coven name appeared on the big screen.

4th Place: Ben Dover's Coven

The roar of laughter only fueled my fury. He still hadn't filed to change their ridiculous team title, and that meant the scouts would be sharing that fucking coven name in their reports to interested enchanters. At least Caleb's coven had a nice ring to it.

2nd Place: The Coven of Inevitable Potential

And to no surprise, Kenzo's team landed at the top.

1st Place: The Roaring Rainbows of Flame and Lightning

My heart raced, waiting for the second category to finish compiling names and reveal one by one who landed among the top ten individual competitors. Pride washed over me when five of my students sat among the top ten competitors today. And honestly, I was utterly surprised to see the jester of innuendos had actually treated this event seriously.

10th Place: Gael Rios-Vega	**26,969**
9th Place: Tatiana Owens	**27,783**
8th Place: Ramsey Miller	**28,802**
7th Place: Katherine Harris	**28,838**
6th Place: Devon White	**28,840**
5th Place: Andrew Johnson	**28,895**
4th Place: Amani Williams	**29,901**
3rd Place: Tara Whitlock	**30,102**
2nd Place: Caleb Huxley	**42,488**
1st Place: Kenzo Ito	**42,490**

Two points stood between Caleb and Kenzo. They had a landslide over everyone else—with Tara only lagging so far behind because she'd ensured her coven's scores didn't flounder. The joy she took in her coven mates' success soared above her ocean of sorrow. It seemed she'd shifted to a support role toward the last quarter of the competition, allowing Gael, Jamius, and Yaritza to claim all the points.

A wave of defeat hit each boy. Kenzo couldn't fathom how Caleb had gotten so close to surpassing him. Caleb couldn't believe he still wasn't able to catch up to Kenzo. Both of them hated ending their fight before truly competing against each other.

The second-year showcase would offer them that opportunity. Chances were they'd both make it to the final round again, with a bigger audience and more experience under their belts. I worried what that battle would bring if they'd emerge finally recognizing each other again, but I knew the time had come.

Kenzo and Caleb needed this.

CHAPTER TEN

TWO weeks had passed since Milo had left for the case, and I missed him, but I had plenty to keep my mind occupied as we moved into the month of March. Once the scouts had left Gemini Academy, the real work kicked in where I had to wrangle my homeroom students together long enough to complete every last-minute project. They'd need to impress guilds with their research essays and magic skillset presentations expressing what made them unique and valuable to the ever-growing industry.

It didn't help that some of my students were high on their success from the results of the Will-o'-the-Wisp tag event. I rolled my eyes and braced for the incoming headache as I stood in the hallway between classes.

Gael had a swagger in his step as he strolled down the hallway with a screeching rooster in front of him. Nearly every student scrambled to escape King Clucks' wrath and pressed themselves against the lockers to clear a path. In his mind, Gael truly walked a red carpet as an audience of eager bystanders stood in awe. The warped reality of his cockiness floated far past his imagination and practically painted a sparkle of camera flashes and cheering fans down the entire hallway.

"That's right, baby. I'm a top"—Gael held a long pause, lowering his sunglasses to the bridge of his nose—"ten contender. Top ten contender, babes."

"Which is sort of last place among the best," Layla said, cutting by him and the rooster unfazed while repressing every ounce of venomous jealousy she had for falling short by a few places. "Sort of puts you at the bottom if you think about it."

"Makes sense to me." Melanie nodded. "Gael being a bottom and all."

"Ain't nothing wrong with being on the bottom." Gael stuck out his pierced tongue and made a face at both girls. "It's a place of power if you know what you're doing."

Gael proceeded to shimmy and dance into the classroom, with King Clucks tapping his claws against the floor in a similar movement. Was the damn bird dancing?

"And I do know what I'm doing because I'm in the top ten—"

"Ba-ba-bawk!"

"Bitches!" Gael smacked his butt and slid over to his seat, kicking his legs back and forth as he sat on the top part of his desk instead of the chair.

Ugh. Gael's success would be the most unbearable experience of my life. How was having him treat his casting and competition seriously more exhausting than when he simply goofed off? He'd likely ride this wave, gloating until the end of the year.

It didn't take long for the halls to crowd back up and I spotted Caleb and Katherine making their way toward the classroom, him holding a stack of books while training with his weighted blocks and her clutching her grimoire tightly to her chest as she playfully shoulder bumped her boyfriend.

"We need to celebrate," Katherine said. "You destroyed that competition. Right now, I bet every single scout is composing a reason and recommendation to their enchanters on why you're going to be a fan-fucking-tastic intern."

Caleb grimaced, fighting an awkward expression where his face twisted anxiously. He wanted to believe that, wanted Katherine's hopes for his success to hold some reality, wanted to see his dedication finally pay off. But this had been a marathon of endurance his entire life and he feared the end of this semester led to a finish line he wasn't ready to cross.

Oh, Caleb. I wanted to tell him this was merely another marker in the endless race. He'd be pacing himself for more laps, obstacles, and competition for the rest of his life as an industry witch.

"Smile." Katherine gave Caleb a very stern face, one where he straightened his shoulders and followed her lead. While she didn't boss him around often, Katherine refused to let Caleb bury his head during his achievements. "You got second place out of 599 people. Everyone sees you as a champion, a threat, an icon. You came so close to outscoring Kenzo. Two points."

"A real Cinderfella story." Kenzo brushed past Caleb, mocking tone in his voice. "And like Cinderfella, you've got your know-it-all fairy godmother sprinkling fake bullshit in your face."

"You know, those two points," Katherine said with a strained smile. "Basically a tie. Which means your branch isn't half as special as you pretend. Or your roots are lacking. Or both."

Kenzo scoffed. "Well, there's that 105-point head start Branchless had. Not much of a tie."

"I wish I had an excuse for my shortcomings at the ready every single time someone pointed them out." Katherine locked her eyes on Kenzo, who'd stuffed his hands in his pockets and walked away.

"No. He's right." Caleb sulked. "I need to do better if I want to stand out."

I pulled Kenzo aside as Caleb and Katherine walked into the classroom.

"Can you maybe not be a little jerk who picks a fight at every opportunity?" I asked. "Maybe just try it for the day."

Kenzo stared absentmindedly, his thoughts quieting, then locked his eyes with mine. "Sure. And maybe you can you try not being a whiny eavesdropping head case, right?"

My face fell flat with shock, wide-eyed and slack-jawed. I had no words.

Kenzo nodded to himself affirmingly. "Looks like we've both got things to work on. Maybe we focus on our *own* business for the day."

Goddamn. And with that, he walked right into the classroom.

I used the last minute of passing time to collect myself. Once the bell rang and everyone had taken a proper seat at their desks, I dove right into today's lesson.

"That demonstration was impressive, and there's a lot of positives I wanna discuss." I stared at their eager expressions, indulging before I popped the bubble of their joy because, quite frankly, we didn't have time to celebrate today. I'd pencil something in for Friday. "But that'll come later."

A collective sigh came from the whiners in my homeroom.

"Today, we're working on interviews because you'll be expected to demonstrate that very important skill soon. Much like the game where we had to impress the scouts, you'll be doing something quite similar with interested guild witches."

"Wait…" Caleb gripped his shaky knee and held back a flurry of confused, anxious questions bouncing through his head. "Interested guild witches? Like enchanters?"

"Enchanters, acolytes, scouts, specialists—hell, Mrs. Whitehurst might even wrangle a few guild masters." I took a sip of my coffee, letting that reality sink into their heads. "This is one of several mini-events second-year students are expected to take part in as we lead up to the showcase itself."

"What questions will be asked?" Caleb had a pencil already pressed to his notebook so he could jot down my response.

"These questions will be similar to what any witch applying to a guild would receive," I explained. "Some of these questions will also be the kind enchanters are expected to handle during a public interview, which makes sense because you'll be interviewed in the auditorium—"

"What?" Caleb clammed up, his vocalized terror louder than most of the surface thoughts asking the same question. "We're being interviewed in front of everyone?"

"Yup."

"Like everyone at the school?" Caleb's face burned bright red.

"No, absolutely not."

"Oh, good." Caleb sighed with relief.

"It'll just be all the second-year students, their homeroom teachers, admin, and, of course, the attending guild witches."

Caleb's entire mind went blank. If it were possible, I thought his head might explode. He simply sat silently.

"And a panel of your peers will be deciding your score." Third-year students who got roped into as part of their internship duties, which meant they'd be extra harsh on those presenting because no one liked to be volun-told for a task.

"Why didn't we prepare for this sooner?" Caleb asked, a mix of anxious anger and some judgment he hurled toward me.

I scowled. I ensured my students had every opportunity to work on the necessary skills they'd need to be successful, finding ways to tie nearly every assignment to a real-world expectation. "Why do you think we have biweekly presentations in here?"

"Because bi pride is the best pride." Gael nodded approvingly as his rooster crowed.

"What?" I quirked a brow. "No. That has nothing to do with…anything."

"Wow. Biphobic much?" He leaned over to King Clucks. "I swear, the gays really are the worst about it."

"Excuse me?" I cocked my head. "I'm not… No. You…"

King Clucks twisted his head in the same swift motion of surprise as me, red comb jiggling and a fierce squint in his gaze. And I swore, for half a second—even knowing it was entirely impossible—I heard that damn bird's thoughts snap back at my comment with, *"Did he stutter?"*

"So judgy. Such a shame." Gael shook his head disapprovingly and ready to drag out this tedious argument for the rest of class.

I took a deep breath because this wasn't an argument. It was a ploy. A tactic. A game meant to kill time. Ignoring the prepped comments skirting around Gael's surface thoughts, I continued preparing my homeroom coven. He had no reason to fuel a classroom debate aside from the fact that he was bored. Far too many times had I found myself dragged into a heated discussion with Gael about utter nonsense only to find out he never really cared about said topic to begin with and merely craved the attention. Gael Rios-Vega was a true agent of chaos and mischief.

"I need you all to focus because I'd like to get through a few of these mock interviews today."

"More like mockery," Jennifer thought, adjusting her septum piercing.

"Oooooh." Gael performed a drumroll on his desk. "I'll go first. I can handle any interview anytime anyway anywhere anyhow."

"Sure. Why not?" I shrugged, believing maybe once the reality of how difficult it was to handle serious topics, he'd simmer down some.

"And I know everyone's curious, but please don't ask how big my cock is." Gael raised a hand over his face as if his rooster couldn't see or hear his still-loud hushed voice. "King Clucks is carrying a bit of holiday weight."

While his familiar flapped in protest and pecked Gael, I sighed, realizing I'd never shake a little fear into him no matter how serious I told him this was. And then suddenly, an idea hit.

"Since this is a practice," I said. "Peer interviewers would be most appropriate."

"Huh?"   *"Seriously?"*   *"He's just lazy."*

**"Might as well make us grade each
other with gold stars, too."**

"Yes. It'll allow each of you to get into the mindset of what the interview process is like from both sides," I continued, ignoring their irritating thoughts because inspiration had struck in the form of another annoyed mind sitting nearby.

With a touch of telekinesis, I distributed the flashcards I'd made a wide selection of questions from and dropped them onto everyone's desks. "You can use these as prompts for your interviews, but you're more than welcome to ask any questions you deem appropriate."

As students flipped through the flashcards, I wrote down interviewer and interviewee pairings off the cuff doing my best to keep it fair since this was completely improvised and honestly, I'd only been thinking about the person who'd interview Gael.

"Jennifer, you'll be interviewing Gael."

She glared. *"You realize fuckboy energy is incredibly wearing on the psyche, right?"*

I nodded as if I weren't linked to Jennifer's mind. *"Oh, I realize. I also want you to know you have complete permission to emotionally eviscerate him.*"

"*Really?*" Jennifer tilted her head, summoning empathic energy that coiled around the classroom.

"*I can think of no one better to give him a little reality check on the difficulty of coasting in the guild industry.*"

Jennifer snatched up the prompt cards and began writing a list of her own questions, smiling the entire time.

"Someone's excited to chit-chat with lil ole me." Gael batted his lashes playfully.

"Just excited by the taste of your tears for when I break you."

Gael gulped, utterly stunned by the sheer delight and contempt in Jennifer's voice.

"Bawk bawk." King Clucks cocked his head with wide eyes giving a very 'you're fucked' expression.

I took a seat at my desk while students prepared for today's practice interviews.

The classroom was an utter disaster. Yes, no one was talking, but no one was learning either. It was just one of those rooms where time ceased, died, was potentially murdered by Mrs. Valson's bland personality. Ughhhhhh.

I sat at the back of the room, glowering at my first-year history teacher and wishing I could be dreaming about something fun. Sure, this memory had Milo and Finn, which I adored, but I could be dreaming about our first date. I could be reliving our first night together. Our first kiss. Our first kink. Instead, I sat in the worst fucking history class of my life during student presentations.

Anxiety wafted around the classroom from nervous students, but all I focused on at the time was Milo. Sure, at fifteen, I pretended I didn't care, but I took the time to scribble in my notebook about random bullshit to distract Milo from his dread. It gnawed at me, the way he was convinced everyone was going to fixate on how unprepared he was for his speech.

He hated public speaking his first year at Gemini. It took him ages to finally get over the fear that consumed him every time he found himself pulled into an interview. Planned. Spontaneous. It didn't matter; the idea of picking one wrong word terrified him. It came down to his clairvoyance, the development of his branch, and how little control he had over it at fifteen. Back then, Milo saw every potential failure but rarely the possible successes. Completely opposite Milo and myself was Finn, who'd volunteered to present his project first.

Finn looked truly dashing, standing at the front of the classroom. Unlike me in my wrinkled academy outfit or Milo, who intentionally wore baggy shirts and blazers with an oversized hoodie to top it off, Finn fit his uniform perfectly. His muscular build already put him on the radar of a few second- and third-years.

There was this annoyingly enigmatic charm he had in front of a crowd. A trait he passed along to Milo. Thankfully, not yet, so we both glommed to each other in the back, hiding from Mrs. Valson's evil eye that "randomly" picked the next presenter.

"For my project, I chose the Sisters of Fate." Finn snapped his fingers, an act to draw attention and show off his telekinesis that he used to click to the slide in his presentation of the divine goddesses. "They represent psychic supremacy. I know, we're rockstars. But seriously, they're like totally psychic royalty, basically the brass ring of casting. Lots of cultures even revered them as goddesses by one name or another."

He twirled his fingers this time, going to the next slide, which showed various names and images of the Sisters of Fate in different regions, religions, and eras. "Of course, they were different covens of witches over the generations, but the reverence remained. Why? Because they possessed the best psychic combination."

Even dating back to our first year at Gemini Academy, Finn used every opportunity to present reasons why he, Milo, and me would make a perfect trio. He did so well, it impressed Cerberus Guild to bring us on as a grouped internship, then hired us as acolytes immediately following our graduation.

"What is the best psychic combination, you ask?" Finn smiled at the class, then pointed to the back of the room where Milo and I hid. "Clairvoyance from the fantastic Milo Evergreen, best known as The Inevitable Future. Telepathy from the majestic Dorian Frost, most commonly referred to as The Ubiquitous Present. And of course, the most grand and important member of all—myself. Finn Summers, best remembered as The All-Knowing Past."

Finn paused for applause. Whether because he was an annoying showman or because our classmates were morons, some of them actually gave Finn the round of applause he craved. I couldn't recall which, but I remembered how it warmed my chest, seeing his smile and feeling his happiness for the display.

"We're basically this generation's Sisters of Fate. Only we're brothers of fate. Well, not brothers." Finn winked at Milo, then turned his coy smile toward me and bit his bottom lip. "*Definitely don't picture either of you as my brothers.*"

My face heated, likely as red as Milo's had become before he hid beneath his hoodie.

"The most fascinating part of the Sisters of Fate is their affiliation with the Celestial Coven, which is sort of the witchy Illuminati. Only they were real," Finn said, moving right back into his presentation like he hadn't just flirted with us in front of everyone. Possibly. We were still sorting those feelings out. "This isn't like conspiracy theory stuff either, but it's definitely not in any of our textbooks. Then again, the amount of relevant historic information they keep out of classroom textbooks is problematic for a number of reasons."

Finn took a breath, inhaling the history he'd etched into the meticulous flashcards he'd written for his project, focusing on the points of his presentation but drawn to the joys of hidden, forgotten parts of history.

"Okay, so basically, the Celestial Coven is an ancient secret society of witches that orchestrated things from the shadows—a shadow government, ooh, aah, ooh la la—influencing events and pushing magical beliefs in certain directions. Of course, then there was the fall of magic." Finn's mind blossomed with wonder. "A much longer story that still has so much mystery. Where did it go? Why did it disappear? Why return after nearly a thousand years of silence? How did magic suddenly erupt back into the world? All very important questions."

Finn eyed Mrs. Valson, who had the driest, dullest face that Finn perceived as boredom. He wasn't wrong. She was a half-second away from knocking Finn's presentation down a whole letter grade because of his tangent.

"But I digress," Finn said, returning to his discussion on the Sisters of Fate and their supposed connection to this Celestial Coven.

As I sank deep into this memory, I couldn't help but wonder why my subconscious had sent me here, to these memories, to this project. Did I miss Milo more than I realized? Despite already establishing a link far across the country. Was this karmic hell because I'd started making my students practice their public speaking interviews? Maybe I missed Finn. Our carefree, drama-free, romance-free days. No. That wasn't it. I would take even our worst date nights or awkward threesomes over this first semester of pining and confusion.

I had half a mind to sink back into my subconscious and yell at those damn personas who were clearly poking me with memories to nudge me this way or that way or whatever.

"I wouldn't say we're the ones trying to tell you anything," a familiar voice whispered.

The shadows of my subconscious danced near the edges of this memory, and one of my personas politely waited for an invitation to crash my dream. The strings of this dream that held me in place snapped loose, no longer keeping me captive to the script of this memory but releasing me to interact with my guest.

"How'd you get up here?" I asked as Nico stepped through the shadows, careful not to disturb anything as if he could actually affect a memory.

"You never know. It's good to be cautious." Nico's casual admission was his way of reminding me that my personas were linked to my thoughts, meaning I couldn't exactly hide anything from a magical extension of me. "And to answer your question, you brought me here, summoned me. Well, you summoned someone you trusted from the subconscious to answer your question about this dream and why we're showing it to you."

"And you're the only persona I trust." I nodded because as much as I wanted to trust the others weren't like the Doppler, his actions warranted my hesitation.

"More like the one you distrust the least." Nico shrugged. "You've always called on me. Well, as a child at least, you'd call on me for the things you didn't understand, explaining them in ways you sort of already kind of knew but weren't ready to comprehend. I mean, you basically made me as a buffer to organize the chaos of the world."

"Fair."

"Just an fyi—your subconscious isn't the root of the dream memories."

"It's definitely not my active consciousness," I said with a bit of annoyance. "I'm not trying to spend my life reliving my worst failures."

"This wasn't a failure. I'm pretty sure you got a C on your project." Nico pointed to the continuing dream as more students presented one by one.

"You know what I mean."

We both stared at each other silently as my memory vibrated, and I held my breath until the lurking horror passed, until the gnawing memory stopped attempting to drag my mind back to the night I'd first failed Finn. The night he was stolen from my life. The night he was taken and tortured and killed. The night I fell into despair and nearly gave up on ever accepting happiness again.

"When you fall into those memories, it isn't the subconscious pushing you toward events. Sure, sometimes you're processing things, but this sort of event. The ones that come out of nowhere and just keep sticking, keep replaying. That's your magic showing you something."

"My magic?"

"Remember when your magic connected you to Finn? To the piece he'd tucked away inside your mind?"

The piece that helped me sort the void vision. The piece of Finn that helped guide me out of my guilt and toward acceptance. The piece that allowed me to let go of the past and find a future with Milo.

"Why would my magic make me keep random dreams with Finn?"

"This dream doesn't seem random." Nico pointed to Finn's highly detailed color-coded flashcards. "A project about ancient magics, on powerful psychics. Plus, your second dream about the Sisters of Fate. Seems pretty important to me."

I squinted, reminded Nico had this irritating way of telling me the obvious in a friendly "you'll figure this out" way.

"Your magic notices things on a different decibel level, hears things you would never hear, but magic can't communicate. Not like us, not in the way a persona can. Well, your personas. Not sure anyone else's personas act outside the range of your typical NPC."

"NPC?"

"OhMyGod, did you seriously stop gaming? You were so good."

I tsked. I wasn't. I sucked. Didn't understand anything about video games. I only tried because my father liked them. Of course, after that deadbeat left, after Nico left—or I made him leave—I stopped playing games altogether.

"Point is," Nico said with a soft smile, the kind that delicately broached a difficult subject change as I'd done what I always did as a kid—I tumbled deep into my overthinking, self-loathing thoughts. Nico had this gentle way of steering me from them. "Your personas, myself included, thank you very much to all the people of the academy"—he took a bow and blew kisses to no one in particular—"we have a bit more animation. We're rockstars, thanks in great part to the magic you've shared. Or the magic you store in the subconscious."

I didn't even realize I did that.

"But I think maybe it's time you took that magic back." Nico got quiet.

His thoughts stirred curiously on what would happen to him, to the many personas buried deep in the subconscious. Would they fade away? Would they lose their charm? Would things stay the same, minus the extra touch of magic in the shadows? He didn't know. All Nico knew was this choice likely led to the best outcome for me. "And I've always had your best interest at heart."

"Because I made you to be my friend."

"No." Nico shook his head. "You made me as a buffer for the big scary world that tried to burrow into your magical brain. I became your friend because you're an awesome person, Dorian."

I turned my head. "Whatever."

I felt six years old again, lost and alone, unable to understand the complexities of the world, but grateful for a friend who explained it all.

A sharp snap caught my attention. I recognized that sound, that crack before the crumble. It wouldn't happen immediately, but this was the first step in those visions breaking loose inside my head. The ones Milo had helped organize, helped push down so they didn't overwhelm me.

"What are you gonna do about the visions?"

"Same thing I always do." I sighed, the strong exhale dragging me from my sleepless slumber, where I stared at my dark ceiling, ignoring the dreamy thoughts of noisy neighbors. "I'll ignore it for now. If they come loose, I'll figure it out."

Part of me wondered if Nico heard my answer. The fact was, I needed to relax because I certainly couldn't pester Milo. He was too far and too busy. And I didn't have time to sulk about my own shortcomings. I'd decided to ignore the vexing headache my telepathy brought at every turn.

An obsessive link to the love of my life. Check. Personas who think they know me better than I know me. Check. Evil persona hijacking my manifestation ability. Check. Several thousand visions I couldn't contain from one tiny kiss. Check.

None of it mattered right now. I had work. I had students whose futures depended on my commitment. I resolved to focus on what I could control while training my telepathy to the best of my ability without allowing it to consume my every waking worried thought.

I organized practice packets at my desk between classes, preparing for the onslaught of aggravation I was about to endure.

Gael pouted, stepping into the classroom and staring at the agenda written across the board. "Testing, again?"

Shockingly, Gael had become my least exhausting student this week. "Ba-ba-ba."

"Ridiculous is right," Gael muttered. "What happened to the importance of interviews? What happened to practicing for them?"

"We'll be returning to the mock interviews soon." Much to my dismay since Gael had walked through Jennifer's questions unscathed. It turned out she couldn't provoke or twist his anxiety because Gael held no shame. Not a trace ounce for her to manipulate on an emotional level. In fact, he'd left her more rattled from their last demonstration.

"Now we're dropping everything for a dumb test that doesn't even matter."

I glared. It did matter. But it was dumb. And it was absurd that admin waited until the last minute to inform us that the Federally Accelerated Practicum testing dates had been changed. The state moved the important test up an entire month, which meant altering lesson plans to account for it. I didn't care for the standardized bullshit, but this covered every subject, from the history of magic to how STEM subjects tied into casting to foundations of language and spell work. It was also the only test accredited by nearly every career field.

Guilds took the score into account. Colleges accepted this test as a substitute for the SAT or ACT. Even the military used these scores alongside their ASVAB.

The last of my homeroom coven shuffled inside as the bell rang.

"I hope you're all ready for the Federally Accelerated Practicum practice test," I said, burying their surface thoughts and ignoring the snickering. I hated this fucking test. I hated the name. I hated how much curriculum time it cut into to ensure students had enough opportunity to practice for the exhausting trick questions of the test.

And they were trick questions, poorly phrased and meant to confuse those who might infer two possible answers. I'd taken the test every single year since I became a teacher just so I could have an idea of what my students faced. My score jumped from top percentile to lowest failure to all over the map in the middle that it basically proved the morons elected to determine educational comprehension didn't know the first goddamn thing about it.

"I am so ready to fap," Gael shouted, the spikes across his arms and legs swelled with excitement momentarily.

I sighed. That was the other reason I hated this test and all the class time I spent ensuring students practiced for it. The jokes never ended.

"You say that now, but you better treat these practice faps seriously," Jamius said with a snicker.

"Oh, definitely," a copy cut in really quick, twinkle of mischief on his face. "You don't wanna under-deliver when the real fapping begins."

"I'm honestly tired of all the fapping practice," Carter said, nudging Gael, who merely rolled his eyes and trudged to his seat with his familiar. "I just wanna fap now and relax."

"How are you not excited to fap?" Melanie asked Gael. "Isn't it like your favorite thing?"

"It's too easy." Gael groaned, having tired himself of the jokes after the first day I'd announced the upcoming FAP test. "Humor requires a level of sophistication mixed with crude undertones."

Oh, how I hated this test name and the person in charge who didn't realize the importance of giving the name an update to avoid all the fapping jokes. I'd honestly heard every single one of them over the years.

"The FAP test is so in your face," Gael continued, gesturing crudely with a jerking motion, and then sighed. "There's no challenge."

"Aaah." Gael tapped his forehead between the spikes in a knowing way, like he'd solved a mystery. "So, you don't like it when people fap in your face? Here I thought—"

"We both know you're the only Gael here who likes getting fapped in the face." Gael made a twisted expression of entertained judgment as his rooster crowed.

Gael's spikes shrank, and his cheeks burned brightly.

"That's what you get for joking about the test like a twelve-year-old," Kenzo said curtly, tossing a practice packet onto Gael's desk.

Kenzo had additional reviewing materials outside of the ones I provided in class. Somehow, he'd convinced Gael's parents to acquire them for him. The memory was fuzzy, but Kenzo held it with pride, the way he'd bonded over the importance of academics, the way he'd impressed Gael's family, the way they found his rigorous study habits astounding—basically giving him a stamp of approval to drag Gael anywhere anytime to ensure he treated his coursework half as seriously as Kenzo. The memory fizzled away as swiftly as it'd appeared, and Kenzo scoffed as his boyfriend sheepishly hid his face behind the pages.

"It's nothing to be embarrassed about." Caleb looked up from his papers, completely unaware of the passing jokes. He showed off his practice tests, delighted by his scores and eager others had additional packets in preparation for the official FAP test, too. "I'm fapping right now."

"Sweetie, no." Katherine leaned close and whispered into Caleb's ear, making his smile crumble away as his face fell into dismayed horror and turned as red as Gael's.

I smacked a hand over my forehead, hiding the exasperation Caleb's comment provoked. The room roared with laughter, everyone aware Caleb had no idea why fapping was funny and how much pride he took in his practice FAP tests.

"Enough," I snapped. "You're not little kids. Some of you are almost adults. It's time to act like it."

The fact was, almost everyone here was seventeen years old, with a few waiting on their summer birthdays to hit that marker.

"In just over a year, you'll be graduating from Gemini Academy. You'll be diving headfirst into the real world. Guild life. College. Workforce. Military. Your parents' basement. Lots of options. So, you will treat the FAP with maturity. You will not laugh about fapping. You will not make fapping gestures. You will not make any more fapping puns in this class." I flicked a hand and shook several empty desks before a single giggle escaped the lips of a student. "The next person who so much as smiles over the idea of fapping will take their test upside down."

I lifted every empty desk into the air and slammed them against the ceiling.

"Cool." Caleb eyed the desks, mind whirling with calculations. *"Bet the level of endurance that'd help improve... Hmm. Would it affect my overall score, though? This is just a practice, so maybe I could extrapolate the—"*

"Caleb." I scowled until he sank into the desk chair and quieted his mind.

Each class was spent reviewing one subject of the FAP test or taking a practice exam on that section. Since it ate up the bulk of instruction time and no one had an ounce of concentration left over anyway, I usually allowed everyone to relax and unwind for the last fifteen minutes of class.

Katherine abandoned her grimoire at her desk and stood beside Tara's seat.

"Yes?" Tara looked up to Katherine, straining to offer a polite half-smile.

"Do you have a date for the unveiling event?"

"Huh?" Tara's blue eyes widened.

"Not like a date date. Obviously, you're not looking for an actual date. Not that you need to look for any type of date. Or that you'd need to look if you were interested in a date. Everyone would be lining up for a date. I'm sure they're already lining up, which is probably annoying. Not that you find dates annoying, just that everyone wants to be on a Whitlock's arm." Katherine scrunched her face, believing every thought that twisted into her head led to another bumbling comment. It didn't.

Her thoughts merely moved faster than her realization and her mouth moved nearly as quickly when spouting out her next comment. I stifled a snicker. The epitome of think before you speak.

"Okay. Factory reset on this convo," Katherine said with a giggle, clearing her mind of the millions of pressing thoughts that weaved around every subject in her busy head. "The unveiling between Harris Enchant Tech and Whitlock Industries. It's coming up. I thought if you didn't have a date, we could go together. Caleb's got work, and it's not that I mind going stag, just seemed like it'd be fun for us... And you're not a second choice. Caleb was never a choice. I mean, he's obviously a choice. He's my first choice. For everything. Except this. Because his work schedule has been keeping him busy this season. Not the winter season, but the…"

Event season. Galas. Balls. Parties of all kinds for only the best of the best at Gemini Academy. Even with so many of our students connected to the guild industry through family, only about a third of them held the privilege of attending seasonal events.

Naturally, Tara held an invitation to everything on Chicago's social calendar; it seemed the Whitlocks had weathered their storm as pariahs and now found themselves leading the pack once again. Katherine's family found themselves thrust into the world of elite prestige thanks to the technological enchantment advancements their company had created, not only finding new and inventive ways to harness tech and magic but for streamlining accessibility and affordability. Basically, the Harris family had gone from average unknowns to brushing shoulders with the top one percent of the state.

"So, the unveiling? Yay or nay?" Katherine asked with a tight grin.

Tara had barely registered the comment, her mind lost in the ocean of thought, enduring the storm that'd recently come to haunt her.

Theodore's impending trial.

My muscles tightened, and pin prickles of anxiety traveled down the back of my neck.

I'd done my best to put Theodore Whitlock out of my mind. His trial was supposed to start months ago, but then there was an incident—an incident my rogue persona indirectly caused. Theodore slaughtered several correctional officers in the MDC, threatened the integrity of their warding system, and nearly escaped. But then he simply surrendered and accepted solitary confinement while the state determined how to move forward with his charges and with his trial.

The Doppler had caused shifts in potential futures, by holding onto Finn, by allowing the chimera another foothold into this world, by causing Peter Graham's possession, and by sending off a message for Theodore Whitlock.

This had shaken loose possibilities in Theodore's future, helped push him back onto the path of destruction, but Milo wouldn't discuss it. Mostly, he claimed it was too improbable, too unlikely, as it'd require the perfect alignment of the stars while rolling a Nat 20 and getting the big-ticket lotto scratch off right when being struck by lightning. Aside from that obnoxious metaphor, Milo didn't elaborate on the subject. All he said was working with the Global Guild would ensure that if that glimmer of horror found a way to wreak havoc on the city again, Enchanter Evergreen would have the backing of the most powerful witches in the nation at his side.

I didn't press the topic with Milo. I wanted to keep Theodore out of my mind. My chest ached, realizing how desperately Tara sought the same thing but couldn't cut the final threads of love in her heart, love for a brother who understood the pain of being a Whitlock, love for the boy who consoled her every time their father berated her, love for the man who'd convinced her that being worthless was okay. That stung.

"That's gonna be a nay, darling." Gael slung an arm over Tara's shoulder, reeling her away from the ocean of sorrow in a way only he ever did. "We've already put a deposit on the hottest bird vest, and obviously, King Clucks has to show it off to the entire world."

The rooster bawked at Katherine. Images of bird attire flashed in Gael's mind, revealing the duo had tried so many matching suits on that a literal dress-up montage played in his mind. He even had a musical backdrop in his thoughts as he reminisced on the outing, finally settling on an emerald-green vest since it'd pair well with the lime dress that some up-and-coming designer had gifted to Tara.

With Milo out of the city, I hadn't stayed in the loop on nearly as many events, but seeing how Tobias Whitlock positioned himself with Harris Enchant Tech as a way to buy back his public favor left a sour taste in my mouth. Then again, that might've come from Tara, who held equal irritation for how her father had manipulated the masses once again, a true Whitlock.

I had so much here at home keeping me occupied between my students, school events, classroom instruction, and the dreams of my past that I didn't have time to dwell on Milo's case. Though, I still hoped he was doing well.

The natural pull of my magic didn't distract me because the manifestation offered balance. Perhaps it was time I checked in on Milo, observed my other half.

CHAPTER ELEVEN

THANKS to my manifestation, I hadn't struggled with the constant flux of my telepathy stretching far across the country. Sometimes, my magic would unravel and coil back into my head. The surge of psychic energy would rocket through my skull and rattle every bone in my body before sending a pulse of electrical snaps like a static shock over my skin. That didn't happen much, and even when my telepathy returned, it whipped back out like a yoyo in search of Milo's mind.

As I graded papers this evening, looking over the shitty rough drafts that screamed first-year incompetence from my second-year students' research essays, I found myself drifting off. Charlie had wedged himself between my stomach and arm as I worked. I rested my hand on his head, rubbing the orange fluff on his face and sinking into the couch to unwind.

I needed to finish grading these essays since I still had a stack of practice FAP tests to get through, plus standard classwork I'd slacked off on grading. Oh, how quickly a few thin sheets of paper piled up into a mountain of horribly written incomplete thoughts filled with garbled talent and incoherent tangents.

I reached out to the tether that connected me to my manifestation, syncing up our perception, our memories, or dual senses. Each time I practiced, it got easier, more bearable, a natural response like something as simple as taking a breath. Yes, there was work involved, so many pieces of the mind and muscle working in tandem, but through instinct, it just sort of fell together. I needed to continue improving, finally master this telepathy, and harness all the missing pieces I'd broken off and dropped into the well of my subconscious.

Milo stayed in Benjamin Oxland's bedroom as the kid recovered. Barely five years old and that child had endured so much loss. His entire life had been stripped away in a single day. Family. Friends. Future. All of them slaughtered and wiped from this world. New futures blossomed in Ben's fateful threads, but Milo stalled in making a major decision on The True Witch because so much of this kid's fate remained tangled in her horrid actions.

No, Ben's future wasn't actually entwined with The True Witch, but the last droplets of her magic still coursed through the boy's body, according to the medical staff who oversaw the full recovery. I hadn't removed every ounce of that ocean, it seemed, but perhaps that was for the best. It offered Milo a stronger link to the witch's trail that he tried to follow. Her thinning thread from the singular interaction she'd had with Benjamin wouldn't last much longer, but it offered Milo the best chance of tracking her down before more unsuspecting people found themselves lost under the weight of Oceanic Collapse.

The strain of carrying the weight of an ocean in his mind for almost two weeks had left Ben in a state of exhaustion. His frail frame, his ghostly complexion, his clenched jaw cracking the two loose baby teeth, and his sunken eyes with deep rings of sleep deprivation. It was as if he hadn't slept the entire time the ocean of magic tried to crush and drown him. Even now, his warding magic worked to shield his mind. I sensed the blue barrier, frightened to let down its guard. The overworked magic seeped out in strange ways, turning Ben's hair a faded blue like the sky on a cloudy day.

More than anything, Milo avoided a decision, a course of action to strike down The True Witch because part of him continued searching for possibilities of Ben finding a happy future. I couldn't glean what potential outcomes lay ahead for the kid, but Milo didn't like the idea of any of those broken horrors.

Benjamin coughed, clearing water from his throat as he'd done every time he woke up, convinced he was still drowning. But he wasn't. He wouldn't ever again if The Inevitable Future had his way.

"There it is." Milo's eyes fluttered, everything in his mind clicking together as the visions aligned in his thoughts, helping him formulate the plan that'd eluded him this entire time. "Thank you, Ben."

"Who are you?" Ben asked, a subtle blue glow radiating from his chest and ready to shield him entirely.

"My name's Enchanter Evergreen." Milo smiled, soft and friendly.

"Where's the other guy?" Ben looked around the room.

"Enchanter Wadsworth?" Milo asked.

"No." Ben shook his head, eyeing the nearby medical staff who tracked his vitals. "He's not here."

"Who?" Milo asked.

"The angry raccoon dragon guy."

Milo snorted. "Wait. Who?"

"The raccoon guy with all the fire," Ben explained, his thoughts opening and an image of me projected on the surface.

Only it wasn't me. I hadn't actually worn that much eyeliner or had fire spilling from my mouth, but in his recollection, I looked like a fucking court jester.

"Raccoon guy?"

"Cause of the rockin' roll face."

Milo shook his head, biting back laughter. "I see. And the dragon part?"

"He breathed fire everywhere. He murdered the water like a rockstar."

I huffed. I didn't spit fire anywhere. I majestically summoned it in the form of a fierce beast to remove the threat of that arcane magic. It was badass. He made me sound like some type of knockoff brand enchanter.

"I'd love to continue this discussion on the angry raccoon-faced dragon guy," Milo said, surface thoughts shifting into memories of the gothiest phase in my youth. Images flashed before his mind with surly-faced stills of my teen years, scowling, flipping him and Finn off, practically growling when they dragged me somewhere. "Unfortunately, we'll have to cut this short so I can fill in my team about your recovery."

"Is the rockin' roll face guy on the team?" Ben asked as nurses came over to check him over.

"No," Milo said, barely able to fight back the wheezing laughter that bounced around his head as he envisioned me with a guitar and whipping my head round and round while breathing fire.

Ugh. I looked like a total tool in both their imaginations. This was the last time I ever helped someone.

"I'll be back soon. I promise." Milo nodded to Ben as the nurses checked him over.

"Okay." The trepidation in Ben's eyes didn't lessen despite Milo's best efforts to offer him a friendly smile and kind words.

It gutted Milo, but he needed to speak with the other Global Guild witches about what he'd seen, about what lined up for him, about how to prevent this from ever happening again.

Milo stepped outside where Enchanter Wadsworth stood perched against the railing of the porch, smoking a cigarette. Gladiatrix levitated in the front yard, cape flowing from the touch of her telekinesis, offering the perfect heroic aesthetic for an audience of no one. I guessed the best of the best were always performing for the watchful world.

"The kid's awake."

"Finally. Now you can focus less on one little life and more on the entire world." Wadsworth sucked down a deep puff of his cigarette and tossed the butt. "Because Enchanter Predicts the Future Sort of Kind of but Not Really definitely needs to prove his clairvoyance is real and not some parlor trick for the Tweeter Face Click Clockers."

I rolled my eyes at his attitude and the way his lack of knowledge had smashed together every social app he'd ever heard referenced.

"I have a plan, a way for us to stop this witch." Milo unraveled the potential futures, eyes fluttering at the continuously shifting subtleties, at the bright light of possibility.

The True Witch's threads of fate presented themselves in the most bizarre fashion, unlike anything Milo had ever encountered. Not from witches, warlocks, demons, or devils. This veiled woman was something entirely different and he considered her frightening arcane branch played a role in how he perceived her possibilities.

"I'm taking every possible calculation into account. Some steps will involve us steering her onto a different course and away from other objectives that might cross her mind."

"What does that mean?" Gladiatrix asked.

"It means he doesn't know what the fuck he's doing." Wadsworth huffed.

"I know you're after the quickest resolution," Milo said, fighting off a frown that tugged at his cheeks. "I can't offer you that."

"You can't offer much of anything." Wadsworth scoffed.

"The result in stopping her sooner is… There's too much carnage in it. I won't be a part of a path that leads to such certainty." Milo wanted to ensure no other towns were laid siege to in the same way as Harmony Valley. He wanted to make sure no one was left orphaned like Benjamin Oxland. He wanted to offer everyone the best possible future, the happiest ever that ever aftered.

"So what are you proposing?" Gladiatrix asked.

Milo had genuine joy on his face, eager to divulge the many facets of his plan that involved intercepting The True Witch in various places, drawing her attention to locations that hadn't fully occurred to her, and luring her to a spot at the precise time that'd all but guarantee a future Milo could take pride in. "It's a big plan with lots of variables that might take a bit—or a lot—longer than the Global Guild wants."

"The Global Guild merely wishes for an end to this witch," Gladiatrix said, looking over at Wadsworth. "No matter what pressures for faster results certain members try to apply."

"Fine." He waved a dismissive hand at Gladiatrix and then turned to Milo. "What's your damn plan?"

"Well, for one thing, we're gonna have to take Ben with us."

"Who?" Wadsworth asked.

"The kid who…" Milo pointed a thumb back toward the house, baffled

Enchanter Wadsworth hadn't bothered learning Ben's name, having the horror seared into his mind, or any sort of empathy in his expression when the realization dawned on the old man.

"Oh. Why exactly?"

"Once we start moving forward with our objectives, things will shift. The True Witch may attempt to pivot, change course, and I don't have a strong read on her." Milo gestured to the house again, where Benjamin Oxland recovered. "Trace amounts of her interaction and magic still linger in the child, which will allow me to maintain a connection to our target."

Milo averted his gaze from the aggravated Wadsworth and stared out into the empty neighborhood. No trace of possibility nearby. Every fate in this town had been snuffed out once everyone had been killed. This barren town saddened Milo, but he maintained his composure and focused on his goal of putting an end to The True Witch.

"Fine. Take the kid, leave the kid, what do I care?" Wadsworth lit a cigarette. "Can we just get a move on already?"

"Almost," Milo said with a minxy grin. The type of playful bullshit he used on me but quickly realized Enchanter Wadsworth had no patience or care for. Cute didn't work on the old man. "We're gonna need a professional tracker."

"You're our tracker for this mission," Gladiatrix said.

"Yeah, for pinpointing where The True Witch will be," Milo explained. "Once we get to her location, we're gonna want a witch that specializes in hunting."

"I'll see who the Global Guild can offer." Gladiatrix reached for her phone.

Milo basked in the bright pieces laid before him, absorbing the possible future he might be lucky enough to cement into reality.

Milo continued working toward unraveling the potential futures tied to The True Witch, but her image remained veiled in light so bright it made the sun seem like a moonlit night. The Global Guild stayed in the town of Harmony Valley while Enchanter Evergreen worked on determining their next best step. He had a thousand plans. Part of him was honored by the belief The Global Guild held in his branch; another part of him froze at the idea their next move came down to his decision, a decision that he needed to determine based on the possible whims of a witch he'd never encountered.

Would The True Witch raze another town that made its fortune on streamlining technology alongside magic? Sure, her motives remained secret, but Milo had pieced together that much. Every possibility of her next destructive destination seemed to tie into destroying those who made casting more accessible, who pushed the bounds of science, who decided magic should come second in this world.

Whoever The True Witch was, her ideology was that of an old belief, that of a woman who fancied tradition, one who prayed when she channeled her magic. He watched countless snippets of altars, flickering candles, sacrifices of earthly goods, tributes of blood made with oaths of loyalty. Few witches continued these practices, not since the earliest days of magics return. Mostly, people adapted, evolved, and we learned that our magic stemmed from other places. We didn't have to pray to the four corners to channel our roots. We didn't have to offer tributes to silent gods to access our branches.

Malice, bitter and filled with disgust, ate away at the edges of the veiled images of The True Witch. Every possibility Milo gleaned revealed how much she despised the world as it was and sought to bring it back to something it should've remained. Milo simply needed to discern which possible act of destruction, of carnage, would peak this vile witch's desires most.

"Well, well, well, aren't you a sight for sore eyes," a sultry voice with a thick southern twang said, pulling Milo from his visions as he took in the sight of a gorgeous man.

He waltzed across the front yard, a swagger in his hips with each step he took. The man was tall, taller than Milo by a few inches, standing at 6'5" or 6'6" and built like a titan with broad shoulders. His physical build was only further accentuated by the sapphire blue corset vest that showed off his tight waist and muscular chest. The corset had a definite allure, drawing attention to his bare arms, too, flaunting his huge muscles. I followed the veins along his flexed biceps, and my eyes traveled down his inner left forearm, where a tattoo spelled out "Texas Daddy" in some fancy calligraphy font.

Seriously? This guy.

I recognized Enchanter Diaz, whose username—*Texas Daddy*—popped up across multiple platforms since Milo and him interacted a bit on social media, given how they both built their audiences on thirst traps showing off their good looks, annoying so-called charm, and skilled casting.

Enchanter Diaz had quite a contradictory style, which he seemed to take delight in as he often wore a cowboy hat with matching boots that were tied together by the laced up satin corset vest.

Milo seemed to like the look too as his eyes traveled down the fellow enchanter's narrow waist and hung on the man's thick thighs that seemed even larger due to the skintight jeans that complimented all of Diaz's assets. Assets Milo continued admiring with each step the enchanter took.

I rolled my eyes. Whatever. We all had crushes, and this lust or pining for Enchanter Diaz went way back to Milo's days as a rookie enchanter.

While Milo fought a daydream boner, I unraveled how well he knew this Enchanter Diaz and why he'd been brought in. It turned out he had worked as a traveling member of The Global Guild for over a decade now, a member who accompanied covens for missions as their tracker. That made sense. Milo's magic would help locate this dangerous True Witch, but Diaz's skills would allow them to pinpoint her presence.

Turned out, Enchanter Diaz had visited Chicago years back when Milo was fortunate enough to partner with the expert tracker and trail a dangerous warlock that led them all across the city until they landed in Gwendolyn's Guns & Gals, the private burlesque club that also served as an illegal shop for magical merchandise.

Milo still recalled the scowl on Cassidy Gardner's face when Enchanter Diaz and Enchanter Evergreen tore her club apart dueling a particularly difficult warlock. A smile crept onto Milo's face at thinking back to how much Cassidy shouted at him, threatened him, and screamed bloody murder at the Global Guild witch, Enchanter Diaz. But when the global witch dropped a hefty apology in the form of buying out the most expensive club in Chicago for the evening, the night turned into a blur of fuzzy recollections.

Flashes of beautiful women, lipstick marks, booze, dancing—so much dancing, Cassidy cracking one small smile, laughter, passion, sweet skin, and desires not quite met as Milo and Diaz both left with different women and never had the good fortune of crossing paths again.

"You remember Vanessa?" Enchanter Diaz asked.

"Yeah." Milo nodded, recalling the petite burlesque dancer who pulled Diaz onto the stage, pinning him to the chair she'd used as a prop and turning the burly man who was nearly twice her size into a play toy. "Pretty sure I do."

Milo's breathing hitched when he recalled the two of them together, imagination already twisting the memory at the edges.

"She finally made an honest man outta me." Diaz wiggled his fingers, revealing the wedding band. His pink and black fingernails shimmered against the sunlight.

"Really?" Milo's bright blue eyes widened, then he smiled with genuine excitement for them. "Here I was worried Cassidy had run the poor girl out of town."

Vanessa was one of her more popular dancers, destined for a bright future in Chicago the last time Milo saw her on stage, but when she stopped appearing at the club, all Cassidy said was, "Good riddance. No one needs her here anyway" and then merely glowered if Enchanter Evergreen alluded to the woman when stopping in to visit his undercity friend. The news served as a reminder that potential futures were potential for a reason and could take a sharp turn from any unlikely interaction.

"Cassidy came pretty close." Enchanter Diaz grinned, a minxy expression almost as captivating as Milo's. "But Vanessa was done with that life, felt like her dances were behind her."

The dance that brought the couple together played in Milo's mind. Diaz's intense stare, the sharpness of his jaw when Vanessa ran her gloved fingers across his face. Vanessa's hauntingly pale porcelain skin under the bright lights, her strut, her stance, the bounce of her black curls. Each perfect movement of her body was etched into Milo's memory.

Soon, the truth of the memory fizzled away, and suddenly, Enchanter Diaz wore a sapphire corset vest. Oh great, Milo's mind had wandered into a fantasy where Diaz and his wife performed a show just for Milo. They grinded against each other and the chair in equal measure, tearing at each other's clothing but careful not to rip the corsets, which Milo found utterly arousing.

Music blared, synced to the dance, to the lust, to the passion. Milo's teeth flashed in his mind, biting and tearing at the strings that held the corsets together. He unraveled a gift meant just for him, and I tried to simmer my connection because while fantasies were normal, I really didn't want to see the hot naked couple my boyfriend pictured in his head. He'd gone from a single musing of bending Enchanter Diaz over to suddenly living out the most erotic club sex his imagination could fathom.

Most people didn't even realize their thoughts had turned into carnal fantasies the first few seconds. Milo's passing thoughts had only been a total of six seconds, yet they felt infinitely long as I waited for him to reel back his desires.

"Fucking hell." I huffed with utter contempt now that Milo's fantasy had fully actualized.

No longer did Enchanter Diaz and his wife parade through the halls of Milo's fetishes. They'd merely been tools for him to piece together his true desire, one he was completely aware of as it bounced around his head.

"Seriously?" I grumbled, half tempted to whisper, persuade, or tempt him back to the hot couple that danced in his mind.

Instead, I watched as Milo pictured me in his head, strutting across the dance stage with a black and scarlet corset vest and matching leather pants. My performance was far better than anything I could ever hope to attempt. In all fairness, I didn't hope much. Here I was in Milo's head, pinned against a pole, crawling down a runway, grinding against a chair, and a million other erotic movements that only further elicited Milo's imagination for all the things he craved to do to me once he'd completed his mission.

"Christ, they sent you?" Enchanter Wadsworth croaked, taking a deep inhale from his cigarette and exhaling his aggravation for the younger enchanter.

Who knew I would ever once find myself grateful for Wadsworth's rude interruption. It immediately popped the fantasy from Milo's mind and settled the lustful aura wafting in the air.

"It's good to see you too, Wadsworth." Enchanter Diaz smiled, bright and unfazed by Wadsworth's venomous gaze. "I see that habit hasn't slowed you down. God truly loves the wicked."

"You know, they used to have real witches with tracking magics." Enchanter Wadsworth shook his head with disappointment. "Now they send incompetent psychics that need more time and bumbling fools that need an animal to cast magic."

A roar in the distance filled the entire block, and a huge brown bear walked down the street. Each step more intimidating than the next. I'd never seen a bear this big. Her body on all fours stretched longer than Enchanter Diaz stood, and her size was more than twice as wide as his broad shoulders.

"Relax, Priscilla." Enchanter Diaz kept his playful grin. "You know Wadesy just likes to run his mouth about the good ole days, pretending they were a real thing."

```
Name: Emiliano Diaz
Branch: Bestial (Familiar)
```

"It used to be those with familiars didn't waste their time applying for the industry," Wadsworth continued as if anyone cared. "We used to have standards in the Global Guild—in any guild, actually. Now witches who need a pet to help them apply in droves. Next thing you know, they'll be letting branchless witches into the organization. They'll nominate warlocks or fiends for guild master jobs."

"Yup." Enchanter Diaz grabbed his chin and nodded affirmingly, a sly glint in his brown eyes. "It's all downhill from here, old man. You should do yourself a favor and hop off the ride."

Wadsworth glared. "Did you and that fat grizzly manage to find any leads?"

"How many times do I have to tell you that she's a Kodiak bear? They're an entirely different breed."

Diaz's surface thoughts popped with facts about the Kodiak species.

For starters, Kodiak bears could weigh up to 1,500 pounds, and Priscilla was a healthy 1,275 the last time she stepped on a scale. She stood at six and a half feet tall when upright. Most bears had incredible tracking skills, and thanks to Priscilla's connection to magic, she could sniff out the faintest trace of someone or something for up to twenty miles. Her claws were four inches long, and with the reinforcement of a mere trickle of telekinesis, she could slice through steel.

Christ. I was suddenly very grateful to have King Clucks in my classroom because I wouldn't trust Gael with a familiar as deadly as Priscilla.

"Bah." Wadsworth waved a dismissive hand. "Fake news."

"The disrespect. You realize she's a killing machine." Diaz held out his arms like he was gesturing to a car, which he might as well have been, considering how giant his familiar was. Priscilla yawned, huge mouth and sharp teeth stretched wide, but she appeared far less deadly when she rolled onto her back and shifted on the ground to scratch an itch. I knew the look. I'd seen Carlie do that a hundred times over, which made me miss my little fat cat. Also, how the hell did Diaz handle his familiar's food bill?

I might've delved into his mind just a tad out of curiosity. Nothing about her eating habits, but apparently, he kept specialized enchantment sigils on hand for her if the climate became unbearable. Oh, Christ. That unintended pun was going to haunt me. Kodiak bears were native to Alaska and required colder temperatures. Priscilla rarely got cooler temperatures on the road or in Enchanter Diaz's home state of Texas.

"I see the boys are all getting along." Gladiatrix levitated outside, hovering between Milo and Diaz and doing her best to ignore Wadsworth.

"Alicia." Enchanter Diaz half hugged the fellow enchanter, then eyed her golden cape and dark clothing. "Where'd all the pink go?"

"Still got it." She pointed to the heart shaped trans flag embroidered onto her outfit, possibly all her work clothes.

"No. You used to have style." Enchanter Diaz sighed, making an exasperated expression, and then flashing his pink and black nails. "We were finally gonna match. Leo's in his pink phase."

"Leo?" Milo asked, eye quirked.

"My kid," Diaz said before pointing to his familiar. "Everything has to be pink these days."

Priscilla, the bear, huffed and rubbed her head, revealing the streak of hot pink that started at the top of her head and trailed down her spine. There were also patchy, tiny handprints along her belly. If I had to guess, this Leo kid was quite young.

Enchanter Diaz's surface thoughts revealed the two children he had. A son and daughter who each got to help their daddy get ready for big cases. Leo picked pink nails, and his sister picked black. They argued and so Diaz compromised by using both.

"Speaking of kids," Milo said, steering the conversation toward their case. "With Benjamin awake and our expert tracker here, I think it's time we finally set out for the next phase of our mission."

"About goddamn time," Wadsworth said, lighting a cigarette.

Milo smiled bright eyed and eager, ready to lead them down a future pathway he believed would offer the best possibilities for everyone involved. The Inevitable Future always wanted what was best and this new pursuit of The True Witch wouldn't change that.

Chapter Twelve

ONCE I'd gotten home from work, I fed the cats, grabbed a beer, had a smoke, and watched really shitty television. Like mind-numbingly awful programming that I couldn't stop tuning into. It was dreadful, and I definitely gave my students judgy, glaring expressions whenever someone had the audacity to bring it up during class. That said, Milo forced me to watch the first season with him, and now I hate-binged it in his absence.

"We don't tell him about that, though." I cuddled with Charlie, who obviously couldn't speak but had very expressive eyes that painted quite the telling narrative. "That means no snitching to Milo even if he offers you a million kisses."

Charlie chirped.

Casually, during one of the most obvious plotlines, I telekinetically waved over the test packets from my bag and started grading them.

Carlie trotted over, whining until I waved a hand to release her treat toys. Milo got them for her. It gave Carlie a bit of a challenge before scarfing down everything.

The show became background static as work enveloped my attention, and I sank into reviewing how my students performed on the practice exams for the Federally Accelerated Practicum. Most of them did decently on the multiple-choice sections, but I'd gathered from their surface thoughts too much of that came down to luck. They couldn't rely on luck during the actual test, so those that I'd peered on guessing their way through parts of the test received a penalty with a note that explained I fucking knew they didn't know and if they wanted to argue about it, bring it on.

"Only, I obviously phrased it nicer," I said to Charlie since he always listened to me when I worked.

He purred in agreement, and I continued making my way through these practice tests.

The written responses for their short answers were harder to gauge. I didn't know if I was being nitpicky or generous half the time when I jotted a comment of praise or improvement. Mostly improvement because, let's be honest, they could use it. Their scoring by the FAP panelist would be subjective too, no matter how much those in charge of the testing procedures claimed to stick strictly to the rubric guidelines. Nothing was a hundred percent foolproof, and the FAP had a lot of fucking fools running it.

The clink of dominos smacking against each other rattled in the back of my head.

I bared my teeth, bracing for the clickity clank of gears shifting, my mind bracing for the visions about to spring loose and fuck up my whole life. Only they didn't do that. Nothing. There was the ding of a bomb about to explode, and then it stopped. I sighed.

"That's not good." I squeezed Charlie against my chest, letting the steady purrs he released steal my attention from the potential horrors awaiting me. "It's fine."

I took a deep breath and shrugged. I would ignore it. It wasn't the first bodily check engine light I'd ignored over the years in hopes that things would resolve themselves. It certainly wouldn't be the last. Besides, no one could help with this. No one except for Milo, and I couldn't bother him. Even if I wanted to. His mission had him traveling across the country in pursuit of a deadly witch. I needed to deal with this on my own.

These visions would spring loose soon, but it'd be fine. It had to be fine. Everything always worked out. Or it didn't. Either way, I survived. Or I supposed eventually I wouldn't. I groaned as I crawled off the couch to my feet while scooping Charlie into my arms because he certainly was in no mood to walk. He had his 'carry me' face on, which meant if I abandoned him in the living room to get ready for bed, I'd never hear the end of it. He'd cry all night until I checked on him.

I tossed him on the bed, using a bit of telekinesis to slow his plop onto the pillows so I could brush my teeth in peace and finish my nighttime routine.

Carlie scratched at the bathroom door, demanding the late-night treats I'd forgotten about. She had the look of utter contempt, patience thin and ready to lay siege to all my belongings as I slept. Of course, only if I didn't pay penance in the form of snacks she'd grown accustomed to.

"This is Milo's fault." I dragged my feet from my bedroom and to the kitchen for the special treats she absolutely had to have because she'd been a good girl.

"They're good for her," Milo's voice echoed in my head, the memory of his sweet smile, his puppy dog blue eyes, the irritating batting of his lashes.

He'd gotten her diet-friendly treats, snacks predicted to help with the fact the vet said she was overweight.

"By three pounds." I side-eyed her, setting a few treats on the countertop. "Might not seem like much, but you're like a foot long."

Carlie devoured her treats and shimmied along the countertop before she hopped off and dashed away in preparation for her late-night antics before she would finally settle for bed.

"Me-meow." Charlie crept at the edge of the hallway, glassy eyes peering out while he hid behind the way.

"I'm coming to bed." I scooped Charlie up once again and carried him to the bedroom because I'd never hear the end of it if he had to walk himself back.

It didn't take long for me to fall asleep, drifting into another repetitive dream. Finn's speech a second time. No deviation from his presentation on the Sisters of Fate, on their psychic supremacy, on the witchy Illuminati conspiracy known as the Celestial Coven.

Part of me wanted to tear loose from the strings; I'd done it unintentionally before. Perhaps I could learn how to change my dreams, turn them into something fun. I'd drag Milo and Finn out of this classroom and run through the empty hallways of Gemini.

Frantic footsteps scampered through the edges of my dream, stealing attention from this memory. Each step beat like a slow drum, a harbinger of the worst about to unfold. The crunch of Caleb's shoes hitting the ground washed away the sound of Finn's voice. The further the void vision crept into my line of sight, the more that empty nothingness ate away at the memory. Soon, everything except for Caleb had vanished.

I took a deep, frustrated breath. The void vision was always the first to appear when the visions came loose, so I braced myself for an onslaught of impending images to bombard me. Honestly, it wasn't simply sightings with these visions. No, I had the luxury of sounds, smells, and sensations of all types.

Would I be able to handle this? Without Milo here, I'd have to navigate the flurry of visions on my own. I knew this was coming. I'd felt it looming for days now, longer really, yet I was still baffled by how I'd sort these bursting visions. I'd have to contain them somehow, ignore them, drown them out before they drowned me.

Fifteen-year-old Caleb ran past me, looking nothing like the kid in my classes now. No, this frantic boy no longer existed, this danger no longer existed, but this goddamn potential future still lingered. Why? Because clearly, the universe was a dickhead. The outdated visions never faded away, always replaying alongside those that were still possible. How Milo handled this, I'd never in a million years understand. If I had his magic, I'd be pissed off all the time seeing useless fucking visions playing on repeat.

I huffed. It was even more annoying knowing Milo managed to smile through his days, considering how this type of shitshow played in his head on a loop. That just aggravated me even more. Irritation actually turned out to be a good thing, a bearable thing, which helped dull the repetition of Caleb sprinting for his life, collapsing to the ground as he died, Kenzo kneeling beside him, furious and removing the enchanted dagger, and Tara somber and filled with so much remorse her ocean of sorrow almost painted the edges of this black abyss.

"Fuck," I muttered, bracing for an onslaught of impending visions. They'd all appear now. I'd endured the routine of it a few times now, and without Milo around, I'd have to cope with the monstrosities in my mind.

Only the pop of a hundred different visions snapping off simultaneously didn't happen. Something new brewed at the edges of my mind. A vision that'd lain dormant among the collection. It boiled and sizzled, seared my inner core, twisting my perception of the mind, a place of my making, into a battlefield of carnage.

Rubble. Debris. Smoke. Flames. Chaos. Blood. Destruction. So powerful and palpable that the sheer devastation radiating off it swallowed every other vision entirely, leaving only the ruin of Chicago in its wake.

Silent screams.

Scorched flesh.

Crying corpses.

The city wept crimson tears, raining down the deaths of millions. Not a few unlucky souls but every single person. Maimed and slaughtered and left to rot on the fractured ground that rumbled with furious satisfaction.

I whirled through every corner of the city, every street, every building, every inch of the sky above and the tunnels below. Death. Death. Death. Everywhere and everyone.

Finally, the vision slowed like a rollercoaster inching its way back to the conductor's station. Here, at the edge of the nightmarish vision, lay twelve bodies.

The fabric of uniformed blazers left burned and ripped. Bloodstained shirts tattered and frayed. Scorched emblems, ruining the golden sheen of Gemini Academy pins.

Yaritza Vargas. Dead. Melanie Dawson. Dead. Jennifer Jung. Dead. Jamius Watson. Dead. Layla Smythe. Dead. Carter Howe. Dead. Gael Rios-Vega. Dead. King Clucks. Dead. Gael Martinez. Dead. Katherine Harris. Dead.

Tara Whitlock. Dead.   Kenzo Ito. Dead.   Caleb Huxley.   Dead.

My entire homeroom coven lay across a sea of corpses, bloody and beaten and broken.

I screamed and shot up, shaking loose from the shadows and limbs that wrapped around my body, my throat. Fingers dug into the scar of my neck and ripped it open, painting blood and pain everywhere.

"No, no, no!" I shouted, gasping and desperate for a single breath.

The attack faded. The limbs that strangled me turned into tangled covers. I took rapid breaths, steadying my erratic pulse before I realized I'd levitated in my sleep. I floated high up off the bed, where both of my cats stared at me from the floor. Their eyes shimmered in the dark of the room.

"Fucking hell," I muttered, releasing the stress of the nightmare—the vision, actually—and descended to the comfort of my bed. "Bet I gave you two a scare."

Charlie hopped back in bed, sniffing my sweaty face and then settling back into a comfortable spot on the bed. I hadn't levitated in my sleep since I was seven or eight. Sleep casting wasn't unheard of, and my telepathy remained active at all times, but I rarely lost control of my roots. That vision shook me to my very core. Quite literally the core of my abdomen where access to the levitation root lay.

I contemplated contacting Milo, telling him about the vision, but he would've already seen it. This was probably another outdated potential future, one he'd resolved years ago. The thousands of visions I'd absorbed from Milo exploded throughout my mind, an eruption of fireworks flickering out too quickly to make sense of but lasting too long to simply ignore. They rattled around my skull, scraping at the insides of my head, tearing everything apart to the foundations of my sanity.

"This can't be real. It can't be possible," I said to myself a few times, repeating it until the truth that this wasn't possible cemented into my thoughts. Only it didn't work.

I grabbed a cigarette and tried to calm my shaky nerves. Continuous flashes played in my line of sight, warping my perception of the dark bedroom. Even the cherry ember of my cigarette appeared blurred when the flicker of some fast-passing vision looped by.

"Fuck it." I snuffed out the smoke and reached for my phone.

Milo answered on the first ring.

"How are you even awake?" I turned the phone to check the time, squinting at the harsh bright light in the darkness of my bedroom.

"What can I say?" He smiled; I felt it in the single breath of his pause. "I had a feeling you might call tonight."

"Damn clairvoyants," I said with a breathy huff, also smiling because only Milo would stay up until three in the morning on the off chance I might have a nightmare vision panic attack and need his soothing voice to calm down.

"I had…" I bit my lip, contemplating because the second I asked for clarification on that nightmare, that past vision, that horrible hellish future, I knew it'd consume me. It'd haunt my every waking breath. My every sleeping one, too.

"Visions came loose, and you saw a really bad one."

"Yes, I saw—"

"An impossible possibility."

"You can't know that."

"I can, and I do. That future can never become reality."

"You don't know that. You always say things can change from the slightest ripple. We both know the Doppler caused more than ripples when he hurled stones into the lake of potential futures."

"Fun metaphor, but unlikely it would put that reality back on track."

"How can you possibly know?" I asked, edge in my voice, barely able to keep from snapping.

"Because I have to be dead in that future. Gone. Poof." Milo chuckled, keeping the silence of that horrifying realization from fully sinking in. "And I don't plan on being dead anytime soon. I've seen my final curtain call, and it's fucking fabulous. I'm sure as shit not cashing that ending in for some knockoff warped reality."

"You've seen your death?" I swallowed the lump in my throat. It hadn't dawned on me, but of course someone with Milo's magic had seen his own death. He'd seen mine before, the possibility, and prevented it. He saw death every day, so naturally, his would be there too, haunting him.

"I've seen like a thousand ish potential deaths for the amazingly awesome Enchanter fucking Evergreen," Milo said with majestic confidence like he stood on a stage, not as a guild witch but as the captivating magicians of old. Top hat. Twirling cane. Silly cape. And a smile that pulled the audience into a trance. I didn't need to be connected to Milo to feel that. His voice, his tone, his every breath painted that perception.

"I'm sorry."

"Don't be. Sometimes, they're funny. Just last week, I saw myself getting taken out from a ham sandwich." Milo burst into laughter, the type of laughter that drew tears to the edge of his eyes as he stifled the joy. He had a joke in his head that he wished to share, to add, but the mere idea of it made him giggle.

I huffed. This joke was probably not even remotely funny. Folks had a way of building up humor in their own head, it hit the right notes at the right time and then they'd burst at the seams in a laughter fest over something ridiculously dull.

"Could you imagine the irony of me being taken out by swallowing a piece of meat? After all those years of mastering my gag reflex?" Milo had an annoyingly charming hint of humor in his voice, playful and hopeful and wishing to steer me out of the storm of paranoia. "I refuse to go out on a joke of a death. Unless it has a hell of a better punchline."

I sat quietly, letting Milo's laughter wash over me, wash away the horror of that vision. I reminded myself Milo was always ready, always here to prevent the worst possible future, refusing to settle for anything other than the best outcomes. That nightmarish future was simply an impossible lie. An illusion cast by a universe who underestimated The Inevitable Future.

"I wish I were there," Milo said. "But I'll be there soon."

"I'm okay."

"You're not. And it's all right to say you're not." Milo got really quiet, like he'd held onto those words from a lifetime ago. "I don't want you sitting there suffering through the rubble of outdated visions when I could do something about it. I should be—"

"Exactly where you are," I interrupted. "You're making the brightest possible future, right?"

Milo didn't respond.

"You're keeping that carnage from my dream an unattainable reality. You're making sure no one suffers at the hand of a scary witch with a serious boner of hate for technology."

Milo burst into laughter. "Boner of hate? What the hell even is that?"

"I don't know." I shrugged, twisting a bit in bed to let Charlie get cozier. "It sounded like some dumb shit you'd say."

"Dick." Milo giggled, incapable of holding in the laughter my absurd comment caused.

It brought pure joy to my thoughts, settling my nerves, easing the tension in my skull, and quieting the visions that'd sprung loose. I wouldn't be able to neatly stack them in the corner of my mind, out of the way of my daily routine like Milo had done for me, but I could bear this fatigue until Milo's return. Knowing his absence was only temporary alleviated the panic, the misery, the world that constantly gnawed at my sanity.

"I should be back in Chicago soon," Milo said. "And then done with the case shortly after that…um, er… I mean, I should be done with the case soon and then back in Chicago after that."

Milo chuckled, carefree with a hint of force to it. I could always tell when he faked it.

"I think maybe you've been up too late," I said. "You sound too tired for conversation."

"I think maybe you're right." Milo took a deep breath and paused. "If there's anything you need, please let me know. I'll do anything I can to—"

"You've helped a lot more than you realize."

The visions sort of bounced around in the background of my thoughts, but I focused on the sound of Milo's voice, the goals I had for work, the nearby dreams of neighbors. It was as if the visions were merely annoying pop-up ads in my brain. If I could ignore the ads in everyday life, I could certainly ignore the advertisements of potential possibilities.

I snorted at my own warped sense of exhausted humor. "I think maybe I'm too tired for this conversation, too."

When I wasn't so tired, I'd tell him about the memory I relived, the one with Finn and the Sisters of Fate. He enjoyed hearing about my memories of us, three guys looking ahead to the future.

Milo and I stayed on the phone, quietly breathing into it and enjoying the silence until we drifted off to sleep.

Because of him, the visions didn't haunt my slumber. Because of him, I fell into a dream memory of our first official date after we'd gotten back together. Because of him, I spent every second of the night wishing for a lifetime of memories we could share.

CHAPTER THIRTEEN

AS we moved into mid-March, I managed to hold out in Milo's absence. Yes, my telepathy remained stretched out to reach him as he traveled the country in pursuit of this elusive True Witch, but here in Chicago I had only myself to rely on when curbing the effects of the visions that'd sprung loose. It turned out, keeping busy with work helped distract me from the continuous crackle and flicker of visions looping throughout my mind.

I sent my telepathy in every possible direction, keeping it spread thin in so many ways that it should've left me so exhausted and overwhelmed I couldn't function. In actuality, it kept my head clear and fresh. The act of having a manifestation hovering close to Milo while also navigating the hallways of Gemini Academy as I stood inside my classroom going over a history lesson before assigning a unit test.

Here I was, bouncing in every direction, which seemed to keep me too active for the visions to bombard my waking mind. Hopefully, I could keep up this pace until Milo returned to the city.

It didn't take long to drift into Chanelle's classroom. I often found myself drawn to her, making observations of her class structure, her dynamic with students, and how, despite the grief and guilt that gnawed at the edges of her thoughts, she never let it change her. Sorrow struck a chord in her heart like the keys of a piano playing nonstop, yet she smiled through it. Chanelle remained so positive, so joyful during her interactions, I almost confused it for genuine. Well, it was. Chanelle wasn't hollowed out with phony happiness, but she held this enthusiasm for life that superseded any depression.

Most of the time, she was fine, but when she worked with Jamie's coven, the worst of her sadness blossomed. Dark blue waves trickled along the sunshine yellow of her aura, but just like the sun would dry up all the water, her happiness worked to erase all the sorrow.

"And how is the spell coming along?" Chanelle signed.

Mostly correct, according to Tia, who had watched Chanelle's sign language progress over their two years together. Thankfully, her interpreter was still there to clarify anything missed in translation. Apparently, Chanelle's gestures were occasionally too enthusiastic.

"Going well," Tia's interpreter said. "Right now, we're trying to find a way to mimic the copycats."

Tia signed a spell, conjuring shadows from the edges of the classroom and pulling them toward her through a cosmic magic she'd read in Katherine's grimoire.

```
Name: Tatiana Owens
Branch: Enchantment (Invocation)
Ranking: 158
```

While Tia used language-based spells, signing to summon magic, and Katherine read from previously written and stored spells, the two girls found a very similar overlap in their particular enchantments. So much so, they shared their knowledge freely, expanding each other's library of casting.

The cosmic magic helped Tia steal darkness from nearby, which she then molded into the form of a shadow cat silhouette.

"Almost there," Vik said. "It's kind of funny, creating a spell to copy a copycat."

```
Name: Vik Smythe
Branch: Arcane (Copycat)
Ranking: 156
```

The shadow cat trotted toward Vik's three shadow cats, joining them as they scurried across the classroom, climbing walls and slipping through cracks before reappearing elsewhere in the classroom.

When Vik's shadow cats summoned a ball of fire, the three of them batted it around, similar to Charlie and Carlie when playing in the house. The fire held no threat as Vik fixed their telekinesis on the element in case their cats got a bit too wild.

Tia sent her cat forward, attempting to join in with the shadow cats since her own attempt at mimicking the fire didn't work. The fireball hit Tia's cat and lit the shadowy fella ablaze.

Tia snapped her fingers, diminishing her spell and letting out a frustrated grunt.

"See," Tia's interpreter said. "I can copy every aspect of the shadow cats except for the actual mimicry of other magics. That involves some secondary provision I can't comprehend."

"You and me both," Vik mumbled, their surface thoughts revealing their shadow cats displayed a fire element magic because when Vik tried to copy water magic, it proved too difficult to mimic. Both were of the primal branch, but Vik found each magic held unique properties, and they weren't skilled enough to memorize or master all the magics of the world.

I winced when making a slightly deeper dive into Vik's thoughts. As expected, they still lingered on Jamie Novak's death, on how they never mastered his whirlpool branch magic. The training effect with the water casting came from Vik's desire to continue pursuing the lessons they'd never mastered with Jamie, with their coven mate, with someone they never got to call a friend. And now they never would.

Chanelle took a seat at the table, ready to review what worked and what didn't and discuss some research she'd done on both of their magics. Vik had the more complex magic, an arcane branch that few possessed and even fewer had documented. A lot of Chanelle's advice would have to be trial and error, which concerned her since she knew Vik had an anxious personality and dwindled when hitting the wall of failure. Not that any of us really took failing in stride.

Tia on the other hand presented her own difficulties since everything Chanelle looked up about invocation came with vocal trainings, harmonizing one's frequency with the melody of their voice, and really all things spoken. That wouldn't help Tia in the least, which meant Chanelle spent a lot of late nights brainstorming ideas to try with Tia.

As Chanelle worked closely with two of Jamie's coven mates, I drifted around the classroom toward the final member of his coven, the one I knew the least about since I didn't have Emmanuel in any classes.

```
Name: Emmanuel Delgado
Branch: Hex (Luck)
Ranking: 333
```

He sat at a table with several classmates, dealing cards as they eyed each other up before another round of poker.

I rolled my eyes. Only Chanelle would turn a card game of gambling into a classroom training project—and actually allow them to bet money, even if it was her ridiculous Chanelle bucks. Though, admittedly everyone kept attentive, shoulders squared, magic finely channeled, and minds whirling in suspicion for their peers.

Chanelle painted imagery with her words, conjuring the best sales pitch when tricking them into treating the game like a battle. In the minds of each teen, they waged a delicate war against an unsuspecting foe.

Emmanuel weighed the amount of luck he'd need to unleash to better his chances while still holding onto enough magic to last several rounds. I didn't realize how finite his hexing magic was in a day.

Tiffany didn't bother with her aloof tricks, something I'd seen her use on Gael and many others during her time at Gemini. As a tiny blonde with a cute face and high-pitched voice, she'd gotten used to being shrugged off as dim. Instead of proving them wrong, she had more fun playing the part. That wouldn't work with her coven since she'd lulled each of them into a trap on more than one occasion.

```
Name: Tiffany Sparks
Branch: Bestial (Familiar)
Ranking: 60
```

So, in this match, she prioritized working with Duchess, her beaver familiar with whom she shared a telepathic link, one even my magic couldn't glean both sides of the conversation. This helped the duo practice their strategizing, predictions, and plotting. A skill Chanelle wanted to further mold.

Much like how I didn't have experience with Emmanuel, I didn't know the next student at the table either. I'd never had her in any of my classes, but I thought maybe I'd seen her hanging around some of my students before. It was hard to recall. It was hard enough keeping track of the hundred-plus kids on my roster, let alone the nearly two thousand roaming the halls of Gemini Academy.

"You all realize I've seen every possible outcome to this little game." Olivia pouted her lips, attempting to add a layer of mystique to her expression, a hint of secrecy, but immediate flashes of the ditzy girl who often tripped over her own feet while laughing at something on her phone appeared in Emmanuel and Tiffany's surface thoughts.

It didn't stop Olivia from continuing to have a cocky attitude as she held her cards close to her chest and performed a three-card spread with a separate tarot deck.

"Hmmmm." She studied her cards, thoughts wrapped in predictions.

```
Name: Olivia Flores
Branch: Psychic (Clairvoyance)
Ranking: 177
```

"I'll take two." Olivia tossed cards from her hand into the discard pile and grabbed two more after gauging the potential outcomes from her tarot spread.

Though she possessed the same branch magic as the great Enchanter Evergreen, they each accessed future images in very different ways. In order for Olivia to glimpse future outcomes, she required the tarot deck as a support tool. If she wanted to predict the future outcomes of others, then she needed them to come into contact with her cards, too.

"This round is mine, so bluff away. I've seen everything you have or will have or could have or might maybe get at some point." Olivia squinted while attempting her most intimidating gaze.

She was quite possibly the only one at the table to actually believe her own bluff.

"Save the heart of the cards bullshit." Emmanuel tossed three cards into the pile and grabbed new ones. "We all know lady luck is on my side."

"If only she were lucky enough to find a better job since hanging on your hip has got to be a real drag." Tiffany fanned herself dramatically, mockingly, and casually showing off two poor cards in her hand to draw attention away from her beaver's careful snooping of Emmanuel's hand.

While Emmanuel, Tiffany, Duchess, and Olivia eyed each other for signs of casting, they underestimated the biggest threat at their table.

```
Name: Ryan Holmes
Branch: Augmentation (Limbs)
Ranking: 37
```

Literally the biggest, too. Ryan towered over everyone at the table, big and broad and thick even sitting down, which might've helped keep him upright with so many extra limbs sticking out of his back.

He'd overwhelmed Gael Martinez with incredible strength during last year's Spring Showcase, but I didn't realize his biggest talent came in the form of stealthy subterfuge. Chanelle did, though, helping him hone his branch in ways even his peers didn't suspect. Sure, every one of them kept an eye on Ryan's many sprouted arms, suspecting he'd use an extra hand to pilfer from the deck of cards, but in actuality, he used his arms to manipulate the casting at the table.

He'd unleashed arms of every shape, from long and gangly to short and muscular, all the way to fat and all thumbs. Each arm moved suspiciously, drawing attention where his literal sleight of hand desired.

This allowed Ryan to brush a few stray hairs from Duchess, dropping them onto the tarot deck and altering Olivia's perception of the future unbeknownst to her. She merely assumed Duchess held the biggest threat to her winning hands and made the unsuspecting beaver her target. After all, why else would the familiar appear in every reading Olivia performed on the card game?

Emmanuel spent so much time gauging the precise mathematical amount he'd require for each winning hand that he didn't notice Ryan run his fingertips along Emmanuel's ankle. That was all Ryan needed. Quick skin-to-skin contact while Emmanuel channeled his luck, inadvertently sending it toward Ryan in waves.

Thankfully, Chanelle made it a rule they explain how they used their magic to outperform each other after the game, otherwise poor Emmanuel would likely spend weeks befuddled by how terrible his math skills were in conjunction with how much magic he actually possessed and how much casting luck truly cost.

Amani watched a few rounds, making a mental note of Ryan's skills but finding the challenge limited. Despite how much she enjoyed playing the game during her first year at the academy, most of Mrs. Whitehurst's review game days left Amani bored. Her illusions were too precise for card games, tricking even her coven mates, who were the most aware of the psychic tells.

```
Name: Amani Williams
Branch: Psychic (Glamour)
Ranking: 5
```

She easily won over everyone, especially without Jamie around. Her breathing hitched momentarily, recalling how soft he'd become during their second year and then how suddenly he was gone. It left a sour taste in her mouth, barbs cast too casually, and compliments never uttered because she didn't have them at the time. Now, a thousand different things buzzed in her thoughts, but dwelling on Jamie was as exhausting as watching her classmates play poker was tedious.

Ignoring all of it, Amani returned to doom scrolling through her phone, watching videos, and messaging friends.

A message from Layla popped up, and Amani smirked.

Wait a second. I cocked my head, focusing my eyesight primarily on my classroom.

Motherfucker. Layla was in the middle of a test.

I twirled my fingers in Layla's direction like casting a fishing reel made entirely of telekinesis, and then I snatched the phone from her lap and pulled it toward me. It snagged, halted by Layla's telekinesis. She practically snarled, eyes a deep golden and filled with fury. Teeth bared and fanged. Claws extended and dug into her desk. She kept quiet, allowing most to remain undisturbed by the slight crunch of her nails.

"*Why are you looking around?*" I linked my thoughts to the few who glanced up from their desk. "*I didn't realize you had finished your test. Wow. Must've aced it if you're done that quickly.*"

And with that, they returned to their own business.

Layla and I competed with our telekinetic grip on her cell phone. Usually, I didn't fight with kids about their technology. There were times when brain breaks were necessary, but I'd be damned before I allowed someone to blatantly disregard my test policies, especially when they had a state test coming up. This type of infraction would invalidate everyone's score. The damn FAP test didn't play.

"*It's mine until the end of the day,*" I thought, keeping my eyes trained on Layla. "*Or you're welcome to have it back now in pieces.*"

Our telekinesis pulled at the phone, each capable of adding more pressure, but that'd most certainly shatter the fragile glass.

"*Even you wouldn't be that—*"

"*Have you met me?*" I glared.

Layla huffed, releasing her telekinesis and allowing me to take her phone while she broke a pencil and pouted. After a few minutes of quiet fury, she resumed her test, thinking profanities about me nearly as hostile as Kenzo during his first year. If I could survive his animosity, I could handle anything from anyone.

CHAPTER FOURTEEN

THE time had finally come. Milo flew through the night sky toward Enchanter Diaz and his bear familiar, who were arriving in the city via some train that had been sequestered for official Global Guild business. Milo nearly rolled his eyes at the ripple effect of unnecessarily altering the lives of so many people attempting to get home, travel on business, or enjoy the scenic route afforded by train.

He buried those possibilities, neatly tucking away the potential futures of strangers he'd never encounter again since his mission carried him far out of reach. They'd gone everywhere, it seemed. Gladiatrix announced her presence from Florida all the way to Maine, flying from state to state to force a shift in their target's plans. Diaz and his familiar hunted along the West Coast without delay. Milo and Wadsworth moved in zigzags across the nation, presenting themselves at every capital city leading to their destination.

Looking through the memories of my manifestation that synced with me revealed Milo's plan involved a lot of separate PR stunts. All of which was intended to steer The True Witch toward an objective he knew how to prevent. One that'd spare another town the horrors that'd fallen upon Harmony Valley.

Now, this Global Guild coven had reunited and traveled toward a destination where The Inevitable Future intended to shatter every horrible possibility The True Witch sought to unleash upon the world.

And Milo did so here. I snapped to attention, almost reeling myself back into my own mind as I sat at home, wondering when my sunshine would return. He had.

Milo was flying through the Chicago night sky. What was he doing here, of all places? Yes, his mind fixated on meeting with Diaz and Wadsworth, but here? Our home? Why drag this True Witch to our doorstep? Was that the only option? Did Milo want to use her defeat here to push some other agenda? I could never keep up with all the futures he juggled; even having thousands of potential possibilities bouncing around my inner core didn't truly offer me insight into Milo's mind. Merely a fucking headache for the ordeal he dealt with.

He reached the abandoned train station, tied off by Cerberus Guild, as he knew they'd move in fast to clear the areas he needed emptied. Enchanter Wadsworth leaned against a pillar, sucking in oxygen from his tank before untwining himself. Such a big mission meant he needed to dispense of anything that hindered his success. I couldn't imagine him fighting, taking on a non-support role, yet the ideas bubbled along his furious surface thoughts.

Outside the train doors, Enchanter Diaz fussed with armor plating on his familiar bear. She playfully bit the gauntlet on her paw until Diaz shooed her off, adjusting her helmet. Each piece of the bear's armor covering her from head to toe was etched in enchanted sigils, symbols that warded or dampened or shielded against magics. Even my telepathy struggled to gauge Diaz's thoughts as he stood close to his guarded familiar.

I searched for the most powerful member in their group but didn't see Gladiatrix anywhere. That was disconcerting. According to Milo's mind, she was still several states away, a day's drive based on the last news report Milo had checked this morning with her helping remove a resurgence of demons from the town of Lumberton, North Carolina.

"Glad you're here," Milo said. "We're gonna have to move soon."

"Well, it might take some time." Wadsworth nodded at Diaz and his familiar. "They've been getting dressed for the better part of an hour."

"Priscilla never goes into combat undressed," Diaz said, tipping his hat. "It's unbecoming for a lady of her station."

"Seriously?" Milo questioned.

"No." Diaz laughed.

"Does she really need armor?" Milo asked. "She's basically already a thousand-pound battering ram."

And according to his surface thoughts, they had the full intention of keeping her distant from combat in a supportive role. I scoffed at that, nearly jolting back to my body. They were going to take the elderly man on literal life support into the fight but keep the ferocious bear on the sidelines?

"Definitely. It's our Sword & Shield Duet." Diaz unsheathed his weapon, revealing a pristine blade covered in symbols similar to his bear's armor.

It appeared the duo served as a perfect attack and defense; formations they'd trained in bubbled along Diaz's mind.

"Look, I get it." Diaz put his sword away and continued checking over each buckle that held together Priscilla's armor. "We're just support on this mission, but that doesn't mean we go in unprepared."

The bear growled and nipped at Diaz.

"Baby gurl, you know I gotta double check those straps." Diaz had a stern fatherly expression, the silent rage of 'let me do my job' on his face.

Priscilla whined, letting out a low growl while Diaz checked the fasteners of her plated armor.

"You know the location, Evergreen," Wadsworth said. "Let's just go. Leave Diaz behind. He's barely a qualified Global Guild witch."

"Oop, I see what you did there." Diaz tipped his hat at the witty pun that Wadsworth hadn't intended.

"Just the organization's way of diversifying."

"I know you're referring to my branch when you say diversify," Diaz said, pointing a finger at Wadsworth. "But you're treading a thin line, old man."

"Bah." Wadsworth waved a dismissive hand, truly finding some branch magics like bestial beneath him.

"We need Diaz and Priscilla," Milo said, earning ire from Wadsworth's glare as he didn't think much of phony psychic magics either.

"I don't need them to face The True Witch."

"Well, if anything, they'll keep her from fleeing," Milo said. "Pretty sure she'll recognize the expert trackers who'll grab her scent the second we confront her."

"Oh yeah." Diaz stretched. "Once I get a scent, it's mine for life."

"Yuck." Milo shuddered, imagining every pungent, horrible smell he'd ever encountered.

"Besides, if I get to play, I can do some real damage with this baby." Diaz pulled out his sword a second time. The symbols glowed now, under his direction, the way he channeled his magic.

That particular blade was expensive and difficult to gain approval for work. Diaz's sword and his familiar's armor plating weren't support tools legally afforded to them, but a casting weapon. In order to use it, he had to pay huge fees and constantly recharge the sigils—which, based on his grumbling surface thoughts, required the aid of a qualified enchantment witch, ward witch, and rejuvenation witch. Christ, he ensured the Sword & Shield Duet came with top-tier magics. That was a big fucking headache.

Every symbol etched onto his gear required yearly testing and evaluations to prove he could wield the weapons without endangering others, injuring them, or causing wrongful deaths.

There was a lot of red tape involved with arming guild witches with extra gear for combat, which was usually why the guild wouldn't front the cash for such exorbitant costs. They generally made their enchanters pay those fees out of pocket—even the undercover case Milo went on to handle demons required the aid of glamoured earrings, which his guild didn't approve his acolytes for, meaning he had to pay the cost out of pocket himself since he was the only one qualified by Cerberus standards. And the use of those glamour tools for a night's work probably matched my monthly salary. Not a cheap bill to buck.

That was why most enchanters relied solely on their magics—since few could afford the upkeep, maintenance, cost, approvals, paperwork, and everything else involved in arming up. Plus, the scrutiny that came with misuse.

All the same, Diaz never felt comfortable going into combat with Priscilla unless she had her armor on. Like any witch with a familiar, he worried for her safety above his own. Diaz's thoughts turned somber until Priscilla rubbed her head against his hip, asking for pets under her chin. She didn't seem to like her helmet much, but she had a goofy grin of satisfaction once she got the best chin scratches ever. I'd seen that happy face on Charlie many times before.

"Alrighty." Diaz slapped his thighs. "Let's get this rodeo started."

"About fucking time," Wadsworth hissed.

And like that, Milo led the way, flying fast and silent. The three enchanters moved so quickly through the city, I barely managed to keep up. Hell, even my connection to Milo didn't help. I staggered behind with Priscilla, who intentionally secured a defensive scouting position as a support role.

When they reached a busy building where the dark aura of The True Witch radiated, I faltered, nearly falling into a puddle of nerves. Atop the skyscraper, the three enchanters closed in on the witch who stood above the illuminated letters of the building.

Harris Enchant Tech!

My heart hitched, stirring anxiously and nearly drawing me back to my body. Some of my students were inside that building at this very moment, celebrating the merger of Harris Enchant Tech and Whitlock Industries. Hundreds of the most elite witches of Chicago were in attendance, completely unaware of the witch who lingered outside their gala with enough power in her Oceanic Collapse to slaughter them all in one fell swoop.

The True Witch carried herself with elegance, carefree and majestic in her pose, in her expression, in her…thoughts? I couldn't glean them. She'd veiled her mind from psychic energy with enchantments, wards, entropy, or some unknown arcane magic. I couldn't determine it. Mainly because I couldn't determine a single thought from her surface. Still, she wasn't hidden from me. Her presence oozed with a toxic horror that sought death, destruction, and the decimation of anything beneath her station.

She stood perched at the ledge of Harris Enchant Tech, ready to drape the entire building in her horrifying branch. I sensed that much, feeling the cold rush of channeled magic seeping from her pores and coating the many floors below, gauging how many people she'd need to cast against, how much energy she'd require, and how long it'd take to drown them all. Milo suspected as much, studying The True Witch in all her glory.

She didn't look anything like I expected. I figured she'd be an old crone of a woman, someone closer to Enchanter Wadsworth's age, but she looked younger than me, a woman barely in her thirties. She wore a tattered black dress, intentionally frayed at the hem leading to two large slits that ran up her legs all the way to her hips, torn at the sleeves, exposing her shoulders, and ripped in the front to flaunt her cleavage. Though her dress hid little, her skin was painted in symbols. Not tattoos for aesthetics but magical etchings strewn across her shoulders, her chest, and the parts of her legs not hidden by the thigh-high boots she wore.

The enchanted sigils matched those carved onto the ivory staff she held, the top a skull with the head bashed in and holding hundreds of glittering small stones. Each gem was a different color and radiated an aura of emotion or magic or possibly both.

The most outlandish part of The True Witch's attire came in the form of her absurd witch hat. A long-pointed hat that'd fallen out of style—if it'd ever truly been in style—more than two centuries back when magic returned to the masses and witch stereotypes fizzled out as we moved toward a modern era. Her hat was bent, the tip hanging low and almost reaching the wide, rounded brim that sat lopsided on her head.

I'd never felt anything like this. It was impossible to explain, to comprehend. There was an aura of mystique, confusion, and pain that radiated off this witch.

"You aged." The True Witch tilted her head, eyeing Enchanter Wadsworth from head to toe, unconcerned by the presence of two other enchanters and a literal armored bear. No. She only had eyes for Wadsworth. "You carry it well. Mostly. Not much. More than expected."

Wadsworth glared, a natural set-in expression for him; the wrinkles creased in a familiar way they'd always done when talking with The True

Witch. A woman whose love he'd seared from his memory. He'd literally had the thought of her exorcised, burned away, holding only onto the details that'd help in his pursuit of ending her life.

She hadn't aged, not in Wadsworth's mind, the same image of her holding a much younger hand of the elderly enchanter. Her French accent had gotten better, more believable, and covered her actual accent, one he never managed to place.

"A glamour from that staff of yours?" Wadsworth asked with a nod to the dangerous gemmed weapon The True Witch wielded. "Or did you finally figure out how to weave those sigils into a solid rejuvenating spell? Something to revitalize your old bones?" He smirked, wheezing as he bit back laughter, actual joy. "I must warn you, reversing the aging process is a delicate and dangerous thing."

"Only for someone with a novice understanding of their branch, such as yourself, Sammy."

Enchanter Wadsworth clenched his fists, furious with the feelings that fluttered from hearing her say his name. So much love and lust and loss clung between them.

"Remember, her staff is where the true threat of her power stems." Wadsworth nodded to the weapon.

Was it a support tool? No. Nothing in Milo's immediate surface thoughts indicated such, meaning she had full access to her arcane branch, Oceanic Collapse, independent of the staff. I swallowed hard, absorbing the thoughts that crossed Milo's mind as he studied the assortment of gems, each housing a different branch magic bound inside the jewels through sophisticated enchantment techniques.

"You bring such a small force to face me," The True Witch said.

"You're alone, Amara," Wadsworth revealed her name casually, letting it spill from his mouth like it meant nothing to him, like she meant nothing. Neither was true despite how he tried to will it. "Rumors suggest your Celestial Coven has finally fallen apart. I suppose that time you spent to find yourself didn't help hold your extremists together."

Celestial Coven? I trembled.

The same coven from the dreams I had. Dreams I had because perhaps my magic became aware of something, wished to warn me of something. Of what, though? And how? How did my telepathy learn or suspect this connection between The True Witch and the Celestial Coven?

"Enchanter Evergreen." Amara tipped her staff toward him, pointing. Her menacing curiosity reeled me away from my paranoid questions. "Your clairvoyance is quite the force of steel. It wormed its way into my choices, my future. You knew every X on the map of my commencement, my reintroduction to the world." She tightened her green eyes onto Milo with an unnerving hunger in her gaze. "You and Global Guild comrades leapt to every marker, every destination so loudly that it steered me here."

"You could've always gone into hiding." Milo shrugged, knowing that was the faintest of chances he gambled by beating The True Witch to every destination she intended on committing massacres at, by announcing themselves loudly and publicly, drawing crowds and media, and ensuring she knew.

"I am no wafter, no feeble child, no frightened rat." Her green eyes flitted and struggled to mask the rage, the offense to Milo's comment. It gave him a direction on how to steer her here and now. "Your Gladiatrix has weaved all across the countryside, has she not? Such a dangerous foe—I was careful to avoid her." Amara studied the three men surrounding her, training her eyes on Diaz whom her expression revealed little knowledge of. There was a twinge of the unknown in the crinkle of her brow. "Yet you chose to face me without her? Without the Gladiatrix?"

"It's just Gladiatrix," Milo said.

"It's actually Global Gladiatrix," Diaz noted. "Though, guess that gets a little redundant for her. Global Gladiatrix of the Global Guild. Whatever, Global Gladiatrix, The Inevitable Future, Annoying Old Man—none are half as catchy as Texas Daddy."

He flaunted his tattoo, but in reality, Enchanter Diaz wanted to let the moonlight glimmer against the enchantment sigils that lined his blade, showing The True Witch that she wasn't the only one with an understanding for support magics.

"No matter," Amara said. "Last I saw your Gladiatrix, only real threat, was in the Carolinas, helping with something as trivial as demons." She spit at the mention of demons as if the word itself left their filth and tar on her tongue. "Figured I should pick a region far from her."

Even The True Witch knew not to challenge someone with supreme physicality. Given the way it enhanced all of Gladiatrix's senses, it might've added a layer of immunity to her wicked arcane magic that drowned people in their thoughts. Either that or she knew Gladiatrix actually earned her ranking as the fourth most powerful witch in the Global Guild unlike Wadsworth who still ranked among the top-ten witches in the world because of his role in founding the organization.

"So, you're here to what? Attack big tech? Corporate Casting Inc.?" Milo shivered, feigning phony fear that he'd weaponized into a slight. "Technology really frighten you that much?"

"Nothing frightens me," Amara said.

"Except for Gladiatrix, clearly." Milo grinned, cocky and meant to shift The True Witch's focus, so he could search, search for possibility layered beneath so many wards of protection.

"These companies, these businesses claim to strive for accessibility." Amara shook her head. "What they offer is simplicity. They brush aside tradition, they ignore customs, and they fail to connect with the universe. All of this. All of it must end. Science is the death of magic."

"The lady doth protest too much, methinks." Milo tilted his head, unraveling futures he'd already glimpsed, tying them into what her feigned response added, layering these possibilities and finding a true motive, a real reason. "That's okay, though. I think it's time we wrapped this up."

"I won't simply hand myself over." The True Witch shifted her stance, channeling magic into her staff.

I braced for the possibility of her Oceanic Collapse hitting Milo, taking down the others. Who knew how fast that drowning arcane magic took effect, but I could counter it. I had before. This wasn't interference; it was merely silent support if needed.

A golden blur zipped in front of The True Witch, and Gladiatrix stood before the other woman, one hand twisting her wrist and forcing Amara to drop her staff, while Gladiatrix snatched Amara by the throat and held her in place.

The grip radiated telekinesis, putting Amara in a full-body stranglehold under Gladiatrix's control. She funneled her physicality into the root magics she wielded, enhancing the power.

"Yield or I'll break all of your bones." Gladiatrix had an expressionless face, calm and in control. I couldn't properly get a read on her thoughts as her mind cycled through Milo's plan, Global Guild protocols, Wadsworth's fears, and her own opinions slipped beneath it all.

"You were a thousand miles away…"

Gladiatrix tightened her hold, choking Amara into silence. "Barely an hour's flight for me."

"Well, suppose I've been bested by the very best of witches." The True Witch had a half smile that faded into a solemn façade. "I surrender."

And like that, they'd defeated and detained The True Witch. Impossible. How? Why?

Enchanter Wadsworth stepped onto an armored truck covered in protective enchantments, dampening wards, and sigils of every type. The guards assigned to the truck had already cuffed and bound Amara in place, making her escape impossible, yet Wadsworth's paranoia matched my own as he studied the witch that'd surrendered without so much as attempting one attack.

Once they closed and sealed the back of the vehicle, the magics triggered and blocked my curious telepathy from further insight.

"So, is the old man actually concerned about the killer witch's escape?" Diaz asked as he unfastened Priscilla's helmet. He wouldn't take all her plating off here, but he wanted her to stop complaining—or so his surface thoughts indicated. "Or is this whole escort thing just Wadsworth's way of dodging paperwork?"

Milo scoffed. "Doubtful. I've been to the MDC, they don't fuck around with paperwork. I had to practically write an essay just to step inside."

And according to Milo's thoughts, Wadsworth planned on following Amara through every single checkpoint of the Metropolitan Detainment Center, examine every glyph, enchantment, and symbol in place to contain the witch's magic, and stand vigilant in the deepest sectors of the facility where they'd hold The True Witch until proper arrangements had been made.

I'd seen the inside of the MDC thanks to the horrid memories of my Doppler, his semi-possession of one of their correctional officers, and his botched attempt to take control of Theodore Whitlock's mind. I shuddered; the mere thought of the vile warlock made the scar on my throat burn with a phantom pain. Supposedly, the MDC elevated their security since Theodore's outburst, and they'd locked him in isolation far from everyone else. Now, if only they'd bolt the door, throw away the key, and leave him to rot.

Gladiatrix floated toward Milo and Diaz. She held the bone staff with the top stuffed with hundreds of gems adorning the cracked-open skull head like a glittering crown.

"Thank you all for everything," Milo said, nodding to Priscilla so she knew he included her in his gratitude. "And for willing to stick around until this is officially resolved."

"But of course," Gladiatrix said. "The Global Guild always sees their missions through to the very end. We leave nothing unresolved."

Was that why Milo lured The True Witch to Chicago? Did he plan on pitting Global Guild forces against any unforeseen potential ripples caused by my evil manifestation and that damned chimera last semester?

"And you're certain of this plan?" Gladiatrix asked.

"As certain as I ever am about the future." Milo grinned, minxy and playful and like he'd shared all his secrets with her, with Diaz, with Priscilla, but it was Milo, and he always had a million more secrets to divulge when it involved the future.

"I'm still trying to wrap my head around it," Diaz said. "Around what we did. I like to think I'm almost average intelligence. Like I play chess, I believe in strategy, but even as you walked me through the plan to catch The True Witch—the ruse of it all, I just…"

Priscilla let out a tiny roar.

"Exactly. Feels like we're playing checkers, and you're playing mahjong," Diaz said to Milo and then pointed to his bear. "And to be clear, she's a tournament-ranked champion at both games."

"It is pretty complicated." Milo laughed. "But I assure you this is the easiest plan I could've concocted."

Diaz and Priscilla turned to each other and blinked with a matching dumbfounded expression. Just the idea of having to plan for every tiny possible detail hurt Diaz's head. I chuckled.

"You and me both, buddy," I said aloud to no one in particular since I was merely silent psychic energy.

"I'm going to take this to the MDC for storage." Gladiatrix lifted the staff slightly and frowned at the idea of all the paperwork she'd have to file just to hand it off to someone to lock in evidence.

She wanted to toss it in with Amara and Wadsworth, but he'd refused to allow The True Witch to be near such a potent weapon despite being held by enough dampening magic to silence a hundred witches.

"I'm gonna call the misses," Diaz said, retrieving his phone and strutting off with his familiar. "See if the twins are still up."

"It's like midnight." Milo checked his own phone. "Your kids don't have a bedtime?"

"They most certainly do," Diaz shouted from afar. "Wasn't talking about those twins."

Milo had a quiet laugh as he stood on the street alone under the night lights of the city. He called out on his phone. The vibration startled me, pulling my psychic energy from him momentarily as I fished my phone out of my pocket.

"I know you have a thousand questions."

"Try ten thousand." I closed my eyes so I could focus my sight purely on him across town without the distraction of my bedroom.

"And we'll talk soon, I promise. I've just got a million and one things to do. I mean, I'm already getting email notifications from every nation Amara has ever wronged, requesting her extradition."

"Then why bring her here? Of all the places—"

"Nope." Milo shushed me. "That's one of your ten thousand questions for later."

"By the time you answer them, I'll have a hundred thousand questions."

"And I'll be fully recharged and able to answer a million." Milo yawned, genuine exhaustion weighing on him. Or he'd done it to manipulate and guilt me since he already knew I was hovering nearby in my extended telepathy form. "We'll talk soon, I promise. I've got a mountain of paperwork first and then some case files to check in on with my acolytes, and I just need a few days to decompress. Don't worry, though."

I wouldn't worry. Or I'd do my best not to worry. At the very least, I was grateful to have Milo home, close to me.

CHAPTER FIFTEEN

MILO was back in the city. Milo had defeated The True Witch. Milo had invited me to his place. Fuck. Only one of those things seemed real. Milo's return. No way would a witch of that caliber simply surrender. Sure, Gladiatrix was an indomitable force, but The True Witch possessed an arcane branch that could shatter a psyche. Had she really not accounted for the Global Guild retaliating?

And Milo invited me to his place. He'd missed me so much that he decided I should come see him. That was truly startling because he never invited me to his place. If anything suggested the world was about to come to an end, it was Milo hosting for a change.

I arrived at Cyrus Bay Estates, the most elegant building in downtown Chicago with marble coated wards to keep out uninvited guests and enchanted windows that promised the best views because they removed anything unwanted when peering outside. The opulence of this building made me quake. Even the door attendants dressed more sharply than I did, wearing fine suits.

I lingered outside, smoking a cigarette and contemplating ditching Milo's invitation and telling him to just meet me at my place. I'd never been to his home. For good reason, too. Look at this elegant fucking monstrosity.

It was modern, magical, historical, and expensive. So fucking expensive. I was pretty sure I'd have to pay a fee just to stand here loitering with a smoke.

It'd already been a few days since Milo had returned to the city, and I was only just now getting an invitation. He might've been too busy to fly over to my house. Or he had to stay home, stay close to his guild, to the MDC, to the Global Guild members likely staying in some equally fancy hotel in the heart of downtown.

One of the door attendants eyed me up, head to toe, definitely with a scrutinizing gaze.

"I'm ah, um, er, hmmm." I backstepped, realizing I still had a cigarette in my hand that felt oddly out of place, like the mere audacity tarnished this pristine place.

"Mr. Frost, correct?" The attendant tilted their head knowingly while the other opened the door. "Enchanter Evergreen told us to expect you."

A quick scan of their surface thoughts revealed Milo had described me in an annoyingly unflattering yet completely accurate manner. *"Keep an eye out for the grouchy guy with heavy eyeliner, wrinkled clothes, likely a smoke in hand and a frown on his face."*

Every layer of this building was met with more attendants, more expensive tastes. I went to the elevator and took it to the top floor where Milo stayed in the penthouse.

When the elevator stopped, I tried to absorb the corridor leading to Milo's door. It took him all of three seconds to whip open the door and greet me with a goofy grin. "You're late."

"Traffic." I shrugged, shaking off the out-of-place feeling of this building.

Milo, Enchanter Evergreen, The Inevitable Future, acted like such an everyman, average guy that it was sort of easy to forget he was also one of the wealthiest people in the city. I mean, for an enchanter. He had nothing on guild masters or those who sat on the boards of guilds, but as the number one enchanter in the state, a recent member of the Global Guilds, and a huge fucking celebrity icon—Milo's take-home income towered over my humble teacher salary.

"Get out of your head." Milo had this knowing smirk, the kind where he studied each worry line on my face and had to remind me that it didn't matter if I fit in this world; I fit in his world, his life, and everything else was just background noise.

"I've missed you." I tried to take in the splendor of the penthouse foyer, imagining even more captivating things further inside, but truthfully, I couldn't take my eyes off Milo.

I was drawn to him. He wore a violet silk dress shirt and light brown slacks that matched his suit jacket. The pants were tight and left little to the imagination, especially since mine currently ran wild with ideas of everything I wanted to do with that hot body. There were certainly discussions to be had, but right now, I wanted to taste Milo's skin, feel his body pressed against mine, sync our minds and sensations into pure primal passion.

I stepped close, removing the distance between us so I could kiss him. Hell, it'd be hard not to mount him here and now, strip off that sexy suit and—

"Hold on." Milo braced with his hands up, pressing against my chest and keeping my lips from meeting his.

"*Someone's playing hard to get,*" I teased him, sending suggestive images when uttering the word 'hard' and grazing his crotch with the back of my hand.

"Dorian, I actually need to tell you something."

I quirked a brow.

"Why hello there, Mister Dorian, sir." The blue-haired kid Whatshis-name walked into the foyer, taking a gentleman's bow that he'd worked on with Milo. The steps played in his surface thoughts, like a game of some sort they panned out. "May I take your coat?"

"I'm not wearing a coat."

The kid's eyes widened, mind buzzing through a thousand contingencies and completely incapable of figuring out what to do next. He'd studied or prepared or assumed, for whatever reason, that he would greet the person at the door and take their coat.

As the anxious confusion bubbled in the suddenly cramped foyer, I found myself feeling bad. Like I'd caused this trepidation.

The fuck?

"How about the tour, Benjamin?" Milo nodded with an encouraging smile.

Oh, fuck me.

"How about a tour, Mister Dorian, sir?"

"I'm okay." I stared, unable to match the enthusiastic smiles coming from Milo or this Benjamin kid.

"He'd love it." Milo nodded, his expression painting a memory in Benjamin's surface thoughts.

"*He's a shy raccoon dragon, the kind that says one thing but really means another because he's the type of dragon that secretly likes to be included.*" The words splattered across Benjamin's thoughts, formed into flaming bubble letters as children had annoying imaginations that seeped out of their youthful, unformed brains.

"Right. Lemme show you around." Benjamin gripped my hand and dragged me toward the corridor. "This is the hallway where picture paintings are kept."

He pointed to artwork Milo had plastered on display for no one in particular since he rarely invited guests. But I knew these paintings, these masterpieces. No named artists and legends were placed on the wall side by side, each personal favorites of mine. Each were pieces I'd seen at one point or another in my youth. And Milo had acquired them, kept them in his home.

Interesting. Something I'd have liked to prod Milo's mind about, but I found myself ushered further through the penthouse, unable to even take in the full beauty of those paintings.

"This is the living room where the TV is located."

"Uh-huh." I looked at the huge, mounted television that took up nearly the entire wall. "A bit excessive."

"It is expensive." Benjamin nodded, convinced excessive was another way to pronounce expensive, then pointed to the couch. "This is where guests can sit and relax or over there or there or there too, I guess."

He continued pointing to the various pieces of furniture in the living room, cluttered with junk.

"And there is the consoles and the toys and the books." He pointed to an array of gaming systems, a collection of children's books, and a ridiculous number of toys strewn about the living room carpet. "I was supposed to pick those up. Hmmm. I will pick those up."

"Okay." I went to pull my hand free, but Benjamin's grip tightened.

"After the tour." He dragged me through the living room and toward the kitchen. "This is where the food is kept, but we're not supposed to eat in here. Cooking and cleaning is for the kitchen and eating is for conversation and community and…"

Benjamin's thoughts glazed over the long-winded tour of the penthouse he'd had with Milo when everything had been explained to him a few days ago. Here, I figured Milo had been keeping busy with paperwork, with the Global Guild, with Cerberus, with the bureaucratic nightmare of detaining The True Witch inside the MDC while every nation she'd ever wronged fought over the right to try her. In actuality, he'd just been helping this kid settle since having his entire life uprooted.

"That seems like a lot of work." I huffed in response to Benjamin's continued tangent about proper mealtimes designed for conversation and yada yada yada.

"Right?" Benjamin smiled up at me, then pulled me by the arm into the next room, where he pointed to the dining room table. "This is where we eat. But snacks are okay wherever. Oh, and toys." Benjamin knelt and picked up a toy that almost slipped under the table.

This tour continued as Benjamin escorted me throughout the entirety of Milo's Penthouse home. I saw every single bedroom, guest room, office space, lounging area, hobby room, home gym, and other space rarely occupied by the busy Enchanter Evergreen. Seriously. He'd spent almost all his free time at my house, cozying up to my cats and making my place his. And it turned out he had a place that could fit my entire house in it three times over. Probably more if we counted the balcony space. Not really a balcony since it had a floorplan of its very own split into several areas, from a patio to lounge, to a barbeque to host, to a pool, a hot tub, and so much more. But

Benjamin couldn't show me everything outside. He hesitated at an invisible line outside near the pool.

"I can't go this way." His heart raced, staring at the clear water of the pool. His sky-blue hair glowed, and his deep brown eyes turned crystal blue, the warding magic he relied on at the ready. "Enchanter Evergreen said that we can't go this far without an adult because the balcony has a dangerous ledge."

"Makes sense to me." I squeezed Benjamin's hand, pulling his attention from the pool. "It's a shifty-looking ledge. Personally, I find balconies annoying."

"Yes, but you need to get used to the balcony, Mister Dorian, sir."

"Oh? And why's that?"

"Because you're a smoker, and you cannot smoke in Enchanter Evergreen's home."

"Oh?" I glowered. "Milo said that?"

"I said that." Benjamin had a stern, unflinching expression, then his face softened, and he dragged me inside. "Let us continue the tour of the home."

After the tour, I finally got a chance to myself to enjoy one of my cigarettes on the cool balcony as the sun set. I savored the precious minutes alone since Benjamin talked to me nonstop since the literal second I walked back into the penthouse. He asked me why I started smoking.

"How old were you? I knew a kid at school who smoked cigarewets."

He asked if I knew the health risks. He asked if I liked smelling weird. He asked if I really thought it made me look cool. "It doesn't. Peer pressure isn't cool."

He explained the academic complexities of being in first grade.

He talked about what subjects in school he was the best at.

He explained math was boring.

He told me how mean his teacher was.

"Ms. Malmay is a bully. *Was* a bully." Benjamin's eyes stilled, locked onto a placemat, and his thoughts cycled through how he'd never see his mean teacher again, how he'd never see his classmates, his friends, his family. How every single person in his life was gone. Dead. Drowned.

It was a thought Benjamin didn't like to dwell on, but he did, and we sat in silence for several long minutes as he quietly processed, considered, and pushed those big feelings aside for another day.

"Do you wanna see my video games?" Benjamin hopped up from his chair, then rushed back in carrying a selection of toys that he fumbled with in his grip. He tried his telekinesis but only managed to drag one doll behind him.

"After you finish your dinner," Milo said, waving a finger and pulling away all the toys Benjamin intended to show off.

He went back to discussing video games for a minute, then shared a secret about good food. He made sure Milo didn't hear, whispering loudly to me about the importance of hot sauce and ketchup ratios.

He talked a lot. He talked while chewing his burger. When he paused to sip his water, Milo interjected, telling a silly story I didn't care about that worked to further fuel Benjamin's conversation. It was never-ending between these two. When we finished eating, Milo brought me to the living room, where Benjamin talked about the games he played and the things he learned and the stuff he disliked and the things he liked and the places he'd traveled since joining the Global Guild.

"But I'm not actually a part of the guild, just a special member."

Enchanter Evergreen had told him his part was integral, he even defined the big word, giving examples of all the possible greatness Benjamin's assistance would offer.

After quite possibly the longest, chattiest night of my life, Ben yawned. He struggled to keep his eyes open during one of Milo's many stories—he had talked nearly as much as Ben without the excuse of having a developing child brain and no filter. Once Ben had completely dozed off, Milo trailed off into some other story and carried the kid off to his temporary bedroom.

"What's with the kid?" I sighed, letting out an exasperated exhale since small children were quite exhausting. Vexing. Talkative. Annoying.

"You think everyone's irritating." Milo strutted past me, confident that he'd read my mind by studying my face.

Admittedly, he was pretty close. Not that I'd tell him.

"True. Thankfully, my tolerance for things I find aggravating has increased since learning to deal with you on a regular basis."

"Aw. You grumpy goof," Milo said, making us drinks and twirling his thoughts into silly songs.

"I get why you dragged him with you," I said in reference to Benjamin. "Dealing with this True Witch—who I have a lot of questions about—but why's he here? Still here, I mean. There's no residual magic leftover." None that I could sense, even with the kid's warding branch shielding his mind and body, I didn't sense the presence of anything else. "And with the threat locked up, surely…"

I waited for Milo to finish my sentence, reassure me, settle the anxious tension that formed at the back of my head.

"We've been dragging this kid all over the country, quick stop here, short break there, new hotel, new hotel, new hotel." Milo handed me a martini I cared nothing for and clinked my glass against his own. "I just thought he could use a real place to crash for a bit. Somewhere not so isolated. I got my acolytes taking shifts to chill with the kid until I find like proper daycare… um…attendants? People, stuff. Baby watchers but for like nonbaby people."

I frowned, partially perplexed and mostly annoyed. Milo had the perfect ability to bring both out simultaneously. "But can't the Global Guild take care of the kid?"

Milo's beautiful blue eyes fluttered, momentarily wrapped in quiet futures I couldn't gain a read on.

I downed my martini, then went to the half-bar in his kitchen and made myself a real drink. It wasn't exactly as stocked as the two separate wet bars I'd seen on the tour. Three. Shit. I forgot about the one outside. Who needed that many bars? It was convenient, though. And truthfully, I just needed the vodka and orange juice.

"So, I'm glimpsing the kid's still around for some whatever loose ends?"

"Yeah, ish." Milo shrugged, truly looking for the words while diving between unknown potential futures. "It's complicated. The Global Guild doesn't really deal with the fallout of survivors. I mean, on paper they do. Their whole helpful cleanup act after those krakens destroyed the oil pipelines and just straight up wrecked the Atlantic. They were there with enchanters posed for every photo op, but when it comes to cases like this…" Milo scrunched his face. "Aside from a few pictures and a really nice interview with Enchanter Wadsworth, the Global Guild didn't have anything planned to help Ben, uh, matriculate? Is that the word?"

Milo looked everywhere else in the kitchen except for at me, squinting his eyes as he tried to find the right words, believing in his heart there wasn't a right way to broach the topic.

I sighed, then sipped my screwdriver, sort of wishing I had an actual screwdriver to scramble my head and turn off my unwanted telepathy. "The future's annoying, huh?"

"You have no idea." Milo groaned. "But I just see a better possible future letting it play out this way. Ben will maybe adjust better, who knows? Kids are weird. The future's unknown. A million variables." Milo shrugged, big grin on his face. "Plus, there are still loose ends with The True Witch, *which*—hardy har har—I'm certain you're curious about."

Wow. Immediately dodged one topic to dive into another where Milo intended to explain how a current open case might play out.

"What are you playing at?" I asked suspiciously since Milo never willingly divulged his cases.

"Sometimes sharing a potential outcome helps steer the future in the right way."

"But only parts of it, right?" I took a big gulp of my drink, finishing the tiny martini glass—seriously, who the fuck thought tiny, rounded triangle cups were a good idea? "So, why did you lure The True Witch back to Chicago?"

"Here's the thing, I didn't lure her. She brought us. She only ever intended to come to Chicago. Everything else she had planned, the attack on Harmony Valley, the sole survivor, her immediate surrender, the political nightmare of fighting over who will put an international threat on trial, all of it went exactly how she expected."

This horrifying sinking sensation threatened to consume me with dread, panic, fear I'd never shake loose, but Milo's bright smile cut through those feelings. His confidence radiated like he didn't care he'd played right into The True Witch's hand. He didn't care that she'd intended on her own escape from the very start.

"Wait. What?" I fidgeted, having trouble reading Milo's mind as my own whirled round and round with concern. "If you were going to do everything the way she wanted from the start, why spend all those weeks chasing her false trails?"

"They weren't false, and it wasn't bravado of the other guild witches," Milo explained. "They were pit stops The True Witch had mapped out. Sort of her road trip of mayhem, slaughtering people for the hell of it, fueling us, encouraging the chase, and distracting everyone from her true objective."

"Which wasn't Whitlock Industries?"

"Not at all." Milo scrunched his face. "Probably. Maybably."

"You're not sure if she actually dislikes the Harris Enchant Tech merger with Whitlock Industries because of extremist ideology or not?"

"The lady is hard to read." Milo shrugged. "She's got a lotta crafty pokers in the fire. Does that make sense? Sounds menacing. And hot. Gotta be real. I see why Wadsworth is such a dick. Like he had a big ole bone for a naughty hottie, and she's a whole lotta scary wrapped in a pretty face."

I stared, not quite glaring but definitely giving him a disapproving expression for trying to shift his thoughts to shipping witch and warlock couples. Playful nonsense that added to Milo's minxy expression when he realized he'd been caught.

"But to answer your earlier question, because I feel like we're jumping all over the place: I sent Gladiatrix, Diaz, Wadsworth, and myself off to every potential destination loud and proud and making the news so that way The True Witch would know we were tracking her, know that I was aware of her, know that even though she believed only a few breadcrumbs had been spilled I fucking CSIed those crumbs and figured out her whole damn recipe book."

"Well, that's a weird metaphor." I poured us each new drinks, as Milo had finished his while spilling his plan and his drink.

"That's the thing, though. I had to show her that I knew it all. It was the only way to steer her from casually killing people to send a message, to lure us closer."

"But if she intended on being captured, intended on being caught, what is her actual objective? What does she really want? And how are you going to actually stop her if she knows that you know? Won't she just plan around that? Could she seriously break out of the MDC? Shouldn't they be made aware their facility is being targeted?"

"Potentially targeted," Milo corrected. That was the downside to clairvoyance. It never held up as evidence in a court of law. It didn't matter that Enchanter Evergreen had never lied or deceived others about possible horrors. They were merely a possibility.

"But now that she knows you know, what can you really do?"

"She knows that I know she knows, but she doesn't know that I planned for her to know that I know she knows so that I can truly catch her off guard with what she doesn't know that I know." Milo sipped his drink, holding his chest with pride.

"I have no fucking clue what you just said."

"All part of the carefully curated plan." Milo winked. "And I'll explain it all to you. Explain everything you should ready yourself for. Because things are about to get royally fucked."

I set my drink down, decidedly aware I didn't want the comfort of a blitzed buzz. I needed to have my senses, needed to attempt to understand Milo's plan. Whatever pieces the great Enchanter Evergreen chose to share with me.

"Come with me." Milo led me through his penthouse and to his master bedroom. "I'm gonna tell you everything I can, but the future has eyes and ears all over the place."

"Wait. Like actual eyes watching?" I stared around Milo's bedroom, barely able to absorb the cheery decorative style as I wondered what looming threat his thoughts twisted toward.

"There's psychics in the air, working with The True Witch. They've got an inside track on how things will play out."

"Another clairvoyant? Like you?"

"Possibly." Milo rifled through a drawer. "There's more to it. She has allies. This Celestial Coven, some reboot on old lore."

They were real. Or some incarnation of them. How did my telepathy detect the presence, the theory, the idea that the Celestial Coven was connected to Milo's Global Guild mission? Maybe it was when I swam through the ocean Amara had left in Benjamin's head. Maybe my telepathy caught something I missed.

"And you're gonna tell me? Actually divulge everything?"

"You want everything?" Milo turned, grinning and holding up an enchantment. "Let's see if you can handle all of it."

I rolled my eyes at the innuendo pouring from his mind. Then I looked at the enchantment he held up, the special incantations it possessed to link specifically to my frequency. The piece of magic he'd bought for us, the kind that allowed him to delve deep into my inner core.

"You're gonna use that on me again?" I made a face, the kind that gave Milo pause, but I couldn't help it. It was different getting used to Milo inside my head, complete and total access. He'd only used the enchantment a couple of times thus far.

"I can wrangle those wiley visions bouncing around your head while whispering a few secret plans in the corridors of your mind."

I'd spent so much time holding the visions at bay, ignoring their constant thunderous rumble, but I did like the idea of Milo tying them down and making my mind manageable again.

He moved in close, licking the paper that held this special enchantment. "May I?"

I nodded, bracing for Milo to delve deep inside me, inside my mind. He pressed the enchantment against my chest; it sparked and sent a warm wave across my torso. I shuddered at the collision of Milo's mind burrowing into mine. It made my knees weak, my teeth chatter, my spine tingle. Every feeling hit as one.

Milo kept me steady, one hand on my waist and the other on my shoulder. While he worked to bind the visions I'd almost grown accustomed to running loose in my head, he also remained firmly planted in the room. There'd be secrets shared tonight, things he wanted me to prepare for, but right this second, the only thing either of us focused on was the presence of each other.

It'd been weeks, longer, since I'd touched Milo. Actually, held him in my arms. Tasted his lips. Caressed his muscles. Smelled his cologne and sweat.

"While I work in there"—Milo pressed his forehead against mine, pushing me backward and guiding me with his hands—"you and I can do some real work out here."

And just like that, Milo shoved me back onto the bed. A piece of his consciousness dived into my deepest thoughts, rooting through the debris of fractured visions and whispering secrets so softly I couldn't register the words. A hidden message to unravel after we'd parted.

The rest of him remained here with me, eyes locked onto mine and the weight of his body holding me down. I moved in to meet his lips with mine, savoring the taste of him, the sensation of being here and now with him while also looped in each other's thoughts and dancing between a thousand different potential futures. Our magics locked together seamlessly much like our bodies.

Chapter Sixteen

I KISSED Milo, lips hungry for his mouth, tongue tasting his own, and a feral bite with each smack. It was too aggressive, too much teeth, too much command, but I couldn't stop. Somehow, it worked. Milo's steady pulse, the way he shifted above me, the subtle drip of his mind into mine…

"So how much are you going to actually tell me about everything?"

Milo continued kissing me, turning my face away and licking my neck, nibbling, teasing.

"Well?"

"How much can I ever tell you? Really? In the grand scheme of things?" Milo pulled away momentarily, wordless but speaking a thousand truths with the shimmer in his blue eyes. They were filled with a yearning desire to plaster the knowledge in my mind, to set up shop inside my inner core and live out his days worry-free and with me. *"I'll tell you everything I can, the dangers lurking just around the corner, the reason this witch came to Chicago, what I suspect anyway, and what I intend to prevent."*

Milo worked his way down my neck, kissing my chest, pulling my shirt up, and grazing my pale skin with his gentle tongue. He teased my left nipple with his fingers, running the tips in a circular motion while playing with my right by kissing and licking and lightly biting.

"Here I thought knowing a potential future messed it up." I moaned, barely able to maintain a steady conversation, completely entranced by the linked sensations we shared because of the enchantment.

He was in my head, I was always in his, and there was this primal surge coursing through him that he held at bay while working on the visions in my head and maintained the link between us.

"Sometimes knowing prevents the best outcome. Sometimes not knowing can be the biggest obstacle in saving the future." Milo unzipped my pants, sliding to the edge of the bed. *"I'm always after the happiest of happy endings."*

He yanked my jeans down to my knees and bit down on the elastic of my boxers. He tugged them, pulling on the elastic to stretch them, which made my hard cock bounce right up; the head of my dick slapped my stomach. Milo had this devilish grin as he held my undies in his mouth, unrelenting.

"Seriously?" I ran my fingers through his blond hair.

"There's a lot I wanna tell you, which I currently am if you're listening closely to the whispers in the back of your head."

I wasn't. He knew that. Probably why that damn grin filled his face the same way my boxers filled his mouth.

He spit out the elastic. As I braced for the snap, I saw he'd already looped his fingers around my boxers so he could yank them down to join my pants that he pulled further off until I was naked.

Mostly. I still had my shirt partially on, which I quickly rectified, pulling it off over my head. In the few seconds it'd taken me to remove the shirt, Milo had straddled my legs, kissing his way up and down my torso as magic funneled throughout the room, carrying the touch of his telekinesis as he caressed my body.

Milo started to play with my dick, gripping it with his hand, licking my balls, and teasing me with every touch of telekinesis he'd conjured.

He licked his palm, stroking my dick from tip to base before he ran his tongue down my shaft alongside his hand.

"Fuck me," I muttered.

"Sort of the plan." Milo ran his tongue from the base of my cock all the way up to the tip, massaging the head with a delicate swirl.

I grunted, reaching out and gripping his head. Unable to contain myself, I thrusted upward, shoving my cock further and further as my hands worked to steadily push Milo's head down onto my dick. It felt amazing, his warm mouth, the way he gagged and gurgled as his throat muscles adjusted. I enveloped his entire mouth, face fucking him.

Before I realized it, Milo had lifted us off the bed with each thrust of my hips. He'd cupped his hands around my ass cheeks, pushing me further and faster while he choked on my dick. We spun in this motion for minutes, me pounding away, Milo keeping a steady stance midair, the two of us twirling round and round, the only thing holding us together being my dick buried deep in Milo's throat. Well, that and the telekinesis he used to control our movement.

Candles lined the room, decoratively placed. I hadn't noticed them at first, but now as my lighter floated from one to the next under Milo's telekinetic guidance, I fucking noticed. He dimmed the lights. He adjusted pillows, seamlessly moving us in a slowly descending circular motion as his lubed fingers entered me.

"Fuck." I grunted, realizing he'd grabbed lube too while giving me the best fucking blowjob. "*Seriously, the technique.*"

"*So, we're done chatting about important world-ending stakes? Good—*" Milo gulped, taking in air and choking on the head of my dick that prodded his throat.

"*That's what you get for making jokes.*" I stifled a chuckle.

The gentle descent faded. Milo pulled away as I collapsed onto his bed, bouncing a bit before his rough collision on top of me held me down and pinned me in place.

"Someone's feeling energetic."

"You've got no *fucking* idea." Milo grinned, kissing me roughly, biting my lower lip as his hands wrapped my legs around his waist. "But I'm gonna give a few *fucking* clues."

"You need better puns," I whispered, nibbling on his earlobe and pulling it with my teeth.

Milo slammed his cock into me. He attempted to ram the full length in at once, filled with a primal hunger for my ass. But I clenched at the suddenness, and he stopped, waiting a few breaths before pushing all the way inside me. Each stroke became swifter as he worked his way into my hole. I yelped before biting down on his shoulder.

"All I need is you." He held the entire length of his shaft inside me, allowing me a chance to adjust.

After my bite had lessened, after my muffled whines had stopped, after my tight grip on his biceps had eased, Milo began pumping in and out of me. Slow and steady, he took long thrusts from tip to base.

I moaned, unable to stop. Each stroke made my own cock throb harder. Precum dripped onto my stomach. Milo pounded faster and harder, releasing the weight of the world from his shoulders as he took powerful strokes to bury all of his stress into me. I could take it. I could carry the world for him; I could offer a reprieve from saving everyone. I wanted Milo to use me, find comfort in me, offer his all to me.

"More." I trembled, twisting my face away and biting on the blanket.

Milo continued, barreling into me with full force. Each thrust fucked a piece of everything else away from me. My job didn't exist as Milo railed me. The thoughts nearby faded to utter silence as I pressed my hands to Milo's chest, easing his rough pace. Visions that rattled in my head calmed to nothingness while Milo heeded my guidance and adjusted his pace. Everything except for Milo vanished, and I clenched my teeth, trying to fight back the climax he brought me to the precipice of.

"Not yet." Milo snatched me by the nape of my neck and pulled me up before tossing me back onto the bed like a ragdoll.

Just as I thought I'd cum, Milo had switched positions. He moved me everywhere on the bed, on the floor, against the walls, floating in his embrace. Position after position to satisfy his cock. This continued for some time. Every second brought me close to finishing, feeling the release, but then Milo would pause, change his pace, move somewhere new to pound me, or do something, anything to bring me right to the edge before taking it all away.

"Told you we had real work to do," he whispered into my ear with a growl before biting my neck.

He kept me pinned beneath him, teeth on my nape, and his arms folded over my back to deepen my arched position as he grunted, taking swift thrusts.

I lay there as he rammed me, sinking into the rhythmic sound of our skin slapping again and again.

Milo spun me around. No telekinesis, just a furious need to pick me up and drop me onto his dick while he pounded up into me. I gasped as I adjusted, straddling Milo, who lay flat before desire consumed him, and he moved to meet me. His lips met mine, kissing and licking and savoring the audible whimpers I released as he continued thrusting while guiding my hips to push me further onto his cock.

He rolled us onto our sides, hugging me tightly as he kept going. Our sticky bodies clung together by the sweet sweat of screwing. Fuck. I never wanted it to end, but goddamn every muscle ached, my dick throbbed.

"Milo…" I stared at him, glossy-eyed and tired. "I'm ready."

"Okay." He nodded, moving on top of me and moving at a pace that brought him right to the edge of cumming.

Then he pushed his cock all the way in and came. Pressing his forehead to mine, his face twisted into delirious pleasure; his jaw stretched as he exhaled ecstasy. I took wispy breaths as he panted, exhaling his satisfaction. It brought me closer, each breath we shared, each tiny inhale of Milo's release.

"Take it." Milo continued his twitchy thrusts into me as he finished, burying his load deep inside me.

I moaned in response, grabbing his back and steadying his shaky strokes. I shuddered, warm and tingling, as my entire body quaked beneath Milo. I busted, shooting my load over both our chests and stomachs.

With that, Milo collapsed on top of me, his mind working diligently inside my inner core, which added to his exhaustion. He hadn't rested in weeks, not truly.

"We need to clean up." I lay beneath Milo, pinned and unwilling to put up a fight.

"Later," he said, licking some of the sticky mess caught between us before resting his head on my shoulder.

We stayed in this embrace until I drifted off to sleep. Sort of. There was no way I'd fall into a dark and silent slumber or into some dream memory with Milo continuing to work on organizing visions inside my head.

I stepped through the dark corridors of my so-called elegant inner core. Geez. Now, it felt pretentious and forced, nothing like the casual modern wealth of Milo's sophisticated place. I really needed to redo my mind, make it something special, not fancy for the sake of being fancy like that somehow made me feel more elegant. It didn't. If anything, it reminded me how many rungs below the—

"Wow, so you're just gonna stand there judging yourself all night, huh?" Milo turned his head, minxy expression, and filled with delight that he could hear my every thought since he had burrowed his way inside my skull with some annoying enchantment.

"I should've burned those damn things."

"But you didn't." Milo wiggled his hips, practically conjuring music inside my inner core as he worked. "And yes, I'll be working all night. Your head is a fucking mess. Like deep clean this pigsty kind of a mess. Seriously, I'm embarrassed for you."

"Hey!"

Milo winked. "You can find my comments, notes, whispers, whatever, neatly tucked away over there. You study up on my super-duper epic plan for the future while I organize this whatever-kabob of chaos you created with my clairvoyance. No, kabobs are a sleek and organized dish. Chili? Yes. Your mind is the chili of chaos."

I glared.

"You know, because with chili, you just toss it all in and mix it together, and it turns into a mushy monstrosity of flavor. It's good. But like…" Milo shrugged, the kind that came with a need to elaborate, until his happy eyes locked onto mine. "Burr, cold. You are chili."

"You're insufferable." I folded my arms and huffed.

"And you're adorable." Milo popped his hip, inside my head and outside, where he shifted the weight of his body ever so as he slept on me.

CHAPTER SEVENTEEN

DID I hover close to Milo with a manifestation despite him being back in Chicago? Well within my extended range of obsessive observations? Yes, but it helped keep my mind grounded where it needed to be by sending my other half to snoop in manifestation form. Sort of like an unopened piece of mail. Even if it had horrid red letters declaring a "final notice" or "urgent" or something that sent a sickening wave of nausea, it didn't actually exist until I ripped open that paper.

I didn't check the thread connecting Milo and me. I kept all my attention fixated on work, here in the halls of Gemini Academy, preparing for the first round of the Spring Showcase, an event where so many of the city's enchanters arrived to observe potential interns.

I bet Milo planned for this absurdity to fall during the Spring Showcase. It kept me at school. Ensured all my students were here. Guaranteed protection from hundreds of industry professionals. I bet Milo wasn't even worried about this True Witch escaping and merely wanted to keep me grounded somewhere safe. So here I stayed safely on the Gemini Academy campus grounds while Enchanter Evergreen worked with his Global Guild coven members, awaiting the escape attempt The True Witch plotted as her Celestial Coven lurked in the shadows.

"Awwww, you two look soooo cute all bundled up!" Melanie side-stepped toward Gael, who held his shivering rooster.

The two of them wore matching green winter hats and scarves because, despite it being the first week of April, the Midwest loved to slap us with a cold front one final time. The bitter chill stretched across the city, lamenting winter's unwillingness to die off and give us a glimmer of spring's gentle warmth before the sauna of summer kicked in.

"If you need a little heat in your life"—Melanie flicked her zippo, sending a serpent of fire swirling around Gael and King Clucks—"lemme know."

"Cl-cl-cluck!" The rooster's furious flapping wings sent the flames cascading through the halls.

I glowered. "*Melanie, if so much as one thing is singed, you'll never see the inside of a guild.*"

Melanie darted off to put out her magic before she set anyone on actual fire.

"Ba-ba-ba-bawk!"

"*She's not being extra. It's called flirting.*" Gael walked into the room with a swagger. "*She just wants another night with this stallion stud—*"

I grumbled, rolling my eyes and tuning out Gael's conversation with his rooster.

Once the bell rang, I gave my homeroom the first fifteen minutes to review the agenda for the week while I reviewed the schedule Chanelle had sent out to staff. Uff. I couldn't believe she balanced organizing the first-year and second-year showcases while also preparing her homeroom coven for internships, teaching classes, and a thousand other things. What an annoying overachiever.

"Did you see Gladiatrix's press conference?" Carter asked, literally floating in his desk as he stretched forward to talk with Jennifer.

"Yep," she said with disinterest while scrolling through her phone, quietly looking for possible events Gladiatrix would attend.

Apparently, she'd come up with the idea of dragging Carter to the next Gladiatrix sighting to surprise him.

News of the Global Guild setting up shop in Chicago had spread quickly.

Gladiatrix worked alongside Enchanter Evergreen, the two drawing all the spotlight attention, which helped the Global Guild slip more forces into the city unbeknownst. Milo claimed they wanted to keep a low profile for the sake of media involvement in The True Witch's transfer being potentially problematic. But we both knew the real reason he wanted the extra forces slipped in under the radar to remain that way.

Since side conversations had taken hold of everyone's attention, my mind started to drift toward Milo, curious and concerned, before I moved to the front of the room to start today's discussion.

"I hope you're all ready for this week." I cleared my throat as the last of the chitchat died down. "You impressed scouts during the Will-o'-the-Wisp games. You caught the attention of enchanters during your auditorium interviews. You secured your academic standing by taking the Federally Accelerated Practicum test. You have all maintained incredible class rankings to ensure you stand out and take full advantage of your educational opportunities."

They basked in the compliments, taking pride in their successes, which almost brought a smile to my face, the joy bouncing around the classroom. I furrowed my brow. Naturally, I needed to humble them.

"But this isn't like those pity events meant to stir up attention while shining a light on every student, saying that you all matter. This isn't a state exam you can spend weeks cramming for. This isn't a class test you can retake if you flunk it. Nope. This is the preliminary round of the second-year showcase. This Friday, you'll have to do everything in your ability to succeed because the chances of enchanter attendance will be low, so if you screw up and get eliminated in the preliminaries, you can kiss any hope of landing a dream internship goodbye."

"What about Enchanter Evergreen? Do you think he'll be attending the preliminary rounds?" Caleb asked with a hand raised, barely able to contain his excitement. He hid his desire to add *"since you're boyfriends"* and jumped right into his follow-up question that eagerly bounced around his maze of a mind. "And do you think he'd bring any of his Global Guild friends with him?"

"Oh, yeah." Gael jumped in, his spikes growing as he flashed his phone to everyone. "Have him bring Texas Daddy! I've always wanted to meet him and Priscilla. She's amazing! So big and fluffy."

Gael scrolled through the recently uploaded selfies Enchanter Diaz and Evergreen had taken together for some case because of course they used *Texas Daddy's* popularity to steer attention from the upcoming transfer, too. It seemed the only Global Guild enchanter who remained stationed at the MDC 24/7 was Enchanter Wadsworth.

I only caught glimpses of Milo's recollections on his conversations with the old man since the MDC had intricate wards to keep out all unauthorized casting including my manifestation that I'd attached to Milo. Wadsworth didn't care for Milo's plan, hating the variables, the patience, the false bravado. I couldn't fault Wadsworth for those feelings since I agreed with the sentiment.

"First off, they're not Evergreen's friends," I said, burying the desire to check in on Milo and prioritizing the upcoming event. "They're called work colleagues."

Layla tapped her sharp claws on the table, her train of thought drifting elsewhere. "*He's only saying that because he's a friendless bag of dicks who only has work colleagues.*"

Ouch.

"Secondly," I continued, ignoring the cutting side thoughts from students. "Enchanter Evergreen—like most highly successful guild witches—doesn't have time to attend the preliminary round."

He'd already arranged everything in his case to unfold this Friday, the entirety of his plan meant to fall apart and into place all at once. My breathing hitched, thinking about everything I knew, everything I had to ignore, everything I had to simply hope for the best on.

"Honestly," I said, practically growling, "you'll be lucky if Enchanter Evergreen or any half-decent enchanters bother showing up to the semi-finals. So instead of wondering who's who in attendance this Friday, focus on not getting eliminated in the first round."

I went over the agenda for the week leading up to the second-year Spring

Showcase with my students while Milo's voice rang in my head.

"Sometimes, the best futures don't reveal themselves until you're right on top of the worst possibilities."

He could've held back his mission, lied about what he knew, what he planned for, but he shared the details. By the end of the week, Milo prepared for The True Witch to break out of the MDC, reveal the identities of her fellow Celestial Coven, and bring chaos down upon the entire city.

"It's scary, having to unravel a hundred thousand potentials and realizing the best option won't show up until the last second on the clock. If you'd prefer, I can lie. Tell you I don't know."

I was grateful Milo shared this piece of himself with me, trusted me with the weight of the world, but I'd be lying if I said I wasn't terrified.

The days leading up to the showcase left me edgy. Would Milo's plan succeed? Would everything fall into place as he'd predicted? Would they detain The True Witch? Stop her Celestial Coven in their tracks?

I zipped down the halls to make the most of my planning period break and have a cigarette to clear my head. Those pounding questions weren't the ones that should've been haunting me. I should've been fixated on how my students would perform. Would they succeed in the preliminary round? Would they impress any enchanters? Would they land the right internship? Were they ready for an internship? Were they ready to graduate and enter into a guild? Christ. That was like a year away, and then they'd be adults. Real adults.

Just last week, Carter asked who you send out dirty dishes to, like it was a laundry service. Melanie and Jamius argued over whether or not Lake Michigan was one of the four oceans or seven seas. And Gael crawled across the classroom floor to Kenzo's desk and then tried to chew through it in some bizarre effort to prove his shark-like teeth were as strong as his spikes.

They weren't anywhere close to being adults yet.

Chanelle's heels clicked as she strode through the hallway; pure delight radiated off her in waves. I weaved around a few students and tried to get to the exit as her eyes widened and locked onto me.

"*Dorian.*" She beelined through the crowd and locked her arm around mine, successfully halting my escape and dragging me with her on her wave of success.

Dammit. I huffed. "Do you mind?"

"Not at all, but I just had to share this with someone."

"How about someone who cares?" I grumbled.

"You care. Or you will. It involves the students."

Okay, admittedly, that piqued my interest, but I kept a sour expression because I refused to allow Chanelle this opportunity to gloat.

"I just finished meeting with the headmaster, and she informed me that the admin team has officially approved my pitch for the preliminary round of the second-year Spring Showcase."

"Which is?" I asked suspiciously.

"We'll be releasing fiends during the first round." Chanelle waved a hand in front of herself like she was unveiling a majestic show for me to watch. "Think of it like our Will-o'-the-Wisp tag but with higher stakes."

"Life-threatening stakes," I clarified. "You're trying to murder our students."

"Not murder. Just some light scarring. A bit of torture. Trauma builds character." She cackled, high on her own joke. "The only thing I'm murdering is enchanter interest in visiting other academy showcases because we're gonna be the talk of the city. Seriously, everyone who misses this performance is gonna be desperate to see how we raise the stakes in the semi-finals and the grand finale."

I doubted that. Once news hit of the attempted escape from the MDC, the way the Global Guild would move in to confront and contain the situation would be on everyone's lips. But I buried that nagging thought and frowned at Chanelle.

"And how exactly are you gonna raise the stakes further? You haven't sent any email updates explaining what horrors you have in store."

Chanelle strummed her fingers together, a wicked glint in her deep brown eyes and a mischievous smile so big it filled her entire face. "Oh, just you wait, Dorian."

Ideas flitted out of her head like a monstrous circus filling the hallways meant to engage and entertain all in attendance. It seemed like chaotic carnage, but I honestly loved the distraction from my own thoughts, floating around Chanelle's mind as she revealed plans on top of plans for future years where she intended to continue outdoing her own performances for years to come.

That said, I still needed to break free from Chanelle and sneak off for a smoke. With the way she rambled, I would end up trapped for our entire planning period. Hell, she was relentless. She might very well keep talking until summer break.

CHAPTER EIGHTEEN

THE time had finally arrived. I'd kept a manifestation of myself latched to Milo all week since my telepathy definitely wouldn't relent during such a stressful ordeal. But rationally, I knew the entirety of the plan. I understood potential pitfalls. I agreed to stay out of it. And I was. Mostly. Splitting my psyche and sending a manifestation kept the rest of my head out of Enchanter Evergreen's big case. I wouldn't actually have to share the events of how today worked out until after work, after the preliminary round of the Spring Showcase.

Even disconnected from myself, the slightest tug of psychic energy held us together, and the anxiety poured from my other half. Being in the know, seeing Milo calm and coolly collected when everything was moments from shattering, kept me less concerned.

He stood outside the Metropolitan Detainment Center with Gladiatrix and Enchanter Diaz, his thoughts stirring to how Enchanter Wadsworth had remained posted in the deepest floors of the jail, stationed outside the solitary cell that contained The True Witch.

Milo checked his phone, then adjusted his tie. "It's about that time."

"Finally." Gladiatrix put on a gold helmet—the type gladiator warriors donned in battle, proving even she deemed this a dangerous mission—then hovered toward the entrance of the MDC, golden cape fluttering behind her with a certain majestic zeal.

That feeling definitely came from Milo, not me. He stared in awe, wondering if the cape ever got in her way during combat.

"You think I could pull off a cape?" Milo turned to Diaz.

"One hundred percent." Diaz focused on stretching, leaning low to the ground and putting his legs out one at a time as he pressed down on his thighs. "Shouldn't The Inevitable Future be a bigger trendsetter? Suits are cool but so…meh."

Diaz shrugged, then stretched his arms high, flexing his bare biceps. The fabric of his gold and black corset vest moved up ever so, revealing his abdomen muscles.

"Hmmm." Milo studied the curve of Diaz's back, the way the corset accentuated everything else. "*I do have the ass to totally rock those. And the wonders it'd do for my posture.*"

He daydreamed how he'd look in different colors and materials, then bubbled with images of me once again in a ridiculous corset before his mind settled and returned to the mission at hand.

I noticed the Global Guild emblem stitched onto the back of Diaz's corset vest on his shoulder blades with the strings of his outfit pulling their symbol together, similar to Gladiatrix's cape that flaunted the GGs. Even Milo wore their logo in the form of a gold pin placed on his jacket pocket over his heart.

"I should be heading on in." Milo paused, taking in Enchanter Diaz as he stood tall and finished stretching. "You sure you're good out here?"

"A little late to change the plan." Diaz winked.

"It's never too late to change things up. Or down. Or sideways. Or no ways."

"You're stalling, Enchanter Evergreen," Diaz said with his southern twang, smiling and confident about the plan to come. "Go kick some ass and save your city. I'll hold the line here."

Milo made his way inside, entering the MDC, where I couldn't follow with all their warding protections. Their enchantment protocol had increased tenfold since my Doppler had slinked through the halls while hiding inside the head of a correctional officer.

Unable to join Enchanter Evergreen, I floated aimlessly around the building and kept close to Diaz as Milo's voice echoed in the enchanter's head, replaying the plan, and preparing for a fight.

Within a matter of minutes, a woman approached Diaz, walking on the empty street of a back road that led to the parking lot of the MDC. Her white tunic hung on her slim body. Diaz studied the golden crown of leaves that held the long brown strands of her hair in place. He studied the symbols tattooed over the arms of her tan skin, her bare feet, eyeing the subtle fluctuation of protective magics cast from each enchanted letter.

"Gotta ask about the getup. The whole ancient Greek vibes is a hot look, but are y'all really trying to pass off as the Sisters of Fate?" Diaz asked with a bravado that matched Milo's in every way. "Or is it more of a way to bring it back into fashion? Because I'm always on board with living your truth."

"We're The Sisters Three, goddesses of fate, prophets of destiny," she spoke with a light lilt, her stance steady but her aura shifting in bizarre ways.

When she said *we*, did she mean herself and The True Witch? If so, where was the third sister? I'd shared my dreams, my knowledge of The Sisters of Fate with Milo, which he used to construct his plan, a plan I still didn't fully grasp. But he believed in Diaz holding the line here and now while bigger threats attacked the facility itself.

"We've weaved the history of the world," she said, her voice deep and raspy.

Her aura moved in overlapping waves like multiple people dancing in place, swimming, floating on her psychic energy alone. Her silhouettes were all white, no emotion to her being, no emotion in a single piece of her soul.

"We see all things fate has in store for you, Enchanter Emiliano Diaz," she said in a harsh voice, piercing and stern, with malice hanging from the edge of her tongue. Even so, her aura painted no feeling. She might've cloaked her emotions, her energy. Such a powerful psychic, veiling her presence while simultaneously oozing her energy everywhere.

"So you ladies decided to fight lil ole me?" Enchanter Diaz shot her a smile. "I'm honored three members of the Celestial Coven considered me a challenge."

"Three? Me?" the light lilt voice asked. "We are The Sisters Three," said the raspy voice. "We are one pillar of the Celestial Coven, not three," added the stern voice.

"Okay. Weird, but works for me." Diaz shrugged. "The wife said no group play without her, anyway. Glad I can keep my word."

"You jest because you're a fool," the stern voice spat.

"I joke because life is short."

"Truly," the light-lilt voice said. "Yours reaching the end of its thread now," the raspy voice said with menacing certainty.

I kept close to Diaz, not so close I'd be noticed, but enough to register his guarded thoughts, the intel Milo shared from his understanding of the visions unfolding. I'd asked for details of what he'd do, not specifics on every component. The Sisters Three acted as one being housed in the same body, witches with a magic mirroring my own trio: retrocognition to glean the past, telepathy to oversee the present, and clairvoyance to perceive the future.

These witches used their power in tandem in a way Milo, Finn, and I never had. They fused their psychic energy into one of their bodies when going into combat. They guised themselves as the Sisters of Fate. They pretended to be deities, all to add some fervor of mystique to the Celestial Coven. That was why my magic sent me those memories, those dreams of Finn's project about the legends of old. Some part of my magic must've felt their psychic presence, their looming power protecting The True Witch, guarding her fate from Milo's viewing. But they'd failed to shield everything from Milo; he'd formed a plan despite what they'd hidden.

Three witches who tracked, plotted, and guarded every step of their coven's agenda. Their magic was so strong it veiled The True Witch over time and distance. That shouldn't have been possible. Their branches were so powerful, it blocked Milo from properly reading The True Witch, prevented me from hearing her thoughts. Then again, I was sort of the poster child of bizarre psychic magic strength.

"Knowing your fate changes nothing," the voice with a light lilt said, stealing me from my rumination and reminding me of the danger that lurked before Diaz. "No, no, no. Fate has decreed we three will slay thee," added the raspy voice before their two voices spoke in unison. "Cherish the knowledge your feeble clairvoyant ally shared; we hope it allowed you the opportunity to live out these last days in peace."

"Ladies, you're talking like you got this in the bag." Diaz channeled his magic, body buzzing with telekinesis. "But I assure you, I'm more than a pretty face."

"But of course," whispered the voice with a light lilt. "You're also a failure," the raspy voice said. "A fraud," screamed the harsh voice.

The psychic energy pulsated in waves, rippling across the street and barely contained by the protective wards of the MDC facility. Even my teeth chattered, a ghostly sensation for certain as a mere manifestation, yet the near collision with their three magics entwined hurt.

They weren't even aiming for me, and the touch held a subtle scalding sensation.

Diaz's eyes had gone wide, his mouth had fallen open, his knees trembled, and his shoulders hunched. Inside his head, they painted a million images of failure. From cases he'd floundered, to tests he'd tanked, to dinners he'd forgotten, to celebrations of his kids he'd missed, to every conceivable regret he kept housed in his mind.

The Sisters Three tore up all the floorboards of his inner core and plastered his shame everywhere, nailing it to the walls and leaving the memories soaked in bloody regret.

```
Name: Emiliano Diaz
Branch: Bestial (Familiar)
```

The worst hellish failure to be splashed across Diaz's surface thoughts, carved into every crevice of his active mind, was that of a tiny bear. Not some horror that might happen when facing off against The Sisters Three, but a truth Diaz had endured. They used the past against him. Regrets. All of them. At once.

Fuck. Everything he'd ever done wrong in his entire life hit him continuously with new realizations of how he could've done it right. The Sisters Three came in with whispers on how to fix his errors, how better men wouldn't have made them, how he had no hope against them, how everyone in his life would be better off. Then they grabbed his greatest shame and slammed it down onto his thoughts, crushing him with guilt.

A scrawny boy of no more than twelve lay beside a dying bear, bloody and bruised and grateful her human survived the terror of a demon. These were thoughts Diaz knew, things his familiar had spoken with her dying breaths. There were years of therapy, acceptance, grief, all the right steps someone like myself would never make, but Diaz had. In this moment, however, he forgot all of them. He forgot how his familiar sacrificed herself when a young witch in a small town far from any guilds was cornered by a demon. He forgot the promise he made her as the life left her body. He forgot how overjoyed he was the day his familiar found him again.

Why? Because the witches hit him with his second biggest regret, the failure that hounded him to harness his magic better every day, the failure that loomed in every awkward conversation he had with Priscilla, the failure that reminded him no matter how great he tried to be—he'd failed the best person in his life twice.

His familiar had found him once again, years later when he'd already graduated from an academy, proven his branch didn't define him, landed at a second-rate guild, but proud of his role as an acolyte in a small town that couldn't afford professional services—services Enchanter Diaz ensured every tiny town between the transit cities of Texas could now afford thanks to his station, his influence, his power.

But that didn't resonate with him. The only thing Diaz saw in this moment, beyond the body of his first familiar, was that of his second. A cub who'd found him during his time as an acolyte. A small creature ready for action, and Diaz believed now that he was ready for combat, surely nothing would happen to his partner.

It did, though. Blood and pain and an agonizing cry that still woke Diaz in the middle of the night after damn near twenty years. Diaz wheezed, choking on the nightmares of his own past. Both of his familiars dead at his feet, covered in blood—the first a grouchy old bear who'd found her partner late in life regretting the bond took so long to obtain, the second a precious cub who believed in fish that tasted of cotton candy and sweet dreams—neither were Priscilla because while witches never lost their familiar bond, the magic and essence that connected them to the bestial branch, the animal partner returned as someone new.

Priscilla didn't possess the memories of her former life—her former lives. She didn't have the same personality. All she had was a connection to Emiliano Diaz, a bond of magic and friendship.

Whether she'd found him after living a full, rich life like Diaz's first familiar or as a young cub confused by this daunting world, familiars had a unique link to their witch partners in how they synced to their lifespan, the human longevity—despite how short it felt most days. It reduced the likelihood of their loss as most animals had much shorter life expectancies than humans. Not with familiars. They could live as long as their witch, sometimes even outlive them, which was always a sad state of affairs.

Familiars who lost their witch didn't gain a new bond mate; their witches didn't reincarnate like the animals. They simply left a vacuum of magic with their familiar friend, who'd spend the rest of their days waiting to be reunited with their other half.

But as much as Diaz feared the chasm his death would cause, the life of his children he'd miss out on, the wife he'd leave alone, the world he'd no longer protect, he quaked at the horrors of failing or abandoning his familiar who he worried for with every breath. Priscilla was the other half of his soul, his magic, his mind and personality. It was something I couldn't grasp.

Despite hearing his fears, his thoughts, I couldn't connect on that level, the degree where someone was you while also themself. Yes, I'd known love, and so had Diaz, but the way he cared for his familiar like a parent, a friend, a child all at once—it was the same bond Gael held for King Clucks.

It was the same connection I rolled my eyes at for every bestial familiar witch I'd taught, met, or interacted with. It transcended the love of a pet, no matter how strong the bond. And yes, I often believed I loved Charlie and

Carlie to the same degree, yet something in those bestial thoughts continued, proving the bond remained stronger. This was your best friend, who you shared every secret with, the parent who offered advice, the child you rooted for. Familiar bonds were unique in their own right in a way that simply transcended thought.

"We can also unravel the fates of your future." The Sisters Three weaved their hands round and round. Each woman danced with a white emotionless aura between the strings of the body they shared. "See now what will befall you, were you to be foolish enough to oppose us."

Bloody images of Priscilla flashed before Diaz's eyes. His broken body slumped over cracked armor, shattered wards, pieces of a blade. Each breath was excruciating, inhaling the possible future that these wicked witches intended on bringing about, holding a future of death in his lungs as a past of horror looped through his memories. The witches bombarded Diaz with every wrong choice he'd ever made, every misstep that led him to this exact moment where he'd die at their hands.

A bear's silhouette tore through the bloody collage stapled onto the surface of Diaz's mind. With a low growl and a swift slash of her large claws, Priscilla linked her thoughts with her human partner, proving no psychic could shatter the connection between a witch and their familiar.

Diaz snapped to attention; his mind released from the glimpses of potential futures The Sisters Three sent in waves. If it was even futures. Clearly one of them was a telepath, she could've merely painted illusions in thoughts, tinkering with fears and tilting Diaz's perception of reality. They couldn't reveal the future so casually, so callously, right?

It didn't matter what they did, because Enchanter Diaz was now aware of the trickery and immune thanks to the aid of his familiar's borrowed thoughts, clear thoughts, thoughts of an animal that couldn't be perceived by the best psychics.

Unsheathing his weapon, Diaz kept the tip of the sharp blade trained on The Sisters Three with one hand while circulating telekinesis with his other hand. Glyphs glowed. Their protective magics worked to push away psychic energy, knocking even me several yards away to hover in silence as his thoughts vanished. A few of the protective symbols snapped and crackled before the light of their magic faded.

"You paint quite the tale." Diaz shifted his stance, readying his blade. "But I've seen your future already. A friend told me every possibility, including the ones you three are ignoring."

Milo. Enchanter Evergreen had prepared every member of the Global Guild, possibly every guild of Chicago, of the events about to unfold. Well, knowing Milo, he'd only shared the pieces of the puzzle they needed to solve the problem.

"Oh? Oh? Oh?" The Sisters Three danced in their body, each caressing their thighs and waist with the aura energy of their hands. They weren't flaunting or flirting, for this action could only be seen by me—who the three of them were unaware of—but instead, they radiated psychic energy, coating their shared body with more of their magic.

Weird. It was as if their body didn't have a trace of psychic magic itself. They seemed wedged into this body; their white auras held strings tangled and hooked into the form they wielded. It was as if they'd possessed a person much like a demon would. No. Not only demons. I had horrible memories shared from my Doppler's days of controlling the minds of others so he could slink through the city while cloaked from detection. Perhaps these three did the same thing. They could be somewhere else, safe and sound, while their minds forced their way into some poor, unwilling host body.

"I've seen the future where I drop you to your knees, shackled and bound and sharing a cell with your friend, The True Witch."

"Shackled and bound," the lighter lilt said with a wiggle of their body's hips. "Likes it rough," the raspy voice said, slapping her butt. "Bound," the stern voice said, moving her finger back and forth disapprovingly. "No, no, no. We The Sisters Three are divine. Divinity cannot be bound, cannot be stopped. We do not predict potentials; we speak of prophecy. Our words are law."

The body stilled, auras of the other two sisters hunched their shoulders, hanging high above their own body in an ominous and foreboding manner. Then in unison they screeched, "Law. Law. Law. You defy the law!" The stern sister's image reeled her sister's white auras back down into their shared body and then said, "You defy us."

Magic buzzed, piercing and powerful, and ready to obliterate Enchanter Diaz in one fatal blow. I felt it in their presence, painting the reality of potential, declaring the future they sought. Clairvoyance didn't feel like this, did it? No. Nothing this foul had ever poured from Milo. Their merger, their branches, their vile minds conjured this horror.

Priscilla roared so loudly it quieted the psychic whistle in the air. The huge bear lunged from above, barreling headfirst in full plate armor. Every glyph coating Priscilla's gear radiated strength, transforming her nosedive of concentrated telekinesis into a fucking explosion.

The Sisters Three had an expression of perplexed shock, naturally unaware of the bear's surprise attack, but they pivoted, moving ever so slightly as the tackle of more than a thousand pounds of pure, unmatched muscle crashed into the street.

It created a huge wave of destruction from the propulsion, the weight, the force of telekinesis all thrust into the street. It shattered concrete, burrowed deep into the sewers of the city. Pieces of asphalt flew in every direction.

"Yeehaw, motherfuckers!" Diaz leapt between the debris, bouncing from one piece to the next while he sliced through the air. The chaos didn't deter him for a second; he'd accounted for it, anticipated it. Maybe. I couldn't know for certain, with his blade's glyphs keeping my telepathy at bay.

The Sisters Three barely evaded the strike of his sword, each slash pushed them back, body and auras. The blade didn't need to hit them to hurt. The glyphs repelled their psychic energy, knocking their footing off, sending a searing pain through their body. I'd been hit by wards meant to dampen psychic branches; it was like your brain was the opposite pole of a magnet being held in place by your skull but desperately trying to claw its way out to escape the magnetic repulsion.

The Sisters Three and Diaz moved so quickly that I struggled to track them through the wreckage. Their levitation and telekinesis propelled them every which way, zipping across this battlefield. Every piece of rock and gravel slowly froze midair, floating in place at the will of Priscilla, who unleashed a ferocious roar that sent every speck of the broken ground propelling toward The Sisters Three like meteors.

The collision created an explosion of dust. It quickly funneled upward, directed by the gentle guidance of telekinesis, revealing The Sisters Three remained unscathed by the strike. *Dammit.*

"You think we didn't foresee such a turn of events?" the lighter lilt asked. "Arrogant, Witchboy. Cowboy. Bearboy," the raspy voice added with a scoff. "We know everything," said the stern voice.

"Even this?" Diaz stood confidently while Priscilla continued clearing away the smoky dust, revealing more witches levitating around them, surrounding and securing the scene.

They wore the same Global Guild uniformed jackets as the medical staff, emblems of gold pinned to their chest displaying their station. These were not elite members of the coveted guild like Enchanter Diaz, like the ranks Milo had recently joined. But these witches were as skilled as any enchanter and worked as support for the Global Guild.

When Milo put this plan in order, he arranged for Chicago to authorize the arrival of over a hundred support witches from the Global Guild. A private military couldn't simply roll in and offer aid; bureaucracy wouldn't allow it. Hell, Milo had to file seemingly endless forms just to gain approval for his casting in California under the discretion of the Global Guild.

The entire force of witches brought in didn't stand here, surrounding The Sisters Three, which meant the remaining forces must already be positioned inside.

A low rumble came from the MDC, followed by a violent shutter of silence. Then an explosion of magic from inside that impregnable facility. Suddenly, every ward carved onto the walls securing the Metropolitan Detainment Center cracked, their radiance of protective magic fizzled away instantaneously and suddenly the minds of thousands of inmates within raged.

CHAPTER NINETEEN

FORTUNATELY, Enchanter Diaz appeared more than capable of handling himself against The Sisters Three with Priscilla and nearly fifty Global Guild witches at his side. Because the instant the protective symbols lining every inch of the MDC failed, I barreled inside, drawn to Milo's mind.

The Metropolitan Detainment Center was a maze of highly secured corridors, layers upon layers of warded checkpoints to prevent infiltration or escape. I understood the layout entirely from the Doppler's time spent here. There were two huge buildings that separated the men's and women's facilities. In fact, the two buildings only connected in three places: the central checkpoint by the parking lot, the correctional officer's locker station, and the underground solitary confinement cells.

I followed the trail of unconscious correctional officers, beaten and bruised but breathing despite the carnage everywhere. Broken enchantments, stray magic, rubble from the crumbling building. In a matter of seconds, every single inmate inside the MDC had been released, and within minutes, the entire facility had transformed into a battlefield.

While the MDC was divided into multiple cell blocks, keeping over two thousand inmates from both facilities separated as a way to prevent rioting or revolts, those blockades were little more than concrete walls, which no longer proved effective since every defensive enchantment and dampening ward had been deactivated. Holes had been blasted through the two buildings, throughout every cellblock. Inmates from the men's and women's facilities coordinated their chaos, ganging up on correctional officers in an effort to escape.

My magic, my curiosity, my concern all reeled me through the long, white corridors of the facility, drawing me closer to Milo, and ignoring the chaotic minds that rioted. Not that it did them any good. As fast as I moved, the blur of my psychic energy darting through this place, paled in comparison to the sheer indomitable force of Gladiatrix who whipped from one end of a room to the other, leaving a trail of fallen foes in her wake.

```
Name: Alicia Lawrence
Branch: Alteration (Supreme Physicality)
```

She shifted between guards and inmates, blocking conflict and separating them. She caught magical strikes mid-propulsion. Literally held magic aimed at destroying something or someone between her hands before smothering it with telekinesis. She prevented battles before the idea was even fully formed.

Each movement held this majestic calculation where Gladiatrix took the entire Metropolitan Detainment Center into account, dividing foes, dropping threats, and protecting the unaware whether they were employed or an inmate. The magnetic pull of Milo's mind simmered as I lingered close to Gladiatrix, watching her unravel Enchanter Evergreen's plan with perfect precision. I had faith in Milo, but goddamn, I had no idea Gladiatrix really could unleash such tremendous strength without breaking a sweat.

One punch shattered steel barriers. A single kick from across the room rippled with the force of a gust to knock down an entire gang. The simple act of squeezing a shoulder with her index finger and thumb dropped men three times her size to their knees. A clap of her hands created a cacophony of echoes to distract crowds. Every step, every movement, every technique used held a purpose.

Her enhanced senses allowed her to hear battles across the MDC, her eyes scanned every room she darted between, her skin radiated with telekinesis sensing the slightest vibration of danger. Gladiatrix worked as an army of one, squashing the riot before a single inmate reached the exits.

All the same, she had a sense of urgency sitting as a heavy pit in her stomach, it churned with the anxiety in her gut. "*Too much time. I need to move faster.*"

Milo's plan required her to drop the number of inmates by half if she hoped her reinforcements stood a chance at stopping this jailbreak in its tracks without a single escape or fatality.

She needed reinforcements? Doubtful.

Someone in a black cloak leapt from out of nowhere. The slight creak in their bones was the only indication Gladiatrix sensed before a sickle's blade swiped past her face.

Crimson washed over everything, filling my sight with a bloodthirsty aura of the witch that attempted to hack through Gladiatrix. She'd spun around, cape whirling, barely escaping the blow, then countered the blade with a backhanded swing containing a powerful blast of telekinesis. The impact knocked the cloaked witch several paces away.

"You're one of the pillars in the Celestial Coven," Gladiatrix said.

"They call me Grim." He swung his sickle, hacking and slashing at Gladiatrix in a continuous motion like the weapon was an extension of his arms.

"*I need to keep him here.*" Gladiatrix easily evaded Grim's careless strikes but had to shove others out of the direct line of the sickle's blade. "*I should've apprehended more of the inmates. This room should've been cleared before he stepped inside.*"

Gritting her teeth, Gladiatrix weaved back and forth, dodging the weapon while telekinetically removing the injured, the unaware, and those still fighting for the sake of violence.

With her focus split onto both goals, Grim took that singular opportunity to lunge forward with his sickle raised. The slice moved so quickly that even Gladiatrix barely evaded, losing a few strands of her hair as she bobbed out of the blade's slash.

Composing herself, Gladiatrix reeled back a fist empowered by her branch and enough telekinesis to level this entire building and struck Grim directly dead center in his chest. I gasped the nonexistent air from my lungs, suspecting the impact had a similar effect on the broken witch that'd come to kill Gladiatrix.

A collection of crackles and breaks popped in the air, signifying the many bones a single concentrated strike had shattered. The sound traveled throughout Grim's body like the webbed cracks of an icy lake before everything collapsed.

Grim flew back, hurled into a wall where the crash led to more breaks. Not the wall, though. No. Gladiatrix used telekinesis to soften the impact against the building and redirected the propulsion of magic. The ricochet of strikes barreled into Grim with waves of honed telekinesis, not unlike a tsunami destroying a city. He lay on the ground with his cloak wide open and body snapped apart into crumbling pieces.

I shuddered at the sight of his body made of bones scattered about the floor. No skin. No blood. Nothing but bones and a few foul organs tied together with twine and attached to the spine. They dangled like hooked meat in a butcher's shop. He appeared to be the most perverse iteration of a grim reaper, the organs dried and losing their color, oozing pus, and leaking magic from his insides.

"Well, that's not very nice." The skull rattled, jaw moving up and down like a talking puppet. Piercing, bloodshot eyes fixated on Gladiatrix. The way they floated in the empty sockets of Grim's skull sent a sickening nausea through me. His bones wriggled and trembled on the floor. It created an eerie tippity tappity of clicks and clinks, followed by a horrifying bellow of laughter that came from the head. "I heard you were tough. How fun."

Cracks, splinters, and breaks mended together. The skull floated at height level as the bones pieced in proper order. He extended a bony hand, staring at the missing index and middle finger. I suspected he'd lost them to the white dust on the floor created from the single hit Gladiatrix had landed.

"If I had to wager, I'd say this is the one Enchanter Evergreen predicts will target The True Witch's staff," Gladiatrix thought through all the variables of

Milo's plan.

The other members of the Celestial Coven remained veiled from visions, but he'd seen three other pillars of support connected to The True Witch, Amara. The Sisters Three, the divine psychics. Now this Grim, a witch made of bone and rotten insides.

Milo had an idea of their motives, how the puzzle pieces of their goals, their agendas, their roles, fit to create the picture of today's future. A future Enchanter Evergreen planned to prevent.

Grim drew his discarded sickle into his grasp with a telekinetic pulse as he draped the black cloak over his skeleton form again.

This was his form, too. Something about his magic, I'd never seen a branch like it before, but he wasn't like The Sisters Three. They wedged their minds into the body of an unwilling host; I could taste it pulsating in vile waves. But Grim…his consciousness fluctuated throughout the entirety of this bizarre skeletal system like his very being had seeped into every bone, his thoughts woven into the desiccating organs stitched to the shambled body.

Grim released a giddy giggle, his teeth chattering. "I can't wait to pick apart your bones. Save the best for my altar."

"Bring it on, you sick fuck." Gladiatrix dug a heel into the floor, cracking the ground beneath her before taking a calming breath. *"Stay in control."*

If she wanted, Gladiatrix could level this entire building, the entire street, with an overzealous stomp of her foot. But that wouldn't resolve this problem; it'd merely injure everyone nearby.

Grim lunged toward Gladiatrix. As their thoughts collided, each with opposing goals, each studying their surroundings, each with a respect for the daunting power the other possessed, I drifted further back. Not drifted. I was pulled away.

Milo. He drew me closer. The same sense of panic throughout the MDC hadn't gripped his heart and seized him. In fact, he zipped through the facility, taking out the occasional threat with carefree admiration for all the allies who'd helped make this possible. The devastation. The destruction. The discord. None of it concerned him because Milo flew down a path following the strands of possibility that shined the brightest, seeing and believing the best outcome was well on its way.

Milo soared past the injured, inmates and guards alike, those who didn't relish brutality, who didn't have the magic to defend themselves, who had become overwhelmed by the chaos in every direction. A pinch of guilt tugged at his heart then, stalling his pursuit of the goal that danced in his mind. Part of him wanted to gamble everything to stop and help these people.

I reached out, willing and wanting to take the burden of that guilt away, prepared to carry all of it as I'd grown accustomed to such feelings of failure. But I didn't need to. Milo hardened his expression, eyes fluttering momentarily, and he reminded himself that sometimes the best future resulted in a few cuts and scrapes along the way. He desperately wanted to shield everyone from every possible pain out there, but even The Inevitable Future knew such things weren't conceivable.

"They'll be fine. We'll all be fine. Everyone will be fine." Milo zipped through long corridors, evading combat, dodging magic, and knocking back persistent enemies who targeted him. His telekinesis rumbled through the halls, cracking the foundation.

Milo arrived at the warden's station that'd been highly fortified by the guards who'd grouped there, by the security defenses that didn't rely on a magical component, by the warden himself who conjured an electrical barrier to prevent anyone from passing. He opened a tiny length, not much wider than the fence posts on a farm, for Milo to squeeze between.

"What happened to those Global Guild forces you demanded?" The warden grimaced, magic straining under such continuous output.

"They're where they're needed." Milo eyed the sealed chamber doors behind the warden, the doors that led down to the deepest sectors of the MDC.

Enchanter Evergreen needed to join the rest of the forces below in the solitary confinement cells.

"You're not seriously going down there, too?" The warden winced, feeling the backlash of his own electrical warding defenses. "You've sent a damn near fifty witches to detain a handful below and left a handful to handle thousands!"

The walls above rumbled. Sparkling scarlet portals opened. Mist seeped between the cracks of the building. Concrete divided, creating a chasm for enchanters to funnel through. The warden's station filled with industry witches from every guild across Chicago, exactly how Milo had planned it. Hundreds of the most highly trained witches surrounded the MDC and stormed into the buildings to detain every threat.

"You're in good hands," Milo said, stepping onto the elevator to join Wadsworth and the Global Guild forces who were stationed to hold back The True Witch. "*Everything is going exactly as expected.*"

Anxiety gnawed at Milo's nerves. Failures of his past crept out of the shadows, stalking him from the back of his mind. Since the protective magics cloaking the MDC had fallen, Milo had a clearer read on the events transpiring. So much of his plan hinged on absolutes outweighing unknowns. Nothing ever went exactly according to plan, no matter how well Milo planned, no matter how many dominos he personally tipped, no matter how precisely he accounted for every possible variable.

Milo used the elevator ride down to steady his breathing and settle his shaky hands. Using his clairvoyance, Milo dived into his inner core, scanning the screens that projected infinite possibilities, and everything seemed exactly on track.

Milo's expression turned sour, fighting back a frown of disgust. For someone who believed deeply in happily ever afters winning out over everything else, he didn't buy this easy success for a second.

The elevator dinged, and Milo looked on in horror as the doors opened. The entire floor was covered in blood and bodies from the reinforcements sent by the Global Guild. Every single support witch they'd sent lay on the ground, barely breathing, barely a thought in their unconscious minds, some already fallen to the dark silence of death.

I quivered, holding back my fear. Fear I didn't wish to pass along to Milo, who stepped off the elevator, assessing the situation, calculating missteps, planning new phases, and searching desperately for an ending that didn't result in more bloodshed.

The True Witch stood in her full garb from the night they detained her, an outfit removed when she was escorted through the MDC. Last time Milo saw her, she was in an orange jumpsuit, much to her distaste, as Enchanter Wadsworth sat across from her sealed cell, shooting daggers with his scowl.

Now, Amara stood tall, floating above a bloody and impaled Wadsworth, staff in her hand and smirk on her face.

"*How'd she get her staff?*" Milo cycled through visions, uncertain of what went wrong.

I found myself drawn to Enchanter Wadsworth. The memory of what happened here bubbled in his fleeting thoughts; each image of the incident seared in his darkening mind. He replayed every step as he took haggard breaths. He second-guessed his decisions as he watched those around him writhe in agony. He expected better of himself from the decades he'd spent preparing for the reappearance of The True Witch and her Celestial Coven.

```
Name: Samual Wadsworth
Branch: Rejuvenation (Healing)
```

In an instance, the wards had fallen everywhere in the Metropolitan Detainment Center except for the underground solitary confinement sector, where the Global Guild forces had already intercepted the circuits, re-tasked the casting, and circumvented any attempt at shattering the barriers that held the most dangerous inmates.

It didn't stop the intruder, though. The fourth and final pillar had barreled into the underground bunker, hacking his way through the forces Enchanter Wadsworth gathered.

Long black hair, a sharp jawline, dark olive skin. These were the only features of the fourth witch from the Celestial Coven that Wadsworth glimpsed in the carnage.

Amara spoke his name only once. "*Lazarus.*" The passion in her voice when she said it, the thrill of her plan coming to fruition, the joy in her eyes when this Lazarus witch destroyed the barriers meant to hold her. It saddened Wadsworth, weighing on his heart.

"*He's a witch with rejuvenation beyond your wildest dreams, Sammy.*" Those words struck a chord. If Wadsworth somehow survived this ordeal, which he found unlikely with each fleeting second, those words would remain etched in his mind forever. A scar that painted the truth based on what Wadsworth saw.

Despite his best casting efforts, most of the witches sliced down by Lazarus had been done so with precision. This expert witch in rejuvenation aimed for arteries, organs, and vital veins, which made it incredibly difficult for Wadsworth to counter, to heal, to save.

He should've focused on himself, a belief of that rang loudly in his thoughts, echoing above the dying breaths of so many. *Too many.* He should've let them perish the second they were struck down by Lazarus, but Wadsworth believed himself better than that, deceived himself into believing no one had to die. Irritation festered for Enchanter Evergreen, who'd caused that foolish, idealistic thought to cross Wadsworth's mind after a lifetime of learning the cruel lesson that it didn't matter who died. Only preventing the worst threats from bringing about more destruction mattered.

Now, he lay in a pool of his own blood with a hole through his chest because he'd been foolish enough to fight two pillars simultaneously while diverting the bulk of his rejuvenation toward those suffering fatalities beyond even his expertise.

Enchanter Wadsworth truly believed he could've faired easily against the rejuvenating witch, Lazarus, and he didn't think The True Witch possessed anything in her arcane branch beyond what he hadn't readied himself for, fortifying his mind against her Oceanic Collapse.

But it was the staff. That damned weapon which offered Amara ungodly levels of strength. A weapon the Global Guild demanded he keep safe for study, a weapon they locked behind a hundred layers of protections, a weapon he should've shattered to pieces instead of logging into custody.

Supposedly, from all of Wadsworth's research, each gem embedded in the skull represented the leftover magic of former members in the Celestial Coven since the dawn of time, fallen but not forgotten, and The True Witch wielded that staff with such tremendous force. A brilliance that'd dropped Wadsworth the second her fingers gripped the ivory weapon.

But how'd she get her hands on it? Wadsworth studied Lazarus' steps the moment he arrived, tracking every blow he landed on his victims, casting countering measures to heal them, replaying every second, yet he didn't once see any indication of Lazarus holding the staff. In fact, he didn't see a single weapon in the man's possession. It took a few fatal blows before Wadsworth realized that Lazarus channeled his telekinesis through his fingers while he held them together and extended like blades.

Once he'd reached Amara's cell, Lazarus broke through with a flat-palmed strike, and the bone staff flung to her grasp instantly. When she gripped it, she struck down Wadsworth and everyone else Lazarus had missed while also burning away her orange jumpsuit and restoring her wardrobe of choice, the tattered black dress, thigh-high boots, and crooked witch's hat with the bent-tipped top. With a snap of her fingers, every other solitary cell had opened, and then Enchanter Evergreen arrived on the elevator.

Tiptoeing along her shoulder, two bone fingers tucked themselves beneath the sleeve of Amara's dress. I knew how she acquired her staff. Grim had done it. Despite being halted by Gladiatrix above, those two fingers I thought had been smashed to dust had actually gone off on their own accord, freeing The True Witch's bone staff. A staff that bone witch likely had the ability to move, seeing as he controlled his bones through some bizarre branch, he undoubtedly controlled this weapon in a similar way.

Wadsworth's desperation pulled at me, holding the same sad and worried thoughts. He wanted to warn Enchanter Evergreen, to share what little insight he had on Lazarus, to prepare him more for what The True Witch was capable of. But Milo worried about something he considered far more grave than any of the pillars from the Celestial Coven.

Fear dripped off Milo's sweat and stole my attention from Wadsworth, who continued feebly screaming his thoughts at Enchanter Evergreen since he remained too immobilized to speak.

But Milo only had eyes for Theodore Whitlock. *Theodore.* My magic crumbled inward, hoping to hide. I eyed every exit, craving an escape while also unwilling to abandon Milo. The sadistic warlock sat crouched among the bodies, holding a semi-conscious witch by the back of the head with a small, crudely crafted blade pressed against their neck. With the cells unlocked, the worst warlock I'd ever encountered had now come one step closer to his freedom, which would surely mean the death of everyone else.

"Enchanter Evergreen." Theodore hummed in the darkness. "I was just thinking of you, of that time I met your *boyfriend*, of all the things left unsaid between us."

He slashed the witch's throat, a shallow and jagged cut meant to mimic how he'd sliced mine, though the dullness in his self-made shiv didn't offer the cleanest cut. Disappointment oozed from his pores.

"You know, I never forget a psychic's touch." Theodore lifted his gaze. His haunting, hollow blue eyes were trained on Milo, but I felt them piercing through me. *"I've missed your magic."*

The memory of slicing my throat blossomed in his surface thoughts. My quivering body in his grasp, my fear tangled in his thoughts with our minds linked that fateful day, and my frightened students staring on in shock. Bloody droplets splashed from the gnarled branches of the petrified tree, representing Theodore's inner core as he offered the world insight into his every musing, craving the attention and carnage in equal measures.

I trembled, nearly drawn back to the rest of my body, the rest of my mind where maybe my other half didn't sink into this all-consuming dread. Where maybe my other half had no idea of the horrors unraveling despite Milo's best intentions to prevent the worst outcomes.

CHAPTER TWENTY

I NEEDED to focus on the showcase about to commence, yet my thoughts continued to wander back to the night I spent with Milo at his place, in his bedroom, where he sorted visions in my inner core while sharing the plans about how he intended on defeating the Celestial Coven, protecting the city, and preventing the escape of Theodore Whitlock.

"You're sure Theodore is her objective?" I asked with a shiver, nearly pulled out of my inner core.

"Yep." Milo continued tinkering with unruly visions. "But there are no worries. I've got it all covered."

"How do you know—"

"Because I'm The Inevitable Future," Milo interjected, playfully shimmying past me and bumping his hip against mine.

"How do you know Amara, The True Witch, whatever is after Theodore?" I swallowed hard, afraid of the response that loomed in Milo's thoughts. I could feel the words, the answer, the hesitation as he attempted to hide it. "Just tell me."

"It's the message the chimera passed along for Theodore." Milo grimaced, an awkward expression meant to convey how he didn't blame me.

Not that he needed to because I blamed myself. That goddamn Doppler.

He ruined everything in my life that he touched. I hated him. He'd interfered, he'd altered futures, he'd manipulated so much… And then there was that chimera, craving to become a perfect devil. Those two ruined my life with every second they fought to exist.

I couldn't believe the chimera, who was dead and gone, still managed to haunt me with his actions. "One letter caused this?"

Milo gestured with his arms, weighing imaginary factors in his hands. "One letter set this in motion. A message Theodore had likely been attempting to send since the day he ended up incarcerated."

"And I helped him."

"Your manifesta—" Milo bit back the word, realizing the extra intricate layers to my magic we'd recently unraveled. "Your evil-ish persona. Well… Not evil, evil. Like neutral evil, lawful evil? Hmmm. I'll put a pin in that for later. Basically, your persona guy helped. Unintentionally. A smidge. The teensiest trickle. To something that Theodore would've likely maybe possibly kind of accomplished even if he hadn't crossed paths with the chimera."

Milo lied. Badly. He'd prevented every potential of Theodore seeking aid from outside the MDC the day he'd locked that warlock away, the thoughts poorly hid behind cheesy lyrics to some of Milo's favorite songs.

But the chimera had required Theodore's assistance to escape from the Doppler's grasp and the confinement of the MDC himself. All he had to do was pass along a single message for Theodore in exchange. I ground my teeth. Of course something as innocuous as sending a letter would bring about utter devastation. It was Theodore Whitlock.

"Get out of your own head." Milo squeezed me into a tight hug, drawing me from my thoughts and the inner core of my mind, and back to the bed where we rested together semi-awake after screwing.

Milo had literally kicked me out of my own mind. Sort of. Despite the amusement I carried for that, I dwelled on the horrors my magic had inadvertently brought about. Sure, the Doppler was the worst of me, but he was still me. Some tiny piece of my faults all stacked together.

"How does Theodore even know The True Witch?" I asked. "The Celestial Coven?"

"No idea." Milo shrugged. "My guess is it's like the Make-A-Wish Foundation but for serial killers."

I struggled against his embrace, annoyed and anxious and feeling completely unworthy of any affection.

"Everything will work out." Milo was unrelenting in his hold and still whispering secrets about his plan inside my inner core. "*Theodore won't have access to his branch. I've got guilds that'll clear every ounce of demonic energy in a ten-mile radius when the day comes. I've got enough enchanters, Global Guild forces, and coven mates of the highest caliber. Seriously, Gladiatrix could probably drop every baddie single-handedly. But I don't wanna gamble any losses, so we're moving in as a small army.*"

"*How can you predict what Theodore will do? What any of the inmates will do?*" I recalled how the dampeners of the MDC blocked Milo's clairvoyant insight, which proved to be a double-edged sword. The warding prevented those incarcerated from using their own magics, but it also cloaked them from magics outside the facility. "*Have you considered reaching out to the MDC? Moving Theodore?*"

"Wow. That never occurred to me, especially with how the wheels of bureaucracy move super quickly." Milo rolled his eyes so dramatically, I almost confused it for an intense vision. "Pretty sure if I file a petition with the state, they'll set up an emergency meeting within six to eight weeks. I'll express the urgency, and they'll reject my proposal. I'll get an email about an option to appeal. They'll respond to my appeal three to four months later, probably with a rejection."

I scowled. "Guessing you've been down this route before?"

"Lemme tell you how the state rejected my proposal about reinforcing the standard demonic energy repulsion enchantments across the city. The inquiry I made to help facilitate events during the Night of the Fiend Massacre." Milo made a face, this dumbfounded, unamused expression. "They sent me the rejection letter six months after the incident. The incident where I'd already saved Chicago from the fiend massacre. Well, not me personally. Obviously, I worked with a lotta amazing witches. But I mean, I was the one who organized the entire thing. Juggling hundreds of variables. Basically, cementing myself as a truly badass bitch."

"And so humble," I teased.

"I can be humble." Milo nibbled on my ear, rousing me from my sleep as he finished sorting visions, finished revealing his plan, finished resting up from round one and craving more of me. "Maybe you can give me some humble pie."

"I don't even know what that means."

Milo ran his fingers down the sides of my torso, delicate and teasing, then squeezed my butt with a firm grip. "Well, how about some humble cake."

I glowered. "*You just told me about how you're planning on fighting a group of warlock extremists—*"

"Witches," Milo clarified because, of course, the Celestial Coven would only be deemed warlocks once convicted of a crime.

"Whatever." I huffed. "*You're putting together a precarious mission to infiltrate the Metropolitan Detainment Center filled with thousands of incarcerated witches and warlocks to stop a coven bold enough to attempt such a thing so they can free a psychopath…and you think I'm aroused?*"

"I mean, my cake-eating can get you there." Milo made a goofy grin, ignoring the weight of the world that lay before him, the mission that held so many variables. "*Look, the Celestial Coven has four pillars. The True Witch and three others who I'm mostly prepared for. As for Theodore Whitlock…I would sooner die than allow the shadows of his ominous presence to ever loom over Chicago or anywhere bright and beautiful in this world.*"

"That's what I'm worried about." My eyes watered, turning Milo's minxy expression blurry.

"You know what might make me feel better?" Milo blinked, making a sappy, pleading face as he pouted his lips. "*Since I'm basically going into war and all that…*"

"I swear to Christ, if you say cake!"

Milo nuzzled the crook between my neck and shoulder, burying his face in my skin. "You've got such a good cake, though."

I smiled a bit as the memory fizzled away, and I found myself drawn back to the stress of the present, wishing I could linger in that memory forever, wishing I could skip past the fear I had for Milo's current mission, wishing I had more to offer him than my quiet support while here at the academy showcase.

Straightening my posture, I tied my hair back into a messy half-up bun, and I did my best to focus on the opening ceremony taking place in the auxiliary gym. It'd taken nearly the entire morning since Headmaster Dower insisted on the formality of traditional introductions. It boiled down to a cotillion-esque charade where each student was announced and then had their magic, accolades, and rankings listed. She wanted to introduce every single second-year student, all 599 of them. I yawned and attempted to focus since the headmaster had finally reached my homeroom, starting the introductions with their coven formation first.

I rolled my eyes when Ben Dover's Coven was announced. Despite the contempt I held for that damn name, the hilarity of it conjured bubbling laughter from the audience. So much so that the joyful emotions radiated in waves that rocked against the shores of my anxiety, washing away my fear like it was nothing more than a sandcastle on the beach.

The distraction pulled me to my senses, helping to ground me here during the showcase. Yaritza and Jamius scolded Gael because he'd forgotten to send in the paperwork to update their coven's name. Gael feigned innocence while grimacing, but truthfully, Yaritza and Jamius shouldn't have relied solely on the jester of their group to finalize the filing. Then again, despite the absurdity of the name, several acolytes in attendance already had Ben Dover's Coven members memorized, and the preliminary opening ceremony hadn't even finished.

Damn. Gael was always craftier than I gave credit to.

"I'm certain everyone is ecstatic about the rules behind the preliminary round!" Chanelle strutted across the stage, enthusiastically working the audience back to excitement after Headmaster Dower's drool commencement ceremony had finally wrapped up. "Obviously, all the students can't compete at once." Chanelle paused for the theatricality that she loved so much. "Well, they could, but we don't want you missing a single second of our students and their outstanding casting. We'll be dividing the preliminary round into divisions based on covens and rankings."

This was Chanelle's way of leveling the playing field. Somewhat. It also meant half of the highest ranked students wouldn't make it past the first round. While I worried about how many of my homeroom coven kids would end up eliminated, I admired Chanelle's strategy. In her own small way, she wanted to flip off the industry ranking policy, offer the less combative an opportunity to shine, and open a few doors for the underdog.

I scrunched my face into an angry frown. She could've had this epiphany last year when I expressed how the system fucked over kids. Whatever. Better late than never. Plus, Chanelle was better at playing the long con than I was when it came to getting what she wanted in the world of education.

"The preliminaries will focus on collaboration, coordination, and conquering your fears!" Chanelle gestured to the covered tanks lining the edges of the arena floor.

As staff proctors like myself telekinetically removed the curtains draped over the glass tanks and revealed the fiends sealed inside, everyone reacted with terror and excitement—students who lined the outer perimeter of the arena, the audience, and even a few staff who didn't realize how big some of the fiends would be. The mixed bag of powerful emotions made it difficult to stay composed, so I focused on Chanelle.

"Competing covens will be expected to eliminate fiends," Chanelle explained, studying the audience as she buried her disappointment. "*Look at this turnout. All those invitations, calls, conversations, sweet talking…and for what? They all bailed. I should've saved the fiends for when the enchanters showed. What'd I do? Where'd I go wrong?*"

She hadn't done anything wrong. Milo had simply diverted a lot of those meant to attend by wrangling together enchanters from every guild in the city. Well, he'd made certain Guild Master Campbell navigated those negotiations. The point was those absent enchanters were protecting our city, ensuring the MDC remained locked down and secure, safeguarding against Theodore Whitlock's escape.

I shivered. Running a hand against my scar, I buried the memory of Theodore's assault. It wouldn't affect today. Milo planned for the four pillars of the Celestial Coven. Milo gathered Global Guild forces, strategically placing them where they were best suited, and kept the alliance of Chicago's guilds strong so they could attack with a unified front.

Ignoring my own concerns, I stared out at the audience. Honestly, despite Chanelle's disappointment, the turnout had been pretty impressive for a preliminary round. The arena seating was completely filled to max capacity. Sure, half of the attendance came down to staff and students dragged from their classrooms or parents who took the day off to see their kid's performance. But there was a big turnout of acolytes in the audience, too. Guessing Milo didn't want many of them walking into the MDC. Not with threats as big as the Celestial Coven…

I clenched my jaw.

No. I needed to stop obsessing. Aside from the fact that half of me was literally already obsessing on my behalf. An extended manifestation of my form currently watched everything unfold. If something dreadful occurred, if things took a turn for the worst, my other half would reconnect with me as a warning.

The entire auxiliary gym rumbled. Enchantments placed along every wall glowed, activating, then went silent with a frightening hiss. The hue of magic turned a sour puke green, and every intricately woven protection carved into the lining of the academy remained nothing more than uselessly written text scrawled on the walls.

Bright blue lights filled the arena stage, rippling portal doorways opening and closing everywhere.

A rapid flurry of explosions hit the arena flooring.

Smoke raged.

What's happening?

My manifestation lunged through the smoke, intent on bombarding me with everything he'd witnessed in the week since I'd divided my thoughts. Here and now. No. I couldn't.

"*He's here.*" My other half had this terror-stricken face.

Our expressions stared back at each other like mirrors reflecting in an infinite loop, my expression frazzled and my manifestation's frantic.

I looked past my manifestation to the clearing smoke, seeing the worst person in the world.

```
Name: Theodore Whitlock
Branch: Arcane (Demonic Resonance)
```

Triumph oozed off him, and delightful destructive desires danced delicately at the edges of his surface thoughts where he had already composed countless scenarios of how he'd eviscerate every single person at Gemini Academy.

The students. The staff. The audience. The few guild professionals.

Here, Theodore Whitlock stood, surrounded by demonic energy, raging minds from inmates hidden beneath the dying smoke, but how'd he get here? Where were the Global Guild witches? What happened to Milo?

My manifestation reached out, ready to fill in the missing pieces, and I readily accepted the answers.

Chapter Twenty-One

MY manifestation leapt through the chaos, barreling toward me. Each moment created a kaleidoscope of dual sensations. When my other half connected, the two halves of my being surged with memories. I could spend hours sifting through these flashes, but only fractions of seconds passed outside my mind.

The results of Milo's plan unfolded before me. Enchanter Diaz and Priscilla versus The Sisters Three, the divine psychics. Gladiatrix versus every single inmate, then against Grim, the living, breathing body of bones. Enchanter Wadsworth and the Global Guild reinforcements versus Lazarus, the rejuvenating witch who killed with a deadly touch. And then Amara, The True Witch, reunited with her bone staff, a weapon she used to drop everyone who opposed her.

Not Milo, though. Not yet. Images splashed in swift succession of Milo reacting to Theodore's release, scanning those in the solitary confinement ward, assessing all the magic at play, and creating new plans with the possibilities that remained.

Enchanter Evergreen had made quick work of several inmates, dropping them before the daze of freedom had worn off. Milo recalculated his plans, his objectives, every necessary step to keep Theodore Whitlock detained.

Lazarus leapt between inmates, slicing those in his path down with his hands that he wielded like blades. Watching the memory unfold, I wanted to shout a warning to Milo, but I couldn't. And I hadn't in the memory, so I watched the collision of my mind from two split pieces, hoping it'd reveal everything was okay. But Lazarus had dropped Enchanter Wadsworth and his reinforcements. Milo was surrounded. Alone. Theodore had escaped the MDC and arrived at Gemini Academy.

In the seconds that ticked as this memory unraveled, I feared the worst. Milo… No. I'd have sensed it the instant something fatal struck. What happened to Finn would never happen to someone I loved again. Not ever.

Milo dodged Lazarus' open-handed strike, assessing the precision of telekinesis at play. While Enchanter Evergreen didn't have a strategy for all the mysterious members of the Celestial Coven and had no insight into their magics, he possessed a mastery in combat and analyzing a situation. It'd taken a few evaded blows for Milo to gain an understanding of his enemy's techniques, branch, the sharp cut of telekinesis woven like surgical blades along Lazarus' fingertips.

With a plan in his mind, Milo grabbed Lazarus under the bicep, moving his foot between Lazarus' legs and preparing to shift the direction of this fight before it turned into something deadly.

A crystalized blue light sparkled, the floor beneath Milo and Lazarus rippled, and both of them fell through a portal that sealed shut as quickly as it'd appeared.

With the sudden snap of Milo's mind vanishing, hurled far away, my magic panicked. It wanted to run and search for Milo. I wanted to run and search. But dread held me still in this underground facility.

"What was that?" Amara scowled at Theodore.

"We don't wanna face off against The Inevitable Future. Not yet at least." Theodore grinned. "E was simply being resourceful as always."

Theodore turned his head to meet the inmate who slinked behind him. A pale, scrawny man who swam in his orange jumpsuit, carefully stepping over blood and bits on the floor. His hands shimmered with trace amounts of magical residue. I knew that warlock.

Name: Ernesto Mendoza
Branch: Cosmic (Warp Portal)

He was one of the warlocks from Theodore's crew, those who helped him attack my students last year. This one fought against Kenzo's coven.

"Return Lazarus." Amara pointed her bone staff at Ernesto, who swallowed his trepidation, pretending to be brave when in the company of Theodore.

"No," he said, forcing the word from his mouth so it didn't slip out sheepish and silent.

Milo's thoughts whispered from afar, perhaps outside the MDC building. Wherever he'd landed, he'd done so safely. Ernesto hadn't sent Milo far and couldn't until his magic returned in full swing. Part of me wanted to follow the tiny thread of Milo's voice, but I needed to know what would happen between The True Witch and Theodore Whitlock.

"Now." Amara clenched her jaw, biting back visible annoyance.

"Couldn't if I wanted," Ernesto said. "Not with him fighting with Evergreen. The two are practically entangled. Bring one, we bring both."

"Leave the clairvoyant to me," Amara said, tilting her staff lower and moving it underneath Ernesto's chin.

"Or we don't listen to you because we don't know you," the girlish giggle that followed Darla's voice had a harrowing effect.

I froze, searching everywhere for her silent footsteps. Even intangible and invisible as I was, even as I merely observed my own memory, the idea of her slicing me apart with shallow cuts again left a sinking horror in my gut.

Name: Darla Monroe
Branch: Hex (Counter)

The foul way she pounced from out of nowhere when stalking her prey. Truly haunting. She'd fought Tara's coven last year when attacking the academy. It'd taken everything Tara had to defeat the warlock. And fortunately,

Gael and King Clucks helped, too.

Darla appeared beside The True Witch, menacing smile on her face and twisted fantasies of bubblegum pink insides that she wanted to pluck from this strange woman she'd never met.

"Who even are you?" Darla's eyes darted from the bone staff to the vital spots every witch harnessed their root magics from, calculating which she'd break, sever, or counter.

But how?

Darla possessed a deadly branch but required support tools to access it. Last time, she wielded two daggers etched with enchantments that helped connect and store her hex magic. Those enchantments also helped her store her counter hex into the blades her warlock comrades wielded, much like the one Theodore struck me with that nearly killed me. But with no weapon in Darla's grip, I wondered how she planned to strike. Hopefully, the Celestial Coven and Theodore's crew would slaughter each other, and Milo's fears of the worst wouldn't come to pass. My fears of the worst.

"We are the coven that infiltrated the most secure facility in your city." Amara stood tall, boasting. "We are the witches who broke the system in minutes, we are the ones who face the most capable organization, and—"

"Who the fuck asked you to do all of that?" Theodore stretched tall, savoring a deep inhale of the bloody mess that poured into the room.

"You." Amara trained her eyes on Theodore. "You demanded—"

"Demanded?" He cackled at the absurdity. "No, no, no. I merely warned your coven of their choices. My early release or execution."

Theodore believed with no uncertainty that his father, Tara's father, Tobias Whitlock, would have the thorn that was his son extracted soon enough.

Theories of his demise danced along the edges of outstretched branches, conspiracies behind the plots his father had organized, and a gnawing belief he'd end up dead before his trial began. Where the proof of these paranoid thoughts lurked, I dared not search, for they dwelled further inside Theodore's open mind.

"You chose to act of your own volition." Theodore brushed his bloodstained hands through his shaggy blond hair. "Boldly, I must contest."

He licked blood from his middle finger; a few droplets dribbled down his chin and soaked between the hairs of his stubble beard. He paraded his mayhem as a distraction, much like he spat his words at The True Witch to provoke her. The coven didn't act. No, not at all. They had to *react* based on Theodore's letter. Whether his psychopathy, narcissism, or his Whitlock education, Theodore seemed to gauge every potential reaction his pawns would make.

The Celestial Coven were pawns, too, in Theodore's mind. Their worthless pieces dangled from branches of his inner core, desperate for interaction, connection, luring a foolish psychic to their demise should they creep closer. Those pawns that hung represented their outlived use in the game he wished to continue playing. That much I glimpsed from a safe distance outside of his deadly thoughts.

Theodore turned to Darla and Ernesto. "They've got a hard-on for my branch. The Celestial Coven wants to control the world, and what better way than with an army of demons at their beck and call."

"You will come with me, Theodore."

"Hmmm. Let me think." He tapped his chin, feigning a thoughtful expression. "That's gonna be a no."

"Theodore." Amara slammed her staff onto the floor, a warning. "The plan is—"

"Foolish." Theodore tsked. "The Inevitable Future knows your plan, your backups, your secrets, your whims, your contingencies. Hmmm. Yeah, no. You're not clever enough to evade him."

This was something Theodore had spent much of his time contemplating while behind bars, so much so it fed into a new philosophy of chaos he hoped to fan.

"Do not concern yourself with the psychic. I will—"

"I'm bored with you," Theodore interrupted again, finding every time he did, it provoked a deeper crinkle in Amara's creased brow, and that made him happier than every dead body at his feet.

"I will take you by force if I must."

"Or…"

He dragged out the silence between him and The True Witch when suddenly the glyphs on her bone staff glowed, and the gems sparkled. I expected pain to follow, shock and surprise, which it did…but from Amara.

She released her weapon and flew back quickly, eyes trained on Darla and Ernesto but not the bloody, writhing body that lifted from among the crowd of inmates Lazarus had hacked down to reach Milo.

"You said her enchantments were gonna be challenging." A man smirked, savoring the hunt and pursuit and carnage almost as much as his leader.

```
Name: Vincent Cromwell
Branch: Enchantment (Brand)
```

I remembered the skill of that warlock, the way he broke through Gemini Academy's security in minutes, yet as smart as he professed himself, believed himself, he'd been taken down single-handedly by Caleb Huxley.

I recalled the brief encounters the Doppler had with him when infiltrating the MDC. Vincent stayed close to Theodore while incarcerated, but despite his brawny build, he didn't serve as muscle. No, he worked as an ambassador, offering tattoos and favors of every kind to build Theodore's numbers. Numbers for an escape attempt they now planned on putting into motion.

The room swirled as I glommed onto all four minds, each clicked into perfect symmetry. Theodore, Vincent, Ernesto, and Darla pieced their parts of the plan together. This entire possibility had crossed Theodore's mind, preparing his closest and most trusted allies, his subordinates, his crew of chaos.

When Ernesto removed Milo, he'd always intended to target a pillar of the Celestial Coven. Theodore had warned of their difficulties.

I struggled as this memory continued unfolding. Each member of Theodore's crew moved to see out his plan, their minds assessing their roles, their purpose, their chance at destruction if they succeeded. Even without communicating, they worked to execute the plan. A plan created on a whim.

It didn't matter that they only had seconds to prepare for the situation, for the attack, their years of connection—of friendship as sordid as it was—offered them certainty. Darla, Ernesto, and Vincent held complete trust in each other, assurance in their skills, and expertise in their own magics.

Vincent had acquired the bone staff, and with the amplification in magic the weapon offered, he used it to link to every single inmate throughout the MDC that he'd tattooed, that he'd secretly inked with alchemic ingredients meant to make them pliable for Theodore's needs.

Darla stalled for time, countering the arcane magic The True Witch unleashed. Despite the commotion from the second this underground facility broke into violence, at some point, Theodore had handed off his shiv to Vincent, who carved sigils necessary for Darla's support tools and then passed it off to her.

She used the weapon seamlessly, sending torrents of magical water lashing back at Amara who now dealt with the effects of her Oceanic Collapse. Images of her drowning mind struck my telepathy.

I ground my teeth, ignoring her agony. Part of me hoped she stayed locked in that state of being forever, feeling the pain she'd unleashed upon tens of thousands, no doubt. Another part of me realized that since Theodore's crew had successfully subdued The True Witch in minutes, it meant the city—the world—would have to contend with these sadistic warlocks.

"Your turn, E." Vincent handed the bone staff to the nervous warlock.

Ernesto swallowed hard. "I've never moved this much at once."

"I believe in you." Theodore wrapped an arm around Ernesto's neck, hugging him as he stood close behind. "And if it's too much for you, then we can kill you, take your branch, and stuff it in one of the empty gems up there."

Ernesto quaked, eliciting a tremble of excitement from Theodore, who relished the easily provoked anxiety in his favorite friend. He clutched Ernesto tighter, savoring the delicious tension the two shared.

"Or maybe we could test the stones." Vincent shrugged, aloof but trained to temper Theodore's whims. "See if one already has a teleporting branch."

"I don't have time for trial-and-error bullshit on hundreds of gems." Theodore chuckled. "Chaos is on a stringent schedule, Vinny."

Calculated chaos. That was Theodore's new life motto. One that would help him obtain his goal and achieve the impossible. Stay off The Inevitable Future's radar. Destroy Whitlock Industries. Dodge the ire of the Celestial Coven and whatever backlash using them might cause. Eviscerate everyone in his path for the sheer pleasure of their agony. How he wanted to feel it. How he wanted to feel.

The new strategy allowed him to conceive every possible idea he could fathom, then abandon it for a new plan. One he'd be ready for since he considered every possibility despite the whim of the moment, which he hoped would make it harder to track. He literally prepared ways to be impulsive. Who did that?

As his warlocks worked, Theodore tilted his head, almost gazing at me. No. He was looking at me.

"*I told you that I never forget a psychic's touch.*" He shuffled toward me, twisting his hateful thoughts into something softer, kinder, phony. "*The way our minds melded before I slashed your throat. Truly artistic. The way you pursued me, chased me in here, stalking my every footstep in the MDC of all places, and bringing a demon with you as a gift. A tribute. I never thanked you.*"

I floated backward, wanting to flee.

There was a wicked cautiousness, like he suspected me a deer he didn't want to startle. "*As much as I like the touch of a telepath, the subtle embrace...*"

He paused, thinking, thinking deep in his mind in some futile effort to lure me somewhere I'd never step foot. Then he reached out and rubbed his hand along my ghostly torso. Even as an invisible apparition of magic that he couldn't form physical contact with, Theodore sensed my presence.

"*I prefer when psychics delve into my thoughts.*" He bit his lip so hard it drew blood. "*I'd love for you to come inside me. Come, come as deep as you desire.*"

There was a smirk growing on his face, eager for me to share in the laugh of his crude joke. The playful expression fell away into this yearning gaze that seemed genuine. Maybe. I couldn't know for certain, and I never would because Theodore Whitlock was not to be trusted. Ever. Not for a second.

My bloody image surfaced in Theodore's mind. The faint agony on my face while I took shallow breaths. The anguish as I lay in a pool of my own blood. It tantalized Theodore. It stirred curiosity in him.

"I'm glad you lived." He smiled, soft and boyish, almost embarrassed. *"I can't wait to see you again. There's so much I want to show you, show Tragic Tara, show the world."*

Ideas leapt from one branch of his gnarled thoughts to the next, but his words offered me a lead on the calculated chaos he weaved. Theodore was going to attack the academy. He'd decided it the second the wards in the solitary chamber dropped. He painted the plan in blood at the roots of his tree, of his inner core where no psychic energy could penetrate without risking his murderous ire.

I had all the information I needed. While Ernesto, Vincent, and Darla tinkered with the bone staff to usher them out of the MDC and to Gemini Academy, I had to run and reunite with my other half, warn myself and everyone at the Spring Showcase.

I flew across the city, seeking my other half.

"It wasn't enough time," I whispered as the memory finished and Theodore stood proudly in front of the fifty-some-odd inmates he'd dragged through a portal to Gemini Academy.

Those who'd been tattooed by Vincent didn't have time to react. They fell and writhed in pain as their ink glowed and subdued them.

The tanks surrounding the arena erupted, unleashing every single fiend prepared for the showcase.

"The arrogance of the industry." Theodore threw his thoughts out, fishing for my telepathy. *"I planned on wisps, here at the schooling home of the future guild witches, or perhaps luring the wisps of the wild, the ones dancing around the city."*

There was a cackle from Theodore. It almost outshined the horrified screams of torment from the inmates who were consumed by fiends. Their tattoos drew demonic energy toward them; it weakened their defenses and prepared Theodore to unleash Hell upon the world.

"The delicious serendipity of the universe delivering me a bounty of fiends." Theodore roared with laughter. *"God really does believe in*

calculated chaos."

CHAPTER TWENTY-TWO

FIENDS were unleashed everywhere, immediately wreaking havoc and causing fear. Each heeded the command of Theodore, whose hatred for the hubris of the guild industry outshined everything in his mind, in my mind. Fuck. The gnarled tree of his inner core cast a shadow over the auxiliary gym that I couldn't escape.

The only relief that came from Theodore's vile mind was how it almost distracted from the searing head-splitting pain of hearing thousands of screaming thoughts whirling about. The audience who stampeded out of their arena seating, shoving and harming anyone too weak to stand in the pack of frantic survival. The staff who cycled through every extra training they'd been forced to attend after my incident last year, the one that nearly got my homeroom coven killed.

"Fuck," I muttered.

My homeroom coven. Their thoughts became entangled among the hundreds of students who scrambled with ideas of how to react.

Were they ready for these fiends?   *Could they face off against warlocks?*

Were those prisoners here to kill them?

Why hadn't any real enchanters shown up at the Spring Showcase?

I pressed my hands against my temples so hard I thought my head might crack from the pressure of my grip. There'd be a brief relief if I crushed my skull. Sure, I'd be dead, but the raging minds that stomped my telepathy into pieces wouldn't ache anymore.

Fiends continued terrorizing the inmates who'd been dragged to the arena floor, dragged into this entire escape attempt from the MDC, dragged to their deaths for no reason other than they were foolish enough to trust Vincent. The warlock who secretly branded them with alchemic ingredients meant to provide the perfect fuel for the demons Theodore sought to unleash upon the world.

Demons.

Teeth ripped into flesh. Tongues lapped at sweaty skin. Magic leached off the inmates. Tattoos glowed to hold them in place. Blood splattered. Limbs broke. Bones crunched. Body parts flew about in the frenzy of feasting fiends that gobbled down their quarry.

The mess and mayhem continued as fiends maimed the inmates, their bodies mashed together in this perverse transformation of sticky tar, curled yellow claws slashed at weaker demonic energy, and jagged golden teeth glistened under the brewing storm clouds above. A scalding heat rose from the fiendish blobs that'd bundled together in a mess of magic and death and hunger. One by one, fiends swelled above the others, a pack leader born to destroy. They boiled and burned with hellish heat that reeked of rotten mold before transcending into truly horrid abominations.

In the center of the arena stood a gorgon with green and golden scales, nothing like the one that'd murdered Finn, but I still shivered at the sight of such a monstrosity. I didn't have time to hesitate, though, to freeze with fear of festering wounds from the past. No, because Theodore had brought a pack of new horrors.

Behind the gorgon, eight scaled heads slithered as faceless mouths snapped their sharp teeth. A hydra wriggled on the stone flooring, finding its footing with tiny legs that barely held its huge body and massively long necks upright.

Hovering beside the furthest hydra head was a fat, bulbous clump of clay and stone held high by the flap of six wings. A gargoyle.

More and more demons revealed themselves as the fiends that Theodore had commanded by the hundreds transcended into twelve frightening foes.

Wisps and fiends continued clawing at the edges of the auxiliary gym, trying with all their might and demonic energy to break into the building as so ordered by Theodore's raging cackle that released his branch magic of Demonic Resonance.

It summoned every monstrous being within the city toward Gemini Academy.

How?

I stared at the bone staff he kept held low, dropping the skull head to the floor at his feet, but he wielded it much like The True Witch intended to wield it herself until her postering proved to be her undoing. Now, Theodore used the power radiating from those gems to extend his range of casting.

His twisted fantasies held orders of mayhem and carnage and the craving for blood and death. He commanded horror in hopes it'd offer him joy. His hatred slinked across the arena, fueling the demons with desire and obedience. An aura so black and foul it would be easily mistaken for the inner core of a demon, a devil, a hellish beast without an ounce of humanity. For there was no humanity in Theodore Whitlock, merely a thirst for pain and brutality.

Chaos ensued. The demons that Theodore had conjured leapt from the arena, powers at the ready, and targeted the strongest guild witches in the audience. The clash created destruction almost immediately. Bystanders and noncombatants were hurled by the few enchanters in attendance. Acolytes scrambled to offer support where they could, but so few had faced off against demons. The ones I'd known to have fought demons—like Enchanter Evergreen's three acolytes—had been tapped to serve as reinforcements for the MDC mission.

A mission I still needed answers about… About what happened to Milo… Where's Milo? My Milo. My…

I ground my teeth, glaring at the demons who tore through the auxiliary gym. Burying my fears, my concerns, and my desires, I prioritized the horrors ahead, knowing so many here needed my attention, not some fool lost in a daze of apprehension.

The few guild members here dove into combat, intercepting hungry demons and preventing casualties. They didn't work independently for long. Staff didn't wait for an organized plan, a meeting, a directive from above. No. Teachers leapt into the fray, scooping students into their arms, shielding audience members, barreling into demons head-on without hesitation, and so much more.

I wanted to help, to prove I could be useful.

There was just too much fear and destruction everywhere.

It dropped me to my knees, unable to compose myself.

Fiends plummeted from above, shattering the glass ceiling and falling into a pit of frightened students.

Chanelle unraveled a whip made from multiple magics that she wrapped together when hurling her potent arcane branch at foes. Fire slapped the biggest fiends, lapping them in flames that Chanelle fanned with the next crack of her whip that held wind. Together, the elements created this huge blaze of burning banishment. Then, without delay, as the staggering forces of fiends continued falling into the auxiliary gym, Chanelle whipped them with ice, then floral, then electricity, steel, light, earth, water, shadows, and every fucking primal element or cosmic radiance she could muster.

It was godly. It left me awed, the way Chanelle destroyed threats from above while eyeing her students, every student, below.

The devastation didn't faze her, didn't stall her, didn't slow her for a second as she banished descending fiends while she also swept away glass like a fucking industry pro.

I wanted to latch onto her mind, ask why she ever walked away from the guilds she surely must've been the best at, but I hesitated, continued hesitating as madness erupted all around me.

Chanelle wasn't the only teacher to move with precision, expertise, composure.

Peterson leapt in front of his homeroom coven and worked with several staff members, shielding students with rock walls that moved and shifted and redirected incoming threats toward a witch at the ready with a banishment.

Thompson, whose voice I'd managed to avoid for almost a year now, belted across the auxiliary gym in an effort to cloak everyone the sound touched. Her homeroom coven vanished beneath the protective cosmic layers of her branch magic known as Fairy's Jacket that hid anything her vocal vibrations struck. Anything while channeling magic, of course, since she was an insatiable gossip, and the entire world would become invisible if the casting merely required her to speak.

It wasn't only teachers but every staff member, from the custodians to the secretaries, who flew across campus to break through the pit of fiends and offer an escape path to the administrators who shielded against fiends and guided everyone to safety. Everyone they could in this carnage.

Headmaster Dower unleashed lava, burning a tunnel for students to dive into, creating a wall of heat hotter than any Hell the demons had come from, and raining magma that lured hungry demonic energy to taste the droplets of primal magic in the air.

Everyone worked perfectly, precisely, passionately, and yet I remained frozen and overwhelmed as my telepathy latched onto the minds of those I cared most about.

Gael's mind called to me above everyone else, concerned and determined to protect those endangered. Not his classmates, not anyone he knew. This desire to help was directed toward people who were trapped in the stands and unable to banish the fiends that surrounded them.

He hurled spikes coated in banishment from his arms, sending sharp projectiles into the demonic threats before banishing enough to clear a path.

"Follow me," a copy of Jamius hovered by the open direction and guided the frightened guests to an exit.

It was a copy as Jamius himself stood beside Carter and Jennifer, allowing them to shield him from threats as he cast countless copies to defend, direct, attack, and everything else he could fathom in the instance of this surprise assault on Gemini Academy.

This attack didn't rattle Jamius. It didn't surprise Gael. Sure, neither expected it, but they were ready nonetheless.

Jennifer ate the encroaching dread that flooded from classmates as they fled the horrors. She remained steady, shoulders squared, and sensory at the ready.

Carter weaved his branch into key members of the audience, fueling those most in need while keeping Gael alert and strong enough to launch more spikes without overexerting his physical limitations.

In mere seconds, the four of them banded together and formulated a plan designed to protect everyone around them. They didn't hesitate because the horrors of their first semester surfaced in their minds. Not in a panicking, traumatic way, but more as a strong reminder of what they'd survived, how they'd survived, and why they picked this career path.

It was mesmerizing. They worked together so succinctly, protecting and fighting and proving they each had what it took to survive in the harsh guild industry. Their casting was on par with the handful of industry witches here who faced off against demons in the deepest trenches of the auxiliary gym.

A flaming ball zipped past my head, nearly setting my hair on fire, and I turned to see Yaritza making her "oopsie" face. Grimacing momentarily before returning to exactly whatever she wanted, which in this case was completely forgivable since she launched countless comets of cosmic magic and infused them with her sensory root.

It was a brilliant use of her magic to pinpoint and strike down demonic threats. She'd turned it into a weird tennis match with Melanie, who controlled the fire around Yaritza's star shower. As they whipped flaming rocks back and forth to tear through fiends or set wisps ablaze, Layla leapt in between the fiery destruction, sniffing out people who were too slow to evade, dodging demonic dangers, and slashing the air while channeling her banishment. The three made for a powerful close- and long-range combination of onslaught attacks.

Katherine soared around the facility, ripping out every page of her grimoire. The spine hung loose, its heavy front and back cover fluttered in a wobbly descent as it crashed onto the ground. Katherine held the spells, hundreds of them, each floating around her like she was swimming in a book.

Whether she used telekinesis to throw the perfect page to someone in need or recited a spell for her own use, Katherine managed to keep a careful eye on all her friends. Not only those in our homeroom but everyone at Gemini Academy that she'd grown to love so deeply. She wouldn't allow anyone to suffer in this horrible attack, not if she could do something about it.

A spell fluttered toward me, and I read it, conjuring a barrier that stopped a fiend in its tracks. Once the barrier faded, I prepared to banish it, but a sharply pointed shadow stabbed the creature first, shattering it into a cluster of wisps I quickly finished.

Tara. She flew above everyone here, studying the environment and doing her part to help.

"I'm going to make sure Theo doesn't hurt anyone. I refuse to let him take what I've built."

I'd never felt such conviction and bravery in Tara's thoughts, such eagerness to cast. But she wielded her magics with incredible talent, casting all five of her branches in tandem with her four root magics. She used them in seamless and intricate ways. Her shadows sprang out like spiked whips meant to banish demonic energy while her icicles stabbed wisps that clustered in large groups. Her Banshee's Wail destroyed the fear and sadness that ate away at stunned bystanders, offering them a chance to flee unharmed. Without hesitation, Tara locked fiends in place with golden seals and transformed would-be victims into intangible forms where they could now swim through the crowd and escape.

"BAAAAWWWWWWK!"

Gael lunged; King Clucks kicked his feet behind as he telekinetically hurled his loudmouthed human at me.

The fuck?

Without any time to brace for impact, I flinched but found myself wrapped in a telekinetic grip and swiveled to a new spot.

"Got your back, Mr. Frosty." Gael stuck out his tongue and winked. *"Gotta protect my boy Evergreen's partner. So, if you wanna mention that to him, you know, on why I'd be a boss intern. Just saying."*

"Cl-cluck."

"Yeah, but like in a casual, cool way. Keep it chill, Mr. Frosty."

Was he seriously using a life-or-death situation to barter internships?

Shaking away the surprise and confusion, I saw fiends tackle each other, snapping their teeth furiously at their missed quarry. Me. They'd landed where I stood mere seconds ago. Where I stood before Gael and King Clucks quickly acted.

They weren't done either. King Clucks led the charge, crowing loudly and carrying waves of banishment in his loud voice.

Meanwhile, Gael moved in this acrobatic dancelike fighting style, telekinetically waving around three stray feathers he'd plucked from his familiar's tail. Those fowl feathers were soaked in magic, Gael's magic, the constant channeling the pair used to maintain their bond. It allowed him to hack through fiendish tar like butter, each feather sharper than a knife and easily swayed with precision thanks to Gael's highly proficient telekinesis.

He'd taught himself this style, this technique, that he was eager to demonstrate during the showcase, revealing his graceful and effective combat skills. Something I was certain the guild witches would've eaten up since the best enchanters solved cases while offering onlookers a true spectacle.

Everyone in my homeroom coven held a certainty few in their class had. Yes, Chanelle's homeroom worked wonderfully together. Yes, students from every class did their best. But my twelve students had tasted an attack on these walls once before. They'd survived an assault from Theodore Whitlock and his warlock crew. They'd battled devils—a devil that stalked me. My students had grown leaps and bounds ahead of their peers. Despite the erratic minds every which way, I latched to the twelve most amazing minds I'd ever had the pleasure of teaching.

A gargoyle cornered Caleb. My breathing hitched, seeing him fight a demon singlehandedly, but his steady calculations calmed my nerves. There was no faltering in Caleb's tactical dodges. His maze of a mind weaved together everything he knew about gargoyles, everything he knew about his surroundings, and everything he knew about his capabilities.

He studied the stone making of the monstrosity that towered above him. Channeling banishment, Caleb determined the best locations to shatter the entity in front of him. If he hit the gargoyle just right, it'd topple over and shatter from fewer strikes, and he would be able to banish the wispy remnants with ease before moving on to help others. Caleb always thought of how he could help others before himself.

He wasn't the only one who fought furiously to help others, but the selfishness in *this* selflessness wasn't missed by me as the angry mind zipped across the auxiliary gym to join Caleb in combat. Kenzo leapt forward, punching the gargoyle across the jaw and shattering half the stonework of its head with a combination of banishment and hex magic working to eliminate demonic energy.

"I have this under control," Caleb shouted.

"Shut up," Kenzo snapped. "I'm here to help you, branchless moron."

"I didn't ask for your help, you…you…" Caleb ground his teeth with a frazzled annoyance as he tried to think of the meanest thing he could possibly say. "You jerk-faced fuck head."

Kenzo blinked. His anger completely washed away when he looked at Caleb. Every thought around simmered as Kenzo and I both shared in a silent laugh at Caleb's idea of bullying others. Picking. Hurting feelings with mean words.

"Just let me help you." Kenzo spun around, kicking the gargoyle that began to compose itself.

"No. I don't need your help." Caleb punched the gargoyle, breaking a piece of its wing when it attempted to counter the witches in front of it. "I can do this myself."

"I know that." Kenzo whirled around the gargoyle, lacing it with hex magic but waiting for Caleb to add the banishment for a combination strike. A combination hit that Kenzo had already proven he could cast independently. "I know you can do anything on your own, you annoying fucker. But I want… I want… I want to help. Let me help goddamn it!"

Caleb froze. Kenzo froze. I froze. The entire world seemed to still as these two stared at each other. I watched their teen forms wash away, replaced by the image Caleb and Kenzo both carried in the forefront of their minds. Caleb saw a sweet Kenny that had a goofy smile all the time. Kenzo saw a scrawny little Caleb with huge green eyes as he carried impossibly big stacks of books everywhere he went. They envisioned who those boys might've grown up to be if their friendship hadn't broken. Kenzo swallowed the hundred kind things he wanted to say. Caleb buried the thousands of questions he had.

"I guess we, um, I guess we, um, well, we could banish this gargoyle together and help with the evacuations." Caleb scrunched his face, bracing for Kenzo to shout, to tell him how stupid his plan was. It needed more steps, more details, but Caleb also worried that if he spouted off an intricate plan, Kenzo would also scold him.

"Great idea." Kenzo grinned, menacing and carrying a desire to break everything in his path. "I go high, you go low."

"Wait." Caleb paused. "Do I have to be on the bottom?"

"Always." Kenzo glared, taking his stance.

"Okay." Caleb readied himself. "That's fine, I guess."

The two lunged at the gargoyle, Kenzo swiping with furious punches that broke stone into wispy remnants while Caleb flew low with his legs ahead of him, pedaling wild kicks at the demonic energy as he banished it.

Each boy smiled at the other, Kenzo looking down and Caleb looking up, but both boys finally saw the other on equal footing. Kenzo wanted to see the world Caleb planned on creating, a world where branchless kids didn't have to dream so big because they were accepted, they had the right to cast freely, they were heroes working in this massive industry. And Caleb… He saw the boy who only wanted the best for everyone, the boy who smiled at strangers before offering assistance, the boy who loved so much that hate seemed like the only way to escape his pain.

Their teamwork spread across the auxiliary gym, carrying potent emotions that didn't hold any confusion while they fought side by side.

It distracted me. Everything here distracted me because I was too incompetent. But the surging thoughts of my students reeled back my attention. Their collaborative coordination had done wonders to clear away demonic threats, but there were still so many threats flooding around.

"I should rework the broken enchantments."

"Everyone's so afraid, I need to steer that fear into the demons somehow."

"Jennifer's in pain. If I redirect my vitality…"

"Kenzo y Caleb son increíbles. Me encanta verlos reparar su amistad."

"Vik's technique has gotten flawless."   *"Those damn fiends keep eating my fire."*

"I need more copies to help with evacuations."

"Maybe if I created bigger stars…"

"I know the plan, but Tara needs us, King Clucks."

A class of first-year students from the audience found themselves locked in the gaze of a gorgon while pinned between several heads of the hydra, which no one seemed capable of banishing. I was the only nearby teacher. All my students were engaged in heavy combat, too far to offer assistance except for Tara. Where'd she gone? My pulse jumped. She'd fought to ensure everyone around her had the best support possible, and now she stood alone, too far for me to reach, surrounded by three terrible threats.

"I'm thrilled and chilled, lil Whitlock." Darla giggled as she slinked around Tara, threatening counter at the ready. "I can't wait to slice you up again. Bet your blood is as sweet as Teddy's."

"We should make this quick." Ernesto popped out of a portal before vanishing and reappearing elsewhere. "She's got a lot of branches. That's dangerous."

"I have infinite branches." Vincent tapped his tattooed sigils on his bare chest with one hand while drawing some horrid spell with his other.

The three warlocks from Theodore's crew circled his sister with animosity in their surface thoughts and not an ounce of remorse or desire to hold back their insatiable ire. They'd each prepared to harm Tara, break Tara, teach her a lesson for daring…

For daring what? For living her life? For not breaking to pieces after the destruction her brother caused?

I furrowed my brow. I wanted to slap the fuck out of each of those warlocks. I had to help Tara. But I couldn't be in two places at once. So many students were trapped by the gorgon's petrification, which slowed victims who were caught in its line of sight; it locked them in place like stone. Then there was Tara, who stood all alone like she'd done too much in her life, fighting against the sorrow inside of her.

"Theo. I won't let you harm the people I love."

Enchanter Diaz darted between me and the first-year students, hacking off the gorgon's head with his enchanted sword.

My heart jumped at his sudden arrival. Where'd he come from? The gorgon who planned on making a feast of teens now fumbled around with outstretched arms to retrieve his lost head, but Diaz hit the demon with so much banishment the monstrosity burst into the goopy tar of desiccating fiends that were mashed into muck by Priscilla. She roared, sending a wave of banishment herself that eliminated the demonic energy entirely.

I didn't have a chance to read his thoughts, not with the glyphs of his weapon active. It didn't take long for Enchanter Diaz to race across the auxiliary gym, shredding demons and clearing a path for Priscilla to usher out those in the line of danger.

I needed to move. To help my students, Tara especially. Was her brother really going to let those warlocks hurt her? He remained perched on the stage, watching the horrors unfold with glee blossoming from his gnarled tree of thoughts.

Purple smoke fluttered around Theodore Whitlock, coiling onto the bone staff he held and snatching it away into nothingness.

"Who the…" He ground his teeth. *"I should've slit her throat when I had the chance."*

Milo appeared behind Theodore from thin air.

"How'd you get here so fa—" A quick fist to his face shut Theodore up.

Milo didn't mince words or let up for a second, belting the warlock with heavy-handed telekinetic punches meant to break and bruise and beat Theodore into submission. Theodore couldn't keep up with the bombardment of well-trained hits, tactical strikes, and the plain ole angry fucking attack. His jaw cracked, his ribs crunched, his knees creaked, and still Milo didn't relent.

Every strike was meant to make up for the lost seconds of this diverted path, every painful hit was meant to apologize to the lives lost because of Theodore, every knuckle-bruising punch was a cry for the mistakes Enchanter Evergreen promised to never make again.

There would be no sorrow. There would be no suffering. There would be no chasms of regret like what he held for Finn.

The certainty and joy Milo always held high in his mind had a chink, a blemish that revealed the sadness he often kept at bay.

I wanted to fly across the arena and hug him, hold him, whisper that everything would be okay. But Tara needed me. Darla continued circling her, searching for any vulnerability. Vincent hurled his own magics from his branded tattoos. Ernesto sprang out of portals, nearly catching Tara with each new attempt.

"Gotcha!" Darla sliced the air, sending a counter meant to strike down Tara.

Gladiatrix intercepted the invisible strike, completely unaware of what the counter would do to her; her body raged as the hex magic burned throughout every cell of her being. I'd felt the effects of that counter or a pale imitation of it from a blade that Theodore used, a blade carved with a brand from Vincent to mimic Darla's branch.

"How are you standing?" Darla's face fell flat, stunned by how quickly Gladiatrix shrugged off the counter.

Her branch was so overwhelmingly strong that the warlock's hex fizzled out, merely dampening the physicality coursing through Gladiatrix.

In a flash, Gladiatrix snatched Darla by the throat.

"Release her now!" Vincent demanded, every sigil on his body lit with a green hue.

Gladiatrix headbutted Darla so hard it rendered her unconscious. In a blink, Gladiatrix had abandoned Darla and barreled ahead, Vincent her next target. A crystalized blue door sprang open, sealing right as the enchanter slipped through, even cutting off part of her cape when the portal vanished.

At least she'd removed Darla, who was the biggest threat of the three.

"What the fuck?" Ernesto tugged his hair, staring at the pulsating blue cracks beside Vincent.

"What's happening?" Vincent's eyes widened when the portal opened back up.

"Impossible," Ernesto creaked. "I sealed it. How'd she do that?"

"You think someone of my caliber can't punch a hole through the cosmic plane? Oh, honey." Gladiatrix made quick work of Vincent and Ernesto before either had an inkling of how to contend with the strongest woman in the world.

Once again, I found myself awed by Gladiatrix's capabilities, even attempting to latch onto her steady and confident mind during this tumultuous attack on Gemini Academy. Her surface thoughts beamed brightly, revealing the missing minutes since I'd last seen her and the other members of the Global Guild.

The Chicago enchanters worked to contain the situation at the MDC. They restrained inmates and offered aid to the injured. Far more injured than expected.

A man leapt between Gladiatrix and Grim. He wore a bloody, ripped shirt. There was something familiar in his set-in scowl. Grim aimed his sickle for the exposed hole of the man's shirt, shattering the blade when it met the finely tuned telekinesis buzzing over the skin.

"Even if you could land a strike with your feeble magics," the man spoke in this gruff annoyance while tearing off his tattered shirt. "You can't harm me in this state."

His literal ten-pack abdomen flexed, every muscle of his body tightened, and with a quick jab, he knocked Grim's head off his shoulders.

"It'll take more than that." Gladiatrix sighed at the laughing skull. "Unfortunately."

"I know how to handle so-called immortals," the man spat before breaking the bones of Grim's body in such quick succession that even Gladiatrix strained to follow the blurred movements.

"About time you came to play, old man."

Old man? Wait. This was Enchanter Wadsworth. This guy who appeared in his absolute fucking prime with muscles I didn't even realize were physically possible to achieve was Wadsworth. Wow. The impatient, elderly enchanter who lay dying underground with a huge hole in his chest had used his rejuvenation, his healing, to literally turn back the clock on his cells, restoring his vitality on a level I couldn't fathom. No wonder he still ranked among the top ten Global Guild witches while in his seventies.

"Grab the psychic and bear boy witches," Wadsworth said. "I'll deal with this bone brat and the other pillar. I need you to find The True Witch."

Gladiatrix listened to the battles outside, the fight between Enchanter Diaz and The Sisters Three had ended when the psychic pillar fled after reinforcements showed. She heard Milo's battle against Lazarus. She extended her senses beyond the MDC, stretching them over every chaotic noise throughout the city, and honed in on the ensuing assault on the academy.

"I have an idea of where the witch is," Gladiatrix said before parting ways with Enchanter Wadsworth.

She zipped through the MDC, snatching Enchanter Evergreen in her grasp. Turning on her heels, she raced in the opposite direction and found Enchanter Diaz with his familiar Priscilla, grabbing them with a telekinetic hold. Bracing them with her magic, Gladiatrix bolted across the city, landing at Gemini Academy in a flash.

Having arrived at the campus, it didn't take long for the three Global Guild witches to assess the situation and neutralize dangers where Diaz hacked apart demons and Milo beat down Theodore.

I blinked away the memory and watched Gladiatrix bolt from Tara's side, having defeated the three warlocks that surrounded my student. She moved from place to place, leveling the playing field and eliminating threats in seconds.

Enchanter Diaz soared between students, hacking down fiends with his sword that banished them on contact, using his glowing glyphs in a deliberate pattern to lure demons away.

While her human worked, Priscilla snatched up everyone in her path, holding damn near a hundred people in her telekinetic grip as she trotted across the auxiliary gym to carry them to a safe location.

Everything was working out. Not like planned, but I slowly composed myself. The erratic emotions were becoming more manageable, especially with Milo nearby serving as a lifejacket amidst this carnage.

Milo had grabbed ahold of Theodore's arm, bending it behind his back to the breaking point. He twisted until Theodore dropped to his knees, gritting his teeth and stifling a wince.

"Of all the places, of all the choices you could've made." Milo tightened his grip, lacing telekinesis down Theodore's arm. "You picked this?"

"Go big or go home, they say." Theodore chuckled, pretending the pain didn't burn across his skin. "I don't have a home, so pretty easy choice."

"Now, you'll have nothing. No choices." Milo contemplated wrapping his telekinesis around Theodore's throat, choking the life out of him, or snapping his neck. ***"No futures."***

If he killed the warlock, he'd ensure nothing like this ever came to pass again, ever held a possibility in the future Milo sought to paint. Another part of him remembered the plan—despite all the horrible hiccups that'd occurred—where Theodore Whitlock would be taken into custody by the Global Guild, dropped into a hole so deep and dark the world would never sense his presence again. Milo knew this because of the warlock's connection to the Celestial Coven and Enchanter Wadsworth's tenacious need to eradicate anyone affiliated with The True Witch.

I wanted to tell Milo to stop. I wanted to keep that spark of joy lit in his heart forever. I wanted to take the burden and kill Theodore myself. But I froze. I hesitated. The Sisters Three materialized out of nowhere behind Milo, and I didn't know what to do.

"The Inevitable Future, I presume." The Sisters Three slinked through purple smoke. "Pale, cheap imitation, sisters," the raspy voice declared. "Difficult all the same," the light-lilt voice added. "We see you weaving your silly little possibilities, desperately clawing at the happiest ever after," the stern voice held utter contempt for the words. "But we have come to only grant zero happily ever afters."

They grabbed Milo by the temples, bombarding his mind with every past regret as they ripped up the floorboards of his inner core. Next, they set their sights on the many vaults where Milo stored visions and sorted futures.

I stumbled forward, struggling against the trepidation that struck the tether where my thoughts and Milo's remained linked. The continuous fear and raging emotions of so many people in the auxiliary gym didn't help.

The Sisters Three attacked the hundreds, the thousands, of staticky screens set up in the Fateful Viewing of Infinite Possibilities, where Milo observed visions. God, how he loved that silly little name, the one that reverberated through his broken thoughts as The Sisters Three smashed each screen, scattering glass and leaving shards at Milo's feet.

As he held back the anguish of so many visions rattling through his mind at once, The Sisters Three surged further into Milo's mind. They barged into the white circular room where Milo kept his Dispatch Board of Destiny, a place to track the many colorful potential threads of tens of thousands of people. Each string represented someone Milo hoped to offer the best, careful not to ruin their choices or push them away from others they might happily end up entwined with. The strings sparked, casting tiny flames in every direction of the board as each thread Milo studied over the years burned to cinders.

The white room where he stored them crumbled and cracked apart, and the office where Milo organized every outdated vision rumbled ferociously. The filing cabinets sprang open all at once, spitting the neatly sorted papers into the air. Each piece carried the weight of a vision that collided with Milo's psyche.

"We're nowhere near finished with you," the light lilted voice whispered. "Let us show you the future we've declared, the future fate has decided," the raspy voice dripped venom. "Quake at the power of your betters," the stern voice said right as raging water poured into Milo's mind.

Milo sank into the depths of the ocean conjured by The True Witch, who materialized beside The Sisters Three from purple smoke, holding her bone staff and no longer fazed by the effects of Darla's counter.

"We told Icarus he dared too much." The Sisters Three cackled in unison, unveiling countless lives they'd professed to have controlled, altered, and manipulated over the course of several thousand years. I couldn't track it; the names and faces whirled by too quickly, mixed together with the flashes of tens of thousands of visions simultaneously replaying in Milo's mind. "Like him, your plummet into death will be ignoble. Because you, Enchanter Milo Evergreen, are worthless to our story. A meager obstacle, hardly even an afterthought."

No.

No.

No.

I had to stop this. They couldn't harm Milo. I wouldn't allow it. I'd rip them to pieces.

"How?" the light lilted voice asked. "It is already foretold," the raspy voice whispered behind me. "You are nothing, Dorian Frost, not even an obstacle in our path."

I backstepped away from the feminine silhouette of one psychic sister who walked inside my head only to bump into another who stood behind me. Her hands wrapped over my temples.

Milo's agony faded. I couldn't remain tethered to him while he suffered so much. While I suffered.

Everyone's thoughts vanished.

The world went black.

Chapter Twenty-Three

IN a matter of seconds, The Sisters Three had torn apart everything in my inner core. They shattered the elegance of my ballroom. They shredded portraits holding recent memories with Milo, with the second chance we'd found, and the happiness we had. They smashed images of Charlie and Carlie. They burned every prideful teacher moment I had.

Then they ripped up the floorboards of my shame, my fears, my failures. I fell to my knees, unable to act as they ransacked my mind. Goddamn, they planned on taking every part of my being and breaking it.

"Don't waste your time, sisters," the light lilted voice said. "This one swims in his regrets every day."

"Pathetic." The raspy-voiced silhouette spat on the memories she'd planned on hurling at me.

Each form of The Sisters Three traipsed about independently while inside my head, their bodies like white marble statues, still merely silhouettes, though. Their faces held no features, and their bodies had curves and a femineity to their build, but they were like dolls. It wasn't some way to leave things to the imagination. No, it was like even as they stomped through my head, invading my every thought, they didn't believe me worthy to lay sight upon their true form, their image, their profound being.

"Heeeeey, sisters. Looky here," the light lilted voice called out as she unraveled the visions Milo had organized. "It's like a sad little imitation of our connection. Their frequencies are almost there."

"But this one's magic is far too *weak* to handle holding onto another being's magic," the raspy voice said, shaking her hips. "Weak, weak, weak."

"He bores me," the stern voice said, throwing the visions around my head, letting them stampede across my every thought.

These three sisters each possessed their own psychic magic yet seemed to use the other's ability as their own. They really were like one entity, one supreme psychic being.

Screams outside my mind called out. Not to me, but to anyone. I tried to open my eyes, but I couldn't see anything beyond the confines of my own inner core that'd been set aflame. Still, the foulest voice in the carnage rose high above everything else.

"You're ruining my game," Theodore snapped. "Evergreen is mine to defeat."

Milo grunted, still lost inside the ocean that was slowly drowning him, but a sharp kick from Theodore made his body react. Theodore's imagination painted a bloody version of Milo on the ground, the one he sought to bring into reality. But now, when he kicked the enchanter, he couldn't relish in the whimpering gasp because Milo lay in a daze created by The True Witch. It sickened Theodore, annoyed him.

I ground my teeth, nearly drawn from the trap of my own mind. A palpable, furious desire to snatch Theodore by the throat and strangle him as he continued kicking Milo, waiting for the joy of his sadistic assault to fill his thoughts. But it didn't. He kicked and punched Milo with passion yet didn't take pleasure in breaking the unconscious enchanter. Each strike broke a piece of my hope.

Hope that Milo would wake. Hope that Enchanter Evergreen had a plan. Hope that The Inevitable Future would save the day.

"Next time, do not touch what doesn't belong to you." The True Witch's staff beamed brightly as the auras of infinite magics and the souls of their fallen casters shimmered at the edge of my mind, carrying this radiance of pure, unfathomable power.

It reminded me of how the chimera collected branches, hoarding them like a dragon. Amara did the same, devilish in her own right, and she had dropped Milo into an ocean.

"I must clean up this mess now." Her voice carried disgust for Theodore's carnage, yet the bone staff's magics flickered and extended the range and ferocity of Oceanic Collapse. "Because of you, I have to contend with this crowd. I'll likely need to clear away the entire city since you chose to throw a tantrum."

"No," Theodore hissed. "You can't do that."

He held contempt for Amara's threat. Not at the idea of her slaughtering the nearly three million people who called Chicago their home. No. It offended Theodore how she dared to take away his goal, his dream, his vision of a burning city. It was his destiny to destroy it. To stand in the rubble, to kick the ashes of corpses, to smile down at his dying father after besting him in his own home.

And with one slam of the staff, The True Witch cast a ripple across the entire campus. Water raged into the minds of everyone.

Gladiatrix and Enchanter Diaz rose to the top, fighting the currents the hardest before tidal waves swept them away.

Chanelle's mind called out, a beacon of friendship, as she swam through the torrents of despair.

Every staff, student, and audience member's mind crashed into each other, trapped so closely in this sea of sorrow, but utterly alone in the depths of water so powerful no mind could escape.

Even Theodore's unconscious crew had their thoughts struck by the dark waters.

The True Witch's branch offered mercy to none, preparing to wash away the lives of every person in Chicago after she finished off those who dwelled at Gemini Academy.

One by one, I found my students' minds, wishing I could help them. Carter Howe. Jennifer Jung. Yaritza Vargas. Layla Smythe. Caleb…

I stopped looking for them. I'd already failed them. I couldn't continue…

I couldn't bear watching my homeroom coven gasp and drown while trapped inside their own heads.

With Milo dying…

With everything falling apart…

With The Sisters Three tearing apart my mind…

I had nothing to offer the world, nothing but more failure. Unable to witness another second, I collapsed into the depths of my own subconscious, desperate to become lost in the abyss of darkness where maybe I'd forget everything, and all these deaths wouldn't haunt me.

"This is where you choose to hide," the light lilted voice asked, diving into my subconscious.

"He's so tragic," the raspy-voiced sister added.

Both carried a white radiance from their forms, illuminating the shadows of my hidden depths.

"Please." I fought back tears. "Please just kill me."

I wanted to die first. I knew this was the end, that this was the worst possible outcome to a future that even Milo hadn't seen coming. There was no victory here. There was no breaking the hold of thousands trapped under the heavy weight of Oceanic Collapse. There was no resisting The Sisters Three who'd outmaneuvered me. But if I died first… I wouldn't have to hear everyone else's demise. I wouldn't have to carry that sadness.

"But you should carry it," the stern-voiced sister spat her words. "Perhaps we should carry you with us."

What?

"Ooooh, his form is cute," the light lilted voiced sister squealed.

"He looks like he requires a lot of upkeep," the raspy-voiced sister turned up her nose at the idea of possessing me.

Wait. I heard her thoughts.

They'd spent so much time professing their superiority, easily overwhelming me and keeping their minds secured from my telepathy. Yet now… Now, the raspy sister's thoughts rang loudly against my magic.

Her name was Lachesis, one of many names she held but a personal favorite she'd had over the course of history. She didn't want to abandon her current host, having finally organized the mind exactly to her liking, and she found my head disgraceful for a supposed psychic. But she knew her sister, Atropos, had a familiar glint in her gaze, a vengeful stare. Guess that was why her voice always sounded stern and aggressive. Atropos considered any slight an absolute offense and would demand recompense.

I'd offended her?

Because I had the audacity to ask for a merciful death, she'd keep me locked inside my head for the next century just to spite me.

She'd possess me until I was old and broken and could no longer contain the glory of The Sisters Three. That was their secret to longevity over the centuries. They always jumped into a new body, a vessel, a new host for their magnificence. But when magic had vanished, when it'd been expelled from this world the sisters slept in silence, waiting for the return of power. Waiting for the Celestial Coven to truly reign.

"Sister, guard yourself better," the light-lilted voiced one said. No, Clotho said. That was her name. Despite becoming aware of how I sifted through Lachesis' mind, she lacked the ability to hide her own thoughts either. "I don't lack anything!"

She pouted, her face forming on the blank head of her silhouette. That made her turn away, shameful and feeling suddenly small for a goddess. They hid their form from those they invaded because the glorious beauty of a divine being was far too spectacular for weak mortal eyes. The way I looked at her face, capturing every detail of her stunned expression, sent a whirl of doubt through Clotho's head.

"You really do believe you're gods." I scoffed. "The arrogance. Literal hubris."

"We are gods. We are divinity incarnate. We are prophecy. We are infinite," Atropos shouted, her booming voice rippled through the abyss of darkness. "You hide down here because you're too weak to face us. You hide down here because you're pathetic and alone."

"He's not alone," my angry-voiced persona bellowed from the shadows as his rage towered.

"Personas," Lachesis hissed. "Pathetic. They hold no power except to hide in darkness."

"Then let us remove the shadows." Atropos waved a hand.

"Yes. Let's show him how it feels to look upon someone else without permission." Clotho uncovered her face, shining brightly beside her sisters as the three unleashed white light across the furthest reaches of my abyss.

Thousands of personas stood as a legion throughout my subconscious. Each was some variation of my emotions, my fantasies, my musings. While their eyes didn't normally glow, each one radiated with a defensive purple hue. They craved the darkness, the quiet, and The Sisters Three had dared to disrupt the routine.

The magic of my personas pulled at the shadows that had vanished, seeking to push away the light and replace it with the abyss.

Magic. My magic.

"Give me my magic," I whispered.

"Personas don't have magic, you fool," Clotho said. "They're simply projections of identity."

"This one doesn't understand even the simplest things," Lachesis said. "Hardly a psychic of any merit. I highly recommend we don't waste time possessing such a brittle body."

"You don't know me." I stood, shuddering every time a tiny pulse of purple light struck me, infusing me with more of my magic.

"How are you…" Atropos quieted, studying the personas who wilted like flowers past their prime. Those who'd returned my magic went to sleep. "They cannot all possess magic. How did you do that?"

I shrugged. "I guess I'm self-sabotaging. I've always had too much power, so I broke off a lot of it and dropped it down here."

"You can't do that," Clotho whined.

"Not possible," Lachesis hissed.

"Maybe for you." I waved my arms, washing the abyss in a sea of purple light before returning to the shadows.

The strength of my magic, the full extent of my branch, was incredible. The first thing I did was restore my mind, my memories, my inner core above. The Sisters Three had trashed everything, but it didn't take long to sort. In fact, even the visions gained from Milo were easy to condense, to bind down so they didn't float wildly in my head. A few months ago, I couldn't manage to suppress a few visions and now I handled thousands with grace.

Once I salvaged the mess in my head, I linked to The Sisters Three, grabbing ahold of their thoughts, their minds, their long lifetime of memories. They were so pliable, insignificant when locked in my grasp. In my mind, I ruled with unmatched supremacy. Squeezing the sisters tightly, I snapped the tether that connected each of them to the body of the woman they'd possessed for more than a decade now.

I searched through the memories behind this woman's crime, the offense she'd struck onto The Sisters Three. A giggle floated in Atropos' thoughts, carrying with it the voice of the woman who'd wronged them. Debra Anderson had laughed during a palm reading The Sisters Three offered, jokingly adding how she found psychic readings a bit silly since no one could truly control the future. That one comment, one explanation, one chuckle at destiny offended Atropos enough to break Debra's mind and keep her trapped inside the deepest cellar of her inner core.

They'd done this to countless others, dating back so far that I struggled to hold all the memories. But I wanted them. I wanted to grab every single memory The Sisters Three held. With them, I'd unravel a way to break the four pillars of the Celestial Coven.

The Sisters Three held no individuality. Not really. Their memories were entangled. They'd fused their minds and magics so long ago, even they didn't recall the days before they weren't one deity. As such divine witches, they sought greatness and joined the Celestial Coven, becoming the Southern Pillar of the Four Corners thanks to their tremendously potent psychic branch.

Three branches, really, that became forever entwined due to their fusion: retrocognition, telepathy, and clairvoyance. But I had an expertise in those three magics, twisting and turning their power back onto them the same way they'd done to Milo, done to me. I'd shatter their being for daring to touch Milo, but I needed answers first. All the answers.

I demanded them.

To become a pillar of the most powerful organization, a witch required immortality, exceptional skill, and an understanding for shaping reality.

Enchanter Wadsworth likely continued fighting against Lazarus and Grim at the MDC. The Sisters Three held intel on those two pillars, the magic they each possessed, the monikers they held, the legends their existence had sparked.

Lazarus had lived life almost as long as the sisters, possessing the ultimate rejuvenation magic of resurrection. He could die, but he always healed, always returned, always worked as the Eastern Pillar of the Four Corners. Even if he seemed to prefer a solitary existence outside of the coven.

Grim possessed the foulest augmentation branch according to the sisters, who considered him a beast, perverse and unsettling. His magic allowed him to grow and control his bones in unique ways. By seeping his being—magic and mind—into his bones it allowed Grim a version of immortality. So long as he performed rituals, old magics that the Celestial Coven prided themselves upon, then Grim found himself eternal.

He was the youngest of the four, but he'd also walked this earth for more centuries than they could count, and he ruled beside them as the Western Pillar of the Four Corners.

The final member, the leader of the Celestial Coven, was Amara. The True Witch. The founder. The Northern Pillar of the Four Corners. She led their coven through this world, shaping it, preparing it, protecting The Sisters Three and other witches when the magic of the world disappeared.

The True Witch worked to bring back magic, worked to bring back the world she loved, worked to bring back her godhood.

"How does she extend her life? Who is she really?" I looked down on The Sisters Three, each white silhouette crumbled on the ground, reaching out to one another, but incapable of moving under the weight of my psychic energy.

I hadn't realized how heavily I'd hit them, how much force boomed off my being.

"Tell me," I roared, carrying a demand that ripped open each of the sister's minds.

They shrieked and cried and presented every memory of their being, incapable of resisting my will and helping me scour for memories that held intel on The True Witch. But they didn't have the answers I looked for. They didn't know how Amara extended her life. They didn't know how to remove her oceans from everyone's minds.

"I see you do know a lot of other things, though." I stared at the seemingly infinite number of memories on display, holding a trove of knowledge. "I'll sort through this later."

"You speak as if you could grasp our glory, our—"

"Quiet." I thought past The Sisters Three, ignoring their feeble attempt to challenge my magic, my psychic power that overwhelmed their minds, and I searched outside this room. Everyone was still alive, still holding on despite the power of Oceanic Collapse.

It'd merely been a few seconds since The Sisters Three had delved into my mind and attempted to torture me.

I needed to be rid of The Sisters Three and then contend with The True Witch. With all my magic fully restored, it might be enough to shatter the oceans from some minds. No. It'd be enough to free everyone. I'd see to it.

"But first, I need to remove you." I stared down at the sisters. "I can't keep you in my head. Well, I could, but I don't want to. You've been here less than a minute and proved to be quite the fucking headache. However, I can't simply let you leave. You'd jump back into poor Debra or some other unsuspecting soul. No. Neither is much of an option. I'll have to end you here and now. Strip away your psychic energy until it's completely depleted."

"You can't do that. You'd be killing us." Clotho had this confusion in her voice. "We don't die. We are forever."

"You've had a long life, longer than most." I shrugged. "Mainly by taking from others, might I add. Taking their body, their will, their future."

"It was ours to have," Lachesis said, truly perplexed I'd question the justification of a god.

"Sisters, join me." Atropos reached out her hands, hoping to harness their magic and escape.

I chuckled.

The idea of fighting me actually frightened them. Three witches who declared themselves goddesses fused as one being, a deity of the psychic branch, was afraid of little ole me.

I turned my gaze onto them. "And you should be. You should be very afraid."

Atropos grabbed her sisters' hands, attempting to merge into their solitary form, but with a wave of my hand, they flew to opposite sides of my subconscious.

"You think I'd allow you to escape? Let you live? After you wormed your way inside my boyfriend's head. After you attacked the love of my life. After you harmed the best person I've ever known." I snapped my fingers, shattering Clotho into nothingness; her light lilt carried a sad, sour note as she faded away. With a flick of my wrist, Lachesis joined her sister in the ether of nothingness. "Maybe there's an afterlife. If so, I hope Hell is kind to you three because I sure as fuck won't be."

"You can't do this. We foresaw…" Atropos widened her eyes, her face fully forming as her memories and magic fizzled to nothing. She couldn't see anything, no futures, no pasts, no thoughts outside the few dwindling ones in her head. "Why?"

"Because you had the audacity to fuck with me. To threaten my future, the happiest ever after that Milo has worked so hard to create." My words carried an echo of authority, a furious snarl.

It shoved Atropos out of my head and to death's door which had long awaited her knock.

Now that I'd ended the Southern Pillar of the Four Corners, I stepped out of my subconscious and returned to the auxiliary gym, where I planned on saving everyone's life by ending The True Witch and Theodore Whitlock.

CHAPTER TWENTY-FOUR

MILO remained locked inside his own head, an ocean burying him beneath currents so powerful that his already shattered mind struggled. The Sisters Three had fractured his inner core, ruining every layer of The Inevitable Future's sanctuary. A piece of my magic had leapt ahead of me, sitting at Milo's side and wishing him well. I wanted to kiss him, to mend the cruel, callous injuries dealt, but first, I had to stop Theodore, who'd moved on from beating Milo's unconscious body and retrieved a knife.

"Wonder how much of this you'll feel." He pressed the blade below Milo's eye, intent on slashing his face to pieces.

"Stop," I roared.

Not out loud but the thought created a thunderous response, literally conjuring a storm above the academy. It swelled and lightning crackled. Not real lightning. Maybe. I couldn't be sure. The raindrops felt real, but they also felt like my sorrow, my sadness manifested into the weather. That wasn't the case. It made no sense. It was timing. The weather had gone foul, and I created a similar projection of telepathic energy.

The lightning. Christ, I loved watching the crackle hit Theodore's gnarled tree. Each spark of electricity broke branches off the warlock's sadistic fantasies. I flew across the auxiliary gym, stopping in front of a bewildered

Theodore.

"What's the matter?" I knelt. "You wanted me to dive deep into your mind."

Theodore panted, uncertain how so many of his thoughts trembled, boiled, burned, faded, stretched into infinite loops. It wasn't that my abilities startled him. He fully grasped the capabilities of a telepath. I even unraveled his most intimate and tender moments with the telepath who loved him.

Dr. Kendall. I remembered our brief encounter where her telepathic touch dropped an anvil into my thoughts. Twisting my magic, I decided to try something similar to Theodore, shattering huge chunks of bark from the tree of his inner core.

"You can't do this." Theodore pressed his hands to his head, attempting to squeeze me out. His years with Dr. Kendall, the way she'd soothe his every thought while dancing naked in his most depraved fantasies, had taught him how to control psychics who entered his mind.

"You should've stayed locked up." I balled a fist, dropping a mountain of telepathic energy onto Theodore's skull.

He screamed. The torment enticed me, encouraging me to unleash further devastation. He'd pay for everything. ***Everything.***

Tears welled up in Theodore's eyes, his hauntingly hollow blue eyes that begged for pity, for me to stop shattering pieces of his memories, of his desires, of his horrible passion for mayhem. It wasn't like I was destroying them forever. That took a lot more time and continuous breaking while also risking the entire psyche. A level of power I didn't plan on committing because, "I'm just going to kill you here and now."

I simply wanted to hurt him first. Like he'd hurt Milo. Like he'd hurt Tara. Like he'd hurt Kenzo. I wanted Theodore to feel the agony of death the same way he'd struck down his victims. I wanted to break his lust for blood. I wanted him to beg.

"Please." He shivered. "Please help."

"All that torture and murder, and now you're afraid to die?" I crept closer, straddling Theodore's waist and wrapping my hands around his throat.

"Can you do nothing on your own, Theodore?" Amara flicked her wrist and lifted me away, pulling me high into the air and then slamming me down.

I gasped at the sudden crash. Everything ached.

Dammit.

Obviously, I needed to contend with her first. I forced my way back to my feet, ignoring the throbbing pain that burned along my torso. As I winced, I locked onto the minds of students, enduring a small piece of the suffering they dealt with while trapped inside an ocean. It reminded me not to complain about a few bruises.

"You're bold and foolish." She tilted her staff toward me, aiming the hundreds of glowing gems in my direction. "I could kill you with a thought."

I stifled a laugh. "Funny you should say that."

Honing in on the multitude of magic stored in each of the stones The True Witch wielded, I heard the many slumbering thoughts. Whispers, dreams, comfort in the will of the Celestial Coven. These weren't unwilling victims but pieces of magics and minds broken off the fallen members of Amara's foul coven. A coven that had many followers, many members who each strived to join the four pillars. Only the pillars never changed, not for as long as The Sisters Three could recall. Still, those gems held dangerous branches that'd make my battle difficult and drawn out.

"I don't have time for that," I muttered, eyeing everyone who fought against the ocean currently drowning them in their heads.

"Seems we're both on a firm schedule." The True Witch lifted her staff, preparing to slam it down, and cast some god-awful magic.

"No." I waved a hand, hurling every ounce of telepathy I could muster.

It sprang forward like a net that wrapped around the bone staff. I yanked my arm close to my chest, reeling the psychic energy with me and ripping out half the gems in one fell swoop.

Not the stones themselves, merely the minds buried in each tiny jewel. The sparkle in the rocks cracked and the glow fizzled away as the magical link had become splintered.

"What have you done?" The True Witch stared at the dying lights of her godly weapon. While she surveyed the losses, I reached out and pulled more fragmented minds from their final resting place, warping the delicate enchantment magic meant to store these magics into the bone staff.

Whether it was from my experience with the chimera's ability to store magics or the fact that I'd harnessed the full capacity of my branch, this proved easier than anticipated. Not in some overly prideful way. No. The world revealed itself to me and I knew that no one could touch me, not unless I willed it. And right now, the only thing I willed was destroying that horrible bone staff.

"Stop it!" The True Witch extended a hand, throwing an ocean at me, boiling hot and icy cold at the same time. Such an enigma, her arcane branch.

I conjured a sun as bright as Milo and Finn's joy, a sun so powerful in my mind it dried up every drop of water instantaneously.

"How'd you…" The True Witch cast another pointless ocean that I shriveled to nothingness the moment the water dared touch my mind.

"You're gonna have to do so much better than that." I cracked my neck and released the last bit of tension I carried in my shoulders.

Since pulling all my magic back together, out of the subconscious, I'd found every thought pounded against my skull from across the city. It hadn't been very long, and yet millions of minds each going about their day whispered. Was this why I created Nico? A child's delusional way of filtering out the world. Was this why I snapped off pieces of my branch to begin with? There was so much power. Despite the pain, I rose above it, feeling impossibly strong.

Thousands lay here at the academy, sinking in the water conjured by The True Witch's Oceanic Collapse. I unleashed every thread of my psychic energy, knowing Amara wouldn't attempt a third cast of her branch.

"What would be the point?" I tilted my head toward her, a mockingly wicked smile on my face and a glint in my eyes that said I'd kill her. *"And if you don't grasp that expression, know that once I've saved everyone here, I'm going to kill you. Going to break you the same way I did your silly little bone staff."*

Her bright green eyes shot open with shock at how easily I linked to her mind. A mind guarded by the many magical tattoos covering her skin.

I broke Milo out of his ocean first, pulling together the shattered memories of his happiest times. He was too exhausted to continue fighting, but honestly, there were only a few fiends left to contend with, thanks to the amazing Gladiatrix, Enchanter Diaz, and Priscilla, who'd wiped out Theodore's demons.

As I worked to remove the oceans from mind after mind, I worked to stitch together Milo's thoughts. He slept on the ground, covered in blood and bruises, and I desperately wanted to hold him, hug him, hear his voice. But he slept. Even in his mind, he slumbered in a deep silence unlike any I'd experienced with him before.

Milo always worked, even when resting. The Sisters Three, The True Witch, and Theodore had broken his mind and left him too exhausted to function.

I clenched my fists, dropping Amara to her fucking knees.

"Did I say you could leave?" I scowled at her continued attempt to break loose and flee.

She pressed her hands against the stage floor, resisting the telekinesis I hit her with. Desperation seethed from her surface thoughts, twisting and twirling between a dozen different languages, but the feelings, the intent, the truth painted the air above her with obvious plots. Fatigue oozed out of her pores. It seemed wielding her staff took a lot of channeling efforts, and losing it hurt even more.

I wanted to savor the deep-seated sorrow that ate away at her. So much power, so much history, and some pathetic nameless telepath destroyed it. Venom dripped from her mind when picturing my face, unaware of who I was and how I held such magic at my disposal.

"You'll carry my name with you to Hell." I turned away from her. "I promise you that."

I'd kill her. I'd kill Theodore. But first, I had to repair their damage, I had to save everyone here, I had to wake Milo. God, how I had to wake him and return The Inevitable Future, the happiest guy I knew, the reason I looked forward to living each new day.

It took a lot of work, effort, and streaming telepathy in every direction, but I managed to slowly piece together Milo's broken mind and remove the oceans drowning everyone in the nearby vicinity. And I did mean everyone nearby. Amara's magic had started to extend beyond the campus grounds, inching toward the businesses and neighborhoods, locking unaware people in a magical ocean.

The relief in every mind struck with this euphoric calm. I'd done it. I'd removed every single drop of arcane magic from The True Witch. I'd saved everyone's life. I'd stopped the worst possible outcome from coming to be. An unknown outcome. A horrible possibility created by the Celestial Coven and Theodore Whitlock.

I turned back to him, to Amara, and prepared myself for the next necessary evil. Taking a life shouldn't feel this easy. Snuffing out someone wicked shouldn't come with such a righteous high. Yet I couldn't hide the satisfaction radiating off my thoughts. I wanted them dead. For what they'd done, what they still wanted to do with each ticking second, and what they'd continue doing if someone showed mercy.

"I'll carry the burden of taking justice into my own hands." I balled my fists, wrapping telekinesis around each of their throats so I could steal the breath of their lives.

Theodore cackled. "How gracious of you."

"*I won't die here.*" Amara's thoughts held the same French accent she used everywhere but slipped into a different dialect with a deeper and darker tone.

I wanted to unravel her secrets, learn who The True Witch really was behind the mask she'd worn over the centuries, but The Sisters Three didn't hold the answers in their memories, not the ones I'd glossed over, and I sincerely doubted they managed to withhold pertinent intel after my demands.

"Looks like you get to carry those secrets to your grave," I whispered, tightening the grip of my telekinesis.

"Too bad," Theodore gasped, struggling to speak but struggling even more to think with the gnarled tree of his inner core fractured. "It's...a... good...secret."

Amara triggered her tattoos, protective sigils which interacted with the broken enchantments across Gemini Academy.

"Time to go, Theodore." Several of Amara's tattoos flickered in this erratic but rhythmic pattern before purple smoke whirled around her and Theodore, stealing the two of them away from my grasp and out of range of my telepathy.

"No," I shouted.

Had they left the city? Left this plane of reality?

I turned to Gladiatrix, who'd begun helping people to their feet. I wanted to call out to her, demand she break through the smoky portal door The True Witch must've accessed in her escape. Gladiatrix had done something similar when bursting through Ernesto's warp portal. Speaking of Ernesto, his mind had vanished, too. All of Theodore's warlock crew members had disappeared. I scanned the crowd as everyone slowly collected their bearings. *Nowhere.* Darla, Vincent, and Ernesto were nowhere to be found.

"*The enchantments...*" Katherine's mind soared above the others. "*How do I stop this?*"

She studied the activated enchantments lining the auxiliary gym. Not activated. So much more according to the growing concern in Katherine's thoughts as she shouted at everyone around her to brace for an attack.

What?

Each sigil lining the academy glowed brighter, fueled and filled with explosive magics that The True Witch left behind as she escaped.

I swallowed hard, lost in the sea of frantic minds without a life raft to help. There was so much terror. I couldn't turn it off. My telepathy couldn't help here. I couldn't stop this explosion.

One by one, the enchantments detonated, carrying a powerful burst of fire and debris. Industry pros followed Gladiatrix and Enchanter Diaz's leads as they created telekinetic barriers over as many people as they could.

Those with branches like Melanie used their control over the elements to block or redirect the fiery destruction, while others with branches like Yaritza used the sheer destructive power of their magic to stop the explosions in their path.

Jamius summoned so many duplicates that he became his own explosion of protective copies meant to shield stragglers.

King Clucks and Gael shouted with a furious duet that carried their telekinesis in waves of early morning crows, bombarding and smothering the rampant fire.

Caleb channeled telekinesis to shield those nearby, and Katherine flew behind him, wrapping her arms around his chest and syncing their casting frequency. This enhanced Caleb's range and control, allowing for stronger barriers of telekinetic energy.

Layla leapt to her cousin's side, shielding them from the destruction, only for Vik to finally master Jamie Novak's whirlpool magic. They summoned the swirl of teleporting water with Tia beside them, signing an invocation meant to reinforce the copy of Jamie's arcane branch. Emmanuel, the final member of their trio, held each of his coven mates by the shoulder and poured every ounce of luck he had into them. As a team, they dragged damn near fifty people through a watery portal to safety.

Kenzo and Gael hugged, creating a telekinetic barrier enhanced by the hexed disruption that shielded them and everyone in their vicinity.

Tara lashed out with shadowed whips in every direction, sealing people with protective golden hues or transforming them into momentarily intangible beings.

Carter pulled Jennifer into an embrace, pressing his hands to her face and whispering something I couldn't hear, something my telepathy had waned during, missing the brief exchange.

Jennifer nodded, anxiously standing closer to Carter. Their heartbeats thrummed so loudly in their minds that it became the only sound in the scattered explosions across campus. Seconds of nervous heartbeats until Carter leaned forward and pressed his lips against Jennifer's.

The two shared their first kiss amidst the devastation. Their connection, their understanding of each other's frequencies, their emotional bond synced their casting. Actually, it did so much more. It harmonized their branch magics, allowing Jennifer to absorb Carter's vitality and cast it outward in waves of emotional radiance meant to empower everyone in the auxiliary gym with confidence and belief and hope.

It seemed nearly every person unleashed their magics, protecting themselves and others around them from the rapid explosions that leveled the entire academy.

I stood alone, lost in the confusion, and so damn tired. The continuous channeling of so much magic made me drowsy. Making a barrier to protect myself seemed pointless. It was work I didn't have the strength or focus for.

My breathing hitched. I wasn't the only one up here on the stage. *Milo!* I needed to find the will to create a barrier and shield him. I needed to… My knees buckled, and I wobbled forward.

"*Dorian.*" Milo leapt toward me, sweeping me into his embrace as we spun round and round. "*I won't let anything ever happen to you.*"

He hugged me tightly, ignoring the pain of the beating he'd taken while unconscious. Ignoring the still delicate inner core that held his broken psychic magic. Ignoring the fates of everyone else that he worried deeply about. In this moment, he didn't care about any of that as much as he cared about me. His love boomed so loudly that it drowned out the world of thoughts, offering me a reprieve from the chaos.

Milo was my life jacket in the storm. I loved him with every breath I took.

I squeezed Milo in return, holding his back gently to avoid the bruising and resting my head on his shoulder as we twirled in the fiery destruction, shielded by telekinesis.

Chapter Twenty-Five

"**THAT'S** right, Trish, the Global Guild already called Enchanter Evergreen away again," Guild Master Campbell said with a sweet, playful laughter. The type of giddy bullshit her PR team expressed would improve her numbers with audience polls since some still questioned her leadership at Cerberus Guild.

She was on the other side of the fucking city, and yet her aggravation for this sweetheart attitude she adopted despite finally sitting at the top reached out and squeezed my chest. It spread like heat, furious and ready to explode.

I wanted to explode, too. Then I grimaced at my thoughts—tacky considering what'd just happened to the academy. My telepathy reached far and wide, so I quelled my branch as I drove to Milo's place. Listening to this station might've been a bad choice, but music grated my eardrums, and silence made the thoughts of strangers easier to absorb.

Guild Master Campbell continued her interview, addressing the great Enchanter Evergreen's absence from the public eye as he worked on a new, secret case. There wasn't a secret case. Unless privately recovering from an assault was the case. That was why I'd grabbed some extra clothes, a few creature comforts, some groceries, and headed back to Milo's place.

I refused to let him recover alone, refused to leave him alone. In the days that followed the attack on the city, I'd spent them with Milo. And it was an attack on the city. Sure, the Celestial Coven and Theodore Whitlock only landed their strikes on the MDC and Gemini Academy, but it wasn't for a lack of effort on their part. Part of me worried that any second, the pair would swoop in and finish what they'd started.

Squeezing the steering wheel firmly, I reminded myself there wasn't a single place in Chicago they could creep through without my telepathy catching sight. Yes, I couldn't keep exact insight of the millions of minds in the city, couldn't hear them clearly, but the familiar ones, the ones I cared about, the ones I knew personally, the ones I hated, they rang louder among the crowd.

It actually helped zeroing in on someone like Campbell halfway across the city. Sure, my telepathy stretched everywhere, but stepping in close to a singular person was like dropping a psychic pin that steadied the erratic onslaught of thoughts buzzing throughout the city.

"It was truly an honor to lead the guild teams in this collaborative effort to restore order at the MDC," Campbell said, pulling my attention back to her careful answers. "Honestly, it's just further proof of the amazing talent and independence Chicago's industry witches possess."

After everything that'd happened, the way the events unfolded, the demand for answers was huge, and everyone clamored for a seat front and center to address the public. Of course, Campbell ensured she led the pack on assuaging fears.

"Well, with the assistance of the Global Guild," Trisha said, in some not-so-subtle attempt to turn the discussion toward Gladiatrix and Enchanter Diaz, who were still in the city but out of the public eye, much like Milo.

"Yes, the Global Guild *helped*," Campbell said, pausing heavily on the word and adding doubt to the meaning for everyone listening—and it worked. Thoughts percolated in this questioning suspicion for how much Chicago actually required the Global Guild's *help*. "But to think, the strongest organization in the world still wanted or needed us when resolving this mission. An investigation that affected the entire world, and we witches of Chicago brought it to an end."

I rolled my eyes. Campbell was one more leading answer away from dropping the stats on fatalities. Admittedly, casualties remained fairly low at the MDC despite the devastation unleashed. And even though Gemini Academy had been attacked by demons, by warlocks, by corrupted enchantments that leveled the entirety of the school grounds, no one was killed except for the inmates Theodore had dragged there and sacrificed to fiends. And The Sisters Three, who I'd executed with my own hands.

Hands that shook as I drove. The high that came from casting absolute judgment had faded and been replaced by something else. It wasn't guilt. It wasn't good, though, either.

And while Campbell boasted about the tremendous success of how events played out at Gemini Academy, I thought about the single email the leadership board had issued. Cancelled until further notice, more news to come, hope that everyone took this time to peacefully recover.

There was a real need to recover too. Emotionally and physically. None of the staff and students had been killed, but plenty were injured. Still, what a miracle they'd lived. Everyone had lived. Milo had lived. I'd lived.

"How's your evening, Mr. Frost?" One of the attendants at Milo's building immediately went to work when I drove up, pulling me from dwelling thoughts.

It'd become a familiar routine of me grumbling some greeting, handing a valet my keys, nodding politely as I went inside, and then taking the elevator to the penthouse floor at the top.

"Howdy, Mister Dorian, sir." Ben swung the door open the second the elevator dinged like he'd stood watch for my arrival. And he had, using a sentinel of security that kept his warding barrier on the front door every time I stepped out of the place.

"You can just call me Dorian."

"Of course, Dorian." Ben smiled, snickering to himself about silly, bubbly thoughts that didn't make much sense with all their bright colors.

"Did you eat while I was out?" I eyed the chocolate smeared around the corner of his lips.

"No," Ben replied, helping add his telekinesis to the bags I floated inside.

I wanted to comment about him using his magic unlicensed, the fines applicable, but he had enough weighing on his thoughts. Plus, his casting was flawless for such a small child. It was tragic, the way everything had clicked for him when The True Witch locked him in that ocean for so long, days, weeks, rotting in his mind. Now, he continued working to hone his root magics and his branch.

"What'd you do while I was out?" I asked, slowly trying to find a way to broach the topic of Ben's need to shield the penthouse when I left.

Seeing Milo return from battle had given the kid the briefest relief before panic and sadness immediately replaced those feelings. Fear inflated in Ben's mind when he saw the bruises on Milo's body, the sling he wore for his dislocated shoulder, the medical enchantments he had bandaged over so many big bruises. It seemed we both believed Milo was impervious to harm until the assault on Gemini Academy, until The True Witch.

"I dunno." Ben brushed a hand through his messy sky-blue hair, forever changed by the extreme casting of his ward branch.

"You know, I was talking to the security outside while having a smoke because the weather's finally bearable, you know?"

"You should stop that."

"Talking to security?"

"No," Ben whined.

"Talking in run-on sentences?"

"Nooooo," Ben whined louder, then frowned, then huffed, and finally rolled his eyes.

"Anyway," I said with a half-smile, enjoying Ben's aggravation because it'd pulled his thoughts away from fear. "They were going on and on about all these intricate wards they have over the building. Like I could not keep up with any of it. Apparently, there's this multifaceted level of protection that not only shields the building but extends with extra barriers per room, then there's this command that contacts local authorities—who you know just rush over, have you seen this place?—and there's defense and attack protocols written into each of the wards, the enchantments, the I don't even know. Just so much protection here in the building. Top-tiered security to keep everyone completely safe."

"Sounds commlicated." Ben pretended not to care, not to worry, but he wondered if the layers of protection were as sophisticated as the ones his daddy used to brag about. He wondered if they were as strong as his mommy's metal armored warding over her body. He wondered if this penthouse even paled in comparison to the complex wards his town of Harmony Valley used. The same wards that didn't stop The True Witch from sneaking into their home and killing everyone.

The idea of Milo dying flitted along Ben's bubbled thoughts. The fear of seeing it pinched at his heart. It tugged at mine, too, making it stutter. The fear of dying, really dying, hit him like a boulder, devastating and inescapable.

"You don't ever have to worry about that," I blurted, unable to subtly shift the conversation, to guide it so Ben would open up naturally. All I wanted was to sweep away this terror that coiled around his every thought.

"Use your telemathy for that?" Ben stared with wide eyes.

"Yeah." I chuckled. "Sorry about that."

"It's okay. I use my magic without asking, too." Ben paused. "I like to put up a barrier sometimes. Before bedtime. When Milo isn't here. When… when you're not here."

"You don't ever have to worry about The True Witch," I said. "I would never allow her to touch you again."

I wouldn't allow her to harm anyone I cared about. I'd track her down the second my magic had fully healed.

Ben's thoughts stirred to the raccoon-eyed dragon guy that spit fire at the ocean and killed the water with flames.

"You know, my branch will always wash away the ocean." I knelt so my eyes met Ben's. "I know that arcane branch is scary, but my telepathy is badass."

Ben smirked at the 'whoopsie' word, reminded of how his mommy would say more whoopsie words when his daddy was at work. Then he thought about how scared his parents looked when the ocean hit them first when all their eyes saw was water.

"But what if the ocean comes back when you're not here?" Ben asked in a whisper. "You can't always be here."

How I wanted to lie and say I could be here whenever he needed me, but I didn't know how things would change in the coming weeks. Soon, the administration would have an official decision on how to handle the loss of Gemini Academy; I was certain I'd end up working over the summer or online or something creative and exhausting to make up for the lost learning time. God, I couldn't even think about that can of worms right now as it opened up a whole new set of headaches. My students… How were they handling this?

"You're right," I said, feeling defeated.

Not the same defeat I felt when The Sisters Three had attacked, not the aching desperation to fall into my subconscious and disappear, but I did struggle to meet Ben's gaze. I didn't have an answer that would erase his all-consuming fear, fear that'd evolved into terror, terror that would soon swell into dread, dread that'd eat away at the last embers of joy that burned in this kid's heart.

Milo or Finn would know what to say. Even if they didn't, they had this enthusiasm, this joy, that carried people through the worst of bad news and kept them afloat. I'd never been like that. I scoffed, wondering how many of my personas had that type of positivity.

My personas.

They were asleep for the most part, declaring they didn't need or require the return of magic to the subconscious. They had their shadows, they rested as the universe intended, and they believed I was finally ready to handle the full force of my telepathy.

But there was one who would gladly accept a piece of my magic, who would offer kind words, who would help because I'd made him to be the best friend I never found as a young kid.

"I'm gonna do something strange." I scrunched my face. "It's a psychic thing."

"Like something Mr. Milo would do?"

"No, sort of a telepathy psychic thing."

"Oh."

I gestured with a single raised finger. "Hold, please."

Which was ridiculous since time stilled to a damn near halt once I nose-dived through my inner core down into the shadows of my subconscious.

It'd changed since my last visit, no longer a land of solid, locked darkness, but more of a murky waterless sea. I floated, drifted, swam through the abyss. Without my magic lurking in this place, it'd become a lot like other subconscious minds.

This place was infinite, endless, but I snapped off a tiny fragment of magic, allowing the purple light to guide me in the dark. This wasn't some simple piece of magic I'd tossed aside. No, I'd conjured it with a directive to find the one persona I knew could definitely help Benjamin.

Weaving around other slumbering personas, the light finally reached the small boy who helped shield me from a big scary world with a goofy smile and a silly story for any occasion.

"Dorian." Nico's face lit up as his eyes glowed purple from the restoration of magic I'd offered. "How can I help you?"

"Not me. Well, I mean sort of me because I don't know what to say to someone else who is actually the person you're gonna help. Maybe. Sort of. Whatever. It's probably a bad idea."

"Words are difficult to find sometimes." Nico nodded in this annoyingly kind way. "Searching for the right words can be a lot of fun, though. It's like a treasure hunt for happiness. If you find the right words, you can make someone's day brighter."

"Ugh." I shook my head. "How'd you come from my brain?"

"Just lucky, I guess." Nico led the way out of the abyss, and we leapt back into the world.

When we jumped out of my thoughts, time had barely passed.

"So," I fumbled for the words. "I'd like to show you something if you're okay with me using my branch."

Ben stared silently, even his thoughts were whispers. Then he nodded. "Okay."

"This is Nico." I gestured to my persona who I'd linked to Benjamin's mind. "He's a persona of mine."

Ben listened intently to the explanation behind personas, how they had a piece of my magic, how they were created with singular purpose, a purpose that differed depending on the emotions and traits they'd absorbed. I did my best to break it down for a little kid minds since his thoughts fluttered with confusion at my initial explanations.

"But I can't do the raccoon-eyed dragon guy stuff," Nico said, revealing he saw the image and wonder floating at the top of Ben's surface thoughts. "Not that I don't wish I could. How amazingly amazing would that be?"

"The most amazing," Ben answered.

"But he is connected to me, meaning I can see through his eyes if I ever need to check in," I said. "Nico and I are linked, and if he's hanging out in your head, then we're linked. Sort of."

"Basically, if any scary witches show up, throwing oceans out, or anything bad, I can alert Dorian the second it happens," Nico clarified.

"You can?"

"Totally. I'd send a message through the psychic link and BAM!" Nico made a big whooshing sound. "Dorian would show up breathing fire until the water or anything else bad just vanished. POOF!"

Nico put on a very dramatic reenactment of how he assumed I'd arrive to battle.

"And even though we're linked, connected by magic, he's still his own person-ish. Persona, yeah," I explained or tried as I felt the muscles of my face contort into this perplexed expression. "His thoughts are mostly his own—along with the quirks—but I guess they're sort of mine in this weird not but are kind of way."

"Telemathy is confusing."

"Oh, most definitely! The most confusing," Nico said. "If there was a crown for confusing magics, Dorian would have a million and five crowns."

"Wouldn't I just have a really big crown?" I asked, rolling my eyes at his logic.

"No. A big crown wouldn't fit. You just have a bunch of crowns," Nico said with an exasperated sigh. "Because you're a bunch of confusing."

Whatever ridiculous logic Nico used seemed to work as a way to ease

Ben, to distract him from his own fears.

"So, I'll just be hanging out when you need me," Nico said with a happy nod.

"Really?" Ben asked with excitement.

"For realio." Nico smiled. "And when you're ready to say goodbye, I'll just head on out."

Ben scrunched his face into a sour frown at that. He didn't like to say goodbyes, something Nico registered right away, something I also caught since Ben had to say a lot of goodbyes recently. Farewells without actually saying goodbye to the people he loved most in this world.

Nico would help. He was a persona created to be the friend anyone needed, the guiding hand when the world was just too big.

I wasn't sure how long Ben would be in my life, but if the thoughts I'd gleaned from Milo were any indication, he didn't plan on sending the kid away or leaving him to deal with the future alone. Ben had lost everything he'd ever known, and Milo wanted to ensure that he found a few new joys on the shifting paths of potentials that'd presented themselves.

After spending the evening watching television with Ben, I read him like five damn stories before bed—because he refused to close his eyes after a story had ended and insisted on only being able to sleep if he dozed off mid-sentence to a new tale. It was a sucker's deal that kept me reading for almost two hours. Thankfully, the kid finally passed out, and I joined Milo in his bedroom. My beautiful boyfriend had slept away the day, and now he slept away the evening.

The blankets were twisted and knotted and bundled around Milo's muscular thighs. He'd completely stripped off the covers, which wasn't surprising considering the sheen sweat on his brow as he snoozed. I continued playing with the thermostat, but it never seemed just right, not perfect for him while he recovered.

Milo rolled over partially. Even asleep, he moved cautiously because of the injuries that seized him if he lay the wrong way. Every time I saw the massive bruise that covered the left side of his face, I receded into myself, barely able to look. The busted lip, the scratch along his sharp jawline, the way his eye had nearly swollen closed. The only thing that kept it at bay was the tiny symbols stitched under his cheek and above his eyebrow. They were meant mostly to heal the detached retina but helped alleviate other damage.

I wished Milo would've stayed in the hospital, would've rested entirely, but he insisted on coming back to the penthouse. Which made sense, his concern about leaving Benjamin with acolytes for the week, leaving the kid unaware and frightened.

But right now, the only thing I worried about was Milo. I hadn't moved fast enough. Theodore had done so much damage. That motherfucker had beaten Milo while he was locked in an unconscious state. He attacked him just to say he could. And I hadn't stopped it soon enough.

Milo's entire torso was black and blue with patches of greenish-yellow. The sigils worked to mend his broken ribs, which meant his poor body had to endure the bruising, the pain, while slowly healing in stages. Steps. Slow steps.

I wanted to kiss away the pain. I wanted to fix his body as quickly as I'd undone the damage in his head. Not all the damage. No, Milo dwelled deep in his thoughts and organized the visions that'd been tossed about carelessly. All I'd managed was to repair the broken inner core and the shattered memories.

Most nights, he slept so soundly that even his dreams were quiet, but sometimes, like tonight, he tinkered with the layers of his inner core, pretending to recover. He deluded himself into thinking I couldn't tell. Even if my telepathy hadn't grown a hundred-fold, I'd know.

"You know, if I wanted, I could drag you out of your inner core and make you go back to sleep," I whispered as Milo lightly snored, playing innocent. Okay, not playing because his body was actually asleep while a piece of his conscious mind made mental repairs. "Let me fix this at the very least."

I tugged the blanket out from the vise grip Milo's thighs had and then delicately wrapped him back up in the covers.

Milo moaned, turning onto his side and cuddling with the closest pillow.

"That poor little pillow never stood a chance." I shook my head at the death squeeze Milo used to crush the stuffed plush in his arms. The dislocation in his shoulder still ached, but not as much as the broken bones.

Carefully, I slipped into the bed and scooted in close behind Milo. I pressed my crotch against his butt, pushed my knees behind his legs, and positioned myself lower so my arms wrapped at his waist where the aches wouldn't disturb him. There was less bruising at his waist than the rest of his torso. When we spooned like this, with my head pressed to the center of his back and our bodies touching, Milo slept so much better.

Maybe I slept better. I took comfort in helping Milo, being with Milo, even in small ways.

With my schedule more flexible in the wake of so much devastation, I used a lot of free time to quietly cuddle up to Milo. I offered him soft whispers while he worked. I gently awoke him when he needed to eat, to take his medicine, to bathe away the grime of sickness. I would stay here and tend to him forever if he required. I would do anything for Milo.

"I love you. I promise I will always protect you." I kissed his back right in the center, and then I returned my head to rest against him. Against the warm, soft skin. "And yes, I know that's your line, but I can occasionally pull off the heroic hero stuff."

"I like it," Milo said, groggy and sore and definitely in need of more rest. "We gotta get you a cape, make it official."

"Rest, please." I scooted up and kissed his shoulder gently as both still throbbed with burning pain.

"I'm fine." Milo turned his head, giving me a weak smile. "Besides, I gotta start working on your heroic comeback. Emphasis on the cum."

I snorted. "You're insufferable."

"We'll start your campaign by bringing back the sexy stage name: The Ubiquitous Present."

"Christ. You obviously have more head damage than I realized."

Milo laughed, wincing and wheezing from the strain of his muscles moving from the joy that swelled inside him. I nuzzled the crook of his neck, kissing him. It offered the tiniest distraction from the pain, from the stress, from the surrealness of events that'd unfolded over the last few days.

We lay like this until I finally passed out, until all that remained was Milo and me until the sound of the entire world fell silent. Milo continued proving he was the world, my world.

Chapter Twenty-Six

IT'D been two weeks, midway into April, and Gemini Academy had issued the lowest form of a stopgap in regard to the lack of a building. We'd moved to online classes. Not remote learning, not virtual classes, but simply teachers posting assignments online and students making their "best efforts" during this difficult time. And I didn't want to hold anyone to the same expectations as I had before the attack on the academy, but I also didn't approve of how administration had dropped the bar. Not even lowered it. Oh no, they'd dropped it completely on the ground and started kicking dirt over it.

This was equivocally an extended early vacation that'd completely screwed up the education of our students. At least the third-year students were still able to report to their internships, and first-years would have a chance to make up for this lost time. But what about second-year students? What was my homeroom coven going to do? It was hard enough getting guilds and enchanters to take individual accommodations seriously when setting up internships. But it was fucking laughable to think they'd make accommodations for the entire student body.

Sure, guilds might promise they would, but then the news would die down, and the immediate tragedy of the events would pass—maybe something new and awful would land on national headlines—and people would return to their lives unable to really care about a situation that didn't personally affect them. I already heard thoughts across the city falling back into place for normalcy.

With my telepathy already soaring every which way, I used this time to check in on my homeroom coven. I couldn't rein in my psychic magic if I wanted, so this seemed like a helpful way to assuage my concerns.

The first psychic pin I dropped was with Katherine and Caleb while he lay out on the couch, and she rifled through the pages of a grimoire in the center of the floor. For a living room, it was nearly as spacious as Milo's penthouse layout and a reminder that the Harris family had a lot of income thanks to the success of their enchantment company.

Katherine had eight grimoires of different sizes and bindings spaced around her. Delicately, she used tools to unravel the pages and cut them from the spines. She kept stacks of pages in an arrangement of various piles meant for storage, clutter, sentimental, and her new grimoire. Sentimental because even the silly spells she'd written as a kid couldn't be tossed out. She'd never use the crayon sharpening spell, but she fondly recalled how proud she was of that wordy little wonder.

Right now, though, she wanted to pull from her old, mostly unused grimoires to recreate the one she'd sacrificed during the attack on the showcase.

"This makes absolutely zero sense." Caleb huffed, becoming visibly frustrated with some of the online assignments he worked on.

One glimpse into Caleb's aggravated thoughts revealed the shitty classwork he contended with. Talk about teachers who dropped the ball. I spent hours modifying lesson plans to help account for the fact no one could really ask questions or work with their peers. Some teachers simply copied and pasted their original assignments without an ounce of forethought—like, say, the fact it required using a classroom textbook that students didn't have access to anymore, but it didn't seem to deter Caleb, who used every online search engine to read up on the information.

Caleb was sprawled out on the couch, lying on his stomach with the laptop in front of him, while he kicked his legs back and forth. The kicks were meant for training, but his strides got more aggressive, and his muscles flexed harder than intended, so Katherine swooped in and snatched away his weighted training blocks.

She looked at the erratic pulsating glow of her carved enchantments and knew her boyfriend was a few kicks away from breaking another set.

"Sorry." Caleb grimaced.

It seemed like a disservice now, minimizing the assignments I'd posted since I didn't want to stress all the students on my roster. Caleb found himself breezing through entire units, which left him stagnant. Having finished his work, he rolled over and sat up, telekinetically grabbing his bag of books. Not to be confused with his book bag, also filled with texts. No, no, no. Caleb sported a new tote bag Katherine had gotten him that easily held ten books, and he'd managed to wedge over twenty in it.

Not satisfied with his classwork and a bit burnt out on his casting research, Caleb moved on to a passion project. He flipped through his notebook to a page where he'd sketched The True Witch.

I shuddered at her image, even if the likeness lacked, I synced to the tiny recollections Caleb held for her arrival, her attack. He'd only seen her for a few seconds before the world turned into water, before he couldn't breathe or think or fight.

But he'd seen enough to draw her hat, her dress, the bone staff. Though he didn't catch the glyphs tattooed on her, and he made her hair impossibly long, reaching her ankles.

The eyes had this startling gaze, where they seemingly followed everything in the room. Caleb drew them exactly as they were: vibrant green—the only part of his sketch he'd colored in.

It was a topic many minds from Gemini Academy lingered on. The news didn't discuss The True Witch. Every media outlet simply pretended she didn't exist. The authorities and guild professions simply acted as if the attack had been fully resolved. Yes, they publicly admitted to Theodore Whitlock's escape, how he now fled the city, probably the nation, but if

The True Witch came up in discussion, the topic was skirted. Avoided. A subject no one wanted to have, so everyone pretended she wasn't real. Still, she silently haunted memories, even the students who hadn't seen her appear on the stage beside Theodore Whitlock, who hadn't seen her and The Sisters Three shatter the mind of the great Enchanter Evergreen, held fear for the ocean that nearly swept them away.

Milo's collapse flashed through Caleb's thoughts, repeating again and again and again, hitting me with a gut punch of guilt until he finally buried images with research, focusing his mind on something different. Something he could offer help on.

"You know, I don't think it's actually a psychic branch," Caleb said, running through his notes before opening a book and flipping through the heavily annotated pages.

"Huh?" Katherine asked, attention still fixated on the order of arrangement she wanted for her new spell book.

"I think it's an arcane branch," he explained, catching Katherine up on where his brain had darted. "The way she summoned the water into people's heads, that was real. All the sensations, and yes, psychics can add sensory details, manipulate perception, but there was this heat, a light, a flash of something…I don't know, cosmic? Primal? Ward? No. Definitely a primal element, though, because of the water. But then another branch to transport it. And of course, the psychic element to invade minds…"

Katherine nodded to Caleb's rambling theories as he accurately assessed the three branches utilized by The True Witch's arcane magic. To think he arranged these puzzle pieces with such little information. He'd make an amazing enchanter someday.

"You're still on this?" she asked.

"Well, it's important."

"Yeah, and important enchanters are probably already deciphering things."

"I just wanted to help." Caleb shrugged.

"Here I figured you were just avoiding your feelings or thoughts on a certain confrontation during the attack." Katherine side-eyed Caleb. "With

Kenzo."

"What?" Caleb tensed. "We didn't fight."

"Exactly. You fought together, had a bromance moment, and now you're pretending it didn't happen while researching some mysterious threat."

"Do you actually think it was a moment?" Caleb bit his lip, desperately avoiding the topic—even in his thoughts. He didn't want to dream about the idea of having Kenny back in his life, didn't know what it meant, didn't want to face another letdown.

"You know, that weirdo witch lady seemed like a psychic to me." Katherine shrugged, noticing Caleb's inability to handle the annoying Kenzo-shaped elephant in the room. "Psychics can do a lot with even seemingly basic magics. Look at what Mr. Frost did?"

"*Huh?*" Caleb and I thought at the same time.

"You know, using his telepathy to remove the bizarro brain water stuff."

And like that, Caleb's mind weaved away from worries and back toward wonders. "You think that was Mr. Frost?"

I hadn't told anyone I'd been the one to remove Oceanic Collapse. Everyone was so deeply entrenched in their own battle for survival that they hadn't seen or felt my actions.

"Who else could've done it?" Katherine casually mused, piecing together intricate ideas about how my branch worked, how it must've pierced through the other psychic magic, estimating vital variables with a whim, then went back to her project without missing a beat.

"I guess I just thought the woman who attacked everyone overexerted herself." Caleb furrowed his brow, adding new notes on the casting capabilities of The True Witch, wondering what the full level of her channeling range was.

I'd also like to know her channeling limitations. They weren't infinite, that much I knew, and without her bone staff, she'd lost a lot of her seemingly immeasurable power.

"Hmmm." Caleb hummed along with Katherine who'd started singing a mnemonic device that she used to use as a child when memorizing the steps required for creating a properly functional grimoire. The song in Caleb's maze of a mind made his thoughts fuzzy, but he continued taking notes on The True Witch while writing a separate note in the corner of the page.

Telepathy Range?

He circled it and underlined it several times as a reminder to revisit his curiosities about Mr. Frost's psychic magic.

I kept close as the two of them worked separately, content being in the same space. I found myself drawn to the other minds across Chicago that worried about The True Witch's magic, about her return, about the ocean that lingered in their nightmares.

If I continued training my telepathy, truly mastering it, I would be able to find her no matter where she'd gone underground. I'd make certain of that.

Gael sat on the floor of his bedroom crisscrossed while he played a video game. The headphones he wore to chat with his gaming team matted down his spiky hair, something he still kept up with even if he'd allowed his dark brown roots to grow out.

Based on the rips on the furniture of his bedroom, I gauged that he preferred scratching up the hardwood floors. Honestly, the tears paled in comparison to Charlie and Carlie's claws of destruction for everything I owned, but I understood how it was something Gael was self-conscious about. Always worried if he didn't watch his every breath, it might hurt someone or something.

Though that protective overthinking didn't concern him now. Kenzo lay on Gael's bed, reading a book. His legs hung off the edge and wrapped over Gael's broad, spiked shoulders like Kenzo was hugging him with his feet. He wasn't, though. They were training Gael's observational skills even in this casual, affectionate way.

Gael had to be completely self-aware of each of his spikes, redistributing them elsewhere as Kenzo occasionally shifted his position, brushing the heel of his foot one way or the other. It was impossible to remove the sharp prick of the spikes, but he could change their size and location with proper focus. Even the ones that seemed to have vanished from his arms had simply shrunk so small they were basically the tiny, hairlike barbs found beneath the larger spikes of a cactus.

"Oh my fucking god, you stupid dumb bitch just shot your load for nothing."

My face fell flat, baffled by how Gael shouted at his game.

"Get fucked, poser. Coming…coming…coming. Gotcha." He shook his head, no fury, just this bizarre cathartic satisfaction. "Looky looky at your little buddy out for my ass. He's not getting it."

I couldn't place it. I'd never seen him like this.

"Yeah, bitch. Came up right behind you and fucked you," Gael growled. "Thought you were something, didn't you? This punk ass team's got nothing."

Wow. This was… I had no words. I'd seen Gael play classroom games, always so happy and giddy for everyone involved. I'd seen him play games on his phone, always so polite and quiet. Right now, his thoughts raged in the mayhem, delighting in the war his team fought. I'd never believed it was possible for someone who spent his every waking minute at school finding ways to cheer up others could also relish in the blood of his victims. Granted, these victims were on a screen and pixilated, but goddamn.

"Get it out of your system, porcupine," Kenzo said, his surface thoughts adding a bit of context to the stress release Gael found when gaming. "Start saying your goodbyes to your basement-dwelling loser friends."

"What're you talking about?" Gael tilted his head back, then jerked right back to the screen. "Not you. What're you doing walking in like that? Back in formation. Shot. Shit. Shoot. Shoot!"

"You've got ten minutes left of gaming."

"That's a school rule." Gael jabbed the controller buttons, thinking profanities in English and Spanish. "School's out for like ever. Maybe. I dunno."

"You don't know because your brain is turning to mush." Kenzo thudded Gael's chest lightly with the heel of his foot. "School might be out, but learning never is. Where'd you put that book you were reading?"

"I dunno." Gael stared at the screen. "Get him. Fucking missed. Where's he at?"

"Gael, if I have to look through your junk…"

"It's not here." He huffed. "Not you. Focus!" Gael craned his neck, Adam's apple bulging as he locked eyes with Kenzo. "It was in my locker at the academy, which is now poof."

"You should've just said that to begin with, porcupine." Kenzo scoffed. "You're so damn difficult."

"You're one to talk." Gael snarled into his microphone, then muted himself to avoid further confusion. "I see you're still not mentioning how you buddied up with Caleb, buried the hatchet—and shockingly not in his head—but like, did you?"

"Excuse you?"

"I'm just saying, I didn't hear an 'I'm sorry' during that demon fight. And Kitty Kat keeps me up to date."

"One, she doesn't know shit."

"Yet, you call her know-it-all."

"Two, why would I apologize?"

"Do you really wanna have this conversation?"

Kenzo didn't reply.

Gael had this obnoxious ability to pry out Kenzo's feelings, his words, his unresolved everything. Kenzo had never experienced something so goddamn frustrating, and he loved it.

But right now, Gael used his skills to pick and poke, which tactically Kenzo admired. Overall, though, Kenzo also had an obnoxious ability over Gael, too. His being a way to center Gael's mind, show him alternative study styles, create habits that wouldn't give him a headache, and make him acknowledge how fucking smart he was.

"That's what I thought. I know I'm not that smart, but I know you're avoiding those unresolved issues, so maybe we don't mock me for being dumb enough to—"

"I didn't," Kenzo blurted. "I wasn't. I was…"

Kenzo struggled to find leisure reading that Gael enjoyed, but he wanted to keep Gael actively growing, even if he thought he was just having fun with a graphic novel. Everything he did was to encourage Gael. It hurt Kenzo, creating this painful pit in his stomach for how he worried about Gael, how he wanted to find ways to keep him smiling. Not simply smiling but smiling with pride in himself. He disliked how someone so clever, so considerate didn't think he was smart enough for his dreams.

I so rarely observed Gael's depression—his infectious optimism always shining brightly—that I forgot he still struggled with his self-worth like so many.

"Yeah, I'm back," Gael said into his headset.

Kenzo sat quietly, allowing Gael to sulk and game away his feelings, struggling to process his own. During a lull in the military murder game, Gael kissed Kenzo's knee with wet and sloppy lips that said sorry. And if Kenzo didn't catch that—which he did—Gael vocalized it.

"I'm sorry for being bratty." He turned off his game. "And no, this is not an apology to teach you how apologies work. How mean would that be? God, how big of a jerk am I for even thinking that? Like I wasn't *thinking* it, thinking it, but it crossed my mind, and if I thought it, you definitely probably maybe also thought it. And it was this awkward elephant in the room, but not a real one. A metaphorical elephant. I just got caught up in—"

"You're fine, love." Kenzo squeezed his legs tighter around Gael, a hug without hugging. An 'I love you' without saying it. Kenzo rarely used names, mostly just nicknames meant to hack down a person's self-worth to match Kenzo's state of being. But very rarely, he'd say love or pet or something else he found equally absurd because it made his heart beat faster seeing Gael get flustered and happy and speechless. God, how Kenzo loved when his talkative Gael was left speechless.

"What's the name of that book again?" Kenzo made a note to buy a new copy. "We can study something else. Maybe you can teach me how to—"

"Or, or, or! What if we replaced study time with an impromptu make out session?" Gael wiggled his eyebrows, hinting how he casually dropped a second vocab word. "I can do that thing with my tongue you like. You know when you pull—"

Kenzo leaned forward, his head upside down when he kissed Gael. "I'm just gonna take this make out time out of your future gaming time."

Gael quirked his brows, smirking with his shark-like teeth. "What if I did that other thing with my tongue that you really like?"

Kenzo smiled, something he often struggled to fight when basking in Gael's cheerful energy. Gael's orange aura radiated as he eagerly delighted in Kenzo's softer side, even if the sourpuss went right back to frowning before he pulled Gael into another kiss.

I drifted away, allowing them their privacy as I continued training my telepathy. It'd grown so much so soon, and if I kept this up I'd be ready for any threat. Any danger that dared step into Chicago.

"Damn." I shook away the last fragments of Kenzo's fury that fanned the flames of my own anger. Anger I held for The True Witch, for Theodore Whitlock, for anyone who threatened the happiness of the people I cared for.

My telepathy fluttered through the currents of summer heat kicking in a bit earlier than expected, even if it was nearly the end of April. Psychic energy rippled aimlessly like leaves dancing in the streets. Finally, I locked in on a familiar mind, a friendly mind, a mind I'd seen struggle with quiet anxiety for years now. A struggle that hit him the day he saved my life against all the odds.

But Carter wasn't nervous about whether or not his branch was good enough to help others. He'd finally grown past that trauma, that lingering fear that ate away at him, and now he fought his biggest, most threatening battle ever.

Christ, this kid's emotional state was a wreck of dramatic overthinking.

He'd kissed Jennifer. He'd finally told her how he felt. He'd reached out and offered every drop of his vitality to protect her from the explosion. And then they'd survived. They'd survived like everyone had survived. Now Carter didn't know what the fuck to do with himself, with his feelings, with his words, with his hands that fidgeted with the zipper of his jacket—a jacket he suddenly hated, feeling overdressed—as he walked to the table to meet Jennifer.

Bev's Pizza Palace was a spot where they loved to dine. Great food. Queer history tucked away in this hole-in-the-wall eatery that was filled with booths, scattered rainbow-clothed tables, and a variety of arcade games. Casual. Cool. And just a fun place to waste a lot of hours with a good friend.

"But are we even friends anymore?" Carter swallowed the lump stuck in his throat and took a seat. *"Can you be friends with someone you kissed? Sure. Maybe. Not if you still like them. Still lo… Jennifer's gonna be so pissed if I don't deal with these dread bunnies and the butterflies. Fuck, feelings suck."*

Jennifer sat across from Carter, her mind a blank slate, completely silent, which seemed skillful at first. I'd almost considered she'd mastered some new degree of psychic precision, but in actuality, her thoughts were quiet because her empathy magic stretched far and wide, linking and unlinking to everyone on the city block.

It kept her calm, clear-headed, too busy to think, to feel, to figure out whether or not Carter felt the same way for her.

"We were about to die." She pursed her lips into a frown over Carter's late arrival, and they ordered their meal. *"He only kissed me because he thought we were about to die. Dead. Gone. Fuck—how nice would that be right now? Did he mean what he said? Was it spur of the moment?"*

They didn't speak, they leapt through their thoughts, and they made the cringiest smiles as they avoided eye contact. Ugh. It was painful to watch. Almost as painful as the small talk Carter led with on the weather.

"Seriously?" I huffed to myself. "The weather? The most generic fucking thing ever."

I wanted to shake these two, to tell them how the other felt, but I just rolled my eyes and hoped for the best.

Jennifer strummed her fingers against the booth, ignoring her scorching hot pizza that'd arrived and fought to keep her words inside. She'd changed her nails, keeping them black with tiny little cartoony explosions artistically stenciled on. Really? Did she commemorate the destruction of Gemini Academy?

"Do you like me?" Jennifer blurted. "Like actually like me, or was that kiss just something to check off your bucket list before dying?"

"What? No." Carter coughed up the drink he'd taken. "No to the bucket list. Not no to the liking you. I do like you. A lot. Obviously, we're friends, right? But I also like you in an unfriendly way, too. No, I mean, in a non-friend way. In an 'I think about kissing you all the time' kind of way." Carter's entire face burned bright red, his cheeks so flushed it'd take hours for the color to fade.

Jennifer giggled, actually fucking giggled, at the sight. It always made her smile, seeing and feeling Carter's awkward confusion since he usually strutted through life carefree and confident. Yes, Jennifer felt the waves of panic he struggled with, and she was always there to offer support. But those feelings were different from shy embarrassment. And she'd know the subtle differences in every emotion as the expert empath.

"I also like you in an unfriendly way." Jennifer blushed. "Your annoying kissable face and all."

"Good, good." Carter sighed. "I guess I was overthinking it. 'Cause our first kiss was…"

"Hot?" Jennifer rocked her head from side to side. "You know, 'cause of the fiery death explosions going off everywhere."

Carter's face stretched into a thin smile, biting back a snicker.

"Too soon?" Jennifer batted her eyes.

"Yeah, no, um…I don't know. It was momentous, though." Carter held onto the word, momentous, having heard it a dozen times over when seeking advice on his kiss. "How do you go about following that up? If I wanna hold your hand, I'll have to fight a warlock first. If I wanna make out with you, I'll have to banish a demon."

"Awww." Jennifer sipped her drink from the straw. "You'd banish a demon just to make out with me?"

"I'd do anything for you." Carter clammed up.

His mind whirled with flashes of a conversation he'd had with Gael and Jamius about the topic, when the two boys who were self-proclaimed experts in the field of romance declared Carter had screwed up by making his first kiss with Gothic Barbie so grand.

Everything popped too quickly to track the fragments of memories but there were lots of lude gestures from Gael as he explained… Christ, I didn't want to know what he explained. And Jamius kept stacking duplicates in some cheerleading pyramid style which I could only assume was a Jenga analogy on romance that resulted in forty collapsing clones who ended up fighting in Carter's backyard.

"I don't know." Jennifer shrugged. "This is a pretty lowkey first date. I think it balances things out to normal."

"Date?" Carter buried his memories. "Right. This is a date. A casual date."

"Are you calling me casual, Preppy Prince?"

"Never, my Emo Queen." Carter leapt out of the booth and took a dramatic bow, dropping to one knee for the added flair.

It made Jennifer snort and laugh and let out this unhinged, wheezing giggle fit of delight. I'd never seen her so ridiculously happy. She looked as bizarre as me with a smile.

As they slipped into comfortable conversation that overlapped with their feelings, their hopes, their thoughts, I silently observed until my telepathy waned, and I was able to unwind for the night.

Tara used her telekinesis to decorate the pool enclosure. She wore a flower-patterned bikini top with a skirt bottom that reached her knees and had an open slit going up to her hip, which revealed a bit of a tattoo on her thigh. I scoffed, knowing that was definitely Gael's influence, and found myself almost drawn back to my other half, where another part of me actively battled against the kitchen stove in some futile effort to prove I could cook dinner.

Tara ignored her nerves, her thoughts about Theodore's escape, the whispers she'd heard everywhere she went. Not that she went to many places with Chicago on high alert and the academy closed. This party was a selfish distraction. It made her wonder if her father threw similar events to avoid his own anxiety over family drama.

At first, a small pool party seemed like an impossible feat. Who would want to go to a Whitlock party? After Theodore had once again caused so much destruction? Despite Tara's nerves, Gael assured her he had everything under control. Now, she found herself setting up for a gathering three times her initial estimates. How he managed, she'd never know, but she was grateful to always have Gael at her side.

While I shouldn't be excited for a bunch of seventeen-year-olds gathered together to drink and smoke and screw around while next to a dangerous body of water without adult supervision, I was admittedly a bit excited to see them all interact together.

I missed the talkative energy they brought into the classroom. I missed the curiosity in their surface thoughts. I even missed the ridiculously asinine questions some students would ask.

"So, are you just gonna be here lurking all night watching teen hotties strutting around in their half-naked bodies?"

Case in point.

Gael stared at the security guard posted at the door of the pool party. This wasn't the security at Milo's building, not that those attendants were lacking in skill, but this guard had biceps bigger than Gael's head. He had six visible knives strapped to his person and three guns and enough hidden pockets in his Kevlar jacket to probably hide a dozen others. Even his thoughts were difficult to read with the number of enchantment sigils and ward symbols tattooed on his skin.

Whitlock Estates was actually one of the most secure places in the entire city since Tara's father had hired private security after Theodore's escape. Muddled minds of several dozen elite witches buzzed at full attention as they patrolled the grounds. Seriously, half of them were fully armed with gear and gadgets and an arsenal of destructive weaponry and magic like the one Gael currently squinted at. These witches were former marines, navy seals, or ex-operatives of all kinds from across the world. Whitlock Industries spared no expense when buying a private army.

Tara folded her arms. "He'll be joining the rest of the little unit survey-ing the grounds outside."

"But your father said—"

"My father is out of the country and has left me in charge of the estate." Tara's expression shifted, almost stern, like she was channeling her inner Whitlock authority. "Besides, if a threat really managed to get all the way inside, past the thirty-some-odd magical military boys swinging their *guns* around, do you think you'll make a difference?"

"Ma'am, I assure you—"

"Leave now before you ruin my party."

He nodded and stepped out of the enclosure.

Gael side-eyed the guard. "You think I can take him?"

Tara giggled, continuing her final arrangements for the party.

"Bet I could take him." His mind shifted to wrestling moves he'd been practicing. "Pin him in under thirty seconds flat."

"That quick, huh?" Tara asked with a grin. "Thought fast was bad."

"Oh, you got jokes."

"And you have a checklist you're ignoring." Tara pointed, channeling her stern expression again, which folded almost the second her eyes met Gael's.

"Fine, fine, fine." He pouted and rushed off to help with the setup.

It didn't take long for students to start funneling inside. Kenzo arrived with Gael, who practically dragged him through the door. But once Gael turned his head for a minute to talk to someone, Kenzo had plastered him-self against the furthest wall.

Katherine arrived with Caleb at her side, literally directing him as he remained with his head buried in a book while carrying a tote bag slung over his shoulder. Not the new one he had, but the kind of bag one might bring for a day spent at the beach, not at a pool party, and he'd stuffed it to max capacity.

So many students showed up, I could barely keep track. It was difficult to hear thoughts, too, given the blaring music and loud as fuck voices. Anx-iety popped, and I followed.

Gael's heart hastened, pounding so hard his rooster fluttered off the pool floatie he rode and went to check on his human companion. When Gael's surprised expression shifted into disgust, King Clucks merely bawked with annoyance and returned to his swan floatie.

"Eeeeww, you seriously invited my ex?" Gael eyed Tara. "You dick."

"What?" Tara waved around the last few kegs to add the final party touches. "Aren't you and Tiff still doing that whole on-again-off-again thingy with your thingies?"

"I'm a sidepiece wonder, but I'm over that life." Gael shrugged. "I can't believe you're still buddy-buddy with her."

"I thought this was amicable. Didn't realize I had to pick sides." Tara sighed. "If you want me to shun her, I will. Easy. Done."

"No, no. Your Whitlock ice-outs hold weight, and on the off-chance Tiff and I reconcile, I don't need you turning her into a social pariah."

"You're making me sound like Layla." Tara bit back her aggravation, finding Layla's need to constantly punch down on others irritating. In fact, she noticed Layla latch onto Melanie and Amani the moment they walked into the party, circling the pool like sharks and sniffing out drama.

Some students certainly missed the angst in their day-to-day school routines.

"You're way worse than Layla," Gael said.

"What'd you just say?" Tara telekinetically shook a can of beer before handing it to Gael.

"I'm just saying, she works for the Queen Bee Top Bitch thing—which, good for her or whateves—but you just roll outta bed with the title." Gael cracked his beer tab. "Like not the bitch thing, though, with a little work, we can get you there. But the queen title? That just happens every time you walk into a room, crown waiting for you to claim it."

He tilted his can away, spraying bystanders with his beer, which Tara didn't realize he'd immediately suspected had been tampered with.

He wasn't wrong about Tara's title. It was something I'd noticed in the halls, in classes, during events at school. As a Whitlock, students often deferred to her expertise in anything; as someone with mastery over her roots and new branch magics continuing to develop, she was the envy of many thoughts. It helped that Tara had this sweet, calm personality that simply drew others in. Something mysterious and distant, yet everyone believed they had a chance to be her friend. After all, she tolerated the most obnoxious boy in school. And I couldn't even believe the number of students who outwardly expressed annoyance for Gael but secretly pined for him. That was a whole different layer of absurdity.

It didn't take long for the party to turn into a noisy kerfuffle of chaos, with teens drinking, diving into the pool, throwing booze and water and anything else they could with telekinesis, casting their branches, and acting like utter fools for the fun of it.

I expected Gael to jump into the revelry, yet he hung close to Tara at the bar, listening to talk about upcoming events she was excited about and the very many she loathed. Turned out, as impulsive and absurd as he was when it came to talking, Gael proved quite capable of being a good listener. The entire party faded from his thoughts as he listened to his friend.

Gael and Tara did a lap around the party, checking in on guests before they joined Carter and Jennifer at another wet bar beside the pool. Seriously, who needed four bars in one room? I mean, the pool enclosure gave most public pools a run for their money in size, but then again, the Whitlock Estate certainly wasn't lacking in funds.

Gael flaunted his new tattoo on his chest over his heart. It was, in fact, a heart tattoo shaded in with black, gray, white, and purple for the ace flag. Which seemed confusing until I realized that Gael hadn't gotten the tattoo to parade his pride but instead his love. Beside the heart was a portrait of King Clucks forever tattooed on Gael's chest.

"Okay, so what's with the new tattoos?" Carter asked.

"How do you keep getting them?" Jennifer asked with aggravation, though secretly curious since she couldn't find anyone who inked teens—unless they lived in a basement and had sketchy needles.

"King Clucks knows a guy who knows a gal who has a cow, and that cow's got a pal who does great work." Gael flexed his chest, making the heart wiggle. "But to answer your question, Carter, the heart's for my bestie. Bestie, show him your heart."

Tara revealed her matching heart tattoo and King Clucks portrait on her thigh, hidden by the skirt of her bikini bottoms. Only her heart was colored pink, yellow, and cyan for the pansexual flag.

"And if we ever break up," Gael said with a shrug, "I'll just lie and say I dabbled in asexuality before deciding my cock was far too glorious not to share with the world."

Tara, Carter, and even Jennifer bit back a laugh.

"One, not funny." Tara held out her raised thumb, sipping her cocktail. "Two, you could just laser it off."

"My cock?" Gael covered his crotch. "You monster."

Tara lifted her middle finger to join her thumb, then finished her drink before telekinetically waving the stemmed glass into the bar sink. "Three, we're not dating."

"We're not?" Gael jested. "But you're the longest relationship I've ever had, and we never have sex. You're basically my wife."

"No, sweetie." Tara playfully patted Gael's head, messing with his faux-hawk. "You're too high maintenance."

"Boo." Gael guzzled his beer. "How am I high maintenance? I'm drinking Bud Light."

"Okay, okay, I get the queer besties tats—love, by the way, and already thinking of ways to get something similar," Carter said, gesturing to Gael and Tara before pointing a finger at Gael's stomach where another tattoo was inked below his pierced belly button. "But what's this one for?"

"Come on." Jennifer rolled her eyes. "You know damn well it's some perverted bullshit."

"I know it's gotta be something ridiculous, but I gotta know the specifics." Carter pointed to Gael's head. "He's a fascinating specimen of epic nonsense, and I will have some *ink*ling of how his brain works before the night is over."

Gael winked. "I see what you did there, you punny little bastard."

"Whatever." Jennifer crossed her arms and awaited the answer Carter craved.

Gael ran his hands over his lower torso like a magician revealing his

"100% Vegan" tattoo neatly tucked between the V-cut indents of his abdomen. "This right here is a healthy reminder to all the guys, gals, and nonbinary pals that I might be slinging sausage in your face, but it's totally vegan, babes."

Carter burst into laughter, face red with delight at the absurd awesomeness that was Gael Rios-Vega. Considering how carefree Carter carried himself, he'd never met someone who genuinely lived freely, saying, feeling, and expressing his every single whim.

I stayed close to the group as they chatted, Carter and Gael leading the conversation since Jennifer and Tara preferred the silence, the atmosphere, the calm joy that boomed from their designated extraverts. When Tara wandered, she took Jennifer with her, and feeling a little emptier without her presence, Carter bid farewell to Gael and went off to search for his new girlfriend.

"See you soon."

"Good luck finding your *girlfriend*," Gael said, smirking at the flustered, giddy expression it elicited from Carter who flushed every time he got to call Jennifer his girlfriend.

I stayed close to Gael at the party, realizing the work he put into reading others, nudging them with varying degrees of crude one-liners. There was a bit of pride in him for Carter and Jennifer. He'd spent the better part of the school year trying to shove those two into a room.

He swaggered over to the pool's edge.

"Damn, baby gurl." Gael raised his brows and pouted his lips. "When'd you get so *thick*?"

Christ. He really just blurted the first thoughts that sprang to mind.

Katherine snorted, slightly amused but mostly annoyed. "Maybe you don't stare at my ass all night?"

"Huh?" Gael cocked his head, barely registering that Katherine was right in front of him. "Oh, yeah. Sorry. Totally missed you there. Looking hawt as always, Kitty Kat. But I was lost on your boyfriend strutting around with all that cake."

"Ba-ba-bawk."

Katherine and Caleb wore matching white swimsuits with golden stars, hers being a two piece and his being a pair of trunks.

"Seriously, Caleb." Gael made a show of nodding his head with approval. "The glow-up is legit. How'd that slip under my radar?"

Caleb's entire face burned bright red, spreading to his neck and freckled shoulders. Gael's very vocalized flattery—as Caleb thought it far too politely, in my opinion—had drawn many eyes to him.

"He's really keeping it all hidden under his baggy academy outfits."

"Those abs..."   *"Talk about buying the stock at zero and watching it soar."*

"Good on Kitty Kat, locking him down."

"Honestly," Gael said. "Katherine, Caleb, if you two are ever looking for a little spice in your life." He gestured to himself. "Or Caleb, if you're ever just curious, curious about the human body, or have a question for— Aaaaahhhh!"

Kenzo shoved Gael into the pool with a bit of added telekinesis which made the headfirst cannonball splash a huge wave of water.

"Asshole."

"Gah, Gael!"

"What's your problem?"

After the crowd simmered, most believing Gael had done this in some dramatic bid for attention, Caleb tensed, worrying Kenzo planned on throwing him in next. It was bizarre how Kenzo had stormed across the entire party to find Caleb. Not so strange he tossed Gael in the pool considering Kenzo had a very short fuse and Gael managed to light it every time they interacted.

"There's a lap pool in the next swimming enclosure." Kenzo frowned at Caleb, practically snarling as he tried and failed horribly to look nicer—per Gael's advice that fluttered in Kenzo's surface thoughts. "Figured you might be the only one here actually interested in training."

Caleb smiled awkwardly. "Oh, um, thank you for thinking of me."

"I wasn't thinking of you." Kenzo huffed. "I was thinking everyone else was lazy, treating this time like some mini-fucking-vacation or some other bullshit."

"Oh, well, that's still nice. Uh, I guess." Caleb's awkward smile strained but didn't falter.

Kenzo glared. "So, did you wanna do some real training, or are you just gonna splish and splash and be a lazy dumbass?"

"My lil poet." Gael slung an arm over Kenzo's shoulder, careful with his spikes but finding he'd gotten quite good at physical contact thanks to the practice he had with Kenzo. Literally. From handshakes to hugs to pats on the back and anything else, Gael avoided over the years since he didn't want to prick someone by accident.

Gael's bright shark-like smile eased a nervous Caleb, who thought back to the exchange he shared with Kenny during the Spring Showcase. They fought a gargoyle together, faced off against a demon, and they buried a piece of their feud. He wondered if maybe Kenzo had buried all of it.

"You cool with me ditching?" Caleb turned to Katherine.

"I already saw the books you stuffed into your towel bag." Katherine playfully bumped her hip against Caleb's. "Figured you were gonna abandon the fun sooner or later."

As willing as Caleb was to go out and explore, try new things, interact with others, all he really wanted to do most days was read, write, workout, practice his casting, and study. Caleb liked hiding in the world of words, learning anything and everything he could get his hands on.

While Caleb and Kenzo headed to the next enclosure, Katherine and Gael made a show of mingling with everyone in a quick social lap before they dived into the pool.

Before they reached the door, Kenzo grabbed Caleb by the arm and held him in place. They stood out of earshot from the rest of the party.

"About what happened during the showcase attack…" Kenzo averted his gaze. "I never apologized."

"Apologized? For what?" Caleb cocked his head, recalling everything that'd happened, everything he'd witnessed, any possible thing Kenny could've done. "You didn't do anything, though. I mean, you were kind of sort of a bit rude, but that's fine. And it all worked out."

"Not for the showcase attack," Kenzo snapped, shoulders raised high and neck turtling in on itself. "For everything. Everything since my parents died. Everything since middle school. Since freshman year. Since we enrolled at Gemini Academy. I'm sorry for being a prick, for questioning your worth, for punching down every single day. I'm an asshole, and I'm not going to change. Fuck anyone who thinks I should. But I am going to change how I treat you. I'm going to work to make up for how I treated you."

Caleb stood speechless, mind whirling in a million different directions.

"I'll start by helping you do some real levitation training." Kenzo nodded toward the door that'd lead them to the lap pool. "Seriously, your form is pathetic. How you expect to be a professional enchanter with such a sloppy stance is beyond me. Bird Brain and Chicken Sandwich have a tighter form, and they just started levitating."

"I forgive you, Kenny." Caleb smiled, then scrunched his face into this contorted, frazzled grimace. "Kenzo. I mean, Kenzo."

Kenzo huffed. "You can't forgive me."

"What? Why not?"

"Because I just apologized. And it was terrible." Kenzo cycled through every well-rehearsed speech he'd practiced, every bullet point he'd mentally prepped, and yet, the second the time came, he word vomited his feelings. "You're not allowed to just forgive me."

"Oh. I'm sorry."

"No, you can't apologize to me!"

"Why not?"

"Because it's…" Kenzo stifled an angry shout. "This isn't going at all how I planned. Just know you can't just accept an apology right away."

"Ooooooookay," Caleb meekly dragged out the word as he studied Kenzo. "And why can't I just accept an apology again?"

"You have to process the apology, think it over, then decide. You can't just forgive someone. Especially someone who treated you like shit for years. Who made it his mission to smash apart your dreams, your goals."

Rage funneled from Kenzo, hurled back onto himself mostly as his emotions twisted into disgust and regret. Part of him wanted Caleb to reject his crappy apology, spit in his face, call him every cruel word in the world, tell him he waited too long to be a decent human being. Another part of him wished he could be as forgiving as Caleb.

"Hmmm. So I've been thinking over the apology." Caleb had a pensive expression. "Well, here's the thing. I'm a fast thinker so I—"

"No! You're not that fast of a thinker. I've seen how long you take on tests." Kenzo scoffed, opening the door and allowing Caleb to go first. "Let's just put a pin in all the mushy gushy feelings bullshit. We'll revisit this awful apology. Maybe I'll have a better one."

"I'm not being very mushy gushy." Caleb blinked. "Am I?"

Kenzo realized he was the one weighed down by feelings, by desires to mend a broken friendship, by confusion on the right way to fix what he'd ruined, by Caleb still being too nice. It annoyed and frustrated Kenzo, yet more than anything he wanted to have Caleb's kind smile back in his life, his wordy nonsense, his absurd optimism.

Kenny wanted his best friend back.

"Whatever." Kenzo jabbed Caleb in the side. "I need you to pay attention to the list of things you're doing wrong when it comes to channeling your roots. It's a long list, so we'll likely be at this all night."

"You know, I actually perfected a root, right?"

"Yeah, and I don't see you throwing out perfected banishment on the regular." Kenzo pushed Caleb forward. "Probably because your technique is sloppy as fuck, and you need a real teacher."

I wasn't even there—that he knew of—and Kenzo still found a way to cut down my teaching methods.

Still, seeing all my students in one setting, enjoying their time away from the academy, recovering, healing emotionally and physically, it helped ease the guilt I had. It also helped exhaust my telepathy since this party had given me a fucking headache. I was able to quell my overpowered branch and settle in for the evening with Milo and Benjamin.

CHAPTER TWENTY-SEVEN

MAY hit, and Gemini Academy finally announced a new plan for next year. Yep, they'd officially washed their hands of this school year, declaring students and staff would be better off finishing with online classes. Not that I complained too much, considering it gave me more time to tend to Milo's recovery while also working on controlling my fully formed telepathy.

The blue filter slowly covering my windshield as I drove reminded me of another very time-consuming adjustment.

"Stop casting," I said to Benjamin.

He clutched his coloring books, eyes darting back and forth at the traffic that zipped around us on the busy street.

"You're worse than Charlie," I said. At least with Charlie, I could put him in a crate and cover it with a blanket while playing classical music since it soothed him on trips to the vet. "If I did that to you, someone would probably have a fit."

"Do what?" Benjamin asked, eyes still on the vehicles that whipped around us in what he considered a bad game of bumper cars about to turn into a ten-car pileup.

"Nothing, never mind." I shook off Ben's fear. "Just chill out."

I'd decided to watch him since the commencement Gemini Academy had planned would take the better part of the morning, and Ben's tutoring sessions were scheduled for noon. The building where Ben socialized with other kids and climatized, or whatever Milo called it, was right down the street from where admin had emailed the announcement would take place. Funny enough, it was also down the street from Cerberus, which wasn't all that funny the more I dwelled on it.

Milo had set up those lessons to offer Ben some type of outlet back when the future Milo foresaw involved more days at work. He'd never predicted the worst would happen. He certainly didn't predict vanishing from the public's eye for over a month now.

Once we pulled up to the event, traffic came to a halt. Every space on the entire block from Cerberus Guild itself all the way to the opposite end of the street where so many damn thoughts bubbled in anticipation for the announcement.

I needed a smoke, but I was already late. "Let's go, kid."

Whipping an illegal U-turn, I drove three fucking blocks to find a place to park.

"Hand." Benjamin raised his tiny hand, flexing his little fingers until I caught the gesture, and reached out with mine as we approached the first crosswalk, then he refused to release his grip even after we'd arrived at our destination.

More families than I'd anticipated had shown up. It seemed every student and family had arrived.

The setup was quite possibly the worst part of this announcement. They kept everyone huddled into the worst blobby mass that filled up the street. It got so bad Cerberus sent their acolytes to redirect traffic. What a terrible decision for the location. What I didn't grasp, something kept neatly tucked away from the surface thoughts of admin, was why they led everyone to this very important destination to deliver an announcement that could've been sent via email.

They didn't even let us inside the building. A building I sort of suspected might be Gemini's new location—but that theory bubbled from the minds of too many curious students who didn't understand the logistics. There was no way this high-traffic spot was going to be the new academy. Right? They'd need the entire street block to come close to the square footage we originally had. And that included pushing Cerberus Guild off the block—which, last I heard, had begun buying up the nearby buildings to expand their office spaces.

Yeah, I highly doubted Gemini Academy had the resources to push out the number one guild off their street corner. Unless, of course, the academy had plans of downsizing. Maybe they were going to drop their roster size, cut a huge slew of students in the name of becoming a more niche boutique program.

I ground my teeth. Fuck, I had to get out of my own head and into someone else's who had concrete answers. Admin might not be thinking closely of the event on their surface, but a slightly deeper delve should reveal something, and who better to pry the intel from than our headmaster.

Headmaster Dower sat at the sidelines, no prepared speech in her head. Weird. A relief since she typically droned on in long-winded metaphors on the beauty of nature and the glory every morning offered or some poetic shit like that. Still, weird that our headmaster didn't have any intention of speaking today. About an announcement for the academy's future. Even if she'd shucked off the task to someone else, as an administrator, it was her obligation to take credit for someone's hard work.

I scrunched my face in suspicion.

"You shouldn't make that face; it'll get stuck that way," Ben said. "Then everyone will think you're always angry."

"I am always angry." I huffed.

Guild Master Campbell practically floated across the stage from the eager exhilaration she held, which turned my anger sour and made me nauseous. Sitting on the stage among the admin was Chanelle, whose thoughts buzzed with a massive checklist for today's event. Of course she had more insight about this announcement than our admin.

Campbell took to the podium. "I'm honored to announce the merger of Gemini Academy and Cerberus Guild."

What the fuck? Campbell didn't believe in slow introductions and dove right into the big announcement on everyone's mind. Tactically speaking, it worked to draw everyone's attention, including mine.

"Our biggest goal as we enter this new journey will be to ensure the best education for all the students at the academy and incoming students for many years to come," Campbell said. "It's a top priority to make sure this new venture doesn't cause students to slip through the cracks, which is why we're bringing on a new role to facilitate this merger."

Chanelle's cheeks burned; she turned away for a second, took a deep breath, and willed herself to appear poised with a loop of positive affirmations as she stepped forward.

Campbell gestured to Chanelle. "Please say hello to the newly appointed Dean of Admissions, Chanelle Whitehurst."

"I'm delighted to stand before you and share insight on my new position and how it'll help make this merger a success." Chanelle squared her shoulders and stood tall at the podium. "I'm here to keep communication strong between both sides, to make sure guild professionals adapt more to their added role of introducing young witches to the industry in small, manageable lessons. It'll be my role to make certain teachers learn how to utilize the shifting resources in the most productive ways to benefit our students. It'll be my job to make certain all our students are assigned to an enchanter for the best possible internship."

This new position gave her the dream job of working one-on-one when necessary while delegating the day-to-day, keeping all the creative control she craved, and allowing her the energy to watch over every student's training, every student's journey. She didn't want to fail her homeroom coven, she didn't want to fail anyone's homeroom coven.

A torch of motivation burned brightly in place of her heart, reverence and healing and a belief that she wouldn't let what happened to Jamie Novak ever happen under her watch again. The snide teen from her class who bullied and berated at every turn, the young man possessed by a demon, transformed into a devil, and freed only to walk his life hollowed out and lost. And when he finally found his footing, found a way forward…that demon killed him.

I swallowed my pain for the role my Doppler played and clung to Chanelle's radiant emotions. She didn't linger on guilt for what happened to Jamie, not even close. It was awe-inspired motivation. She carried Jamie in her heart, promising to wake up every day and do a little better each time.

"But you're all probably wondering what this merger means exactly, how we came up with something so outside the box, so grand." Chanelle's smile filled her face as she positioned herself to slip away from the podium after her introduction. "I'd like to present the brain behind this brilliant concept that's going to move the industry of casting to the next level, carrying future generations higher."

Enchanter Evergreen descended from the rooftop of the draped building behind, joining Chanelle and Campbell on stage. He'd shown up in a trademark suit, wearing a light gray with a lime green tie to match Chanelle's dress. He strutted toward the podium, a swagger in his hips and a smile on his face as he waved. The crowd went wild. Their great Enchanter Evergreen had returned home after his latest mission—the story every media outlet spun. As they looked on in amazement, I tensed.

Milo had returned to work.

I expected him to return eventually, but today? For this merger? A merger I still didn't fully understand. I couldn't believe Milo. He pretended to be asleep when I left this morning. Poorly, might I add. But I figured he was just plotting to exercise beyond the limitations of his medical advice again or that he'd make himself a stack of cool whip-covered chocolate pancakes he didn't want me to know he was having—because, again, not what he should be doing when on the mend.

"This merger is the next step in fully immersive casting educations where guilds will offer their funding, their resources, their industry insight to help teachers provide well rounded educational opportunities." Milo's response went over well with the audience.

Admittedly, I concurred with the concept—what I understood at least. There were already whispers of the state shifting its eighty-percent proficiency goal in the next few years, feeling it was too optimistic. That basically meant they threw too much money toward education and wanted to reallocate those funds elsewhere. But with a guild backing an academy, they wouldn't have to limit their scholarship students. Families wouldn't have to rely on the state for a voucher, and kids from any background could gain a license.

I still didn't like the idea of academies and guilds collaborating in this exclusionary deal with internships, which Chanelle's surface thoughts revealed. Her mind showed a lot as she cycled through every question she'd likely face in today's panel. A panel where they'd address how every student at Gemini would have an internship with a Cerberus enchanter. How their acolyte permits would be fully funded for three years—much better than the one-year expiration academies offered graduates. How students wouldn't be obligated to apply to Cerberus and Gemini would help ensure every graduate was offered letters of recommendation to any guild they applied to after their internship.

"This merger is something I've thought about for years," Milo explained. "It's something I envisioned bringing about the best possibilities for so many future generations. But I'll be honest, it's happening sooner than expected."

There was a pause, a moment of silence for the horrors faced at the academy, the dangers The Inevitable Future hadn't put a stop to, but when that moment passed and Enchanter Evergreen smiled, so many released these bated breaths and smiled with him.

"Not that I'm worried because the brilliant minds in charge at all levels are prepared." He gestured to Chanelle, to Campbell, to Dower. "I'm honored to watch these women use their expertise and dedication to lead Gemini and Cerberus forward."

The audience listened intently, quieting their minds so they could absorb the words shared by their Enchanter Evergreen. Even up at that podium, surrounded by the thousands in attendance, everyone really believed Milo was reaching out and talking to them personally. He had this obnoxious ability when it came to public speaking.

"I actually approached Mrs. Whitehurst with this silly little idea years ago," Milo said, which was a lie. He'd brought it up less than a year ago based on his surface thoughts. "She was able to take my musings and transform them into a real plan. Since then, she's been helping make this a reality. Helping connect all the educational dots I just don't understand."

"Honestly, I didn't do much." Chanelle smiled. "I'm just honored to have helped The Inevitable Future bring his vision to life."

The audience roared at that, partially because a lot of students and their families loved Chanelle—her efforts every year didn't go unnoticed—and partially because everyone loved Enchanter Evergreen and hearing his stage name lit a fire of excitement in many hearts.

"I'm just thrilled she'll be taking on such an important leadership role, guiding this ship forward." Milo waved his hands, casting delicate telekinesis that unveiled the building behind him to the audience.

The new Gemini Academy building was still under construction, but damn if that sign didn't sparkle.

"We'll be holding tours across the intended facilities this upcoming fall semester," Guild Master Campbell explained. "Then we'll have a Q&A that'll offer everyone here an opportunity to address any concerns."

Campbell hadn't intended on mentioning Milo's role, and her aggravation for his inflated ego bubbled at the surface of her thoughts. But he was the perfect person in these circumstances to gain an audience's trust. Many families were nervous about returning to Gemini next school year, and having Enchanter Evergreen's seal of approval went a long way. What really struck me was how Campbell also wanted to offer Milo an easy return to the public eye, a chance to gain his footing on his terms, because despite how much he annoyed her, Campbell held genuine concern for his wellbeing before and after his assault.

They chose to host this event with staff, students, family, and guild members of every level because this should be a transparent experience. They could've held a press conference and let everyone in this room know through an email or a robo call or on the off chance they watched the news that day. But they wanted to be honest with everyone.

I was proud of Milo, of what he'd created with Chanelle and Campbell. But I couldn't help wondering where my place in all this was. The academy was changing so drastically. This year was going to be swept aside, finished online, and forgotten. I never had the chance to really say farewell to my homeroom coven, to send them off to their third and final year.

It seemed things were ending.

More importantly, it seemed time was running short. I turned to Ben. "Let's go."

"But I wanted to take the tour."

"You have your tutoring class thing in like twenty minutes."

"Ugh, I hate it though. There's people everywhere. They just ruin it."

"I concur. People tend to be the worst part of going places." Despite Benjamin's mild tantrum about leaving, I managed to drop him off without too much protesting.

I had errands, plans for today, little surprises for Milo by checking off some of his to-do list—but he'd dropped the biggest surprise returning to work.

I sat on a bench, smoking cigarettes and quelling the minds of millions. Easier than expected since my mind bustled with a thousand questions on where I fit in all of this, where I belonged, how I'd help, what I'd do next year, and if this new model—as great as the idea seemed—was something I wanted to invest in. It'd be another ten years before this approach found a good flow, its footing. That'd mean years of doubt, of questioning what the fuck I was doing and goddamn professional learnings created by people who'd never worked at guild or in a classroom but ready to charge thousands for lessons meant to motivate and prepare us for all the unknowns.

Fuck. I think I'm at one of those annoying career crossroads.

I sucked in a deep inhale, letting the nicotine offer a rush of relief.

Staring at the buildings across the street, I lingered on the flashing sign of a salon. I needed a change of my own, needed to control something as everything around me evolved. Somehow, I ended up inside the salon, setting up a walk-in appointment and buzzing with anticipation as I waited to be called. When I was finally brought to the back, I sat in the chair, which offered a reprieve, a distraction, a secret excitement. The beautician draped a black cape over me, brushed my hair back, and smiled.

"So, what are we thinking?"

"Cut it all off."

So much was changing around me. So much would have to change soon. I needed to change, to grow, to keep up, to be prepared for what would come next.

As much as I knew what I needed to do, I still wasn't sure if it was what I wanted to do. For now, all I wanted to do was bask in my reflection as it quickly evolved into a new look. A new Dorian.

CHAPTER TWENTY-EIGHT

THE beautician did a fantastic job on my haircut, buzzing the sides and back short. My neck and shoulders were free. She'd kept the top longer, ruffled with an easy-to-follow product regimen. I'd enjoyed the new look so much, I allowed her to add the blond streak in my bangs that were curled backward above my forehead in this pompadour style, which basically looked like a knockoff Elvis.

Carlie immediately squinted when I walked inside, likely judging how I found the time for a haircut but not her mealtime. Charlie, on the other hand, avoided me, nose raised high as he strutted around the kitchen. He was mad. For weeks now, I'd spent so much time at Milo's place during all my free time, stopping home less than when I worked in a building.

To be honest, assigning lessons online, walking away, and only returning to supposedly grade them wasn't work. Not the work I was used to, not the work that'd help shape young witches into productive citizens who'd mastered their magics.

Once I'd fed Carlie and set up her treat toys, I walked into the living room and called over to Charlie, attempting to gain his love. I lay out on the floor, head pressed against the carpet and arms outstretched, begging for Charlie to come cuddle. It took time, lots of time, patience, but he finally rubbed his head against mine and playfully bit my new haircut.

My betrayal had been forgiven. "Thank you, Charlie!"

After kissing and hugging and holding Charlie, my telepathy was drawn to Enchanter Evergreen, who winced as he flew across the city, making strategic stops meant to draw attention and quietly announce his return. Based on the buzzing thoughts, that quiet announcement would be raging in a matter of hours, which was probably the intention.

Milo arrived at a secluded dock end with empty warehouses based on the lack of thoughts—except for one that wasn't a warehouse building at all. Merely a glamour. Not that I could tell, but Milo had some opinions on the shoddy craftsmanship. Rushed work with easy tells.

"Relieved to see you doing well," Gladiatrix walked toward him, dressed down in a pair of jeans, leather jacket, and heels. "The city has missed you."

"It's been calm in my absence, too." Milo nodded to her. "Thank you for that, Gladiatrix."

"It's just Alicia today." She smiled, then gestured to the warehouse door to usher Milo inside.

Despite keeping her profile almost completely hidden from the public eye, Alicia discreetly dealt with any issues that threatened the city beyond guild capability, which turned out to be few and far between. Still, to imagine one of the strongest witches in the world setting up shop to protect Milo's city sent a rush through his body, energizing him.

It made sense she'd taken off her garb as Gladiatrix, it allowed her to handle problems without drawing massive media attention which was something the Global Guild wanted to avoid in Chicago all things considered.

Once they'd stepped inside, Milo was greeted by a smiling Enchanter Diaz, posing beside his familiar with his phone raised high for a selfie.

He wore a black corset vest with magenta laced strings and embroidery that matched the hot pink cowboy hat he and his familiar wore. "Her fans have been missing her candid shots."

I wasn't sure he knew what candid meant. Or maybe I didn't.

"This place might be on the DL, but we gotta update her followers on something." Diaz smooshed his face close, kissing Priscilla's snout. "She's got an unbearably loyal fanbase."

The bear pawed at Diaz's head, nudging him away.

"She's never been a fan of my jokes. Not an ounce of humor in her. And she's got a lotta ounces."

Priscilla roared.

"Kidding, baby gurl."

Wadsworth stepped into the room, looking like his old self. Quite literally, in fact. His wrinkled brows furrowed into a deep frown.

Relief swelled inside Milo as he took in Wadsworth's approach. Even if the enchanter had healed his wounds, Milo saw his impaled chest, and he sensed the various outlier possibilities where the extensive casting pushed well beyond Wadsworth's limitations.

Wadsworth took a deep drag off his cigarette and then exhaled his aggravation. "If you slackers are done goofing off."

"Slackers?" Milo asked, aghast in the phoniest sense possible. "I've been on the mend, healing. Recovering from—"

"Lazy." Wadsworth scoffed. "All of you."

"You've also been recovering." Gladiatrix folded her arms. "Doing nothing."

"Yeah, old man. You're a bum, too." Diaz tipped his hat. "Welcome to the slacker's club."

"We meet every third Thursday of the month," Milo said with a smirk. "Although, we tend to skip the meetings, slacking off and all."

Diaz snorted. "I heard jacking."

The pair nearly exploded in a fit of laughter until Wadsworth's scowl tempered their teasing.

"I'm not young and spry like I used to be," he explained. "Accessing my full rejuvenation form hits a lot harder at a hundred and thirty-eight."

"*What?*" They all thought with slack jaws and utter disbelief on their faces.

And for good reason, everything in the media said Samual Wadsworth was in his seventies, but I supposed a co-founding member of the Global Guilds could manipulate details over the many decades. Very many decades in his case.

Unwilling to offer any more explanation for his comment, Wadsworth led them deeper into the building. Further inside, this glamoured warehouse started to resemble the Global Guild-level detainment facility that it was, something privately funded and off the books, according to Milo. I wasn't sure whether the sinking pit of skirting around government sanctions came from me or Milo.

The security was top-notch. It held wards meant to repel psychic magics, yet I slipped inside all the same. Whether I'd intuitively retained some of the sleuthing under the radar skills my Doppler shared before his demise or my fully formed branch simply overpowered the protections put in place, I didn't worry. Too much, anyway. Wadsworth had special forces positioned throughout this small facility, rotating through actual guild members like himself, Gladiatrix, Enchanter Diaz, and Milo.

"We keep the place moving," Wadsworth said, going on a long tangent explaining the primal and cosmic magics used to move the building from one location to the next undetected.

"Cool deal." Milo nodded approvingly, mind scouring potential futures where this place would be compromised, yet given his calm expression, I'd wager he didn't see any.

"I should've just done this to begin with," Wadsworth said with a huff. "But knowing that trashy True Witch, she would've attempted putting up a real fight the first time we'd grabbed her if things hadn't gone her way."

"In a nutshell," Milo said.

Convincing The True Witch her plan was working seemed like such a clever idea at the time, planning around every potential scenario and luring the other Celestial Coven members out. And while she was still out there, Theodore was out there with her, I took refuge in the successes. Three pillars of the coven had been stopped. Two were captured and now detained in this private facility. The third, The Sisters Three, had died and finally gone from this world.

Wadsworth stopped at a completely sealed chamber made of glass. Multiple layers that looked like smaller transparent boxes locked inside of each other until the final glass box about the size of a milk crate. It hovered in the center, each glass box rotated continuously, and the light of the room revealed the subtly carved enchantments on the glass.

In that final box lay a pile of dust.

"This is what remains of the skeleton witch," Wadsworth grumbled. "Not how I hoped to detain him, but the fucker kept coming, so I had to smash him."

"Guess we don't have to ask pass or smash." Milo grinned.

"Nope." Diaz wheezed. "Wadsworth is smashing all them bones."

"And making sure he kept *coming*," Milo added.

Those two dolts burst into laughter because they had the sense of humor of twelve-year-olds.

"I did it so he'd stop coming," Wadsworth interjected, clearly missing the phrasing that played through Milo and Diaz's minds.

"There's gotta be better ways to stop bones from coming," Diaz said with a bellowing laugh.

"Oh, trust me. There are lots of ways to handle a bone that's coming." Milo clutched his ribs, ignoring the slight pain that came from laughing, lost in the joy of joy with his new annoying enchanter friend.

They both laughed so hard they floated momentarily, one light breeze away from twirling round and round.

"Anyway," Wadsworth glared at the pair, waiting for them to finally stop laughing.

That didn't happen until Gladiatrix flicked them both on the back of their ears, sending a searing pain reminiscent of a really horrible piercing experience. Not that either of them knew what that sensation felt like, but I'd drifted in enough minds to retain the awful feeling of a needle jabbing the skin in the wrong way and lingering for hours or days to come.

"He's still in there, still radiating magics," Wadsworth explained. "But our psychics can't find much of a foothold to investigate his mind."

No wonder they couldn't. His thoughts were as shattered as his bones. The teensiest fragments of memories floated around his being like algae. If he weren't a member of the Celestial Coven, the Western Pillar of the Four Corners, I'd have sworn he was dead and gone. I couldn't fathom how a mind this broken could ever piece itself back together, but Wadsworth seemed certain, Milo seemed certain, and I'd watched Grim repair every broken bone after Gladiatrix punched them to bits.

"Are we gonna tape him back together or what?" Milo asked.

"We'll wait patiently," Wadsworth said, which was absurd since he was the most impatient member of their group and possibly the only person in the world who wanted The True Witch dead more than me.

Still, his thoughts, those on the surface, didn't carry cunning or calculated deceit. He was genuine, it seemed.

Wadsworth moved them to the opposite side of the facility to an iron chamber filled with dozens of chains looped every which way and holding a bloated, rotting body in the center like a forgotten meal in a spider's web.

Each link of the chains held a sigil meant to prevent this corpse from escaping, prevent anyone from entering.

"Yeesh." Gladiatrix grimaced, biting back the foul taste that wafted down her throat like sludge from a single poorly timed inhale through her nose.

Despite the layers upon layers of iron walls, the fact they observed this corpse through a camera in the neighboring room, the enchanter with supreme senses still caught a whiff of the terrible odor.

"Why are you keeping this one?"

"I killed Lazarus twice in combat when he tried to escape the MDC," Wadsworth said, mind flashing back to the difficult battle he faced while pitted against two pillars of the Celestial Coven. "Little bastard got back up almost instantaneously like death hadn't gripped him."

"Maybe it hadn't." Diaz shrugged.

"Trust me," Wadsworth said with flashes of his battle surfacing. Images of Lazarus' snapped neck, of his bloody heart in Wadsworth's grasp, of a thousand other injuries inflicted that brought each witch to the precipice of death. "I know how to kill someone."

"I figured it out." Diaz slammed a fist into his palm. "He's got cat magic, and it gives him nine lives, but now he's run outta lives. Game over. No save file."

Milo shook his head. "That's not a magic."

"He's playing dead." Wadsworth glared at the corpse his team had taken every precaution to trap, but not one to preserve the corpse.

There was a spike of hate from Wadsworth, a whisper of hope that the witch felt some pain, some disgust in the rotting shambles of his being.

I doubted Lazarus felt anything in his current state. His magic and mind had stilled. I didn't understand the full extent of his resurrection branch, but as I glossed through the memories I'd acquired from The Sisters Three, I found glimpses of Lazarus in similar conditions awakening and healing without a trace of death lingering in his body.

It was a bizarre sensation, rifling through memories that weren't my own. Sorting through thousands of years of knowledge seemed impossible, yet when I searched for some in specific, the memories appeared without question. It was sickening, like having a search engine at my fingertips from the minds of three witches I'd slaughtered. Ultimately, I felt worse for their victims, the tens of thousands, and the millions more they intended on killing.

"So, what's the next step?" Milo asked.

"We wait for these two pillars to recover, then you do your psychic mumbo jumbo, we get a lead on where The True Witch fled, hopefully more intel on the identities of the other coven members, and then we fuck 'em all up."

That was right. Despite the four most powerful core members of the Celestial Coven attacking the city, they had many others over the centuries. From the flashes of memories I'd searched from The Sisters Three, they seemed to keep twelve witches at all times, one for every branch. When a witch died, their essence was transferred into the bone staff that I'd destroyed.

There was so much more that The Sisters Three had answers to, yet I needed to find it buried in the memories I'd taken. They'd walked the world for thousands of years, one of the pillars beside The True Witch, and yet she still kept so much of the workings a secret. I wasn't sure if The Sisters Three didn't have the identities of current members in the Celestial Coven or perhaps they'd destroyed that memory before I took it. Seemed like something spiteful those *goddesses* would've done.

I reeled my telepathy away from Milo and his Global Guild comrades, delving deeper into my own mind so I could hopefully unravel some of the mysteries behind the Celestial Coven.

In the corner of my eye, at the edge of my inner core, sat the visions I'd absorbed from Milo's mind more than a year ago. The visions I couldn't make any sense of for the longest time. And now, I'd warped them into small marble-shaped lights so they'd be easier to store.

One in particular shined a bit brighter, the crimson sparkle carrying an allure.

I'd mostly ignored Milo's visions after I'd finally learned how to keep them under control. But this one called to me, similarly to a strong mind that reached out. I'd say my connection to Milo provoked this spark. Although, every vision stored in my head came from my connection with Milo. Surely, there was something special about this one. Something that urged my magic to reveal it above the others. Something to indicate why it held so much pain in a tiny glimmer of light that radiated through my body as I attempted to work.

Pulling the vision from the pile, I held the tiny light between my hands until the images of an unknown possibility revealed itself in the form of a fast-moving scene throughout the city.

Not an unknown possibility. I'd seen this vision before, this terrible and horrifying vision of death. Death everywhere in Chicago. Death that took everyone. This vision had awoken me weeks ago in the middle of the night, haunting and horrible, yet Milo promised it was impossible to achieve. A future that required his death first. A future he'd done everything to divert. This awful night would never happen.

I shivered, taking in the reality of Milo's near fatality, the reality of this vision.

Fire burned. Buildings crumbled. The earth had split open and swallowed thousands. Debris and death hit with every single breath as I whirled faster throughout the city, looping to the end of this vision.

Visions weren't always literal, not an actual depiction of how the events would play out. That much I'd learned from Milo's experiences. But my chest still tightened when I reached the mountain of corpses, finding my home-room coven sprawled across the sea of bodies. Former homeroom coven. It was almost summer. They were done with their classes, and they'd be third-year students focused on internships and reporting to the newly appointed Dean of Admissions, whereas I'd find myself working with a new batch of first-year witches again.

I panicked, averting my eyes as I hovered over the bodies of my dead students and reached the peak of this disgusting mountain.

The perpetrator of this destruction and devastation stood proudly with a smile painted in blood on his face. Theodore Whitlock.

His shadow conjured monstrous silhouettes of demons, demonic energy he controlled, and hellish beasts he sought to unleash upon the world.

I leapt forward, startling poor Charlie as I returned to the living room of my house, blinking away the splotchy remnants of the worst possible future in existence.

And it was possible, too. Despite everything Milo had done to prevent this potential outcome, to change fate, Theodore Whitlock had escaped with The True Witch. He roamed the world, conjuring new and awful ways to hurt, to maim, to torture, and slaughter everyone.

But I could stop him. I'd come close during the attack on the academy. I'd come close to finishing him and Amara.

The academy. The academy that continued changing, growing, evolving into something better. A better brighter version I couldn't see myself involved in. Not currently. Not until I'd done something about this impending vision. I wouldn't allow it to become a reality.

Chapter Twenty-Nine

DESPITE the horrid vision, I had a bit of a pep in my step as I walked into Milo's place, feeling fresher, newer, ready for anything. It was a damn good haircut, long overdue. There was also a serious conversation I needed to have with Milo, something I'd have to tell him before the end of the school year—not that it was much of an ending. But I wanted to celebrate his return to guild work even if it made me anxious. Even if it reminded me of losing Finn. Even if my chest tightened every time I thought back to when he collapsed on stage, surrounded by The Sisters Three, The True Witch, and Theodore Whitlock.

I buried that fear, that worry, because Milo wouldn't be deterred, and I did support him.

Stepping through the foyer, I fought back the disappointment that came from that lack of a farewell, all the things left unsaid before the school year ended, the months of preparation now lost that my homeroom coven would never get back. Well, they would. They were all dedicated. They'd find time to make up for that lost learning. I hoped, at the very least.

Milo shimmied across the living room to the kitchen, adding a bit of levitation for a real pep in his step as music blasted from every room of the penthouse.

He'd changed his suit, no jacket, tie, or dress shoes—definitely his way of unwinding for the evening. His blond hair was curly and slightly damp, clearly shower-fresh from the smell of his body wash.

I kept quiet, enjoying the swagger of his hips as he floated around the kitchen island, meal prepping for the week, because for some god-awful reason he genuinely enjoyed chopping, washing, sorting, cooking, and organizing a bunch of fruits and veggies for snacks during long workdays.

Work. Milo was back to work, taking on cases, preparing for how to capture Theodore Whitlock, how to infiltrate the Celestial Coven, how to fight against The True Witch.

I swallowed the wafting trepidation. Not merely mine but the fear nearby, too. With my mind floating throughout the entire city, it became somewhat second nature to sync to certain emotions. Then they struck me harder, heavier, so much fucking worse.

Okay, maybe I wasn't quite ready for this conversation.

"Where's Ben?" I asked, not sensing his surface thoughts anywhere in the building.

"He's chilling with my acolytes tonight. Figured big case stuff going on today, plus…" Milo turned off the stereo, clinging to the song lyrics freshly plastered in his mind, humming softly before he smirked. "You know they all got an apartment together?"

"Your acolytes?"

"Yeah, and you know that's because—"

"They aren't paid," I interrupted. "The system is cruel? Guilds are greedy and use loopholes to exploit free labor for years? Capitalism is the ultimate magic?"

"No." Milo's face fell flat, thoughts fizzling into disappointment. "Sad face. I was gonna say 'cause they have confusing feelings to work out. My version was Three's Company poly vibes. Your version makes me feel bad about the economy. Sadder face."

"And maybe for exploiting your acolytes?"

"I'm not exploiting them. I've been handing them top-tier cases while working this Global Guild investigation."

"And babysitting duty."

Milo frowned, a pouty, sour expression that showed he hadn't really seen it that way, but he was too stubborn to admit I had a point. Too stubborn to even think it, the song lyrics played louder along his surface thoughts.

"We're gonna have to get him a real nanny soon."

"We?" Milo asked.

"You, sorry." My face warmed, flustered a bit by the very confusing situation. And it was confusing. Milo had taken Benjamin in temporarily for the sake of a case, for the chance to offer the kid some stability. Now, though, even as everything continued spiraling toward potential chaos, things seemed to have unfolded better for the kid. I wasn't sure if it was Milo's doing, if it was Milo's hope, but I sensed Milo had no intention of letting Ben slip through the cracks of the system. "Whatever. I just included myself in the equation in case you needed help. Whatever. What do I care? It's whatever."

"Alrighty, you've clearly got zero fucks to give or *whatever*." Milo smirked in his annoyingly minxy way, surface thoughts revealing the conversation he'd had with Ben about staying longer, about the conversation Ben had with me, about how I'd offered him a manifestation wrapped in the form of a persona to protect him if the ocean ever returned.

"Maybe I give one or two fucks." I shrugged. "Whatever."

Milo's eyes fluttered momentarily as he wrapped his thoughts around visions—some still fractured and tumbling chaotically around Milo's mind. "I also sort of figured we'd need to have a serious convo."

Damn. He knew what I wanted to discuss. Of course he did. He was Milo fucking Evergreen. He knew everything about me, everything I'd ever contemplated.

"And that hair has serious convo written all over it."

"You don't like it?" I ran my hand through the back, feeling the short buzz before reaching the ruffled top.

"I love it. But I am gonna miss yanking you by those long locks." Milo winked. "Now, to this serious conversation. I know it's coming. So—and this is the first time you'll hear me say this so savor it—just spit it out."

I ground my teeth to stifle a small bubbling laughter. *Damn clairvoyants.*

Milo playfully batted his lashes, teasing and always knowing what was on my mind, with or without his magic. Our connection in itself was magical, bonded and linked on a level I'd never fully comprehend. That said, I wanted to spend our lives together figuring it out.

It didn't seem like this was a conversation to avoid, so I dipped my toe into the topic. "You really did a thing today, huh?"

"The merger between Cerberus and Gemini was part of this long game plan." Milo scrunched his face, fighting back aggravation for how much improvisation had popped up since fate had deviated so far off the careful paths he'd arranged.

"I know. Sort of glimpsed that much during the reveal."

"Oh, man. I was so upset." Milo made his angry face, his overdramatized angry face where one poke in his stomach would result in a giggle fit because only one of us wore a scowl well in this relationship. "I had all these plans of having a statue of an Orthrus—which is basically a two-headed Cerberus— which would've been amazing. Sort of like an homage or a tribute or something. Gemini and Cerberus overlapping because, you know."

"Gemini is the twin sign, and Cerberus is the demon dog." I nodded. "And this Orthrus is the demon dog but twinning?"

"Twinning!" Milo laughed loudly, obnoxiously, then stopped immediately and shot me an overly serious face. "But they said I couldn't use it because of trademarking. Apparently, some guild in *Milwaukee* uses the Orthrus demon as their emblem, and we can't because of copyright and blah, blah, blah."

I always found it strange how the Midwest used so many demon names for their guilds. Of all the things they could've picked.

"I think what you created, what you're creating, is amazing." I paused, contemplating. "It's gonna open so many new doors in the industry. It's the big picture guilds and academies never grasped."

"It's also a big picture that folks can scribble all over and ruin if we're not careful," Milo said. "But that's a problem for the future, one I'll redirect if need be. Thankfully, Gemini has some awesome educators. Seriously, Chanelle's a boss ass bitch, the way she sat down with the Cerberus board and just… Wow."

"Gemini is in great hands, which is why I think I'm okay walking away."

"What?" Milo's quickened heartbeat rang so loudly it thrummed alongside his worried thoughts.

"I'm leaving Gemini—leaving teaching—for a while. I'll take a sabbatical or something." I took my time with the words, biting back my own feelings while tiptoeing around Milo's. He'd seen this possibility, clearly alluding to it when mentioning the serious conversation we needed to have, but I doubted he believed it'd actually cement into reality. I honestly couldn't believe I'd emailed the headmaster with my request, a request to leave. "It's just the right thing to do for right now."

"There are lots of right choices, Dorian. Some are more extreme than others." He glanced at my chopped-off hair.

I huffed. "Subtle as ever, Evergreen."

"I do like it. I just want you to know it's a big choice, a permanent choice, a guiding decision."

"Yeah, but think of how much I'll save on shampoo."

Milo rolled his eyes. I knew he meant leaving education, but maybe I'd stolen some of Milo's great avoidance through sass technique.

"I'm losing my homeroom coven to their third year anyway. They're going to be prioritizing their internships. Teachers don't get to follow their students up to graduation anymore."

"What about your other students? Your history classes? Won't some of your homeroom coven kids being taking your advanced history?"

"Probably, but Dower will find someone to fill in for the coursework." I shrugged. "I won't be any good to my students so long as I'm carrying this weight."

"Weight?"

"You make it look so easy." I smiled at Milo, simply awed by everything about him.

"Make what look easy?" His brow crinkled in the cutest way when he didn't know the answer to something. An expression I rarely saw, with him being a clairvoyant and all.

"Carrying the weight of the world," I said, soaking in his flustered expression, his soft pride, his lingering guilt for still not having an answer for every problem in existence. "I can't return to the industry forever, I'm not built for it, but I need to see this case through to the end. I know I have the right magic, the ability and conviction to stop The True Witch and Theodore Whitlock."

"You mean kill them?" Milo swallowed hard, holding back his concerns, the ethics, the desire he had to do the same.

"I don't know," I answered honestly. In the heat of the moment, it felt right, righteous, but now… "I just know I have to help stop them. What happens when I find them… I'll cross that bridge and carry that burden. But I can't allow them to stay out there, hurting people, plotting against the future, your future, the beautiful and wonderful happiest ever after that ever aftered you are creating."

I brushed my hands over his face, resting them on his shoulders and squeezing his tight muscles. Careful to be gentle.

"Dorian—"

"I want to return to Cerberus as an enchanter. I want the resources, the access."

"You're lucky you know a guy." Milo kissed me, sloppy and wet and silly because the vulnerability, the fear he had for this path, this journey made things far too serious. "I suppose I can pull some strings, but you're gonna have to pull something for me. Well, more of a yank. A gentle tug, actually."

I shoved my hand down Milo's pants and gripped his semi-hard cock.

He stifled a moan. "What am I saying? You know what you're doing."

I continued to jerk Milo's cock, guiding his backward steps with my eyes as we reached the bedroom, where I immediately stripped off my clothes. With a delicate touch of telekinesis, I unfastened Milo's pants and yanked them down to his ankles—feeling the spike of aggressive lust radiating from his core.

I rubbed my palm over the head of his dick, playing with the precum that dripped and teasing his sensitive tip. It only took a few more tugs for him to get fully erect.

He wanted me this second, every which way, but mostly, he wanted to feel me buried inside him. Milo craved my passionate touch, my carnal hunger, my primal roar as I fucked him.

I couldn't, though. Not yet. The bruises had finally faded, and the broken bones had finally been mended, but I wasn't ready to be rough. Waving over the lube, I applied some as I continued stroking Milo. Then I gently worked my mouth over his body, planting kisses. On his lips. His cheeks. His neck. His shoulders. His chest. His biceps. His abs. And then all over again, all the while running my hand up and down his cock.

The great Enchanter Evergreen had returned to work, declared himself ready and eager to protect the city—but I only saw the sweet man I declared that I'd protect.

"Fuck me." Milo leaned forward, biting my ear and shouting his demands on a loop. He wanted me to make him scream aloud. He wanted to feel my every inch.

With a hand pressed to his chest, I shoved him back, giving him that authority he sought. But only for the moment, only to push him deeper into the soft mattress.

As he lay back, legs spread, I slipped in and spread his cheeks, licked his hole. I dribbled spit and licked and lathered his pretty hole. I took my time, running my tongue up his taint and taking his balls into my mouth before returning to his hole. Milo convulsed, releasing a satisfied whimper every time my tongue poked a bit deeper.

With Milo quivering, I wanted to ram my cock into him this instant. Every fiber of me demanded I plunge deep inside and grant his desires. Instead, I used the lube and stuck my fingers inside him, readying him for my cock, readying myself too, perhaps.

Every time his lust and longing sent me spiraling into this primal hunger, I held back and pushed my fingers deeper and faster, watching his hard cock bounce as he moved back and forth, demanding more.

I finally moved in closer, sliding my cock into Milo. He groaned, biting his bottom lip and lifting his head back.

"Wait." I tilted his head forward, locking his eyes back onto me. "I wanna see your face, see all of you.”

Milo returned his gaze with his beautiful blue eyes. I took gentle thrusts, maintaining the same steady rhythmic pace, watching his face scrunch, expressions shifting between pain and pleasure.

I panted, keeping my strokes slow and giving him my entire length, letting him feel every inch.

“Don't hold back.” Milo tightened his thighs around my hips, locking me in place. “I'm fine. I can handle it.”

“I know.” My gaze shifted, unable to keep eye contact with him. “I just…I, um…I…I'm feeling this.”

“You're lying.” Milo didn't say it, but we both knew I only ever drew passion from my partner's pleasure.

I'd get fucked every night if it made Milo happy. I'd fuck him into the ground gasping and begging for cum if it made him happy. My only true arousal came from bringing my partners off. Finn and Milo, their needs were always my needs.

So when I declared I craved something, it was the weakest of lies on my part.

“I don't want you holding back. I want to feel you, all of you.” Milo wrapped his arms around my shoulders, running his fingers through my freshly cut hair and returning my eyes to meet his. “Please don't do that.”

“Do what?”

“Don't treat me like I've changed.”

“I'm not…” I pressed my forehead against his. “I'm afraid I've changed. My magic, yes, but also what I want, what I need to do moving forward…”

“Does this change include me?”

I widened my eyes. “Always. That's never a question.”

Milo's eyes watered a bit. “It's just the future is always shifting, and you're making new decisions and this coven, this horrible coven… I don't know if I have all the answers anymore.”

“Whatever future lies ahead, I want you in it.”

Milo rolled his eyes up, doing his best to fight back tears because he felt splotchy and not sexy, then closed them tightly, unable to look at me. “I'm sorry I'm so damn dramatic sometimes."

"You're never dramatic." I kissed his eyelids. "And you're always sexy."

"Dorian," he whispered, unsure what to say next but wishing to say so much more.

So I spoke, I filled the silence, I quelled his worries, or I hoped I had.

"I'm sorry I ever gave you those doubts." I kissed him. "I'm sorry I spent so many years lost on myself." I kissed him again. "I'm sorry you ever have to worry that I'm not in this." I kissed him again. "I am. I am yours for as long as you'll have me. I belong to you. I will never leave you. I will never stop trying to make you happy. I will always serve at your altar because you're my everything."

Milo kissed me until we couldn't breathe, until everything except our lips had vanished. We parted and panted, and then he leaned in and whispered, "Fuck me."

I'd give him my everything. I moved closer, pressing my chest against Milo's, kissing him, hugging him tightly as I pumped into him faster.

I pounded him, eliciting moans.

"You can do better than that," I growled, demanding the sweet sound of his surrender. "This is what you wanted, right?"

He whimpered, gritting his teeth, and taking sharp, quick breaths.

"Take all of me." I railed him. "Fucking take all of me."

I fucked faster and harder until his gasps turned into shouts, aloud and internally, his every thought lost on the slap of our skin and the feel of my cock. Milo's eyes got glossy, lost in the swift thrusts I took. His breathing hitched, and I wanted more. I wanted everything. Delving deep into Milo's mind, I stepped completely inside him, embracing the warmth of his body and the bliss of his memories.

Every pinky touch, every hug, every kiss, every quickie, every romantic evening, every rough fuck, everything intimate between us floated here in Milo's inner core. The ones between him and me, the ones between Finn and him, the ones he'd watched between Finn and me, and of course, every experience the three of us shared together.

Fuck. I took a sharp breath, entranced by the sweeping memories and pounded harder into Milo. Each thrust made him grunt, and I kept going until he screamed.

Craning my neck, I listened outside his mind until he shouted, and then I slapped my hand over his mouth, muffling his voice and giving him the rough fuck he sought.

"Look at me." I panted heavily against my knuckles, my lips pressed to the back of my hand and craving the taste of Milo's lovely lips. Another part of me surged with ecstasy every time he whimpered into my palm, begging for more.

I kept my eyes locked on him, showing my attentiveness, but I fixated more on the inner core he continued working at repairing.

Most of his memories were intact and organized exactly as they should be, but the visions continued bouncing around. So many had been sorted and fixed in the three layers of his inner core. I wanted all of it restored, so I waved my hands and guided those straggler visions. Thousands, tens of thousands, fought against me, enjoying their adventures throughout Milo's head.

I snorted, fighting to keep from laughing aloud and alerting Milo to my actions. But the way some visions scampered away, hiding in the shadows of Milo's mind. It reminded me of when Charlie got outside and went on an adventure. He even wriggled free of my telekinesis—mostly when he cried, pretending the grip hurt him.

One by one, I captured the visions and moved them to where they belonged. I couldn't see them clearly, the images they presented, but with my mind synced so precisely with Milo's, I instinctively knew where to place them.

After I'd tucked away the final vision in a filing cabinet, I stepped out of his inner core and rejoined him fully. I released my hug, holding my arms on the sides of Milo's head and watching his face jerk as his glossy eyes fought not to roll back.

"How'd you…how'd you do that?"

"The visions?" I licked his neck, continuing to pound him. "I listened to you, to your needs, to your guidance."

"So, you just psychically connected on such a level you managed to put all my visions where they belonged?” Milo blinked a few times, playfully, but also holding back the groans my strokes caused. “Even though you…even though…you can’t see them? Can’t see my…my…my full system?”

“You’ve got an easy system to follow. I mean, the Fateful Viewing of Infinite Possibilities and the Dispatch Board of Destiny? They’re brilliant. Plus, the…” I quirked a brow. “Do you have a name for the office area?”

“It’s just The Office,” Milo gasped. “It’s iconic.”

“Well, it’s all practically labeled, so thank you for helping me help you.”

“I can’t believe you did this for me.” Milo had his weepy gush face.

“It’s nothing you haven’t done for me.”

“And you used the names.” Milo let out a long, drawn-out moan seconds from his release.

“I’d do anything for you.” Even use those ridiculous silly names for his inner core.

He grunted and shot his load. Three powerful jets shot out; the first hit my stomach, and the second and third streamed far, landing on Milo’s chest.

I kissed him, then pulled out of him and worked my way down his chest, running my tongue against his sticky skin so I could taste his cum, taste him.

“Wait,” Milo wrapped his legs around my back, using them to push upward. “Finish.”

I really only wanted to feel his orgasm, taste his climax. Make him happy. Everything was to make him happy.

“I wanna taste you, too.” Milo’s yearning drew me in.

Scooting up his body, I straddled Milo’s chest, positioning my hard cock and shoving it into Milo’s open mouth. He’d stuck his tongue out, inviting me to ram it right down his throat. I ran my fingers through his curly blond locks, controlling his head and bobbing it forward while meeting him half-way, knocking the head of my cock further but stopping shy of the back of his throat.

“Goddamn.” Every sensation of his warm, wet mouth hit my nerves. I didn’t want it to end. Not yet.

I twitched, dick throbbing, pulsating. “I’m gonna…” I sucked my teeth. “I’m gonna cum.”

I went to pull out, to jerk my cock the few needed strokes, and let out my load. But Milo gripped my ass and pushed me down onto his face. He gurgled and gagged, taking in the full length of my shaft, and the instant my dickhead met the tight muscles of Milo's throat, I came.

"Fuck." My body jerked, taking uncontrollable thrusts as I milked the rest of my load into Milo's mouth, savoring the sound of his choking. It made me cum harder.

Milo lay there grinning as I slid off him. I kissed him, wiping the slop of spit that ran down his jaw. I lay on top of him, enjoying the sweet, gentle embrace while continuing to kiss, to wrap each other in fluids and lube and sweat. I couldn't help but bask in this blissful sensation.

But after ten minutes, Milo was done with tender touches.

I rolled over, resting on the pillow, while Milo scooted over, snuggling close. He wrapped his arms around my stomach, playfully rubbing the hairs on my belly. Our sweaty bodies clung together as Milo pressed in closer, taking these easy breaths of satisfaction. I loved it, loved how effortlessly our breathing synced.

"You know," Milo whispered into my ear. "With a performance like that, I might be able to pull some strings."

"You're insufferable."

Milo laughed, loud and obnoxious.

I smiled, the grin filling my entire face because of how wonderful Milo's happiness rang in the back of my ear.

"If you ask nicely"—I moved his arm down my waist and put his hand over my slightly erect dick—"I can give you some more incentive. You know you want more."

Milo played with my dick, moving his hand over my balls and cupping them, rubbing them. Then he pulled his hips back and bumped my butt with his already stiff boner.

"Seriously?" I chuckled. "Full attention already?"

"Not quite." Milo grabbed the lube and stroked himself a few times before slipping his dick between my cheeks, the head sitting right against my hole. "I've missed this."

"Me too." I whimpered as he pushed inside.

"Relax—it's just the tip." Milo kissed my shoulder, letting me adjust. "You feel so good."

Milo took gentle strokes, easing the full length of his cock into me one inch at a time while he nibbled and kissed my shoulder, my neck, my nape. I craved his lips, lifting my head back and searching for his touch. Milo teased me, leaving pecks along my cheek, my jaw, but missing my lips every time. My mouth wasn't the part he teased. He'd fisted his hands loosely around my erection, guiding me with each thrust of his hips. They bucked me forward and back, running my shaft through the lubed hand Milo kept at my cock.

I moaned, begging, pleading, craving every single touch. Every part of me was in Milo's grasp, in his control, and I wanted to offer him more. I always wanted to offer Milo more.

"I love you." Would that be enough? Would my love be enough? I hoped so. How I hoped I was enough for Milo.

"I have always loved you." Milo kissed me, running his tongue lightly over mine, similar to how his body had slightly positioned itself on top of me now, even as we lay on our sides. "I will always love you. I will love you in every possible future. I've loved you in versions of the future where our paths never crossed, futures where I lost you, futures that we'll never meet, and futures still yet to unfold. You are my forever, Dorian. You are the piece of me that wakes me each day, the piece that pumps my heart, the piece that makes me smile. Dorian, you are my everything."

I collapsed into ecstasy from his words, from his touch. Before I came, I arched and pushed fast and hard to the base of Milo's cock, clenching around him. When my hips convulsed, Milo's bucked in a similar motion, each of us cumming.

Milo kept his flaccid dick inside me, scooting closer and hugging me tightly. The stir of his thoughts told me that he had a long night planned. For now, he rested, buried deep.

"I don't know what lies ahead." I pushed against him, dozing off. "*But please know that I'll do everything in my power to give you the happiest ever after that ever aftered.*"

Milo kissed my shoulder, nuzzling into my neck. *"And I will do the same."*

We rested, minds syncing to all the beautiful thoughts that ran freely throughout Milo's mind.

CHAPTER THIRTY

SUMMER break had officially hit. There were no final tests, no yearbook signings, no farewells. It was just a goodbye without the closure. Even if I was stepping away from the classroom, parting ways from my homeroom coven after two life-changing years, I wasn't abandoning my responsibilities as their teacher.

I shared with Milo how the vision reappeared to me, fully formed and revealing Theodore Whitlock as the culprit. It was one Milo had seen many times, one Milo had adverted, but now it rattled inside his inner core; the devastation held a glimmer of possibility because of Theodore's escape. That possibility wouldn't last. I'd snuff it out soon.

"You ready?" I asked, stepping into the living room.

"I should be asking you that," Milo said, joining me. "You sure you wanna do this?"

We'd circled back to this conversation more than once. Milo triple checked every day about if I was sure I wanted to take a sabbatical, if I was ready for the guild industry again, if I was prepared for the stakes of a mission this big.

"I'm certain." I nodded. "I'm the only one who can."

Somewhere out there, Theodore Whitlock roamed the earth, his thoughts and feelings too faint for me to pinpoint with ease, but not impossible. We shared this bizarre connection. It was small and similar to the trickle that connected me to my homeroom coven, to my friend Chanelle, to Benjamin after removing the ocean from his mind. In Theodore's case, it was disgusting. But it existed and served as something that allowed me to sense him.

It'd formed the day he poured his thoughts into my head then slit my throat. It grew when my Doppler slinked inside the MDC and observed Theodore's mind. It was cemented when I dove into his inner core and ripped apart his gnarled tree as I choked the life out of him.

"And you're comfortable sending a manifestation off on its own?" Milo asked.

"Yes." I gestured for him to join me on the floor where we would channel our magics.

I wouldn't be sending one manifestation after Theodore. I'd summon multiple manifestations at once and break off a tiny piece of magic for them to explore as far as they could. They would each be me entirely—no personas involved, especially since all but Nico continued slumbering deep in my subconscious.

Even with full access to my magic, the ability, the range, I worried it would be too much. Hence why Milo was here. We sat down facing each other. Milo extended his hands and I grabbed ahold, shuddering at the subtle embrace of our channeled magics, our frequencies melding. He anchored me through all things in life; of course, he made the perfect anchor as we channeled and I unleashed telepathy in waves.

"And you're sure you can summon multiple manifestations at once?"

"Yes." I kept my eyes firmly shut but could feel Milo looking at me, judgy face on full display. Okay, I heard his surface thoughts gauging my furrowed brow to determine my current level of concentration. "It's a ten. On a scale of zero to ten, my current concentration level is a ten."

"That's a lie." Milo smirked; I could feel it. "If it were a ten, you wouldn't be eavesdropping on my thoughts."

"You know what else isn't a ten."

Milo let out an exasperated gasp.

"Please take this seriously."

"I am. And I'm seriously still a little concerned about you summoning more than one manifestation at a time."

"Right now, my telepathy is stretched across the city." I glowered. "I'm enduring several thousand mental ramblings at this moment. Mostly keeping them on the back burner of my attention, but that takes constant work."

"That's because of the full range of your telepathy?"

"Yes, so summoning more than one manifestation will be easy enough." I shrugged. "Hell, it might even dim my branch some, which would ease the number of thoughts funneling through my head all at once."

"Okay." Milo squeezed my hands, fully invested in channeling with me. "Let's do this!"

Manifestations leapt from my being, our vision, our senses, synced and then severed because I couldn't handle such an overwhelming outpour. They left the penthouse and pursued Theodore. They'd scour every inch of the planet if necessary. There was nowhere Theodore could hide that I wouldn't locate him. And once a manifestation found him and had a precise location of the warlock and Celestial Coven, that piece of myself would report back, and I'd share the intel with Milo. Then, the great Enchanter Evergreen would move in with the Global Guild forces and eradicate this threat once and for all.

Such an endless quest, roaming the psychic plane, veiled in the magics and bright energy of voices across the world as I searched for Theodore. Occasionally, I crossed paths with other versions of myself who also skirted along the temporal plane. This was the fastest way to move everywhere at once. It wasn't like with Milo, where my magic sought him instinctively. No, my hunt for Theodore relied on more patience.

When the sharp, sizzling hatred snapped in the distance, I froze. If Theodore detected me, he could overpower my manifested form. Even if he did, I'd still have the intel. But I supposed the real worry came from how deranged and vile Theodore's thoughts would get once I crept in close enough to identify his location. I didn't want to carry his memories in my mind; I didn't want to linger any longer than necessary.

I shook away the anxiety and dove out of the psychic plane of existence and into a dark room where the familiar twisted sadism resided. The hatred didn't bubble over, though. More of a simmer. Here, I suspected that faint, hollow flow had to do with Theodore's distance.

Not at all the case. He sat on the wet, gravel floor a mere few feet away. His expression was vacant, much like his surface thoughts that merely fixated on a dried stain. I quivered. It wasn't a stain—it was dried blood caked between the crevices of the ground and beside a limp, lifeless arm.

What the fuck?

I backed away, taking in this room. A dank, dark dwelling that didn't look much bigger than Theodore's solitary cell at the MDC.

The arm was the least disturbing thing around Theodore. A body lay beneath a blanket. Dead, which I gauged from the lack of thoughts coming from it. Another body was propped against the wall nearest a metal door. A rotten corpse burned all over with squishy pockets of popped pus. Truly revolting—enough to make me want to hurl. It held the foulest, most disgusting smell. My senses might've been lacking as a manifestation of psychic energy floating about like a ghost, but I had the misfortune of syncing to the sensory details Theodore experienced.

There was an aggravation for the smell, a smell he couldn't get out of his nose after all this time. A smell that clung to the roof of his mouth. I recoiled. How long had he sat surrounded by these bodies? Who had he killed and why?

I scoffed. It was Theodore. There was no why, merely a need for calculated chaos.

"You should leave little telepath," Theodore whispered with a cracked voice, already aware of my presence, but remaining against his wall, staring around his tiny cell.

I wanted to ask him what happened.

His hair was unkempt, his eyes red and sunken in, his lips chapped.

Dry blood clung to his hands, picked at but not washed away. Grime under his nails. The clothes he wore were filthy and seemingly the only set here. His orange jumpsuit from the MDC was balled up in the corner, soaked in blood, and beside a bucket.

I almost linked to his thoughts, almost asked him how this transpired, but I felt the memory scrape against his surface thoughts, dragged raw along his mind as it played on a continuous loop while he remained locked in here.

Purple smoke filled my vision as I entered Theodore's exposed memory, finding him land in this tiny cell the day he'd escaped with The True Witch months ago.

Theodore's eyes were heavy, with purple and black splotches lining his vision as he coughed, spurting the teleporting mist out of his lungs. Each wheezing exhale was a chore, a battle to stay awake, but that came from the groggy state I'd left him in when I attempted to strike him down during his assault on the academy. Correction, his second assault on the former Gemini Academy.

"You are infuriating, Theodore." The True Witch had a scolding tone which only further exhausted the menacing warlock. "Two pillars of the Celestial Coven captured. One slain by some no nothing psychic. The mess you have brought to my doorstep. Theodore! Are you listening to me?"

He wasn't listening, the words were barely retained, and even now they only came through so crisply because he'd replayed this memory multiple times.

Sleep clawed at Theodore, luring him with a lullaby of rest and recovery. But a piercing yellow glow cut through the smoke, carrying a high-pitched squeal and the smell of sulfur as adrenaline stabbed at Theodore's insides. He took a deep breath and raised his head high, seeing The True Witch stand before him with a single tattoo radiating a yellow hue and releasing a rejuvenating aura meant to startle those she'd taken into a state of awareness.

"Where've you taken me, old crone?"

"Do not speak to me in such a way." The True Witch clenched her jaw, the tension tempting Theodore to further antagonize. "Perhaps you will show some respect if I take away your pets."

"I'm no one's pet." Vincent bared his teeth.

"Might be anyone's pet if the mood suits me." Darla coughed, clearing away purple smoke. "But I'd like to see you try. Teddy's already told us everything about you."

"And you don't even have your staff anymore," Ernesto added, crouched behind the others.

"You think that was my only weapon?" Amara extended her arms, revealing the light shimmer along her many tattoos.

"Your brands are artful, but they're nothing compared to mine." Vincent's tattoos radiated a light glow of channeled magic, and he prepared to harness more than thirty spells simultaneously.

"Cute." Amara kissed her hand with a heavy, wet smack. It smeared lipstick onto her palm which she blew off with a seductively puckered mouth and a touch of delicate telekinesis. "But I've got so much more than ancient enchantments and wards paired with my ensemble."

The flecks of her makeup fluttered until they reached Vincent's mouth, choking him upon contact. He gasped, clawing at his throat. His tattoos continued burning brighter and brighter, absorbing more channeled magic until they popped like broken bulbs. It was sudden and startling, and it didn't stop until each brand etched onto Vincent had pus and blood oozing from it.

His skin reddened, and he scratched and gnawed and burrowed into the rotting flesh of his body. How quickly his body twisted in on itself, feeding and eating.

"It's a delicious venom made especially for your little friend, Theodore." Amara knelt in front of Vincent, watching him flail, watching him struggle, watching him crawl to the door he'd never open.

I'd seen his body when I arrived, squishy and burned and merely a rotten corpse.

"You bitch." Darla swiped her arm quickly, three times, carrying counters in every strike meant to capture any of the buzzing magic building from The vile True Witch.

Vile. That word clung to Theodore's throat, preventing him from shouting, from warning Darla. He wanted to tell her to flee, to escape. He wanted to move beside Vincent and hug him during this excruciatingly agonizing death. He wanted to plead with The True Witch, tell her to stop, tell her the point had been made.

Instead, he froze.

"Fool me once." Amara flicked a finger back and forth, waving it with disapproval. "Shame. On. You!"

Her tattoos sparkled. Somehow, they diverted Darla's hex magic. Between the spelled makeup and the tattoos, neither Theodore nor myself considered this timely preparation. She'd had these magical defenses stored and at the ready upon her arrival to the MDC. It was merely happenstance that Theodore's crew caught The True Witch off guard earlier. An opportunity that wouldn't present itself again.

With a twist of her hand, Amara balled a fist and dropped an ocean into Darla's mind. The warlock who'd sliced into me a hundred times over, the one who nearly killed Tara, had now collapsed to her knees, locked inside her mind while she held her breath—truly believing she was drowning.

"Stop," Theodore forced the word out. "You've made your point."

"I do not believe I have." Amara stood tall, her stance imposing and godlike in Theodore's memory.

He shuffled toward Darla, crawling on all fours as he reached his friend, his lover, his perfect killer. Now, he'd lost Vincent to some sick, perverse entropy magic, but he knew The True Witch's ocean could be pulled back.

"Awww, Theodore." Amara channeled magic into her fist. "It pains me to see you suffer so."

With a sudden whip of her arm, she lifted Darla's body and hurled her headfirst into the rocky floor, bashing her skull in.

Blood splattered over Theodore's face, his stunned, baffled, and frightened face.

"I still get my vengeance; you don't have to watch her slow death." Amara giggled. "We both win. It's compromise. I do not offer compromise lightly. It is my love for you, Theodore. Remember that."

"Your love for me?" He seethed with rage, with hate, with power. "You've struck what is mine. You've harmed two of—"

"Three," Amara corrected, pointing a finger at Ernesto. "Because he's not leaving here alive."

Theodore's eyes widened, staring at his fidgety frightened friend. His skittish ally. His gentle lover. His soft murderer.

"Run," he mouthed.

"Four, technically." Amara chuckled. "I forgot I killed that trollop doctor of yours. To think your father sought to keep her alive, to continue using her research for merging magics where they don't belong. Despicable."

"You killed Kendall?" Flashes of the doctor telepath that soothed Theodore's destructive desires funneled through his thoughts. Her image was beautiful and dangerous and seductive and now coated in a red filter of death.

"Ages ago, darling." Amara had this smile that faded into an expression of utter contempt. "She was meant to guide you, teach you while I was away. Instead, she exploited your youth, your ignorance. No, no, no. She had to go."

Crystalized blue shimmered throughout the cell, and Ernesto leapt through a portal.

"Her death was truly exquisite." Amara licked her lips, almost like she relived the torture she'd most certainly dealt Dr. Kendall. "Nothing like this fodder that you play with as if any of them were your equal."

Ernesto screamed and shouted; his body flailed and fought to escape his own blue doorway, splashing water into the room and blood and chunks of flesh. Theodore leapt to Ernesto's aid, gripping his hand to pull him to safety. It didn't help. Something horrible dragged Ernesto back, and his portal door sealed, slicing off his arm that now lay in the cell, rotting.

"What've you done?" Theodore collapsed to his knees and dry heaved.

"I thought the *hack* to his destination was quite skillful." Amara stepped over to Theodore and patted his head. "You'd think with all the time he spent at your side, he'd have done better when swimming with sharks."

"I hate you."

Amara mused, her vibrant green eyes softening ever so. "What child doesn't hate their mother when being reprimanded?"

Child? What? The True Witch was Theodore's mother? The memory swirled as I struggled to fathom this revelation. The True Witch, a pillar and leader for an ancient coven that sought to control the world was Theodore's mother. Tara's mother.

"Your tantrums have gotten much worse in my absence." She shook her head. "Your father was never any good at discipline. It's why my sweet goddess still lacks in harnessing so much of her power."

"This was never about me, was it?" Theodore looked up at Amara, at The True Witch, at his mother. "You finally came back because it's time for Tara to fulfill her destiny. The MDC, my release, all just a minor pitstop on your destination to supremacy."

"It's time for you both to fulfill your destiny, my love." Amara brushed the back of her hand against Theodore's cheek as if meant to wipe away tears, but he hadn't shed any—he wouldn't give her the satisfaction. "You are the vanguard of the new world order, the return of gods. You will be the commander of an army. You will be the right hand, the vigilant knight, to your sister who will reign as queen goddess over everything."

When she said everything, it sent a shiver through my spine, through Theodore's too, because she didn't mean everything here. She meant everything everywhere. The True Witch sought to tear down the walls of every plane and rule over them with her children: Theodore and Tara Whitlock.

"But first, you can stay here until you learn to appreciate and respect all I have given you." Amara slammed the door closed and left Theodore to rot in this cell with the corpses for months now.

I sprang loose from the memory as it continued playing in Theodore's mind, resetting to the very beginning and looping through the deaths of the three most important people in his life.

"Well, well, well." The metal door that sealed Theodore inside his cell was flung open with Amara bathed in the light outside. "If it isn't the psychic that struck down one of my pillars. Naughty, naughty."

She could see me, even as a ghostly manifestation.

"Know this, witch. The next time we face each other, I will have the full force of my Celestial Coven and an army." She hurled an ocean, enough to shatter my fragmented being away from her secluded hiding spot and sent my broken being back to the whole of my body, my other half.

I gasped, taking in another manifestation. A few had returned over the summer empty-handed and mostly depleted of the magic I'd loaned their form. Nearly a month and nothing learned. But this new one carried answers. Not the location, not yet, but so much worse.

I had to find Milo, had to share this information. Most of all, I had to figure out how to protect Tara from her mother. Protect the city from Theodore. I had to protect everyone from witches who sought to unleash gods and demons onto the world.

THE END

...UNTIL THE FALL SEMESTER OF
THE THIRD AND FINAL YEAR.

BRANCHES OF PAST AND FUTURE CODEX

For unknown reasons, a little over two hundred years ago, magic returned to the world. When everyone gained access to magic, people were referred to by two different titles.

Witch – Law abiding citizens using their magic for good.

Warlock – Corrupted people who cast their magic selfishly.

THERE ARE TWO TYPES OF MAGIC:
Root magic – Standard magic that all witches have access to.

Branch magic – Unique magic that differs person to person.

ROOT MAGIC
There are four root magics. Every witch in the world has access to these same four root magics; however, the amount of control is based on training and skill.

Telekinesis – The ability to move things with one's mind.

Levitation – Harnessing gravitational polarity in the core of one's body to float.

Sensory – The ability to track and pinpoint demonic energy.

Banishment – The ability to repel demonic energy from the mortal world, exorcising the unnatural presence.

BRANCH MAGIC
There are twelve types of branches. Each branch has their own unique attributes. Most witches are born with only one branch magic. Some people are born branchless, meaning they have no unique magic. In rare cases, some people are born with multiple branches.

Alteration – This branch focuses on altering a witch's physical limits. This can involve enhancing strength or senses. It can also involve manipulating and altering what a body can do such as invisibility or duplication.

Arcane – Unique and rare unclassified magic. Witches who possess arcane magic are often coveted because of their power. Arcane magic is usually a mix of two or three types of branches in such a way that it becomes impossible to classify the magic into any other branch.

Augmentation – Altering the physical nature of a witch's body. This can include added appendages such as tails or wings. It can also include the removal or replacement of certain limbs or organs. There are many varieties to augmentation magic, some major or minor, but it's important to understand this differs from standard physical anomalies. Most augmentations are interwoven in such a way that they link the nervous system and the magic of the witch together.

Bestial – This branch connects a witch to the animal kingdom in one form or another. There are dozens of different varieties to this branch, all revolving around animals. Some witches are born as therianthropes, which allows them to take on the physical attributes of an animal. Others can shift entirely into an animal form. Some can communicate with animals. Many witches with a bestial branch are born linked to one animal in particular that becomes their familiar. These familiars share the magic with their witch.

Cosmic – Magical energy that is drawn from the stars and astral plane of existence. This can include things such as manipulating light or darkness. It can also involve moving through the astral plane through things such as teleportation or portal doorways.

Enchantment – A written and spoken form of magic. This is where the traditionally known form of spellbooks comes from. Channeling magic into symbols is a common form of enchantment magic that allows anyone access to the spell so long as the witch who created the spell freely shares it. Enchantments can come in the form of words on parchment, reciting key phrases, combining ingredients into a potion, and storing magic into sigils.

Entropy – Often regarded as the most shameful branch in existence. This magic deals with things like poison, venom, toxins, and other diseased aspects of necrotic rot. Because of the deadly nature of this branch, entropy witches are shunned by most of society and blamed for the sickness in the world.

Hex – A darker magic that allows a witch to manipulate probability around them. Hexes can counter or weaken other magics. They can warp the senses of another person. Some hexes can breathe life to curses, striking down foes with in simple or severe ways.

Primal – Elemental control. This can come in the form of controlling or creating an element through magic. Most witches can harness either control or creation, but some can do both. Common elements include fire, water, earth, air, electricity, ice, and steel. There are many others including unique minerals, types of florals, and combinations of elements.

Psychic – This type of magic delves in mental control beyond normal limitations. Psychic magics have the widest array of types. There are lots of mental magics from reading minds, sensing emotions, predicting the future, observing the past, manipulating thoughts, conjuring illusions, and countless others. It is often said, if a person can think it, the psychic magic is likely out there somewhere.

Rejuvenation – This is a healing type magic. While rejuvenation can be used by a witch to heal themselves or others, there are often limitations. Many healing magics are only temporary as the magic is a shortcut. Most of the time, when the magical effects wear off, the injury returns even in a mild form. Severe wounds must be looked at by medical professionals before the rejuvenation magic fades away.

Ward – This is typically a binding or barrier type magic. In most cases this is used to protect individuals or entire areas. Schools, hospitals, and government facilities are often covered in warding magic.

TYPES OF DEMONIC ENERGY

This type of energy is unnatural to the mortal world. Demons claw their way through dimensional barriers so they can feast upon the magic in the world. When demons break into the dimension, they often shatter into pieces.

Wisps – fractured droplets of demonic energy usually in the form of small white lights. They act on instinct alone, seeking out magic.

Fiends – Tarlike creatures made from a collection of wisps. They are feral, low level demonic beasts that crave magic. If they absorb enough magic, they'll ascend to demons.

Demons – Otherworldly creatures that crave magic to sustain their existence in the mortal world. They must constantly consume magic as they will perish without a steady supply. Demon bodies leak magic quickly, making them regularly hunt witches for more substance. There are tens of thousands of types of demons. Most monster lore is inspired by actual demons such as gorgons, vampires, sirens, hydras, and so much more.

Devils – When a demon possesses a human host, they transcend to something far stronger and harder to kill. They don't leak magic, and they become almost impossible to detect. However, hosts can't contain a demon for very long and most possessions end in the body rotting inside and out.

PROFESSIONAL WITCH RANKINGS

There are many types of government and private sector jobs that require magic. The most aspired to position is a guild witch.

In order to legally cast magic, a witch requires a license, waiver, or fledgling permit. Without official government documentation and approval a witch can face fines or even jail time for illegally casting their magic.

Guilds – Private companies that work to protect citizens within a particular territory. Many guilds compete for popularity and work to be the most successful in an area. Some take on jobs by the city, picking up the slack. Many work for private citizens. Others specialize in particular magics.

Acolytes – These are young witches who are recently licensed and seeking to become professional enchanters. They usually work for free as assistants and sidekicks to gain experience in the industry.

Enchanters – Professional witches who are deemed the best in their field. They keep the streets clean of demonic energy, dangerous warlocks, and anything deemed a threat to society.

Guild Masters – The leading witch of a particular guild. They oversee all the enchanters and acolytes of a particular guild. While proficiency in magic is significant to claim this title, it is important to note that guild masters are not always the strongest witch in an area, but simply the most calculating. To become a guild master a witch requires approval from the enchanters working there and from the board that funds the guild.

ACKNOWLEDGMENTS

I really hope you enjoyed this installment of the Branches of Past and Future series. 2023 was an exhausting year for me. A lot of great things happened. I published three books and found readers who loved my little queer magical worlds. It's been wonderful. Sadly, there were also difficulties with my health. I had a heart attack which led to surgery and time and lifestyle changes (still adapting) and A LOT of relearning habits. Even my daily habits, my routines.

Zero Happily Ever Afters was the first book I wrote after my surgery and recovery. I'm so proud of this story. I'm so glad I've been able to share it with readers. If you enjoyed it—or even if you didn't—I hope you'll consider leaving an honest rating and/or review. They're very helpful, especially in the further installments of a series.

Now, let's discuss a few things that have been on my mind since drafting this beautiful story. For starters—that ending!!! The True Witch is related to WHO?!?! Looks like the Celestial Coven might be here to stay…at least long enough to create some more drama for Dorian and his homeroom coven, along with Milo and his Global Guild.

Speaking of the Global Guild, I had an absolute blast creating the dynamic between the three members introduced. Gladiatrix is iconic. I'm so glad I found ways to highlight all of her OP abilities without it taking away from the fight sequences because while I adore Wonder Woman and Supergirl, I love a brilliantly choreographed battle. Next up, Texas Daddy! Seriously, I might have to write a brand-new series revolving around him because I adore Enchanter Diaz so much. I also loved developing his family (the wife and twin kids) who didn't get nearly enough page time. And finally, who can forget our grumpy old grandpa, Wadsworth. He was irksome and entertaining—at least for me.

As I delve deeper into this world, it's such a joy to explore more characters while highlighting those who've been around since book one. There was some definite resolution in student arcs this installment, which means books five and six might introduce some new drama their way. One thing I've prided myself on since the first book is the development of my characters. Honestly, character creation is my favorite part of any story, learning who they are, and spending time with them.

BUT I HAVE TOO MANY CHARACTERS! I introduced a few new folks which meant I had to cut down on some others. Here's a huge shout-out to Milo's acolytes for rocking it out off the page, being amazing young witches in the city of Chicago. Let's applaud Chanelle Whitehurst for being the most fabulous teacher at Gemini Academy. The way I keep outlining these massive plotlines for her and her homeroom coven only to chisel those words or ideas away, so Dorian's kiddos get their scene time. And honestly, can you blame me? We need more pages with grumpy Kenzo, sweetheart Gael, flirty Gael, oblivious Caleb, and so much more!

Plus, I had to make time for the villains. Le sigh. Unfortunately, I find myself enthralled by The True Witch, her coven, and her darling psychopathic son.

It's been such a pleasure inviting you into the wonderful world of branch and root magics. I hope you'll return for the third and final year to follow Dorian, Milo, the homeroom kiddos, and EVERYONE else I throw onto the page for the next two books.

AUTHOR BIO

MN Bennet is a high school teacher, writer, and reader. He lives in the Midwest, still adjusting to the cold after being born and raised in the South.

He enjoys writing paranormal and fantasy stories with huge worlds (sometimes too big), loveable romances (with so much angst and banter), and Happily Ever Afters (once he's dragged his characters through some emotional turmoil).

When he's not balancing classes, writing, or reading, he can be found binge watching anime or replaying Dragon Age II for the millionth time.

Author website:

https://www.mnbennet.com

Amazon page:

https://www.amazon.com/stores/MN-Bennet/author/B0BLJJK5NF

Goodreads page:

https://www.goodreads.com/author/show/23017668.M_N_Bennet

Patreon:

patreon.com/MNBennet

Newsletter:

https://mailchi.mp/e2ee2caea89a/newsletter-sign-up

Find All My Stuff:

https://linktr.ee/mnbennet